W9-BZY-076

The Archaeology *of* Brittany, Normandy *and the* Channel Islands

The Archaeology *of* Brittany, Normandy *and the* Channel Islands

An Introduction and Guide

Barbara Bender
with Robert Caillaud

ff
faber and faber
LONDON · BOSTON

First published in 1986
by Faber and Faber Limited
3 Queen Square London WC1

Printed in Great Britain by
Butler and Tanner Ltd
Frome Somerset

British Library Cataloguing in Publication Data

Bender, Barbara
The archaeology of Brittany, Normandy and the Channel Islands: *an introduction and guide*.
1. Channel Islands – Antiquities – Guide-books
2. Channel Islands – Description and travel – Guide-books 3. Brittany (France) – Antiquities – Guide-books 4. France – Antiquities – Guide-books
5. Brittany (France) – Description and travel – Guide-books 6. Normandy (France) – Antiquities – Guide-books 7. Normandy (France) – Description and travel – Guide-books
I. Title II. Caillaud, Robert
914.23′404858 DA670.C4

ISBN 0-571-09957-2

Library of Congress Cataloging-in-Publication Data

Bender, Barbara.
The archaeology of Brittany, Normandy and the Channel Islands.
1. Brittany (France) – Antiquities – Guide-books
2. Normandy (France) – Antiquities – Guide-books
3. Channel Islands – Antiquities – Guide-books
4. France – Antiquities – Guide-books
5. Great Britain – Antiquities – Guide-books
I. Caillaud, Robert II. Title
DC611.B85B46 1986 936.4 85-16123

ISBN 0-571-09957-2

In memory of Robert Caillaud and my father

For Polly and Tom

Contents

Illustrations

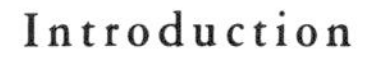

Introduction

Brittany

Côtes-du-Nord

Finistère

Ille-et-Vilaine

Loire-Atlantique

Morbihan

Normandy

Calvados

Eure

Manche

Orne

Cock of the menhirs the hired deaf-mute
Leads the way through bracken and stones,
Scrabbles with a rope-tied lantern
For a hole in the Mound of the Martyrs' Bones.

Over the red waves the wind still blows...
The narwhal shudders on the rocky shore...
Shade of the bone-ghosts brought by the moon
Hunts from their stiffness marten and boar...

There! it laughed, there by the man-shaped oak
Swallowing the sound of the may-bugs! C'Havann!
Sea-urchins prickle out on a rock.
The shadowing student works at night,
Unworried by the lightning stroke.
Under his pillow the stone fight.

Alfred Jarry (1873–1906)
From 'Les Minuits de Sable'
(translation: Jan Farquharson)

Acknowledgements

I wanted to write this book with Robert Caillaud. He became my friend and mentor, starting many years ago when I found him digging tranquilly at the great multiple passage grave of la Hoguette, Fontenay-le-Marmion, in Calvados. I had arrived, somewhat wet behind the ears, intent on writing a thesis on the Stone Age farmers of Normandy; I stayed and dug with him at la Hoguette, and then later at the gallery grave of Bardouville in the Eure. They were marvellous, meticulous excavations that raised as many questions as they answered. And we talked. He was an archaeologist-anthropologist-philosopher-naturalist-artist. An autodidact who paid no heed at all to academic boundaries. At a time when most archaeologists were still immersed in artefact typologies and the delimitation of time and space dimensions, Robert talked about prehistoric social relations and how and why they might have changed through time. I was often mystified, but I wish the conversations could have gone on. Shortly after we started this book, Robert became very ill. He died in the spring of 1981. I hope he would have liked our book.

So many archaeologists gave me advice and help that it is hard to know where to begin. But most particularly I should like to thank Jean L'Helgouach for his encouragement, for showing me many sites, for giving me information and providing photographs. Likewise Guy Verron in Normandy, and Roger Agache in Picardy – to whom I owe an apology. Originally the book was going to be even more wide-ranging and the coverage was to include the Somme and Picardy; but eventually I had to cut back and all his advice remains to be used another time. Patrick Galliou and Mark Hassall helped with documentation on Gallo-Roman sites. Gerard Baillaud located recalcitrant stones in the Carnac area (and his wife offered great hospitality at the Hôtel de Tumulus). P.-R. Giot pruned a long list of potential sites and C.T. Le Roux and J. Briard gave me plans and photos of many important sites and finds.

On the Channel Islands, Rona Cole on Guernsey was welcoming and informative and Bob Burns gave me unpublished information and provided photos. P.M. Wilson helped me with material on Alderney. John Renouf showed me many fine corners of Jersey and gave me an excellent unpublished manuscript that he had written with Jim Urry on the archaeology of the Channel Islands. Margaret Finlaison and the Société Jersiaise were very generous with plans and photographs. Ian Kinnes, at the British Museum, kept me up-to-date on the excavations of the extraordinary multi-phased site of les Fouaillages, Guernsey and gave me plans and photos.

I would also like to thank Glyn Daniel for sage advice, and the publisher, Giles de la Mare, for encouragement and tolerance beyond the call of duty in the face of much procrastination on my part.

Finally, I thank my family. They came on endless field trips with me. Just occasionally Jan ran a red line through some particularly mean and remote stone, embedded in brambles; and sometimes, after a plethora of menhirs, Sam was heard to murmur 'not another and another'—but mostly we enjoyed ourselves.

Content *and* Layout

The Introduction

It will be clear, leafing through this volume, that the majority of entries refer to stone monuments built by Neolithic farmers. It seems logical that in the general Introduction and in the Introduction to the Channel Islands more space should be devoted to the Neolithic than to other periods. But it is important to get a feeling for the enormous length of time of human occupation in this region, of the long history of gatherer-hunter-fisher societies, and of the changing geographical and climatic configurations. And to understand also how, as the stone- and then metal-using communities developed, they were affected by developments far beyond their borders; how sometimes the Atlantic seaboard was a major artery of communication and exchange, and at other times it was more of a barrier between rather isolated Atlantic communities that were peripheral to developments in the interior of Europe.

The Introduction ends with the Roman Empire; the Inventory also includes Romanesque churches, for it seemed that a diet of dolmens and menhirs, mounds and hill forts, might happily be leavened with an occasional church or cathedral crypt.

The Inventory

Sites in Brittany and Normandy are often hard to find. I have tried to give quite detailed instructions. The upper map reference on the right-hand side locates the site roughly, using the *Michelin* 1:200,000 maps. *These maps are essential*, and for Brittany the numbers are 58, 59 and 63, for Normandy 59, 54, 55 and 60. The lower map reference on the right locates the site precisely on the *Carte de France* 1:25,000. These are expensive and are probably only worth buying if you are going to stay for some time in an area. Very recently, folded 1:25,000 maps have been introduced, each covering two of the earlier maps. They divide the area into East and West, so that the new East map covers the old 3/4 and 7/8 maps, the new West map covers 1/2 and 5/6.

Some sites are hardly worth a great detour; some are on private land and are really almost impossible to get to (for example the fine corbelled grave of Ile-Longue, Larmor-Baden, or the bifurcating passage grave of Toulvern, Baden); some are deep in brambles, though this may, of course, change with time. I have wanted to give a rather full coverage, but to counterbalance this I have tried to warn off the saner visitor from some of the less remarkable sites. On the other hand, some sites, while unexciting in themselves, provide a marvellous opportunity to explore wild and remote areas. This too I have tried to indicate.

The sites are usually unprotected. Often they have been vandalized. P.-R. Giot once refused to write a French guide-book because he feared for the safety of these prehistoric monuments. I hope that the reader of this guide-book will be careful and respectful of the sites. *I hope also that no one with a metal detector buys this book*. They are fine for combing beaches and footways. They are pernicious destroyers when used on archaeological sites, for it is the context of a find, not the find itself, which is of vital importance.

Dating

Two sorts of relatively precise dating are given in the text. There are carbon-14 dates, based on calculation of the rate of carbon-14 breakdown in organic matter, such as charcoal or shell, found on a site. The plus/minus figure gives the parameters within which the date is to be located, i.e. 1000 + − 150 means that the date has a reasonable chance of falling between 850 and 1150. *Carbon-14 dates are indicated by lower-case bc*. Carbon-14 dates have, however, been shown to suffer anomalies, due to differing amounts of carbon-14 present in the atmosphere at different times. A more accurate method, still being elaborated, is to use bristle-cone pine dating, based on dating the tree-ring sequences of very long-lived species of pine and then cross-checking with the carbon-14 dates. In the text the resulting *calibrated dates are given in brackets, with an upper-case BC.*

A chart of carbon-14 dates and calibrated bristle-cone pine dates is given on page 59.

Key to Maps

Romanesque

Museum

Axe polishing stone

Stelae

Tumulus

Roman

Camp

Megalith

Menhir

Above 3000 ft

River

Sea

Coastline

Main Road

Dèpartment boundary

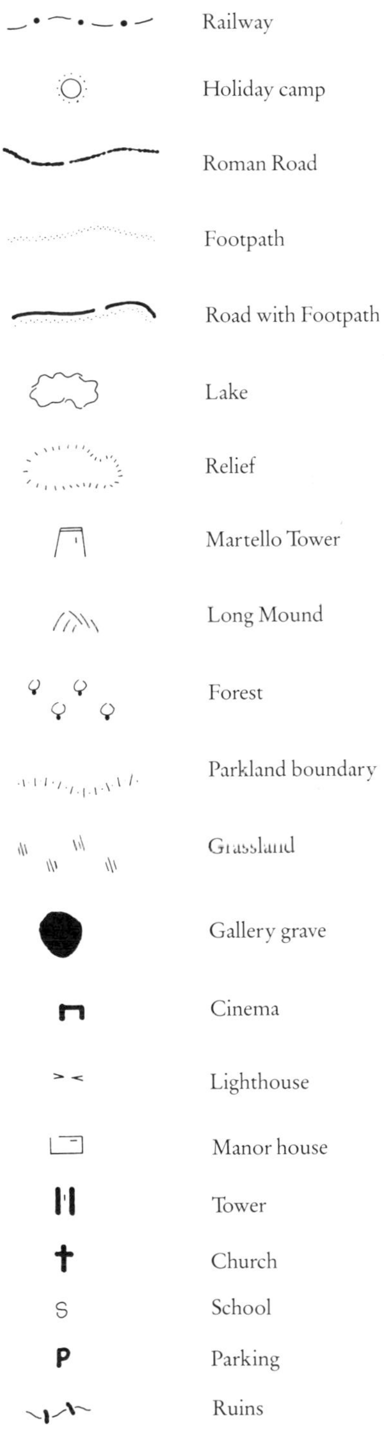

Railway

Holiday camp

Roman Road

Footpath

Road with Footpath

Lake

Relief

Martello Tower

Long Mound

Forest

Parkland boundary

Grassland

Gallery grave

Cinema

Lighthouse

Manor house

Tower

Church

School

Parking

Ruins

Introduction [1]

Brittany, land of the Bretons, was named after the fifth-century incursions from across the English Channel; Normandy, after the tenth-century invasions by the Northmen. But there was an earlier name for Brittany and Lower Normandy, the Celtic name Armorica—Land of the Sea—a name that outlives the individual histories of the area, that emphasizes the impact of that endless coast of inlet and headland. Four thousand kilometres of seascape, provider of fish and shellfish, beach pebble and drift wood, pumice and, on occasion, amber. The sea was a barrier but also a means of communication, a link between far-distant places. There were times when Armorica seemed like the rim of the world, a distant outpost to continental Europe, other times when it was central to a great Atlantic network of exchange and trade.

The Breton interior is called Argoat—Land of the Woods. It is an old granitic outcrop, part of the oldest geological formation in Europe, much eroded, rarely rising above 300 metres. The soils are thin and acid, better for pasture than for cereal growing. Only the coastal plains and narrow valleys are more fertile. But the ancient rocks are rich in fine hardstones and contain tin and lead, even a little copper and alluvial gold.

This old massif stands in sharp contrast to eastern, or High, Normandy. High Normandy forms the western end of the great chalk Paris Basin that cradles the Seine and its tributaries, river highways between the continental interior and the Atlantic. Within the wide valleys, terraced deposits of gravel and loam mark the rivers' history of alternating down-cutting and deposition, responding to the rise and fall of sea-levels. These stratified terrace deposits, long quarried for building material, contain some of the best evidence of early prehistoric occupation, and many of the quarry sites along the Seine and the Somme have given their names to Early and Middle Palaeolithic industries—the Abbevillian, Acheulian and Levalloisian.

The chalk soils are often capped with loess, a wind-blown deposit that forms on the edge of ice-sheets. It gives a light and well-drained soil ideal for early cultivation. There are also cappings of clay-with-flint which provide an easy though rather poor source of flint. Better quality flints come from seams within the chalk.

Between the chalklands of the Paris Basin and the Armorican massif of western, Lower, Normandy, lie the humid valleys of the Pays d'Auge and the calcareous plateaus of Caen, Argentan and Alençon. These were often frontier zones, affected by developments to both east and west.

Prehistoric developments in Brittany and Normandy began some 300,000 years ago, during the last great Ice Age, the Pleistocene. During the Pleistocene there were long glacial periods when the sea-waters were locked in the ice-sheets and sea-levels dropped far below their present range. In such periods Jersey and Guernsey and the other islands off north and south Brittany formed part of the mainland,

[1] Sites italicized in the Introduction are described in more detail in the Inventory. There is a glossary of archaeological terms on page 245.

and the whole area was in the grip of periglacial conditions. There were also shorter, warmer interglacials when the sea-levels rose and the 'islands' became islands or were even totally submerged (the chart in Figure 5 shows the major glacial and interglacial divisions). The final retreat of the ice accelerated around 11,800 years ago, and the Pleistocene gave way to the Holocene.

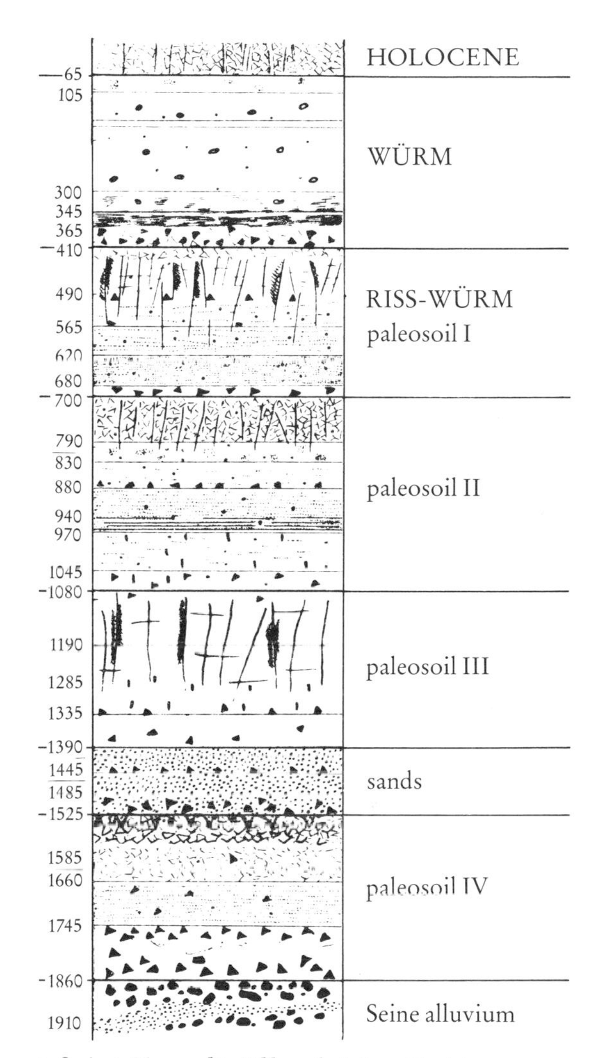

1 ***Saint-Pierre-lès-Elbeuf****, Seine–Maritime, section through the quarry*

Lower Palaeolithic Hunter-gatherers

300,000–90,000 bp[2]

Around three hundred thousand years ago, during the Mindel-Riss interglacial period, when conditions were quite similar to the present, there is occasional evidence of hunter-gatherers in High Normandy and Brittany.

In High Normandy very crude Acheulian pebble tools are found on the beaches and in the lower Seine alluviums; somewhat finer bifacials, of much the same date, come from the quarry of *Saint-Pierre-lès-Elbeuf* further up the Seine, and in this quarry there is a sequence of Acheulian deposits that spans the Mindel-Riss interglacial, the following Riss glaciation and the beginning of the Riss-Würm interglacial (Figures 1 and 2). There are technological improvements through this long time span. Tools gradually begin to be made with a soft hammer-stone, permitting greater control and thus a more varied range of blade and flake tools.

In Brittany and Lower Normandy (including the Channel Islands) only occasional stray tools document the Early and Middle Acheulian.

[2] Carbon-14 dates are either not available or only very approximate for much of the Palaeolithic. The dates are therefore simply given as an approximate 'before present' (bp).

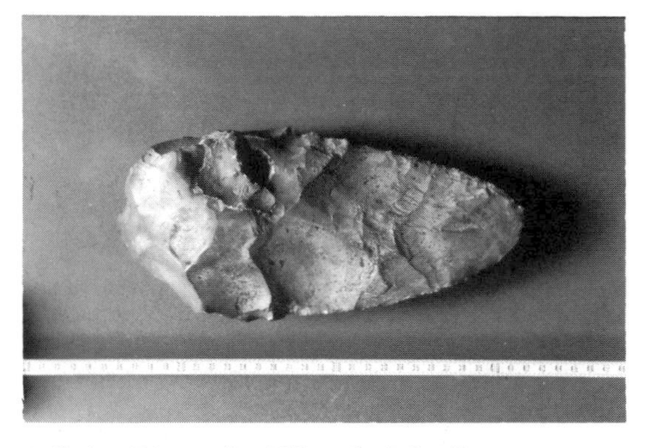

2 ***Saint-Pierre-lès-Elbeuf***, *Acheulian axe*

3 ***Epouville***, *Seine-Maritime, Mousterian tools*

Even the Late Acheulian is represented by only a few sites.

For the whole of this long Lower Palaeolithic occupation, over two hundred thousand years, there is not one human skeleton, not a house-floor, nor a grave from north-west France. All we know, from one of the Breton sites, is that the Late Acheulian people were capable of hunting or trapping a wide variety of large game including reindeer, horse and mammoth, and that they were prepared to go to some trouble to obtain good quality stone for their tools.

On the basis of evidence from other parts of France, from sites like Lazaret and Terra Amata in the south, it is probable that the makers of the Acheulian tools were pre-*Homo sapiens* hominids, *Homo erectus*, or, towards the end of the Lower Palaeolithic, an archaic form of *Homo sapiens neanderthalensis* (Neanderthalers). *Homo erectus* had a smaller brain, less dextrous hand and a more shambling gait than *Homo sapiens*. But these hominids, at least in southern France, were already able to hunt and trap a wide variety of game, could process shellfish, build huts, control fire and dig pits. They did not bury their dead but they had notions of ritual and belief; sometimes they kept aside the skulls of the dead, sometimes they removed the brain.

Middle and Upper Palaeolithic Hunter-gatherers

90,000–10,000 bp

The Middle Palaeolithic is distinguished by changes in the human population—*Homo erectus* develops into *Homo sapiens neanderthalensis*—and in the stone technology whereby more effective tools are made by preparing stone cores so that more carefully controlled flakes and blades can be struck. This Middle Palaeolithic industry is known as the

Mousterian (Figure 3). There were also important changes in social organization.

In Brittany and Normandy occasional Mousterian tools appear around 90,000 bp at the close of the Riss glaciation, somewhat more substantial evidence emerging around 70,000 bp at the onset of the Würm glaciation.

The Würm was the last great glacial period. It was marked by fiercely cold conditions, particularly in the middle stages. Brittany and Normandy were lands of tundra and steppe. But although bleak and cold, these conditions were ideal for herds of reindeer, mammoth, woolly rhino and musk ox, and human occupation probably increased. The evidence, however, has largely been covered by the sea, for, during the Würm, much of the sea-water was trapped in the ice-sheets. Jersey was part of Lower Normandy and Lower Normandy extended to include the bay of Mont-Saint-Michel. The present-day cliffs of northern Brittany, formed in the earlier Riss-Würm interglacial, were stranded far inland and overlooked a wide coastal plain, and the present-day islands off south-east Brittany were still part of the mainland. Neanderthalers must have exploited the low-lying coastal areas, and when the sea rose again after 10,000 bp the evidence of their sojourn disappeared.

In Brittany the relatively rare sites cluster at the base of the abandoned cliff-line, where cliff and cave provided some shelter from the elements, although a couple of quite large sites have also been found in the high interior. In Normandy there is again some evidence from the Seine terrace deposits, from levels that lie above the Acheulian. But the best evidence comes from the caves of St Brelade and la Chêvre cut in the cliffs of Jersey. Cotte St Brelade, in particular, has a series of stratified hearths that show that it was occupied on and off for nearly thirty thousand years. Quantities of artefacts were found: in the lower levels fairly rough tools, later increasingly effective Mousterian tools. A great range of animals was hunted and apparently woolly rhino and mammoth were particularly valued, for their skulls and bones were purposefully heaped up against the cave wall.

At St Brelade a few teeth and part of a skull indicate that the occupants were Neanderthalers. These are the only skeletal remains for the whole of Brittany and Normandy. Evidence from other parts of France shows that *Homo sapiens neanderthalensis* had a brain that was as large as *Homo sapiens sapiens*, was capable of speech and of formulating concepts of self and group. In other parts of France they buried their dead, often lavishly covered in red ochre, and placed grave offerings—tools and food. There is the beginning of regional cultural differentiation, and evidence too of more varied and more specialized activities. There are sites for butchering or plant-processing, for tool manufacture, game-spotting or home-base activities. On the whole, however, the Mousterian evidence from Brittany and Normandy is limited. Only the stone tools remain to indicate the increasing functional and cultural variety.

In north-west France these Mousterian industries continued for over sixty thousand years, through to the final, less intensive Würm III glaciation. They seem to linger on in the north, to be only slowly affected by the changes that further south demarcate the beginning of the Upper Palaeolithic around 40,000 bp. In southern France, for example, there is evidence of the emergence (or arrival) of *Homo sapiens sapiens*, of increasing concentrations of people, of more permanent settlement, and of an overall intensification of social exchange, technology and subsistence. The southern French cave art and finely engraved portable objects indicate a growing emphasis on ritual and a degree of social differentiation. But these very significant developments are barely recorded in Normandy and Brittany (and not at all on the Channel Islands).

In High Normandy the upper levels of the great quarry sequences are more or less sterile, and most of the evidence for the Upper Palaeolithic comes from stray finds, with only occasional sites and a couple of decorated caves, at Gouy (Figure 4) and Orival, both north of Rouen in the chalk cliffs above the Seine.[3]

In Brittany there are rare sites along the north coast, including a reindeer-hunters' camp, huddled against the granitic rocks on the Ile de Bréhat (Côtes-du-Nord) with arcs of stones that perhaps held down skin tents. Another group of sites lies south of the Loire.

The evidence from these rather thin sources is of an increased range of equipment, including more specialized scrapers, a great increase in engraving tools reflecting the increased importance of bone working, and a microlithic element—tiny blades that could be mounted in a bone or wooden handle and used as a knife or saw, or used to tip an arrow shaft, or to make a grating tool for processing tough roots. The use of microliths greatly enhanced the flexibility of the stone tool-kit, and they became increasingly important in post-glacial times.

Post-Pleistocene (Mesolithic) Gatherer-hunter-fishers

8000–4000 bc

During the later Würm glaciation (III and IV) conditions were less extreme than in the earlier glacial periods—the Ice Age was on the wane. Certainly after 8000 bc—the formal end of the Pleistocene and the beginning of the Holocene—conditions rapidly warm up, and as the ice melts so the sea-levels rise once more. From the great low of more than − 100 m at 16,000 bc, the sea-levels rise to − 40 m around 10,000 bc, to − 22 m at 7800 bc, and by this time tongues of sea begin to separate Guernsey and Alderney from the mainland. By 4000 bc Jersey is severed from the mainland, the bay of Saint-Michel fills up and many islands off the Loire-Atlantique are formed. (Others, like Gavrinis and Er Lannic at *Larmor-Baden*, Morbihan; or Hoëdic and Téviec at *Saint-Pierre-Quiberon*, Morbihan; or Guennoc, *Landéda* and Ile Carn, *Ploudalmézeau* in Finistère remain attached to the mainland till much later.)

As the sea-levels rise, sandbanks form, filling

4 ***Gouy****, Seine-Maritime, an Upper Palaeolithic engraving in the cave*

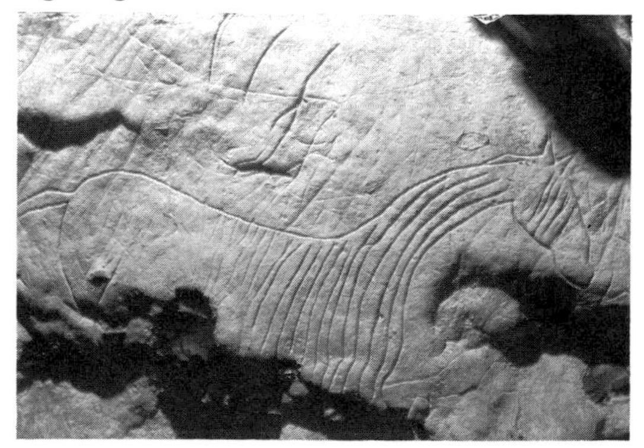

[3] Gouy is not open to the public. It is a rare outlier of the main concentration of decorated caves in southern France and northern Spain. On the fragile walls of a narrow gallery are engraved birds, cattle, horses, mammoth, human silhouettes and signs. At Orival there are simply a few traces of engravings on the ceiling and of red paint.

the estuaries and bays and providing long tidal stretches rich in shellfish and plant foods. There are also times of minor retreat when these tidal zones turn into soft-water marshes that teem with fish and fowl.

The sea-levels rise, the land warms up, the vegetation changes (Figures 5 and 6). In the pre-Boreal phase, 8000–6000 bc, pine colonizes rapidly, followed by birch, then willow, and towards the end elm and hazel. By 6000 bc, the beginning of the Boreal, conditions become still warmer and rather drier, and pine and then hazel come to dominate. Somewhat later, but still within the Boreal, oak and elm become more extensive and more rarely, alder and lime. Such conditions last till 5000 bc, and then, during the Atlantic, while it remains warm it gets wetter, and the forest covering becomes increasingly dense. The encroachment of forest is particularly marked in the second part of the Atlantic when Brittany and Normandy are colonized by massive stands of oak or mixed oak, as well as alder in the more humid zones, and hazel and pine on the drier, more porous soils.

Right through into the Atlantic, c. 4000 bc, northern France remains the domain of gatherer-hunter-fisher groups. Brittany seems to have been more heavily populated than Normandy, and the Channel Islands seem to remain unoccupied. The Post-Pleistocene groups had to adapt to the very different environmental conditions. Most of the large herd animals disappear; instead there are huge cattle, deer, boar and a wide range of small game, as well as a great increase in plant foods and, as the sea invades and the rivers are pounded back, marine and riverine resources. The Upper Palaeolithic groups had already perfected a great range of specialized tools and these could be adapted to new subsistence strategies. No doubt there were also changes in social organization; the large groups associated with co-operative big-game hunting probably broke up, at least for parts of the year, and individual hunting with bow-and-arrow and fishing by individuals or in small groups became more important. The Post-Pleistocene gatherer-hunter-fisher groups have tended to be viewed by archaeologists as the shell-shocked survivors of the Ice Age, unable to cope with the encroaching forests, limited to the

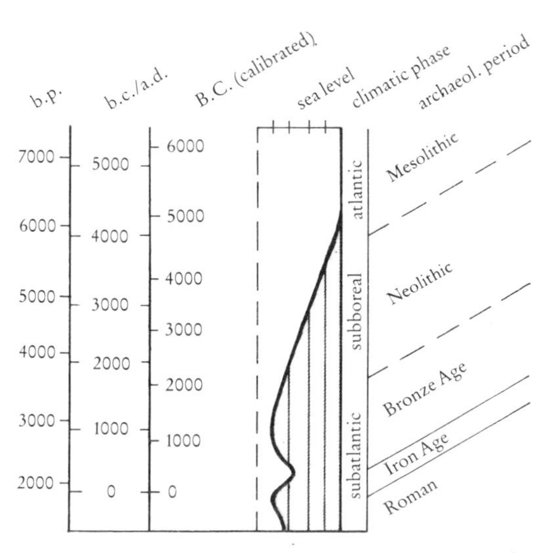

5 Climatic phases and sea-level changes from the Mesolithic to the Roman period

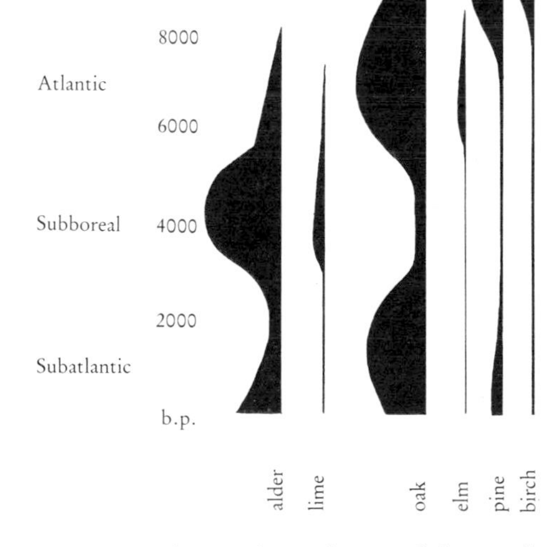

6 Vegetation changes from the Mesolithic to the Iron Age

poorer, sandy soils, armed with poorer tool-kits, operating in smaller groups and bereft of artistic expression. This is almost certainly a misreading of the evidence. As conditions warmed up, cave sites and rock shelters were abandoned, and open-air sites, often more difficult for the archaeologists to find, were occupied. They were probably small, and, as fishing became an increasingly important activity, were located down on the coastal plains or close to river banks. They are now deep under the sea or covered with thick alluvial deposits. The small sites found inland on the sandy soils may often have been only seasonal camps optimally located to exploit the hazelnut groves. In the case of Brittany it has recently been suggested that the inland sites would have been used when the winter tempests raged around the coast, and the seasonal 'retreat' would have provided an opportunity to replenish lithic materials, in particular quartzitic hardstones.

The heavy industry of the big-game hunter was no longer necessary; a lighter, microlithic tool-kit, more rapidly made and perhaps more rapidly discarded, would have been advantageous. Wood was now readily available and probably many tools were made of this perishable material. Certainly there is a dearth of ritual manifestation, at least as expressed in cave paintings and mobile art, but, like the rich ritual paraphernalia of contemporary Australian aborigines, items may have been made of perishable materials. Indeed there are indications, albeit rare, to show that at least some Mesolithic communities were involved in co-operative ritual enterprises that seem to focus around funerary ceremonies. Some evidence of this comes from Brittany. There are Mesolithic groups scattered along both the north and south coasts and inland as well. It is the south and south-western groups that provide some interesting insights. Associated with large accumulations of shell debris, on what are now the small islands of Hoëdic and Téviec, but were then part of the Quiberon coast, are cemeteries with indications of funerary ritual and of some minor social differentiation.

The shell middens contain inhumation pits. At Téviec tightly flexed bodies were placed in pits that were sometimes paved and usually demarcated by a stone setting and a slab cover. Small fires were lit on these slabs, and offerings, often the jawbone of a boar or deer, were placed in the ashes. Then a small cairn of stones was erected. There were also free-standing, carefully constructed hearths. At Hoëdic, *Saint-Pierre-Quiberon* (Morbihan), there was a roughly paved area close to the cemetery. Usually only one body was buried, but sometimes several were placed together, or a pit was reused. Nearly all the graves contained grave-goods. At Téviec there were fine flint blades, and bone pins apparently especially made for the burials. Many had ochre, some had shell beads, and at Téviec two were exceptional in that a beehive of large antlers had been placed over the individual. At Hoëdic one grave was singled out by an offering of worked antler pieces placed around the head. All this suggests a degree of social cohesion, involvement in collective ritual and some—probably slight—social differentiation. It has often been maintained that gatherer-hunters are egalitarian, but social differentiation, or leadership, does not necessarily contradict this. A person may have authority yet be socially constrained to share all that he has. Such authority would be gained through personal qualities—through an ability to organize economic and social undertakings such as hunting ventures, initiation, marriage and funerary ceremonies, inter-group gatherings and fertility rituals. Such intra- and inter-group activities are essential to the maintenance of social and economic relations and are as significant for gatherer-hunters as for the later farmers. But such activities, which involve feasting and exchanges, make demands on people's material resources. It may be that such social demands on production played a part in encouraging early attempts to manipulate plant and animal resources. At the sites of Téviec, Hoëdic and at la Torche, *Plomeur* (Finistère), among the abundant remains of shellfish and wild animals, are occasional bones of domesticated dogs, small cattle and perhaps sheep and goats, all of which perhaps represent local attempts at domestication. It may be that in Brittany gatherer-hunter-fisher groups gradually become farmers, and that there is an affiliation between the Mesolithic graves embedded in the shell middens and the Neolithic stone graves embedded in artificial mounds. The early Neolithic passage graves at Dissignac, *Saint-Nazaire* (Loire-Atlantique), and at Larcuste, *Colpo* (Morbihan), seem to have been built by farming groups employing local microlithic tool-kits.

Such developments could not, however, occur in isolation. Cereal crops were not native to Brittany and would have to be procured through contact and exchange with farming communities in other parts of France, or even in Iberia via the long Atlantic seabord. There are elements in the microlithic industries of south-east Brittany (Loire-Atlantique and Morbihan) that evoke such contacts.

This pattern of continuity and contact may also be faintly recognizable on the Channel Islands. The Upper Palaeolithic population appears to have been sparse or non-existent; the evidence for the Mesolithic is also limited. Nonetheless, at les Fouaillages, *Vale*, Guernsey, there are Mesolithic flints, and then, apparently in the Early Neolithic, a circular paved area and a small cairn containing a domed cist were constructed. These are not unlike the Breton shell-midden structures and there may well have been Mesolithic midden burials on the Channel Islands that have been washed away.

Neolithic Farmers

4000 to 2200 bc

calibrated 4850–2850 BC

From the point of view of the visitor to Brittany, Normandy and the Channel Islands, the evidence for the three hundred thousand years of Palaeolithic and Mesolithic occupation is neither easily visible nor visitable. The impact of these gatherer-hunters on the landscape was marginal, only small sites and work-floors, occasional middens, and, towards the end, small-scale firing of the woodland to encourage young plant growth and to concentrate the game. Thus the evidence is mainly encased in museums and it requires some effort of the imagination to turn these stray stones and bones into once-living communities.

Early farming does not in itself immediately improve archaeological visibility. Clearance was still modest and the coastal plains, which, at least in Armorica, provided the best soils, have largely disappeared below the rising sea.

Settlements too, though more permanent, were out in the open, small, and built of perishable material—all that remains are post-holes and hearths, rubbish pits or pits dug to obtain building materials. And again, in Armorica, most of the settlement would have been along the coast and has been obliterated. At Curnic, Guissény (Finistère), where there is evidence of a long occupation, the last few post-holes are now being eroded by the sea. Only occasional promontory sites remain, and these were probably refuge points rather than settlements. A rare exception in Brittany is la Butte aux Pierres, la Brière (Loire-Atlantique), where there is a large occupation site on slightly higher ground above an extensive stretch of marsh.

What does remain is, first, far more extensive

evidence of stone-working areas—great work-floors of flint and hardstone. The best known is the dolerite A workings at Sélédin, *Plussulien* (Côtes-du-Nord), in western Brittany, which cover an area of one square kilometre and supply forty per cent of the Amorican lithic requirements. Great flint work-floors are also found in Normandy, at Olendon in Calvados and Blangy in the Seine-Maritime, and flint mines, with passages extending out from bell-shaped pits, have recently been discovered at Bretteville-le-Rabet, Calvados.

Increased lithic production must reflect, on the one hand, the need for a more massive and extensive tool-kit for land clearance and agricultural work, and on the other, an intensification of social exchange. The repertoire of stone-working now extended to pecking, grinding and polishing which gave an extremely durable commodity but also involved a considerable expenditure of time, and put a premium on better quality stone. Polished stone tools and weapons would thus have been highly prized and would often have been used as socially prestigious exchange items underwriting social transactions, especially the *rites-de-passage* of a tribesman's life. Polished stone tools and weapons would have circulated along with many other, less durable commodities, and group leaders would enhance and maintain their position by exerting control over the production and exchange of a range of such socially valued items. There must, therefore, have been quite complicated distribution patterns. Groups close to raw material sources would either produce rough-outs which they bartered to individual groups or group-leaders, or would simply permit access to outside groups who processed the raw matrials themselves. Groups with more or less direct access to the raw materials would exchange these prestige items over a much wider area. In general, circulation would fall off in direct relation to the distance from source, but there would, of course, be variations caused by local exchange relations. Work is beginning on such patterns and, for example, the range of contact, and the general fall-off rate of the dolerite A axe-trade from *Plussulien* has been mapped (Figure 36).

The other line of evidence is the widespread funerary and ritual structures. The Neolithic farmers often built elaborate monuments of durable material and sited them on higher ground. It is the distribution, form and content of these that provide much of the information about Neolithic developments.

There are two, if not three, distinctive developments in the early Neolithic of the region. One centres on Brittany, the other on High Normandy, while the third, encompassing the Channel Islands and Lower Normandy including the plains of Caen and Alençon, is clearly affected by developments to both east and south-west.

The Breton culture, known as the Breton Primary Neolithic or Carn, is first recorded around 3800 bc (calibrated 4600 BC); that is, the monuments seem to begin around that date, though it is quite possible that farming settlements with less impressive and less durable architecture occurred earlier. Around 3800 bc, along the coast of Brittany and extending some way into the higher southern interior and around the Loire, the Stone Age farmers built communal graves, often grouped together, with burial chambers made of dry-stone walling and/or large orthostats, with a slab or corbelled roof and an entrance passage that permitted the tomb to be reused. The chambers were covered by a large stone cairn or mound skirted by one or more revetment walls and often by a paving. The mound protected the grave, and made it more conspicuous, more of a landmark. There might be one chamber below a round or oval mound, or several below an elongated one (Figure 7). More exceptionally, two mounds might be joined, as at Barnenez, *Plouézoc'h* (Finistère), or a large mound might incorporate an earlier, smaller, passage grave mound (for example, the great *Carnac* and *Locmariaquer* mounds in Morbihan). Often the orthostats in the passage or chamber were engraved or pecked with a multitude of symbols. These might be scattered over the stone surface, or concentrated in panels, and sometimes, in the multiple passage graves, they were limited to certain chambers that were architecturally distinctive. Often too, orthostats within the chamber or in the encircling wall of the mound were roughly shaped to human form.

Very similar monuments were constructed in Lower Normandy and on the Channel Islands, the difference being that, initially, the builders seem to have been of different cultural stock, Cerny and Chassey, originating further to the east. Drawn into contact and exchange with the Breton mainland—occasional axes from Plussulien have been found on the Channel Islands—they organized themselves in a similar fashion; more specifically, they used monumental architecture as the material expression of their ritual and social relations.

At les Fouaillages, *Vale* on Guernsey, a triangular mound of stacked turves, with a stone facing that included a monumental eastern façade, covered a small forecourt and slab-roofed chamber, and an unroofed double-chamber of slabs and dry-stone walling. It also covers an earlier cairn and circular paved area. This structure dates around 3500 bc (calibrated 4850 BC), and this 'mixed' monument seems to provide a link both to the Mesolithic shell-midden inhumations—it is noticeable that the use of shells as part of the funerary deposition continues long into the Channel Island Neolithic—and with some undated but apparently long-lived long mounds with cists scattered through Brittany and Normandy (for example,

7 Multiple passage graves at la Hogue, ***Fontenay-Le-Marmion****, Calvados*

Manio, *Carnac*, Morbihan; Croix-Saint-Pierre, *Saint-Just*, Ille-et-Vilaine and *Colombiers-sur-Seulles*, Calvados). More conventional passage graves were also constructed at this time, both on the islands and in Lower Normandy.

The Breton graves, because of the acid soils, contain almost no skeletal material, and it is the multiple-chamber mounds on the plain of Caen in Normandy that provide information on who and how many were being buried in such structures. The information is a bit piecemeal, but it would seem that usually six or seven, or up to fourteen or fifteen bodies, would be placed in a chamber. These would be male and female, young and old. They would usually be placed in a tightly flexed position, although sometimes bodies were moved to one side to make way for later burials. When mounds come in pairs—as for example at *Fontenay-le-Marmion*, Calvados—they may have been used in somewhat different ways, for of the two at Fontenay, la Hoguette had intact flexed burials, while the chambers at la Hogue seem to have been used as ossuaries and often contained only partial inhumations. In particular the skulls were often missing, and it is possible that these were buried separately at settlement sites.

The grave-goods in these early Neolithic tombs of both Lower Normandy and Brittany are not extensive—a few stone tools, a little pottery, a few perforated shells or stones.

There were certainly associated rituals. Hearths were built in or in front of the passages, pottery was placed on the pavement in front of the encircling walls. Moreover, the engravings on the orthostats and the statue menhirs were expressions of a widespread cult. Among the engravings, a frequent symbol, formerly called the buckler motif, is in reality a female figure, perhaps echoing the rough statue menhirs found in the chamber and peristalith. Sometimes the 'buckler' is associated with, or replaced by, U-signs.

Much time was lavished on the construction of these monuments, and often stones were transported over considerable distances. Clearly this was not the quickest or easiest way to bury the dead. But these monuments fulfilled many different functions. They provided a community focal point; they brought together small groups of related people. They were associated with specific groups, and hence could act as territorial markers. And the building—by communal labour—and the use of the tombs would have been an important focus of ritual activity, ritual that was essential to the well-being and survival of the group. As the context of ritual, they were probably also the context in which leaders gained much of their authority, acting as mediators between the living, the dead ancestors and the gods. The tombs were, most probably, the resting place for past leaders and their families or lineages, for even allowing for destruction through the ages there are insufficient monuments to serve the entire community. The burial of a leader, the feasting, ritual and exchange, would also have created a setting for the validation of a new leader.

There had been leaders in gatherer-hunter societies, but ritual authority could be further enhanced within farming communities. Gatherer-hunters often experienced delays on the return of their labour, technical delays when dams or traps were constructed, social delays on marital and material exchanges. But with farming, technical delays were built into the cycle of planting and harvesting. So heavier commitment to place and group was enforced and a greater interdependence between generations. The leaders could take on additional roles in planning agricultural activities, building, and defence operations. Moreover, since production was no longer limited to what was available in the wild, it could gradually be controlled, and could be intensified to meet social commitments. Leaders could use the labour of their family and kin to accumulate and redistribute produce and could create debts and obligations. Thus they could intensify and extend the network of exchange relations, and increasingly control the circulation of socially valued items, a circulation which ties in again with ritual, initiation, marriage, the underwriting of significant events in the life cycle of a Neolithic community.

The extent of social differentiation varied in different parts of Brittany, Normandy and the Channel Islands, and varied also at different moments in time during the Neolithic period.

Armorican passage graves went on being built until 2500 bc (calibrated 3250 BC). As time went on the most highly differentiated societies seem to emerge along the south Breton coast. Indeed, in this area we may be witnessing the move from a Big Man society, in which position is largely achieved, to a chiefdom where it is ascribed, thus inherited. On the one hand, the great mound at Gavrinis, *Larmor-Baden*, covers a magnificent passage grave in which both the long passage and the chamber are covered with panels of engraved symbols. The chamber is small and may only have held one or a very few individuals. On the other hand, there are even larger mounds at *Carnac*, *Locmariaquer* and *Arzon* (all in Morbihan), which, though they often incorporate a peripheral and probably earlier passage grave, basically protect a series of small closed cists that were clearly not intended to be reused. These cists were excavated very early and not very well, but at Carnac the central cist was larger than the others and was filled with quantities of rich grave-goods—fine axes, beautifully polished, never used, made of a variety of hardstones (including jadeite which may have come from some small undiscovered local source or may have originated in the Alps), and thousands of variscite beads. In addition to these elaborate structures—the resting place, perhaps, of great chiefs—there were other passage graves in southern Brittany that were more modest; they seem to represent a structurally more economical version of the multiple passage graves. Regional variants include a single compartmented chamber, a transepted chamber, a chamber with lateral cells, or a chamber with cells going off from the passage. Rather similar and contemporary cruciform graves are also found on Jersey.

It is interesting that social change is signalled by internal changes in the chamber architecture. The form of the mound and the great facade seem to remain unchanged. Indeed often, earlier graves and their mounds are included and the new façade extends to encompass them, giving a feeling of unity. There seems to be a public emphasis on continuity and a reference to the past that perhaps served to disguise quite radical social change.

There is also evidence of non-funerary activity in the third millennium, for now large stones are erected, singly or in lines, or occasionally in circles. Some of these have engraved or bas-relief symbols on them. Some of these only stood out in the open for a short time and then were purposefully broken up. Sometimes the fragments were reused in the burial mounds and chambers. They have been found in large passage graves (for example at Mané-Rethual and la Table des Marchands at *Locmariaquer*, at Gavrinis, *Larmor-Baden* and at le Déhus, *Vale*, Guernsey) and in the great mounds with cists (Mané-er-Hroëk, *Locmariaquer*). Perhaps these decorated menhirs were associated with individual leaders and were broken on their death. Such rapid displacement suggests that they would not have been used for astronomic sightings, but it is quite possible that other uprights were used in this way—not for precise astronomical observations, but rather as a means of making rough predictions of lunar movements including eclipses and other calendric reckonings. Knowledge vital to agricultural

8 Neolithic Pottery from Brittany
1 Primary Neolithic or Carn ware
2 Vase-support
3 Le Souc'h ware
4 Lower Conguel ware
5 Upper Conguel ware
6 Collared flask
7 Seine-Oise-Marne pot
8 Kerugou pot
9 Small, perforated, polished hardstone axe and Grand Pressigny dagger

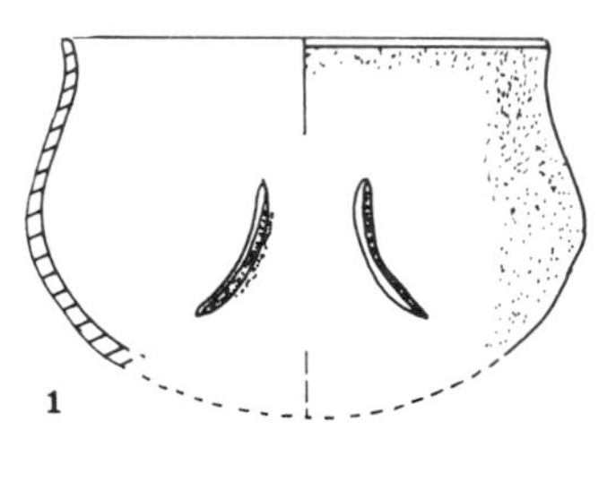

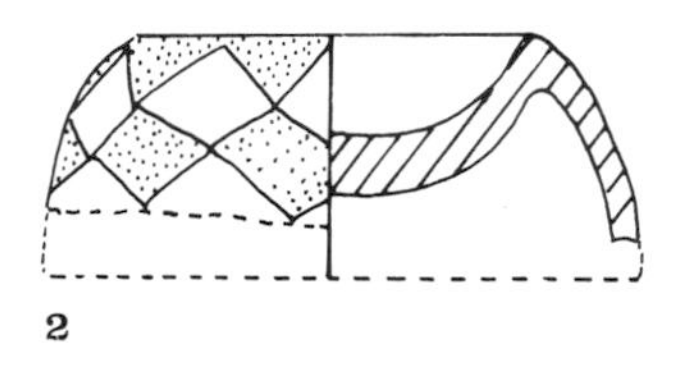

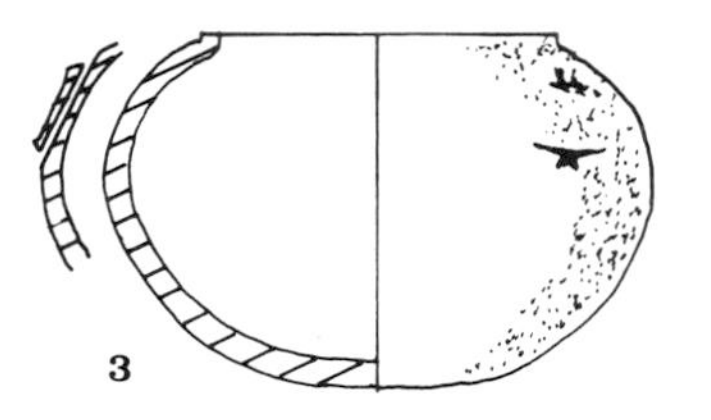

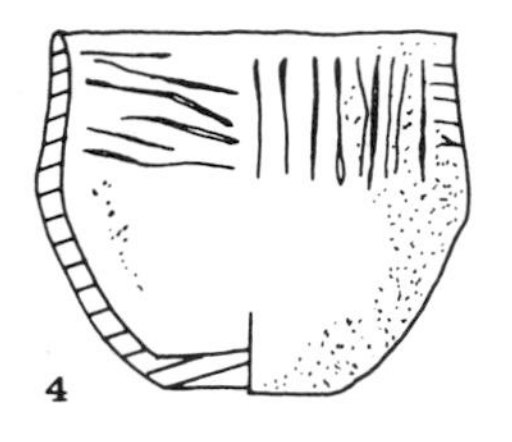

undertakings would thus be embedded in ritual observation which would be in the hands of specialists interceding on behalf of the people. Another office, another 'bond' between leader and followers.

This increased social differentiation in the third millennium required increased exchange to enhance and maintain prestige, which in turn put pressure on production and encouraged specialization. The early third millennium Neolithic exchange networks extended far beyond Armorica. In particular there is more evidence of contacts with the Paris Basin, mainly in the form of imported or imitation Chassey ware, especially decorated vase-supports. (A local Breton variant found, for example, at Larcuste, *Colpo*, Morbihan, and Dissignac, *Saint-Nazaire*, Loire-Atlantique, or at Barnenez, *Plouëzoc'h*, in Finistère, consists of a fused vase-support and vase [Figures 8 and 9].)

Increased specialization in the third millennium involved both the manufacture of prestige ware and of fine polished axes. On Jersey numerous vase-supports were made, mainly for internal funerary consumption, but also for exchanges which extended down to Er Lannic at *Larmor-Baden* in Morbihan. And at Er Lannic—now an island but in Neolithic times still firmly attached to the mainland—not only a local variant on the vase-support but also fine Castellic ware was made in considerable quantities. Er Lannic was also a manufacturing centre for highly polished axes made of fibrolite that came from across the bay at Port Navalo. Er Lannic lay close to the fine passage grave of Gavrinis, while the great *Locmariaquer* mound lay just to the north and the *Arzon* mound to the east. This area of Morbihan must surely have contained one of the richest and most powerful chiefdoms in Armorica. The associated settlements probably lie, alas, below the shallow waters of the gulf.

Other evidence of intensified axe production

comes from the dolerite A work-floors of Sélédin, *Plussulien* where production shifted into high gear; the earlier rather makeshift methods of extraction were replaced by more systematic open-mining, and rock platforms were created for roughing out blanks.

Meanwhile, Early and Middle Neolithic developments in eastern, High Normandy took a rather different form. Here, the first farmers were certainly not indigenous. They were colonizers, although occasionally they may have made contact with local Mesolithic groups.

Normandy was at the very tail-end of the great Bandkeramik migrations which began far to the east in the Balkans and the eastern plains of Europe. In eastern and central Europe the Bandkeramik people colonized the fertile loess soils, stringing out along the valleys in solid villages of wooden long-houses, growing a range of crops and keeping stalled animals. There appears to have been little social differentiation and ritual activities seem rather muted.

The Bandkeramik colonists that finally reached Normandy were probably few in number. The loess soils were running out, more varied landscapes had to be exploited and a heavier tool-kit had to be assembled. Some of the Bandkeramik cultural uniformity was lost, and the massive long-houses became rarer. All that remains, in High Normandy, are a few post-holes from lighter structures, a few inhumations, an occasional pit or stray find.

The evidence suggests a first, rather feeble, infiltration of Rubané colonizers—a Rhineland variant of the Bandkeramik—probably in the late fifth millennium, reaching no further than the plain of Caen. By 4000 bc (calibrated 4850 BC) a more regional grouping, the Cerny, emerged within the late Bandkeramik province. There is scattered Cerny material from High Normandy and from the Channel Islands (Mont Orgeuil, *St-Martin* and le Pinacle, *St-Ouen*, Jersey, and les Fouaillages, *Vale*, Guernsey). A

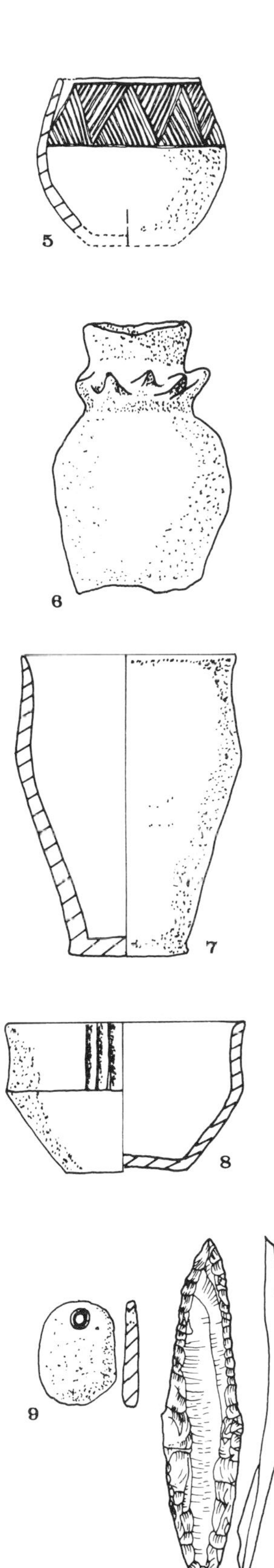

9 Fused vase-support from Larcuste, ***Colpo****, Morbihan*

little later, c. 3800 bc (calibrated 4600 BC), the Cerny groups seem to have co-existed with, or perhaps were assimilated by, a further influx of colonizers, the Chassey people, originating from south-east France. In general, these north Chassey groups seem again to have been rather egalitarian. The evidence is not, however, conclusive; most of the sites found are defended promontory camps, which, as in Brittany, were probably only refuge points. Otherwise there are the great flint work-floors with occasional traces of small huts, and the odd individual pit burial. However, as mentioned earlier, towards the west, on the plain of Caen and on the Channel Islands, Cerny and Chassey groups moved into the orbit of the Armorican passage-grave builders and, perhaps through involvement in a more intensive exchange network (in which fine Chassey pottery played a part), moved towards greater social differentiation, signalled by the increasingly elaborate Channel Island passage graves.

It is only in the late third millennium bc that the east/west cultural divide between the Armorican province on the one hand, and High Normandy and the Paris Basin on the other, breaks down. The cultural distinctions tend instead to follow a north/south axis with a 'Seine-Oise-Marne' province (the name a hopeless misnomer) extending across the Paris Basin through High and Low Normandy and much of north and central Brittany, and a southern Kerugou-Conguel province across southern Brittany.

The Seine-Oise-Marne development is not well understood. It is possible that one of the features that lends unity to this very extensive northern province is a shift in the economic base, a shift from a mixed agricultural economy to one with a greater emphasis on livestock. This in turn, may in part relate to a climatic deterioration. Around 2500 bc (calibrated 3250 BC) the Atlantic phase gave way to the Sub-Boreal. Conditions were cooler and drier, the mixed oak forests retreated and were replaced by a thinner spread of beech and pine, sometimes hazel, and in low-lying areas alder. Under such conditions agricultural yields would have declined and any attempt to boost yields by shorter fallowing would only further exacerbate soil impoverishment. A further option would be to open up new tracts of land. This option became more readily available in the late third millennium as plough and ox-traction spread through northern Europe. Livestock thus became a valuable commodity. But the new lands were often more marginal and easily degradable, so that, once again, agricultural yields would dwindle. An emphasis on herding presented a more viable alternative, but then led to renewed land hunger since herding requires more land per person. Competition and conflict may, therefore, have increased. In Late Neolithic

Brittany there is good evidence of widespread clearance and of settlement on the poorer soils of the interior, while in High Normandy and the Paris Basin (Brittany as always suffering from a dearth of skeletal material) a considerable number of deaths by violence are recorded.

Such developments, widespread throughout Late Neolithic Europe, may have been exaggerated in Brittany because of the existing social conditions. Within a socially differentiated society many additional demands are made upon production. In a society where the level of farming technology is still relatively low, these demands might be met by increasing the size of the individual household. A combination of limited technology, deterioration in climate and increase in population could well have strained productive relations to the point of collapse. The hierarchical system would revert to a less onerous system of more autonomous communities based on extended kin-grouping. In conjunction with the greater emphasis on livestock, groups may also have been more mobile.

So in northern and central Brittany and in Normandy (more faintly on the Channel Islands) a radical social change is reflected in the funerary architecture. Instead of passage graves utilized by only a fraction of the population, there are communal ossuaries. In northern and central Brittany and Lower Normandy these are long, parallel-sided, orthostatic chambers, covered with great slabs, with an antechamber and often a terminal cell, all set below a long, low mound. They are usually isolated, and built close to rock outcrops rather than in commanding positions. Eastwards, on the fringes of High Normandy, as the granite gives out, the graves are cut into the ground forming a long trench, which is roofed with slabs. The rather crudely notched stone that usually separated antechamber from chamber in northern Brittany is replaced by a fine carved porthole stone sometimes complete with stopper. This transitional area is also marked by other variants, small chambers known as dolmens, or circular pits covered with slabs. Still further east, on the chalklands of the Paris Basin, the whole 'edifice' is carved out of the soft rock.

There is, as usual, no skeletal evidence from Brittany, but the contents of the Normandy trench graves make it clear that these burial chambers served whole communities, with twenty, fifty, a hundred, even two hundred, inhumations, with much evidence of bones being pushed to one side to allow for new depositions. The grave-goods are modest, mainly coarse, relatively unvaried, domestic ware with occasionally a rather crude copy of a collared flask—particularly in the north of Trégor, Côtes-du-Nord (Figure 8). The original, much finer, collared flasks come from the North Sea area. There are also personal ornaments—perforated miniature axes and segmented discs, occasional copper, amber or variscite beads or Grand Pressigny flint objects.

The antechamber of the gallery grave was generally left empty and used for ritual. It contains hearths and in some instances engravings on the uprights. In other cases, the terminal cell is the cult focus and contains many engravings. Very occasionally the 'grave' was never used for burials but was purely a cult house, as for example the enormous monument at Roche-aux-Fées, *Essé*, Ille-et-Vilaine.

The engravings indicate that the main focus of the cult was a female deity. There was far less mystification than in the passage grave representations, though the form varies greatly. On the soft chalks of the eastern Paris Basin the whole female—face, breasts, arms, necklace, 'crook' and belt are depicted. Further west in High Normandy only the face, breasts and necklace appear, while on the hard granite of Brittany, representation is often reduced to one or several small plaques with pairs of breasts (Figure 10). In Brittany these are often juxtaposed with engraved weapons—a long, wide, tanged blade or an occasional axe. The female cult is not only expressed in grave art, but in occasional menhirs—two from Guernsey, one from Kermené, Guidel, Morbihan, and one from Laniscat, Le Trévoux, Finistère. The Kermené stone was, like those at *Locmariaquer*, broken up and placed in a mound.

Ordinary menhirs and small alignments are also associated with the Seine-Oise-Marne culture (one recently uncovered at les Fouaillages, *Vale*, Guernsey is associated with a timber structure, and a similar juxtaposition is found in the Ille-et-Vilaine, at le Moulin, *Saint-Just*). But these are much more modest than those of southern and western Brittany.

So there is a cult that transcends cultural boundaries, a general cultural homogeneity that encompasses a large part of northern France, but also, it should be stressed, considerable regional variation, consistent with the differing local histories within the Seine-Oise-Marne province. For example, in northern Brittany local passage grave antecedents and contemporary passage grave developments in the south were both important. In Trégor, Côtes-du-Nord, for example, hybrid lateral-entrance gallery graves were in vogue.

In southern Brittany these rather dramatic Late Neolithic social developments are much less evident. The more hierarchical societies seem to maintain a holding operation. Perhaps these southern communities were to some degree buffered by their heavy reliance on the continuously bountiful sea. While the massive mound graves of the great chiefs are no longer built, community leaders continue to have distinctive burials, sometimes only in reused passage graves, but often in fine angled passage graves, the walls of which were dominated by anthropomorphic engravings. But communal effort and ritual seem now to concentrate more effectively around non-funerary monuments—on the great

10 Anthropomorph on the upright in the trench grave of ***Dampsmesnil****, Eure*

stone alignments that often lead up to oval stone-girt sanctuaries. Those at *Carnac* (Morbihan) are but a fraction of their original extent and throughout south and west Brittany there are the remains of many others, as well as many individual menhirs.

Prestige items are still being produced and circulated. The great dolerite work-floors continue to flourish, using more sophisticated techniques. Foreign materials are imported, in particular the honey-coloured Grand Pressigny flint from the Indre-et-Loire. These flints and other hardstones are often made up into artefacts that mimic the rare metal objects circulating in parts of western Europe. The Grand Pressigny flint is made up into metallic looking daggers, dolerite is used for square-edged axes and hornblendite for the boat-axes with imitation metallic seams. These objects are exchanged up and down the Atlantic seaboard, and up the valley of the Loire. Nonetheless, there may have been some decline in specialized pottery production; the Late Neolithic southern Kerugou ware and other localized wares are not so fine and are more limited in distribution.

Bell Beaker Complex

2200–1800 bc
calibrated 2850–2250 BC

Throughout most of the third millennium the societies of Brittany, Normandy and the Channel Islands continued to depend upon stone technology, although there were sporadic contacts with distant metal-using communities. At the very end of the third millennium, within the context of the late Seine-Oise-Marne development, more coherent and distinctive assemblages containing small copper and gold items appear. These Bell Beaker assemblages, dating between 2200 and 1800 bc (calibrated 2850–2250 BC), are named after the easily recognizable well-made red beakers with horizontal bands of cord or comb impressions (Figure 11). Such beakers may once have held gifts of food or drink. They are often associated with copper or poor quality bronze daggers, small tanged spear-heads, bow-and-arrow equipment such as fine barbed-and-tanged flint arrowheads and schist wristguards, and with ornamental thin gold plaques or bone and jet buttons.

These assemblages, or individual elements, appear quite suddenly and are found scattered, or in concentrations, from Spain to Holland, from Britain to central Europe. There is evidence of regional variation, particularly in the pottery, and of much exchange, contact and local redefinition. In Brittany, for example, the majority of the beakers are of the Maritime type, probably locally made but showing strong affinities in form and decoration with the Portuguese ones, but there are also imports of all-over-decorated beakers, probably from the Low Countries, and there are local variants where the Maritime form is covered with all-over decoration.

Sometimes the context of the assemblage suggests an intrusive group. There may be individual burials below low mounds that are markedly different from local traditions, or burials that are clearly intrusive within older megalithic structures. Where skeletons are preserved the physical type may differ from the indigenous population. Sometimes there are habitation sites where a coarse ware, the domestic counterpart to the fine beakers, is found and differs from the local pottery. But at other times and places such distinctions are not apparent, the Bell Beaker elements appear to be intimately associated with the local material. In Brittany, where there are heavy concentrations of beakers mainly on the coast but also inland, there are apparently no individual mound burials, but there are examples of intrusive individual burials in reused megalithic chambers (for example, at Goërem, *Gâvres* in Morbihan), and of Bell Beaker elements that apparently form an integral part of the Seine-Oise-Marne grave-goods placed within gallery graves. In Normandy, where the distribution is thinner and more strictly coastal, there is a little enclave of intrusive individual mound burials at Bernières-sur-Mer, Calvados, while in the Eure, at Porte-Joie, two collective graves contain inhumations accompanied by Seine-Oise-Marne and Bell Beaker ware, gold plaques, variscite beads, barbed-and-tanged arrows and an amber

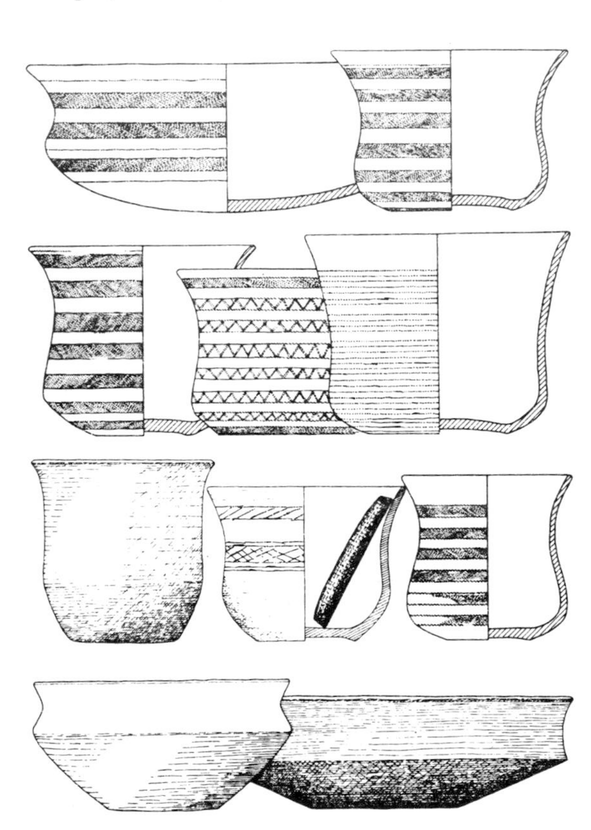

11 Bell Beakers from the gallery grave of Men-ar-Rompet, ***Kerbors****, Côtes-du-Nord*

bead. There is nothing to suggest that this Bell Beaker component is intrusive. On the Channel Islands large numbers of beakers, often rather distinctive island variants, are placed with secondary burials in reused passage and gallery graves.

It seems probable that the Bell Beaker elements formed a prestige assemblage, access to which was controlled by a small section of the society. In some cases it might be an intrusive group that held power over the local population through the control of socially valued items; in others it might be powerful indigenous élites, able to manoeuvre within the widespread Beaker network of alliance and exchange. In north-west France the Bell Beaker elements would not appear to be indices of great power but rather of social differentiation on a rather modest scale achieved by individuals through controlling the labour and produce of a relatively limited number of people. Production and exchange would not have been limited to the durable commodities that remain for the archaeologist. It may well be that with the inception of the ox-drawn plough, human labour, especially female labour, was increasingly freed and could be used in craft production—not only for potting, but also, with the increase of livestock, for textile manufacture. It is noticeable that the beaker designs are very reminiscent of weaving and of geometric textile patterns. Another possibility is that with the deterioration in climatic conditions and the greater use of marginal soils, barley became a more important crop and barley could provide the basis of a fine alcoholic beverage. The Beaker pots circulating in the context of feasting may well have once held a powerful brew.

There were places in Brittany and Normandy where the local populations held aloof from these transactions, and perhaps operated within contemporary but different exchange networks. On the north Breton coast, for example, the Late Neolithic groups that constructed lateral-entrance graves seem to have had little contact with the neighbouring Bell Beaker communities, their links—seen in the use of collared flasks—seem to be northwards with the coastal Low Countries. Or again in Normandy, the unique Seine-Oise-Marne crematorium built on the site of an earlier multiple passage grave mound at la Hoguette, *Fontenay-le-Marmion*, Calvados, had collared flasks but no Bell Beaker elements.

The widespread Bell Beaker distribution gives evidence of a very extensive network of prestige exchange. It presages a still more intensive and probably rather differently organized network among the increasingly bronze-orientated societies that emerge after 1950 bc (calibrated 2450 BC).

Early Bronze-working Societies
1950–1400 bc
calibrated 2450–1700 BC

The first area within north-west France to be drawn into the bronze-working network was western Brittany, and perhaps, very marginally, Lower Normandy (mounds at la Hague, Beaumont-Hague, Manche). Over the rest of Brittany, Normandy and the Channel Islands the Bell Beaker circuit crumbled, Bell Beaker copper metallurgy went out of circulation, and the more widespread Late Neolithic social and technological configuration was reasserted, although it was no doubt affected by the emergent west Breton chiefdoms.

These chiefdoms were small, powerful, hierarchical societies, in which individual authority was largely achieved through the control of the production and circulation of prestige items both within the society and with other élite groups within a context of lavish feasting and display. Quite possibly these élites were the successors to the local Bell Beaker users—the individual burial, the 'heroic warrior' accoutrements, including very similar arrowheads and wristguards, suggest such continuity. But Beaker pottery was supplanted as a prestige item by the more effectively controlled new bronze repertoire. And the specifics of this new technology greatly affected the extent, the intensity and the form of social relations, as well as bringing new pressures to bear on the underlying subsistence economy.

The new bronze technology could have enhanced productivity— the sharp bronze axes and palstaves would have speeded forest clearance, spear heads would have increased hunting proficiency. But these utilitarian uses came later, basic tools continued to be made of stone, and the new technology was geared to the production of prestige items. Because the new technological processes, alloying copper and tin, were more complex, production could more easily be controlled, thus lending itself to more systematic élite monopolization. The combination of hammering and casting increased the potential range of form and style and was conducive to intensive, and no doubt competitive, exchange relations. No doubt, too, some of the functional innovations, including more sophisticated weaponry, permitted 'alliance' to shade into coercion.

The uneven distribution of the raw metals gave further impetus to trade. Brittany, for example, had a fair amount of alluvial tin, lead, a little gold, but almost no copper, and this had to be procured, first from Britain and Iberia, and a little later, from the Alps. An extensive network developed, with an important axis extending from Ireland, with its gold and copper resources, through Wessex to western Brittany. There were rarer contacts with central Europe—the halberds, triangular daggers and low-flanged axes may have been inspired by central European Unetice forms. The trade is documented in Early Bronze Age Brittany by occasional hoards or isolated finds: a few fine gold crescentic lunulae, Irish in origin or inspiration, imported or copied halberds, occasional daggers, flat axes, or axes with slight flanges. The uneven spread of the metal sources also meant that the chiefdoms had to tap the resources of a wider hinterland, and in this way more remote parts of Brittany and Normandy formed a necessary periphery to the chiefdoms. The thin distribution of bronze objects, often of rather modest types, in these areas probably marks the filtering down of prized objects in exchange for local resources.

Looking more closely at the Early Bronze Age materials, there is, yet again, a dearth of evidence on settlement, indeed a dearth of most sorts of evidence other than funerary. There is, therefore, no documentation of metal-working processes or organization. And the funerary evidence is mainly from a series of large mounds that cover one, or at most, a few, individuals, and represent only a very small proportion of the total population.

French archaeologists have tended to divide the mounds into two series suggestive of change through time. The first series dates between 1950 and 1650 bc (calibrated 2450–2050 BC) and includes at least four distinct types of mound burial probably corresponding to social divisions. The best known, because the finds are so spectacular, are the thirty or so huge mounds found mainly in the west along the coast, although there are a couple inland at Ployé, Finistère, and Saint-Fiacre, *Melrand*, Morbihan. These huge earthen mounds enclose a stone cairn that seals a central individual inhumation placed in a cist made of wood or dry-stone walling. No question here of tomb reuse. The wooden cists are concentrated in the north-west, in the Côtes-du-Nord (Tanouedou, *Boubriac*; Saint-Adrien; Mouden-Bras; Pleudaniel), and this area, with the neighbouring northern

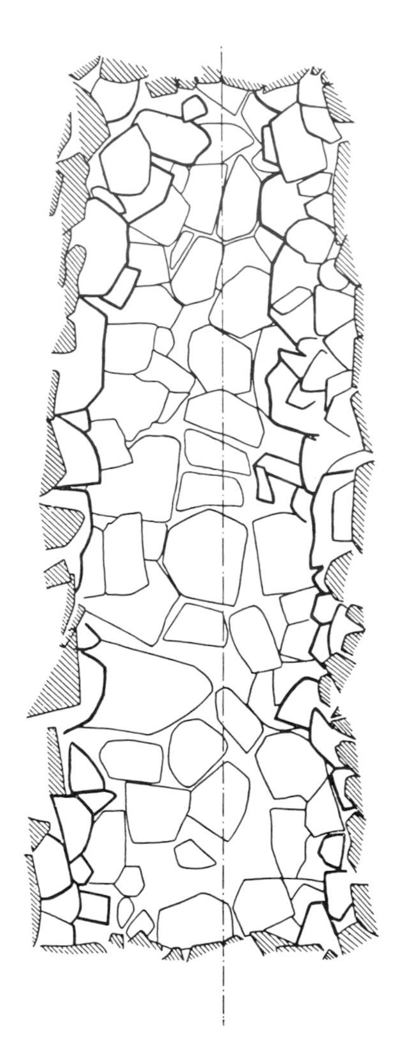

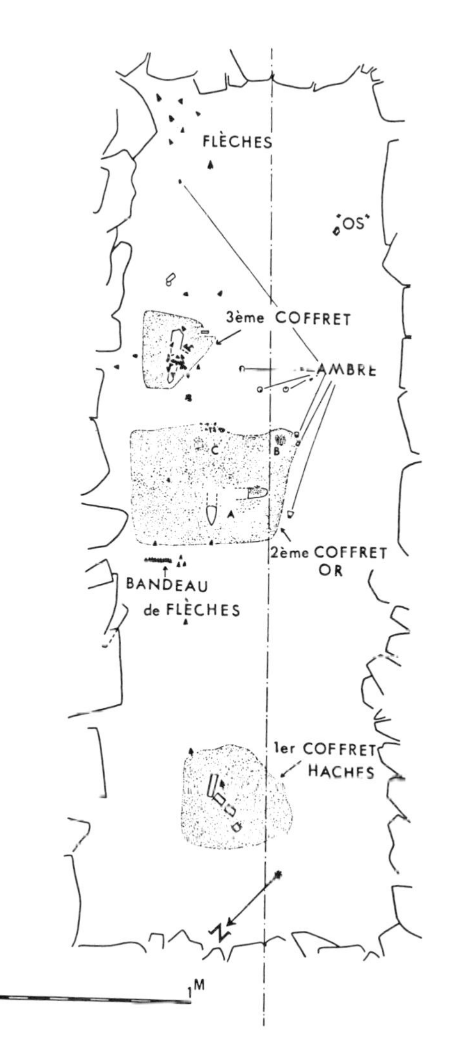

12 Plan of the Early Bronze Age burial floor below the mound of Kernonen, ***Plouvorn****, Finistère*
(*flèches* – arrows, *os* – bone, *3ème coffret* – 3rd cist, *ambre* – amber, *2ème coffret* – 2nd cist, *or* – gold, *bandeau de flèches* – quiver, *ler coffret* – 1st cist, *haches* – axes

Finistère (Plouvorn; Juno-bella, Berrien), may be the earliest bronze-using areas in Brittany. The individuals buried below these mounds were warriors who seem to have taken much of their individual wealth with them. One of the finest graves, excavated at Kernonen, Plouvorn in Finistère, has been reconstructed in the museum of *Penmarc'h*, Finistère (Figures 12 and 13). Among the lavish grave-goods were imports or copies of daggers with geometrically patterned gold-studded hilts and particular forms of amber beads that are very similar to ones found in the Wessex graves.

Other large mounds often placed close to this first type may have been used for important female burials. Again the body is placed in a wooden structure but with almost no metallurgy, and instead, some decorated pottery. At Saint-Jude, *Bourbriac*, Côtes-du-Nord, such an assemblage was placed inside a fine solid mortuary house made of thick branches (Figure 14). It was protected by a stone cairn covered by another, sloping, wooden roof. This mortuary house may, perhaps, give a clue to the construction of the totally missing domestic architecture. Yet other mounds contain a number of small cists, no central chamber and minimal grave-goods, and finally some seem to have no internal structures or grave-goods, and may not have been funerary mounds.

It is assumed that the second series of Early Bronze Age mounds are later in date, 1600 to 1400 bc (calibrated 1975–1700 BC). The distribution overlaps with the first series and the main concentration is still in Finistère, but there is also an inland penetration, to the Monts d'Arrée in southern Finistère and up the small valleys of Morbihan. These second series mounds are sited on poorer land and there are more of them (about a hundred, compared to the thirty of the first series). They tend to be smaller, more varied, and to be placed in groups (for example at Berrien, Finistère). They still cover a central rectangular, dry-stone walled pit or schist cist, but there are far fewer grave-goods, often no more than a biconical vase (of which one regional variant is a fine four-handled pot), a small bronze dagger and a little jewellery. Occasionally cists without mounds have also been found in these areas.

Since the dating is by no means very secure—there is very little difference in the carbon-14 range for the two series—two interpretations are possible. The second series may represent a belated, more insular, more impoverished development, and the wide distribution may reflect pressure on the land and a colonization of poorer soils. Or these mounds may be, at least in part, contemporary with the first series groups and represent somewhat more peripheral or lower-ranking sections of the society. For example, one of the second series in northern Finistère (Ploudalmézeau; Plouarzel; Trézéen; Plourin-Ploudalmézeau), apparently associated with a particularly fine group of decorated menhirs (Kerloas, *Plouarzel*, Kergadiou and Kergouèzel, *Porspoder*, etc.), lies close to the tin deposits of Saint-Renan. This might be a peripheral group, retaining strong Neolithic-Megalithic traditions, supplying tin to the neighbouring, more hierarchized, societies.

13 Bronze dagger with gold-studded hilt, amber wristguard and flint arrowheads found with the burial at Kernonen, ***Plouvorn****, Finistère*

14 Saint-Jude 2, ***Bourbriac****, Côtes-du-Nord*
a Plan of the timber-lined funerary pit
b Reconstruction of the funerary chamber

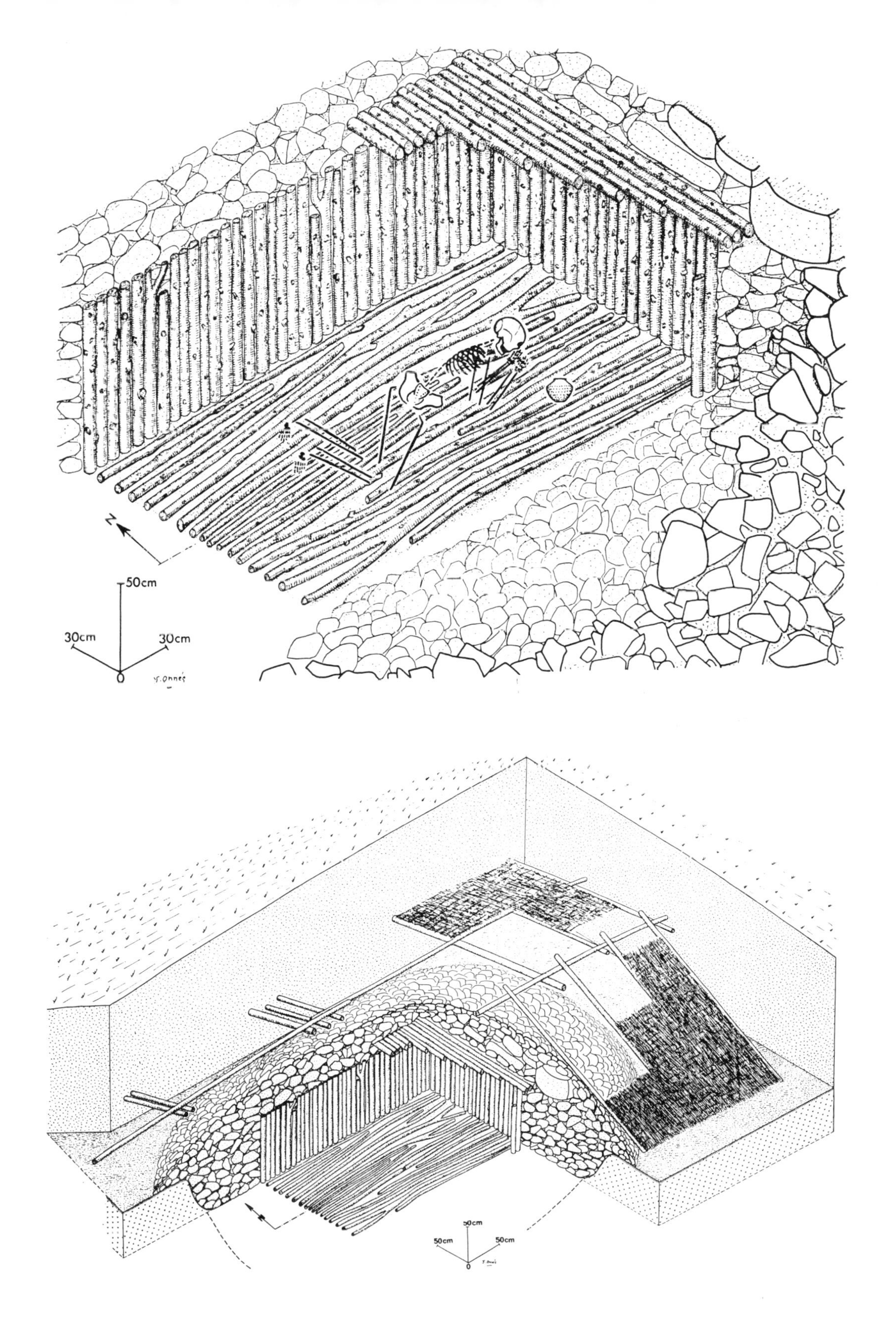

50cm
30cm
30cm
0
50cm
50cm
50cm
0

Middle Bronze Age
1400–1000 bc
calibrated *1700–1250* BC

Large or small, the burial mounds stop being built by about 1400 bc and the funerary evidence becomes very meagre—poorly dated cist graves, occasional cinerary urns, sometimes placed in earlier megalithic tombs (a few are found on Jersey and Guernsey, although the islands remain peripheral until almost the end of the Bronze Age). Settlement sites continue to remain extremely rare, little more than the occasional coastal midden, small coastal site (Roussellerie in the Loire-Atlantique) or promontory site (*Trémargat*, Côtes-du-Nord; Mont Joly, *Soumont-Saint-Quentin*, Calvados; the Hague-Dick, *Beaumont-Hague*, Manche, and the huge site of Bierre, *Merri*, Orne). Instead there is a new and rather difficult class of evidence—great hoards of metal objects.

In general, the Middle Bronze Age seems to be marked by the evolution of a number of tightly articulated, though independent, chiefdoms along and across the Channel. With bronze objects serving as a major form of prestige and power, there was every incentive to perfect the technology and to innovate in form and style. There is clearly considerable regional specialization allied to rapid dissemination of products and ideas. Alongside the material and marital exchanges, there must also have been exchanges of personnel and of expertise. The Channel linked rather than separated.

Two of the major production and distribution centres within this Atlantic province were located in Brittany and Normandy. In Brittany the hoard distribution shows considerable continuity with the earlier Bronze Age mound groupings. Some twenty hoards, known as the Tréboul series, are located in the same western coastal regions. (There are occasional hoards further afield, at Vicomté-sur-Rance in the Côtes-du-Nord, and Rennes in Ille-et-Vilaine.) The main elements of the Tréboul hoards were heavy flanged axes and palstaves. Weapons included decorated socketed spear heads with rivet holes that are clearly related to, if not derived from, southern England. Fine swords with bronze hilts are also made and traded up the Channel to the Low Countries and south as far as Lyons. There were also the beginnings of a tool inventory—socketed hammers and chisels.

In contrast, the Norman bronze manufacturing centre in the lower basin of the Seine seems to have no local antecedents. Like the contemporary lower Thames development, it was ideally located to utilize Channel, coast and interior lines of communication. Middle Bronze Age production in the lower Seine may have begun a little earlier than in Brittany, hoards such as the one at Muids in the Eure with decorated axes probably pre-date the Tréboul palstaves and swords, but in general the range of objects is much the same and is mainly differentiated by stylistic features—the Norman axe and palstave have wider blades and more cast decoration.

As time goes on, the hoards become larger and more specialized. In Brittany over a thousand objects were found in a Late Tréboul hoard at Languenan (Côtes-du-Nord), with large numbers of palstaves, often with rather minimal decoration and with a high tin content suggesting that local tin resources in northern Finistère and probably Morbihan and the lower Loire were being exploited. In Normandy fifty late Middle Bronze Age hoards from the Eure and Seine-Maritime contain one and a half thousand palstaves. The Norman palstaves show closer contact with southern England; the trident motif, for example, is found on both sides of the Channel and also the occasional loop attachment. The Norman palstave is exchanged over a very wide area, inland to the Yonne, north to the Somme, south to the Loire.

Increasingly, in the later Middle Bronze Age, the hoards comprise mainly tools and ornaments. Weapons—particularly swords— are more frequently found as isolated objects. It may be that weapon-making was a specialized, perhaps more centralized craft, while the tool/ornament hoards are the work of local smiths. Perhaps the large size of the hoards indicates that smithing was a seasonal occupation and that the smiths, working from a fixed abode, then supplied the local population, or supplied the chief who then redistributed the objects. Raw materials or recycled old bronzes are not part of the hoards, nor were they part of a separate trade sphere. They were, therefore, presumably exchanged in a more haphazard fashion against a variety of commodities.

Towards the end of the Middle Bronze Age contact with the great Tumulus chiefdoms of central Europe seems to assume more importance. Certainly many of the ornaments—the massive bracelets with engraved geometric panels (Ille-et-Vilaine and Normandy), the incised and ribbed pins (Seine hoards)—derive their inspiration from the east. However, the heavy gold Yeovil torques dotted through Brittany and Normandy—with one example on Jersey (St Helier)—derive, as the name suggests, from southern England (Figure 15).

15 Gold Torques 1 ***Cesson-Sévigné,*** *Ille-et-Vilaine 2* ***Saint-Jean-Trolimon,*** *Finistère*

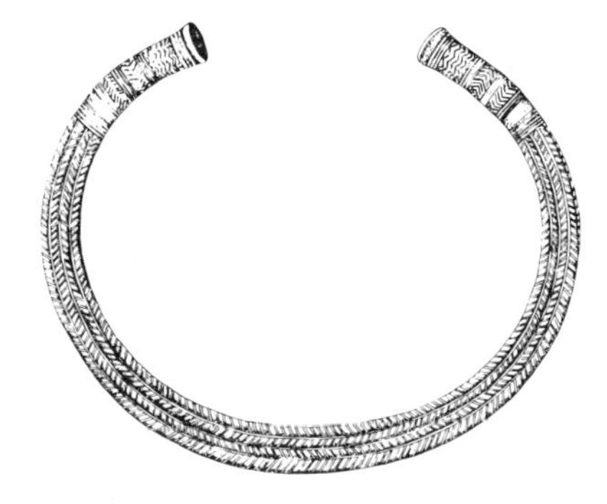

Late Bronze Age

1000/900–500 bc
calibrated 1250/1100–600 BC

By the beginning of the second millennium the eastern links are still more pronounced. By this time the Late Tumulus/Early Urnfield chiefdoms had spread westward to the middle Rhine and eastern France, and were meshed into a flourishing transalpine trade network. The demand for metal ores to feed their burgeoning bronze industries increased rapidly and the Atlantic groups were well placed to respond to this demand, either with their own metal resources or by acting as middle men between less developed societies with metal deposits and the Urnfield traders. In exchange they probably received copper ingots and salt, and certainly considerable quantities of bronze objects, particularly ornamental weapons. These were then copied, added to the Atlantic repertoire, and filtered through to the more remote sources of raw materials, for example southern Wales and Ireland.

So in the early Late Bronze Age, in both Brittany and Normandy, the distribution of hoards is wider and the variety of objects found in them greater. The north Breton Rosnoën hoards, for example, included hilt-plated rapiers of Urnfield (Rixheim) origin, median-winged axes and razors also of eastern type, and a wider range of small tools, as well as massive palstaves that derive from the earlier forms. An important centre developed around Nantes on the Loire, with easy access to the interior of France. And in Normandy, alongside the earlier local forms of palstave and incised bracelet, the Rosnoën-type palstaves, hilt-plated rapiers, basal-loop spearheads (another eastern element), and the wider range of small tool types began to be produced.

The Urnfield influence was maintained in the later hoards (Late Bronze Age II) on both sides of the Channel, in the Wilburton of southern England and the Saint-Brieuc-les-Ifs hoards of Brittany and Normandy. For example, the Urnfield leaf-shaped slashing sword (the Erbenheim) was introduced and then made locally.

The contents of the hoards alter in two respects in the Late Bronze Age. First, the repertoire increasingly served more utilitarian ends. The wider range of tools—chisel, axe, socketed gouge, knife, razor—probably means that bronze was being used by a wider section of the community and that increasingly it was used in the subsistence and domestic sector. In consequence, some of the bronze objects were 'devalued' and dropped out of the prestige sphere.

Secondly, with the increased demand for metal ores and finished goods to meet both the more extensive home market and the Urnfield demand, there was a greater premium on the accumulation of old stock for recycling. The Saint-Brieuc hoards are rarer, particularly in Normandy, but much larger and contain old and broken bronzes, copper ingots and sometimes moulds and scories.

All this no doubt reflects changes in the organization of smithing and in the relationship between the smith and his élite, or more humble, customer.

In the prestige sphere of exchange, weaponry becomes a major component. The fine ornamental forms are concentrated in the richer centres of production, the lowlands of southern England, the Breton and Norman centres. The disproportionate number of swords dredged from rivers (for example, fifty Saint-Brieuc swords from the Loire) suggests that they may have been thrown in as part of some important ceremonial or ritual undertaking. The emphasis on weaponry probably relates to increased competitiveness, and the particular form of the Late Bronze Age sword suggests that this competitiveness is beginning to take a new form. The new slashing sword is not simply a reflection of stylistic change but of a change in warfare. It must be associated with mounted warfare and, although no horse has yet been found in Brittany or Normandy, it must have been introduced at about this time, for there are horse-bits and decorative elements from horse gear, and the wheels of a small ritual chariot from Longueville in Calvados. The introduction of the horse must have had important long-term repercussions on the organization of warfare, and on the ability of chiefs to assert and maintain power.

The eighth and seventh centuries witnessed both the apogee and the end of the great Atlantic bronze-trading developments. The Carp's Tongue founders' hoards—named after the widely traded Atlantic slashing sword with its very pronounced ricasso and tapering blade—are far more numerous, very large (often over a thousand pieces) and display a still wider range of objects. In particular, socketed axes begin to be manufactured in great numbers, with a heavy concentration in Brittany. Other tools include anvils, chisels, saws, scythes and gouges, hog-backed knives, even a few hammers and hoes. Weaponry includes swords, daggers, spearheads and helmets (nine, placed neatly one inside the other, were found at Bernières-d'Ailly, Calvados), and among the ornaments are torques, bracelets, buckles, pendants, pins, fibulae, and for toiletry, razors and tweezers.

Urnfield contacts are reflected in the winged axes (and in the imitation wings on the local socketed axes), and the bronze-hilted Mörigen swords, the hollow-cast and solid bracelets and neck-rings, and the occasional vase-headed pin.

The intricate Atlantic network of alliance and exchange now extended far to the south. It included the bronze-working centre in north-west Iberia, which utilized the rich local tin resources and, increasingly through the eighth century BC, tapped the copper resources of south-west Iberia. With this southern extension the Atlantic system hooked into the Phoenician network, probing northwards from its south Iberian colonies. So from the Somme to the Gironde and on into Spain, and up the rivers of the Seine and Loire, and across the Channel to south-east England, the network penetrated. Even the Channel Islands were involved; a few large hoards are found on Jersey and Guernsey.

But the system was vulnerable. From an Atlantic perspective the Bronze Age must have seemed an heroic age, but from the viewpoint of central Europe and the Mediterranean it remained 'a peripheral zone of motley people using archaic bronze technologies and weapon fashions long outdated in Central Europe'.[4] And by the end of the eighth, beginning of the seventh century, new developments in central Europe and the Mediterranean increasingly isolated the Atlantic communities. For now iron began to be worked north of the Alps and slowly the demand for tin and lead from the west declined. Moreover, as new trade networks began to open up between the Early Iron Age Hallstatt C communities north of the Alps and the Greeks and Etruscans in southern France, the Po valley and the head of the Adriatic, the copper and other commodities that had once been traded westwards were deflected to the south. This copper was vital to the Atlantic industries. And then, by the end of the seventh century Spanish tin and copper ceased to circulate northwards, for the Phoenician colonies further to the south were cut off by the expansion of the Greeks, and the centre of power in Iberia shifted from the Atlantic coast to the south. By the sixth century the disruption of raw material supplies, coupled with over-production of bronzes for a dwindling and unstable market, registered both in a noticeable decline in the quality of the bronzes, the Breton socketed axes being rendered more or less non-functional by the excessive percentage of lead, and in the burying of vast numbers of hoards, perhaps because they had lost value or as part of a rather desperate attempt to maintain some scarcity value (Figure 16). In Armorica some 36,000 axes were buried in over two hundred and fifty hoards!

16 Late Bronze Age socketed bronze axe hoard from ***Marchésieux****, Manche*

[4] D. L. Clarke, 1979, 'The Economic Context of Trade and Industry in Barbarian Europe till Roman Times', in *Analytical Archaeologist*, pp. 263–331.

Bronze/Iron Age Transition, Hallstatt C/D

600 BC to 450 BC

The burgeoning Early Iron Age societies of eastern France and Germany have no counterpart in Normandy and Brittany or on the Channel Islands. Instead we witness the collapse of the Atlantic bronze network and the transition to a more fragmentary and insular, less hierarchical and more competitive society.

The Atlantic is no longer a major communication corridor; exchange, on a much more limited scale, is orientated to the east, so that while once-flourishing maritime provinces are marked by dwindling numbers of Carp's Tongue and socketed axe hoards, the more easterly interiors of Normandy and of Brittany, fed by the Seine and Loire, import and copy—often in bronze—a restricted number of items from the Iron Age centres in Burgundy and the Marne. Burgundy was directly meshed into the Rhône corridor trade with the Greek colony at Massalia and with the north Italian Etruscans. The Marne was in tight relationship with Burgundy; and the Seine and the Loire were the peripheral contact arteries by which the Marnian groups gained their necessary exchange commodities. These probably included tin from the alluviums of the Loire and Morbihan in Brittany, salt from lower Normandy and Brittany (Lion-sur-Mer in Calvados; Préfailles in the Loire-Atlantique), products of the forest (timber, pitch, resin, honey, furs and leather), and, beginning in the Early Iron Age and becoming increasingly important, slaves. In return came personal adornments—bossed bracelets, fibulae, a rare torque, or beads of coral, blue glass or amber, or an occasional iron spearhead or iron sword with antennae (one, for example, dredged from the Loire at Guesne-en-Crossac, another placed in a rich burial at Ifs in Calvados—reconstructed at the Musée de Normandie, *Caen*). An occasional metal bucket (situla) was imported and then locally copied in pottery (another rich grave at le Rocher, *le Bono* in Morbihan had a bronze situla for the ashes, covered with a bronze cup of Etruscan form). A griffin head (Etruscan or a south-east French copy) was dredged from the Loire and two bronze oxen were found in Ille-et-Vilaine.

Probably contacts were somewhat intermittent, and such exchanges would not have been sufficient to underwrite a highly differentiated élite. Indeed, the evidence from the cemeteries suggests that while there were more important personages in the local societies, they were not set far above the rest. On the plain of Caen and Bessin in Normandy there are small cemeteries (Longrais, Soumont-Saint-Quentin and Ifs, Calvados) of flat graves, generally orientated south-south-east, containing individual extended or flexed inhumations in shallow pits (Figure 17). There may be a grave marker; there are often hearths and sherds to suggest ritual feasting. Grave-goods are modest, but there are distinctions, the imported jewellery is primarily in the centrally placed graves. And again in Brittany, among a plethora of different types of burial (cremations below small mounds, cinerary urns in flat graves, some inhumations), there are small cemeteries with individual cremations in urns placed in cists or pits within a circular stone revetted area, covered with a low earthen mound. Here, too, there are variations in the quantity and quality of the grave-goods (le Rocher, *le Bono* in Morbihan).

There is little evidence of where these people lived—a ditched farmstead from Kerlande, Brandivy, Morbihan may prefigure the dispersed pattern found in the later Iron Age; promontories and hilltops are occasionally defended, for example at Toul-Goulic, *Trémargat*, Côtes-du-Nord, Fossé Catuélan, *Cap d'Erquy*, Côtes-du-Nord and *Jerbourg* and Mont-Orgueil on Jersey.

Iron remains a rare commodity.

17 Early Iron Age burial from the cemetery of pit graves at Ifs, Calvados

18 Bronze helmet with bronze and iron decoration from ***Amfreville-Sous-Les-Monts****, Eure*

19 Iron Age stele, from Ruat, ***Ploudaniel****, Finistère, diameter 1.8 m*

Later Iron Age and the Roman Conquest

450–56 BC

In the mid-fifth century BC (the beginning of the La Tène), there are shifts in the centres of power further to the east, with the most vigorous and politically dominant chiefdoms centring on the Marne and Middle Rhine. These are associated with changes in the southern axis of contact and trade, with the Rhône corridor losing out to transalpine contacts with the Etruscans of northern Italy. The power of the Middle Rhine groups owed much to their location close to rich sources of iron ore, while that of the Marnian chiefdoms seems to be sustained by their ability to siphon in materials from far-flung areas, including the Atlantic seaboard. South-east Brittany with its tin, iron ore and salt supplies was one such area, Lower Normandy with iron ore and salt another. Strabo, the Greek commentator, recorded an important trading emporium at Corbilo on the Loire, and isolated finds and hoards of bipyramidal iron ingots attest to one aspect of the trade (thirty-eight ingots were found at Kercaradec, Moëlan-sur-Mer, Finistère, thirty to fifty at Saint-Connan, Côtes-du-Nord). In return Marnian or Etruscan imports are found, though still on a very modest scale—an elaborately decorated Italian helmet and an oenochoe at Tronoan, Saint-Jean-Trolimon (Finistère), a sword in a richly decorated sheath from Kernavest, Quiberon (Morbihan), a fine helmet from Amfreville-sous-les-Monts (Eure), and metal vases, which are then imitated in fine local pottery (Figure 18).

Meanwhile, a local iron industry begins to develop. It produces both utilitarian items—tools, utensils, nails, etc.—and prestige items. The utilitarian items permit more extensive forest clearance (for example at Mont d'Arrée and Montagnes Noires in Finistère), and more intensive farming (ploughmarks are found below the dunes at Plougoulin, Finistère). One reason for intensification may have been an increase in population. Another that land was becoming an important commodity. In earlier Breton and Norman societies elders and chiefs had gained and maintained position by manipulating kinship networks and alliances and by controlling the flow of prestige objects. The necessary surplus for feasting and exchange was extracted from the individual's household, from kin or debtors. But now, in the later Iron Age, it is possible that a more direct control of land and production began to be exercised and that status began to be defined, not only in terms of lineage affiliation, but in terms of landed and non-landed divisions. Thus by the late fifth and fourth centuries BC petty chiefdoms began, once again, to emerge, but based on rather different social relations.

There is evidence, particularly from Brittany, of more permanent field boundaries; evidence of isolated farmsteads or hamlets, often on high ground or on small islands (Ile Gaignog, *Landéda*, Finistère), surrounded by ditches and banks that may be a defence against wild animals, but also against humans. Evidence, too, of defended camps, sometimes hilltops (Kercaradec, Penhars, Finistère; Péran, *Plédran*, Côtes-du-Nord), often promontories (*Cap d'Erquy*, Côtes-du-Nord; Camp de César, *Ile-de-Groix*, Morbihan; Castel Coz, *Beuzac-Cap-Sizun*, Finistère, and a series of small camps on Jersey and Guernsey). These camps were usually very small, a refuge and a place for seasonal gatherings or exchanges. Other camps, still small but with multiple defences, may have been the locus for a petty chief, perhaps also for craft specialists producing prestige items for local and more distant exchanges. At such camps there may have been resident smiths and specialist potters. The smiths combined iron and bronze technology to make an array of bracelets and rings (sometimes incorporating imported blue glass), fibulae, and weaponry, including large swords, helmets and horse gear. The potters began to turn out fine hand-turned or wheel-made ware, metallic in shape, metallic in sheen through the addition of graphite or by controlled firing, decorated at first formally with classical geometric motifs, and then, by the late fourth century, with free-flowing Celtic derivatives. Other seasonal specialists, whose product was also probably controlled by the chiefs, worked the numerous salt-production sites along the coast—by the late Iron Age one hundred and twenty sites are known for Brittany alone, and there are others in Normandy and on the Channel Islands.

At some of the early La Tène sites, particularly in the territories of the Veneti and Osismi tribes of Morbihan and Finistère, there are underground chambers cut in the rock, entered by a passage or shaft. They contain remarkably little. They could be for storage, and pots have been found in them, or more probably they were 'cult' sites—two stelae had been placed in one of them, and they all appear to be very carefully sealed up.

Status was not generally signified in burial form or grave-goods. In Brittany inhumation and cremation continued but now in flat cemeteries. Ritual at such cemeteries often involved the erection of stone stelae. At Kerviltré, Saint-Jean-Trolimon, in a cemetery with eighty cinerary urns there were half a dozen stelae.

Other stelae are found that are not in direct association with burials. Some, particularly, though not exclusively, in the Veneti territory, are low and hemispherical or spherical in shape; others are taller, with an angular or round cross-section (Figure 19). The largest are found in Finistère, and there are certain regional styles. Fine grooved examples come from south-west Cornouille, Cap Sizun and Pays Bigouden. Occasionally they are decorated (Sainte-Anne-

Trégastal, *Trégastal*, Côtes-du-Nord).

Through the fifth to the later second century, Brittany and Normandy remain rather insular. Then, quite rapidly, these areas are drawn into the orbit of the Roman empire. During the second century, the Romans had pushed northwards into southern France, and by 120 BC, having defeated the Arveni in the Massif Central and made an alliance with the Aedui, they created the province of Narbonensis, which stretched from the Upper Rhône to Toulouse. For the next sixty years they consolidated their position in the south, and entered into treaties with the tribes of central Gaul, and more tenuous trading alliances with more distant groups. They called unconquered Gaul *Gallia Comata* (long-haired Gaul), after the Celts' fearsome habit of spiking out their hair with limewash. Trade was mainly in terms of slaves, but also involved tin, precious metals, corn and salt (very highly prized for seasoning, preserving, supplementing cattle fodder, etc.). In return the Romans sent wine and fine bronze serving sets. In central Gaul the greatly enlarged volume of trade permitted certain chiefs to expand their retinues, armies and territories at the expense of others less well placed. Great fortified *oppida*, proto-towns, developed and an oligarchic system emerged that curtailed at least some of the intense competitiveness. But Normandy, Brittany and the Channel Islands, while drawn into the sphere of Roman trade and exchange, obviously remained more peripheral. Caesar, and other Roman commentators, and the great epic tales of Ireland, which refer back to the Celtic Iron Age societies, talk of an élite—an equestrian aristocracy, land-owning but not immediately involved in production—then of a class of freemen, farmers (who also doubled as retinue, soldiers and charioteers), craftsmen, religious specialists, and finally a class of unfree men, ranging from temporary debtors to slaves. There was mobility between classes and it was a highly competitive society. Warfare for land was endemic. More land gave more produce and more personnel, including hostages. Power was measured by a man's retinue and by his ability to feast. Feasts were the locus of hospitality, and the arena in which status was claimed—and disputed. Diodorus Siculus reported that 'they also invite strangers to their banquets, and only after the meal do they ask who they are and of what they stand in need. At dinner they are wont to be moved by chance remarks to wordy disputes, and to fight in single combat, regarding their lives as naught.' They drank—alarming quantities according to the Romans. The local brew was a wheaten beer prepared with honey, but one of the attractions of the second-century trade with the Romans was wine, for which, it is said, they were prepared to give a slave for every full amphora (twenty-five litres).

How far we can take these accounts back, and how far the details remain true for the more peripheral Celtic societies of Normandy and Brittany is open to question. It may be that the free/unfree distinctions were less true in Armorica than for central Gaul; but the competitiveness, the emphasis on martial prowess and plunder, the feasting, the land hunger, probably holds true for the whole of the Celtic world.

Probably, then, in Brittany and Lower Normandy and the Channel Islands, there were petty chiefdoms that perhaps acknowledged a common regional name, and accepted a symbolic central figure—a paramount (the king in the Irish traditions). There might be, as Caesar recorded, a council of elders, but again their position was vulnerable.

One of the most powerful Breton tribes in the second century was the Veneti who occupied the south-east. They acted as middlemen in the long-distance Roman trade. The Corbilo emporium on the Loire seems to have faded out by the second century and although trade continued via the Rhône corridor, most Roman commodities probably came across southern France, along the river Garonne, up the Atlantic and were then trans-shipped in Morbihan (at Vannes) and transported by the Veneti around the coast of Brittany and across the Channel, or overland to the river Rance and down to Alet at *Saint-Malo* and from there, perhaps with a stopover on the Channel Islands, to Hengistbury Head in southern England. The overland route involved passing through the territory of the Coriosolites and it appears that there were close relations (possibly not entirely equal) between the Veneti and the Coriosolites. The Veneti—according to Caesar—had a fleet of some two hundred leather-sailed ships. They shipped wine in amphorae (mainly Dressel IA), many of which have been found on the Quiberon peninsula. The strength of their political and economic position is suggested by their minting of gold coinage in the late second century. Such minting had, earlier on, been monopolized by the Arveni in the Massif Central, but after their defeat in 120 BC, the way was open for other powerful groups to mint their own coins. At first it was gold based and the figures derived from the Arveni coinage and ultimately from the gold stater of Philip of Macedon. It was a restricted commodity—an item circulated as payment within the prestige sphere. By the end of the second century, as other Armorican tribes meshed into the highly competitive network, they too minted coins—the Riedones, Namnetes, Osismi and eventually, in the mid-first century, the Coriosolites (Figure 20). As the conquest approached and trade increased, and the need to pay armies, more base metal was added—the Coriosolites' coinage was mainly copper, with up to twenty per cent silver.

As well as—and no doubt feeding into—this long-distance trade, there was, in the second century BC, increasing inter-tribal cross-channel and Armorican trade, in which the Veneti also played an important part. Again Alet at *Saint-Malo* (Ille-et-Vilaine), in the territory of the Coriosolites, was probably the most important port, with Hengistbury as a counterpart on the other side of the Channel. St Peter Port on Guernsey was probably an important stopover point, and parts of Lower Normandy were also drawn into the network. There were, for example, regional Norman and Breton pottery centres and Hengistbury and St Peter Port (King's Road) on Guernsey, received graphite-coated ware that was probably produced in Finistère, black cordoned ware from Lower Normandy/ Trégor, and rilled ware from an area west of Trégor.

Such active trading and craft production may well have stimulated larger and more centralized settlements, and the large defended camps of Armorica and High Normandy probably began as political and economic centres, and then, as the Roman conquest approached, became the rallying points for tribal resistance. There is a huge, thirty hectare site, the defences of which were never completed, at Lesouer, Guégon, Morbihan, on the tribal border of the Veneti and Coriosolites; another, of twenty hectares, at Poulailler, Landéan, Ille-et-Vilaine on the eastern border of the Rediones; another large one in Unelli territory at *Petit-Celland* in the Manche; and a vast one, rallying point for the west, at Camp d'Artus, *Huelgoat* in Finistère.

In the north, in High Normandy, on the southern borders of the Belgic tribes (Celts too, but centred towards the Somme) there was a whole series of great *oppida*, stretching along the Channel coast, the Seine estuary, and up the river (Incheville, *Bracquemont*, Auppegard, Heugleville, *Veulettes*, *Fécamp*, *Sandouville*, Saint-Nicolas-de-la-Taille, Saint-Samson-de-la-Roque, Bouquelon, Caudebec-en-Caux, *Duclair*, Orival, Saint-Pierre-d'Autils and *Vernon*). Some of these may only have been thrown

20 Tribal territories in Brittany and Normandy, and routes to southern Britain

up in the mid-first century as a defence against Caesar, but others were involved in the pre-Conquest cross-Channel and Armorican trade. These camps were probably larger and more permanent than those in Brittany, and some have extensive cemeteries (Orival is associated with the cemetery at Caudebec-lès-Elbeuf or Moulineaux; Caudebec-en-Caux with Saint-Wandrille-Rançon; Bracquemont with Caudecôte), and, more generally, there is a great concentration of cemeteries along the river routes of High Normandy and, in particular, on the confluence of the Seine, the Eure and the Andelle. Some of the cinerary urns from these Norman cemeteries show marked similarities with the English Aylesford series, whilst others, for example from Caudecôte, suggest contact with Armorica. Occasionally, individual graves within these cemeteries, and also in the late Iron Age cemeteries in Brittany and on the Channel Islands, deviate from the normal rather minimal grave-goods, and give a glimpse of a warrior chief, with items that emphasize both the importance of martial skills and of prestige accoutrements gained through warfare or trade. At Notre-Dame-du-Vaudreuil (Eure) a cremation was placed with a helmet, sword and fine pottery (museum of *Louviers*), whilst an inhumation at Tronoan (Finistère) in the territory of the Osismi has a sword, spearheads, pottery, a gold statue and coins. The 'warrior graves' in western Guernsey and at St Peter Port in eastern Guernsey contain swords and their belt rings, shield fittings, spears and, more occasionally, knives, amber, glass, jet and bronze rings, as well as fine cordoned and graphite decorated vessels.

In 57 BC, Caesar, secure in southern France, moved north-east to conquer Belgic Gaul. The *oppida* along the Seine were fortified and refortified by the Belgae. Known as the Fécamp series, the defences comprised an encircling wide flat-bottomed ditch, a dump rampart and an inturned entrance. Often the camps were never completed. Caesar picked them off one by one and the different Belgic groups capitulated.

Meanwhile, his ambassadors were sent to Brittany; the Armorican tribes appeared to submit, but only in order to retrench and combine forces. They began to refortify their *oppida*, using a different technique to the Belgae. They dug V-shaped ditches and sometimes constructed what Caesar called a *murus gallicus*, a rampart comprising a criss-cross of horizontal timbers kept in place with thousands of nails, a vertical stone-facing through which the ends of the timbers protruded and a rubble infill (for example at *Petit-Celland* and Lithaire, both in the Manche). Sometimes, as at the vast Camp d'Artus of the Osismi at *Huelgoat* (Finistère) or at *Plédran* (Côtes-du-Nord), the timbers were fired (on purpose or accidentally) and stone and timber were vitrified into an almost impenetrable barrier. But often the defences remained half-finished, and often there is evidence of violent destruction. For in 56 BC the Veneti killed the Roman ambassadors, and Caesar attacked. He dispatched Labienus northwards to ensure that the Belgae remained quiet, and Crassus southwards to Aquitaine to prevent southern reinforcements. Sabinus, with three legions, pursued the Coriosolites and their allies under the leadership of Viridorix of the Unelli, and defeated them, probably at *Petit-Celland* in the Manche. And Caesar himself marched against the Veneti. They were holed up in their promontory hill forts and, he admitted that 'it was impossible to approach them by land, when the tide rushed in from the open sea ... and they were also difficult to reach by sea because at low tides the ships would run aground on the shoals.' So he attacked in concert with Brutus who took on the Veneti fleet off the coast of Morbihan. The Veneti had two hundred high-prowed, square leather-sailed ships, the Romans had faster, low galleys powered by oars. The Romans rowed in among the ships and, with long-armed sickles, cut the stays of the sails. In addition, the winds dropped and the Veneti ships were becalmed. The slaughter was great, and Caesar's vengeance on the leaders was terrible.

What happened to the defeated tribes? Some, at least, of the Coriosolites may have sought refuge on the Channel Islands. The huge flight-hoards of Coriosolites' coinage on Jersey (four at Le Câtel de Rozel, *St Martin*, one with nine hundred coins, one with seven hundred, and one at La Marquanderie, *St Brelade*, with twelve thousand) suggest the mint may have been shipped to the island. The small enclosed site of Tranquesous, St Saviour on Guernsey with some fifteen defended huts seems to have been a settlement of the Coriosolites.

The Romans had to spend another sixty years subduing *Gallia Comata*. Caesar mentions that the Lexovii (around Lisieux) amd the Aulerci (in the Eure and east of the Orne) rose against their own council of elders for having been too 'docile' in 56 BC and tried to come to the aid of the Unelli, and again in 52 BC, at the instigation of the College of Druids, these and many other tribes joined under Vercingetorix of the Arveni. The chief of the Aulerci directed the defence of Lutetia (Paris) and fell in battle. Others fought, and lost, at Alesia.

During this second part of the first century the Romans ruled through the intermediary of allies among the Celtic chiefs. Many local chiefs continued to flourish and, for example, the Belgic tribes handled much of the trade down the Seine and over to south-east England. The Seine *oppida* continued in use. In contrast the Armorican tribes continued to resist, and the trade route between Alet and Hengistbury ceased to function. It was not until 27 BC that Augustus embarked on a far more thorough-going Romanization. By the mid-first century AD the Seine *oppida* had ceased to serve as tribal centres.

Post Conquest *to AD 400*

One reason for the Romanization of the administration in Gaul was a desire to implement a more systematic tax system. Augustus and his lieutenant, Agrippa, undertook a major census of land holdings, values and usage, and then within the four major provinces of Gaul (Narbonensis, Belgica, Lugdunensis and Aquitania), they reorganized further subdivisions known as *civitates*. The *civitas* corresponds, more or less, to the old tribal area and within it the administrative centre was often at a tribal focal point. Brittany fell within the province of Lugdunensis and the five *civitates* centred on Condevicnum (*Nantes*, territory of the Namnetes), Condate (*Rennes*, territory of the Riedones), Darioritum (*Vannes*, the Veneti), Fanum Martis (*Corseul*, the Coriosolites) and Vorgianum or Vorgium (*Carhaix*, the Osismi) (Figure 21). Normandy was part of the provinces of Lugdunensis and Belgica and comprised some eight *civitates* conforming to the territories of the Abrincatui, the Unelli, the Baiocasses, the Viducasses, the Essuvii, the Lexovii, the Aulerci Eburovices, the Velliocasses and the Caletes.

Epigraphic evidence from Rennes shows that in AD 135 there was a senate with a magistrate; the *civitas* was subdivided into several districts, and there was a fairly complex organization of the Imperial cult. It is probable, though not proven, that the other *civitates* were organized in much the same way. On the other hand, the Channel Islands seem to have fallen, for all practical purposes, outside the administrative network, although they may have had some importance as ports of call in the Roman wine-trade network. On Guernsey a small second- or third-century settlement at St Peter Port obtained Roman imports, and two wrecks, probably first century AD, with wine amphorae, were found close to the port. First century AD Spanish wine amphorae and other Roman wares, as well as Breton pottery, was found at the small village of Coriosolites at Tranquesous.

Unlike other parts of Gaul, Roman Brittany and Normandy had relatively few, and quite small, towns. Urban industry appears to have been limited, and often the main function of the town was administrative, involving the collection of tribute and taxes. Such activities necessitated an effective network of roads, and by the second half of the first century AD the

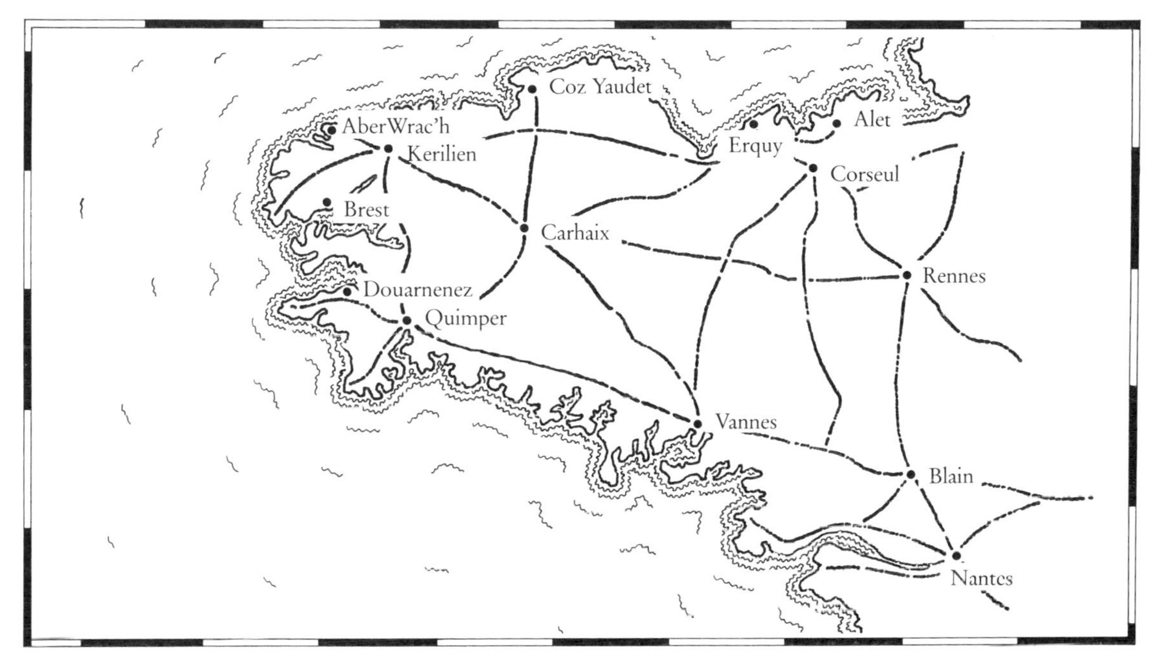

21 Roman roads in Brittany

countryside was laced with small and large roads. The towns were at nodal points, often combining river or sea navigation with inland transport systems. Some of the towns also served as points of entry for imports of wine and oil, or Samian ware from south and central Gaul, or pottery from the workshops in the territory of the Arveni. Many of the towns were constructed on a tight orthogonal plan, with *insulae* (street-blocks) of artisan workshops, administrative buildings, public baths and theatres. Shrines, sometimes occupying a room off the town hall (*basilica*), were erected, and the indigenous gods were often associated with, or replaced by, the Imperial cult. Condate (*Rennes*), for example, was built on such a plan in the first half of the first century AD, and covered about a hundred hectares. By the early second century a temple to Mars Mullo, a basilica, huge baths, suburban villas, and pottery workshops had been constructed. *Corseul* covered over one hundred and thirty hectares, and aerial photos show a similar orthogonal plan. But other towns were more haphazardly arranged, with a more dispersed series of *insulae*. At *Quimper*, Finistère, there was the small port at Locmaria, with workshops (bronze-smiths, probably potters) and modest houses, and then there were urban *insulae* strung along the river Odet. Roads radiated out to Vannes, Carhaix, Morlaix, Kérilien en Plounéventer, Crozon, Douarnenez and Tronoën. One such *insula*, close to Locmaria at Roz-Avel had some fine private dwellings, baths and a large civic building.

But throughout the Roman occupation, much of the population and much of the wealth was located not in the town but in the countryside, on the agricultural estates. Probably many of the early villas replaced Iron Age farmsteads, and were the domain of rich, Romanized Celts. Others were new establishments sometimes on newly-cleared land. In Brittany the densest concentrations were along the coast, particularly around the Bay of Saint-Brieuc and the Gulf of Morbihan, but there was also a scattering of villas in the interior. Many place-names suggest the sites of villas—often names that end in -y or -ay or -ey, or sites with names like le Bosquet, le Bus, l'Épine. Mézières or Masures suggests ruins; la Tuilerie, les Tuileaux, le Perrier, the ubiquitous Roman tile.

There are several recognizable villa-styles; the 'cottage-house', found, for example, in the first phase of building at Kéradennec, Saint-Frégant (Finistère); or the villa with a corridor façade flanked by two turrets, or with wing extensions. Phase two at Kéradennec has a corridor with turrets, so does Valy-Cloistre, la Roche-Maurice, Guilligomarc'h, also in Finistère (Figure 22), and Saint-Aubin-sur-Mer (Calvados). There are also larger, and later, courtyard villas with buildings around one or two courtyards, with access via an ornamental porch. The courtyard villa combined a luxurious abode including baths, with farm buildings, barns, forges and labourers' quarters. So, for example, in the third century, Kéradennec was transformed and enlarged on the courtyard plan, and incorporated a fine bath building (Figure 23).

Such estates were probably of the order of two to three hundred hectares and might employ or maintain several hundred people. They produced much wheat, probably also hemp and flax, and animal products, and since much of it was for export, they were closely linked to the road network.

There were also specialist work-sites. Iron, for example, was exploited in High Normandy at a series of small sites in the forests of the Pays d'Ouche in the Eure. In Brittany the indigenous salt industry was greatly extended. Along the bay of *Douarnenez* in Finistère, centred on Plomarc'h Pella, are the remains of considerable work areas. There were rooms for preparing fish (mainly sardine, but also tunny fish), and a series of square vats, 3 to 4 m long, 2 to 4 m deep, often set in rows and protected by tiled roofs, for salting and for *garum* (fish sauce) preparation. There were lodgings, too. Other salt-working sites are found at Lorient in the Loire-Atlantique and in the bay of Saint-Brieuc.

A number of detailed excavations in Brittany make it possible to outline the changing fortunes of town and country. Conditions appear relatively stable until almost the end of the second century; then between AD 170 and 180

22 Plan and reconstruction of the villa at Valy-Cloistre, La Roche-Maurice, Finistère (below and opposite)

some villas were fired. At Valy-Cloistre, la Roche-Maurice (Finistère), part of the family treasures were left behind in the destroyed building. Kéradennec, Saint-Frégant, was burnt but then reconstructed on a larger scale at the beginning of the third century. The unrest may have been internal, and may have been widespread, since similar destruction is recorded in Belgic Gaul. Such unrest, and more general dislocations within the Imperial administration, may have affected the towns still more acutely, for it would appear that, despite the sporadic destruction of rural sites, the richer town-dwellers began to move out from the towns and established themselves on larger, more luxurious, defended, rural estates. Quimper, for example, seems to decline in the second century, and many of the larger private buildings fell into disuse, while the rural villas were often rebuilt and redecorated. At Kéradennec, Saint-Frégant, the painted plaster was renewed with decoration imitating marble panelling, and at Kervenennec, Pont-Croix, the painted mortar floors were replaced by stone inlays, stucco and sculpted decorations, and shell-encrustations. The flight of wealth to the countryside is perhaps suggested by the find of 14,000 coins below the floor of the villa at Mané-Véchenn, Plouhinec.

In the mid-third century conditions worsened. There were Germanic attacks along the Rhine and Danube, Frankish, Saxon and Frisian pirates raided up the Seine and around the Cotentin, even rounding Armorica and attacking the lower Loire. Despite the garrisons at Rouen, Rotomagus, Coutances and Avranches, which were part of the Saxon shore defence line, the Franks and Alamans pushed into northern Gaul and by AD 277 Evreux was fired. Lisieux was sacked twice in the third century, and the survivors retreated to a small fortified area; Vieux, ten kilometres south-east of Caen, and the capital of the Viducasses *civitas* was destroyed at the end of the third century. Armorica was less immediately affected but the unrest led to hoards being buried and to hasty attempts to build up a second line of defence behind the Saxon shore defences. So coastal towns like *Nantes*, *Brest*, Alet, *Saint-Servan* (which had

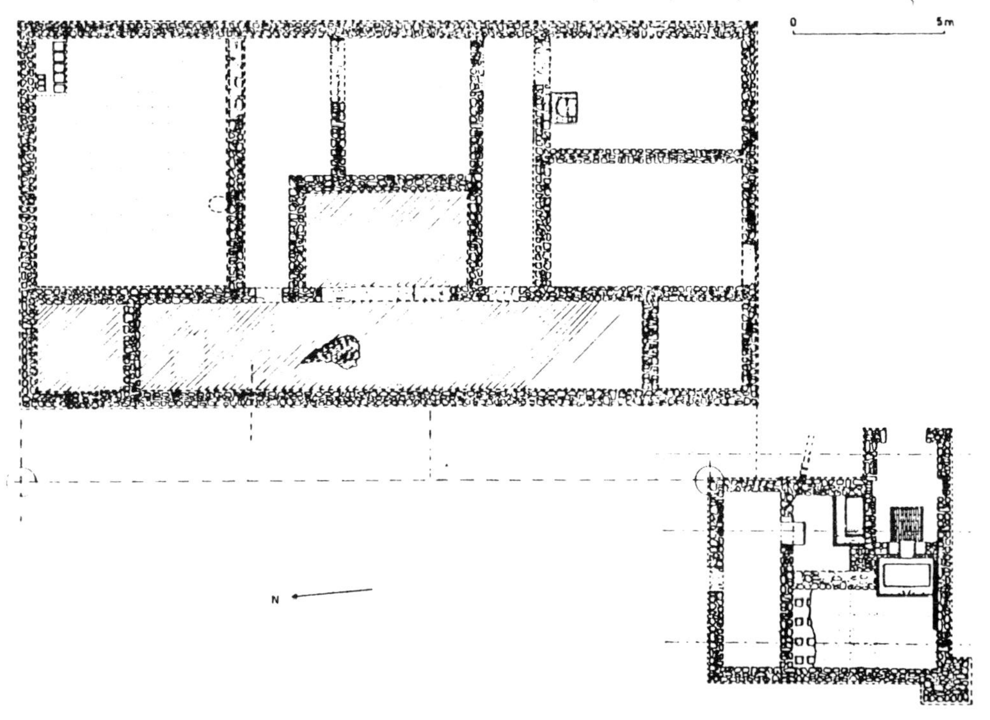

lost much of its importance in the first century AD), *Vannes*, and inland *Rennes* were all fortified or refortified between AD 275 and 300. Even on Alderney, the Nunnery site fortification was thrown up. To no great avail. The towns were burnt, the villas at Kervenennec, Pont Croix and Kéradennec, Saint-Frégant, were abandoned between AD 270 and 280. Much of the countryside seems to have been depopulated, there was a sharp decrease in cultivation, forests regenerated, commercial links were severed, the fish-salting and *garum* industry at Douarnenez stopped.

23 Villa (courtyard house phase) at Kéradennec, ***Saint-Frégant****, Finistère (scale 1 cm : 5 m)*

Some of the destruction may have been caused by local uprisings, and some, at least, of the villas were reoccupied by indigenous squatters. At Kéradennec rough walls were built to repartition rooms and an oven was installed in the bath house. But some of the squatters, for example at Kervenennec, still maintained some Roman links, and it may be that they were 'official' Celtic immigrants from southern Britain and Wales arriving by order of the Roman authorities in the early fourth century.

There may have been a brief reprieve in the first part of the fourth century; Roman imports pick up for a while. By the mid-fourth century there were more incursions, internal uprisings, firings and devastation. Villa and town alike were abandoned.

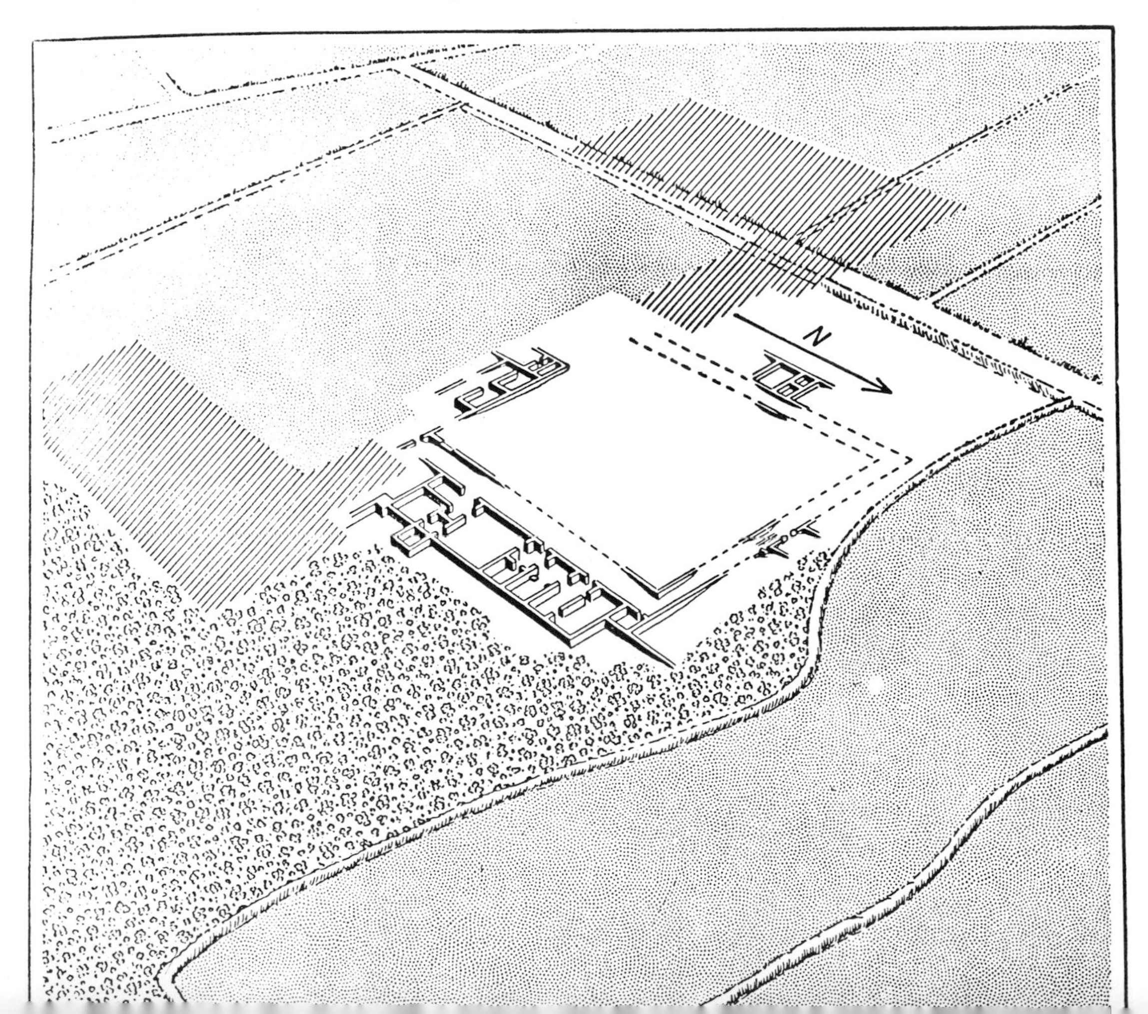

Carbon-14 Dates

A sample of dates from the Mesolithic to the Iron Age. The Neolithic dates are plotted on the diagram in Figure 24.
For an explanation of the difference between bc and BC dates see p. 16.

		bc	BC	lab. no.
Mesolithic				
Brittany	Saint-Pierre-Quiberon, Hoëdic, Morbihan	4625 + − 350	5480	GSY 227
	Plomeur, la Torche, Finistère	4020 + − 80	4875	GRN 2001
	Saint-Nazaire, Dissignac, Loire-Atlantique	4300 + − 150	4095	Gif 3823
		3390 + − 150	4835	Gif 3822
		3830 + − 150	4620	Gif 3820
Neolithic				
Megalithic Monuments and Mounds				
Brittany	1 Colpo, Larcuste II, Morbihan	3540 + − 120	4400	Gif 2826
		2660 + − 110	3440	Gif 2454
		2030 + − 110	2560	Gif 2453
	2 Saint-Nazaire, Dissignac, Loire-Atlantique			
	Primary phase	3830 + − 150	4615	Gif 3820
		3990 + − 150	4830	Gif 3822
		4570 + − 150	5435	Gif 3823

24 Carbon-14 dates for a range of Neolithic sites and monuments (site names are given in the carbon-14 lists)

Secondary phase	2990 + − 140	3775	Gif 3821
3 Perros-Guirec, Ile Bono, Côtes-du-Nord	3215 + − 130	3405	GSY 64A
	3245 + − 300	4035	GSY 64
4 La Forêt-Fouesnant, Kerleven, Finistère, chamber A	2875 + − 125	3665	GSY 111
	1950 + − 120	2455	Gif 809
5 Plouezoc'h, Barnenez, Côtes-du-Nord			
chamber G	3800 + − 150	4590	Gif 1309
chamber A	3500 + − 150	4375	Gif 1310
	3150 + − 140	3935	Gif 1116
chamber F	3600 + − 140	4450	Gif 1556
6 Landéda, Ile Guennoc, Finistère			
cairn IIIc	3850 + − 300	4630	Gif 165
IIIc	3125 + − 140	3910	Gif 1870
IIIe	2250 + − 120	2910	Gif 813
7 Ploudalmézeau, Ile Carn, Finistère			
South chamber	3440 + − 150	4315	Gif 1362
Central chamber	3390 + − 250	4235	Gif 414
Central chamber	3280 + − 75	4070	GRN 1968
North chamber	2890 + − 150	3675	Gif 1363
	2210 + − 120	2875	Gif 810
8 Gâvres, le Goërem, Morbihan	2480 + − 140	3225	Gif 1148
	2150 + − 140	2755	Gif 768
9 Carnac, Kercado, Morbihan	3890 + − 300	4670	Sa 95
10 Saint-Just, Croix-Saint-Pierre, Ille-et-Vilaine	2308 + − 120	2980	GSY 31
11 Carnac, le Castellic, Morbihan	3075 + − 300	3860	Gif 198B
12 Saint-Quay-Perros, Crec'h Quillé, Côtes-du-Nord	1790 + − 200	2215	GSY 344
	1810 + − 120	2245	Gif 814

	13 Saint-Philibert, Mané-Kernaplaye, Morbihan	2635 + − 200	3405	GSY 88
	14 Quessoy, le Champ Grosset, Côtes-du-Nord	1870 + − 200	2335	Gif 283
	15 Penvenan, Tossen-Keler, Côtes-du-Nord	2550 + − 260	3310	Gif 280
	16 Guidel, Kermené, Morbihan	2080 + − 100	2635	GSY 73
		2440 + − 140	3155	Gif 1966
	17 Laniscat, Liscuis, Côtes-du-nord			
	cairn I	3160 + − 110	3945	Gif 3099
	II	2500 + − 110	3245	Gif 3944
	II	2220 + − 110	2880	Gif 3585
	III	2250 + − 110	2910	Gif 4076
	III	1730 + − 110	2140	Gif 4075
Normandy	**18** Fontenay-le-Marmion, la Hoguette, Calvados	1800 + − 120	2230	Gif 1347
		2350 + − 120	3030	Gif 1346
		2770 + − 130	3550	Gif 1514
		2850 + − 130	3635	Gif 1513
		3050 + − 130	3835	Gif 1345
		3610 + − 150	4460	Ly 131
	19 Porte-Joie, Eure	2090 + − 180	2655	Ly 703
	20 Colombiers-sur-Seulles, Calvados	3200 + − 130	3990	Gif 5150
Channel Islands	**21** Vale, les Fouaillages, Guernsey			
	Neolithic	3640 + − 50	4475	BM 1892
	Neolithic	3560 + − 60	4415	BM 1893
	Neolithic	3330 + − 140	4140	BM 1894
	Beaker	1900 + − 50	2385	BM 1891
	Beaker	1880 + − 50	2350	BM 1897
	Beaker	2050 + − 60	2595	BM 1895

Carbon-14 Dates

Neolithic				
	Land-clearance, Settlement, Quarrying			
Brittany	**22** Guissény, le Curnic, Finistère	2650 + − 200	3430	GSY 47A
		4030 + − 150	4875	GSY 47B
		3560 + − 250	4418	GIF 345
		3390 + − 60	4230	GRN 1966
	23 Plussulien, Sélédin, Côtes-du-Nord	3320 + − 140	4120	GIF 1877
		3200 + − 140	3990	GIF 1873
		2840 + − 110	3625	GIF 2328
		2750 + − 150	3530	GIF 1540
		2100 + − 130	2670	GIF 1539
	24 Brignagon, Finistère	3030 + − 120	3815	GIF 75
	25 Saint-Michel-de-Brasparts, Finistère	3450 + − 60	4325	GRN 1983
		1820 + − 65	2255	GRN 2175
Normandy	**26** Soumont-Saint-Quentin, Calvados			
	Bandkeramik	3780 + − 150	4575	Gif 2139
	Chassey	3190 + − 140	3980	Ly 149
	Chassey	2990 + − 200	3775	Ly 135
	Chassey	2840 + − 150	3625	GSY 39
		2610 + − 120	3380	Ly 134
		2590 + − 140	3360	Ly 148
		2040 + − 140	2580	GIF 2321
		2080 + − 150	2640	GIF 2323
Channel Islands	**27** Le Pinacle, Jersey	3070 + − 110	3855	BM 370
Bronze Age				
	Tombs, Mounds, Settlements			
Brittany	Berrien, Ligollenec, Finistère	1550 + − 130	1900	GIF 1866
	Bourbriac, Saint-Jude, Côtes-du-Nord	1480 + − 160	1800	GIF 166

Region	Site	Date	Calibrated	Lab ref.
		1830 + − 100	2250	GIF 2686
		1920 + − 100	2485	GIF 2687
		1810 + − 100	2240	GIF 2688
	Guidel, Cruguel, Morbihan	1320 + − 200	1615	GIF 235
	Melrand, Saint-Fiacre, Morbihan	1950 + − 135	2455	GIF 863
	Plouvorn, Kernonen, Finistère	1960 + − 100	2045	GIF 805
		1250 + − 120	1550	GIF 806
		1200 + − 120	1495	GIF 807
		1480 + − 120	1815	GIF 1149
	Saint-Adrien, Run Bras, Côtes-du-Nord	1700 + − 35	2095	GRN 7176
	Saint-Brévin-les-Pins, l'Ermitage, Loire-Atlantique	1225 + − 200	1520	GIF 193a
		825 + − 200	1000	GIF 193b
	Saint-Michel-Chef-Chef, la Roussellerie, Loire-Atlantique	770 + − 200	945	GIF 194c
	Brandivy, Kerlande, Morbihan	870 + − 100	1060	GIF 2378
	Guisseny, le Curnic, Finistère	1225 + − 160	1520	GIF 159
		1270 + − 110	1570	GSY 47c
Normandy	Merri, la Bierre, Orne	850 + − 120	1030	Ly 465
		790 + − 110	965	Ly 466
		370 + − 100	435	Ly 464
Iron Age				
	Settlements			
Brittany	Erquy, Fosse Catuélan, Côtes-du-Nord	550 + − 100	755	GIF 715
	Erquy, Pleine Garenne, Côtes-du-Nord	320 + − 110	410	GIF 1302

Brittany

Côtes - du - Nord

Bégard

menhir 59/1
Neolithic
Lannion 7–8
186,50/118,95

In Bégard, opposite the church entrance, take the small road marked to the Hôpital; then immediately, turn right (→ Guénézan), then first left (→ Saint-Nicolas). Then take the third road left (500 m beyond the hamlet of Saint-Nicolas). The fine menhir, 6.4 m high, is in the third field on the right, 100 m from the road.

Boquen

Abbaye de Boquen 59/14
Church

Marked on the Michelin. On the edge of a great forest; well signposted. A beautiful monastery, founded in 1137, pillaged and more or less destroyed during the revolution, and painstakingly reconstructed since 1936 by monks from Tamié in Savoy. It is now used by a closed order of nuns. The twelfth-century nave and transept, the chapter house and part of the cloisters can all be visited.

Bourbriac

1 Church 59/2

The foundations of the village church are tenth and eleventh century, the transept-crossing is Romanesque. The Merovingian sarcophagus of Saint-Briac lies behind the sixteenth-century tomb of the saint.

2 Tanouedou
tumulus Bronze Age
Guingamp 5–6
194,60/98,80

Marked on the Michelin. In Bourbriac take the D 22 south-east (→ Plésidy) and after 2.57 km turn left (→ Tanouedou, Langoat). At the further end of the hamlet of Tanouedou, as the road bends left, take the track to the right. After 50 m, at the fork, keep left, and after 300 m the large mound rears up through a gap in the hedge on the right.

An early, rather summary excavation uncovered an individual burial chamber cut into the subsoil below the mound. It contained bronze objects, tiny gold studs and a small electrum torsade.

Close to Tanouedou, at Saint-Jude, two large, low mounds have recently been excavated and provide more information on the internal structure and grave-goods. One of these, Parc Monten, contained a wooden mortuary house within a stone cairn, covered in turn by a huge mound of loess. The other mound was similar, though the wood was less well preserved, and both contained a little Bronze Age pottery and a few pieces of copper and bronze (Introduction page 38).

Corseul

59/5–15

Corseul was an important centre of the Coriosolites tribe and then became the capital of a Gallo-Roman *civitas*. It was built on a grid plan and flourished in the first and second centuries AD. Then during the upheavals of the third century it decreased in size, and was in part abandoned. It was to some extent

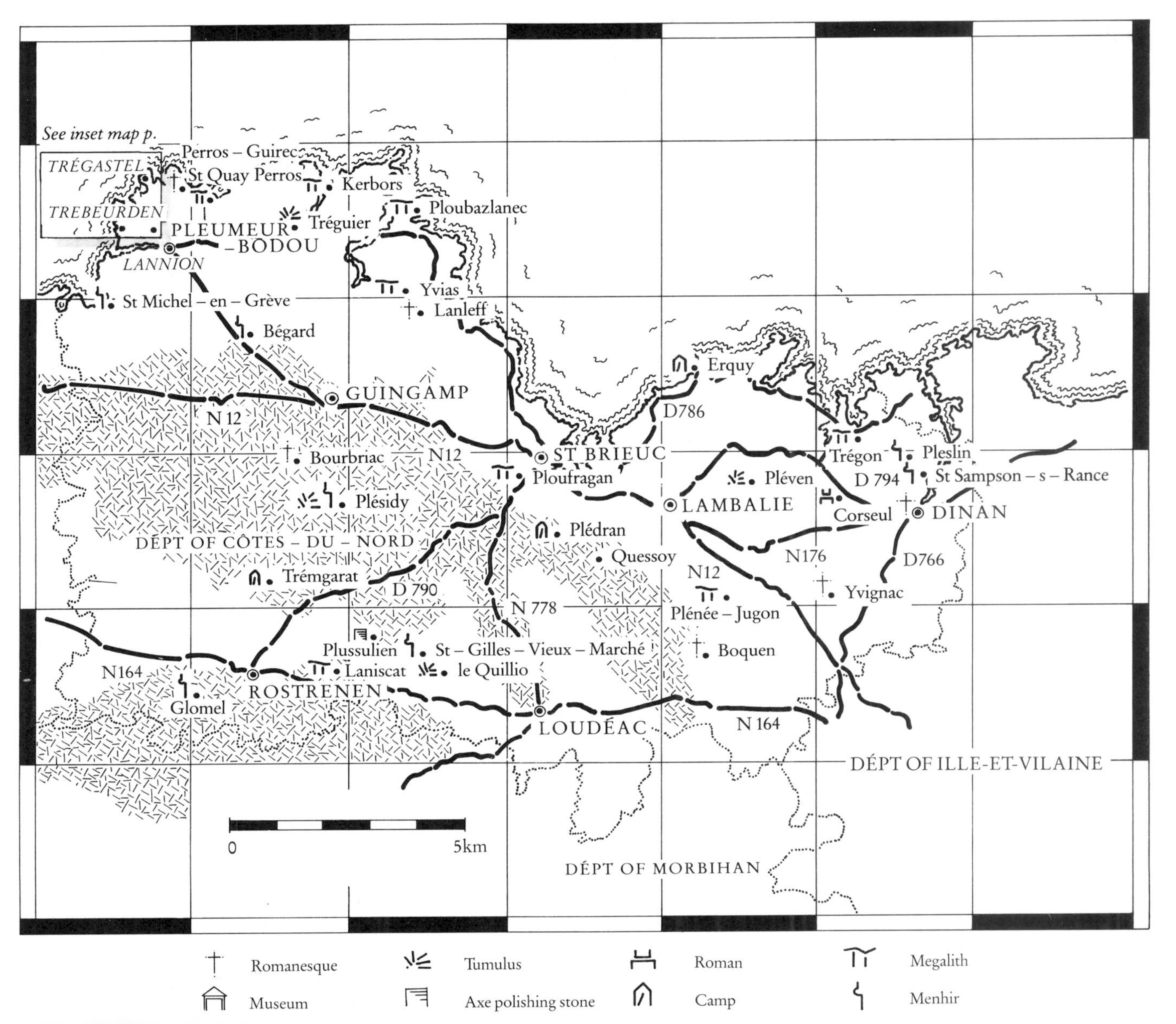

25 Département of Côtes-du-Nord

resuscitated in the fourth century, although the centre of the *civitas* became Aleto (*Saint-Servan-sur-Mer*, Ille-et-Vilaine). Outside the city was the great temple, the Fanum Martis of Haut-Bécherel—in area the largest in Brittany, if not all Gaul. All that remains of the temple is the cella (see below).

1 The Mairie
museum Museum
The upper storey of the town hall houses an interesting collection of local prehistoric and Gallo-Roman material. In the public gardens, alongside the Mairie, are some Gallo-Roman architectural fragments.

Open weekday mornings.

2 Le Champ Mulon
Gallo-Roman remains Gallo-Roman
200 m from the town centre, near the sports field there are a few remains of the Gallo-Roman town.

3 Church Gallo-Roman
There is a fine Roman stele in the church with a funerary inscription dedicated to a woman from the Roman provinces in Africa.

4 Fanum Martis
(Figures 26 and 27) Gallo-Roman
Dinan 5–6 268,60/95,60
Marked on the Michelin. From Corseul take the D 794 south-east (→ Dinan) for 2 km, then turn right to the 'Temple de Mars'. After another 0.5 km it is signposted again, to the right. Go through the farm and up the track ahead for 100 m. The ruin lies to the right.

The precinct has gone, although various reconstructions have been attempted, all involving a degree of imagination. The most probable plan, Figure 26, dates to 1870, and suggests a huge central court open to the east and lined on the other three sides by two parallel walls, the first of which probably supported a colonnade. The sanctuary, on the west side, comprised the hexagonal cella—*all that is now visible*—made of mortared rubble faced with small blocks and with iron joints. It was surrounded by an ambulatory, and was reached by a monumental entrance opening onto the west colonnade. A tile from this monumental entrance had a crude scrawl on it identifying the building as a shrine to Mars. Coins found in the vicinity range from Augustine to Constantine.

A large urban villa, built on a horseshoe plan, was excavated nearby. It opened onto a paved street. There was also the remains of a bath-house dating to the fourth century.

Most of the objects from these sites are in the Mairie at *Corseul*, but some are in the museum of *Rennes*.

26 Plan of the temple of Haut-Bécherel at ***Corseul***

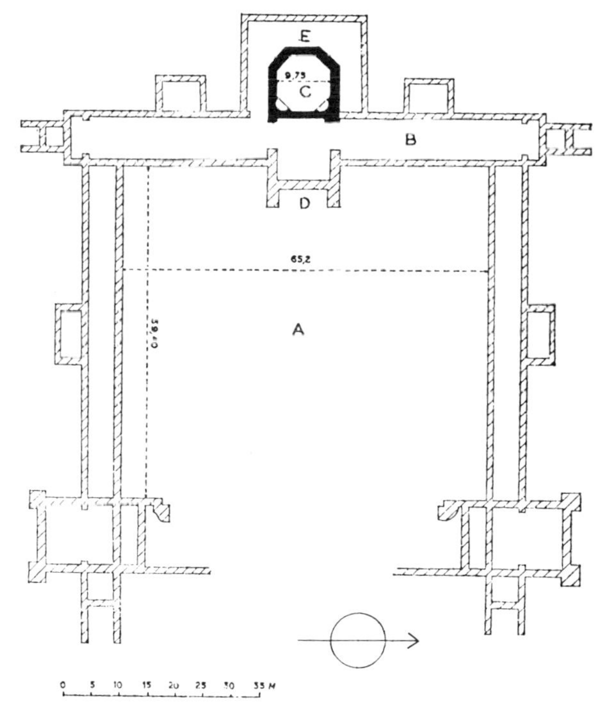

Dinan

Saint-Sauveur 59/15
Church
The church was almost entirely rebuilt in the fifteenth

and sixteenth centuries but by great good fortune the lower part of the façade, which dates to the late twelfth century, was preserved. It has the most elaborate Romanesque portal known in Brittany; the doorway, crowned by a tympanum showing Christ, is flanked by two blind arcades both incorporating a pair of twisted columns resting on sculpted animals. The columns, plain and twisted, have deeply sculpted capitals illustrating various sins and their attendant punishments. The twisted columns suggest a Byzantine influence, probably arriving by way of stone masons from Poitou.

The south wall of the nave is also twelfth century.

The old part of the town, with many fifteenth- and sixteenth-century buildings, lies just west of the church.

Erquy

Cap d'Erquy — 59/4
hill fort — Iron Age
(Figure 28) — Saint-Cast 5–6
244,80/116,20

From the lower town of Erquy take the small road north (rue le Hamel) up to the promontory (→ le Cap). Near the top of the promontory turn left on the rue du Four à Boulets and when this forks keep left. The end of this road cuts a neat section through the inner rampart.

The first defences, the inner Catuélan bank and ditch, were thrown up in late Hallstatt times and protected an area of 15 hectares. The bank seems to have had irregular stone revetments on both flanks, the ditch was shallow and there is a slight counterscarp. Only a small amount of pottery has been found, mainly domestic ware of the Late Bronze Age or Early Iron Age. A carbon-14 date reads 550 + − 110 bc (calibrated 755 BC). Below the Catuélan bank a level with burnt twigs dating to the Middle Neolithic seems to indicate that the promontory was cleared long before the defences were erected.

During the La Tène period, another bank and ditch were constructed 450 m outside the Catuélan defences. This system, the Pleine-Garenne, protects 35 hectares. The main bank has an internal stone core 4.5 m wide, supported by horizontal wooden cross-beams. This is capped with earth bordered by small stone retainer walls. Along much of its length this bank is doubled by another, made of tightly packed sandstone blocks. Beyond this lies the ditch, 1.7 m deep and 2 m wide.

The Pleine-Garenne defences have a carbon-14 date of 320 + − 110 bc (calibrated 410 BC).

Glomel

menhir — 58/17
Neolithic
Rostrenen 3–4
175,15/74,15

In Glomel take the D 85 east (→ Saint-Michel). After 0.5 km the menhir is signposted to the left. It is to the right of the track—a really vast stone, 9 m high.

Kerbors

Men-ar-Romped — 58/2
(or Ile-à-Poule) — Neolithic
gallery grave — Tréguier 5–6
195,45/141,80

A modest monument but with a marvellous view out to sea.

Marked on the Michelin map. In Kerbors take the V 1 north (→ Ile-à-Poule, allée couverte de Men-ar-Romped). Well signposted all the way. The last 200 m are down a rough track to the left of the road.

The chamber is only 6.7 m long. A small pillar marks the division between the chamber and antechamber, while the terminal area, 1.8 m long, is demarcated by a sill-stone and a fine large flat paving stone.

This grave was reused by Beaker people who left a rich collection of grave-goods, including forty Bell Beakers, with much variety of shape and decoration, and a wristguard.

Lamballe

Notre-Dame — 59/14

The church of Notre-Dame is a great fortified Gothic structure lying high above the town. There are a few remains of the earlier, late twelfth-century church—a fine rather austere north door with multiple archivolts falling onto a series of colonettes and an even plainer south door.

27 *The temple of Haut-Bécherel at* ***Corseul***

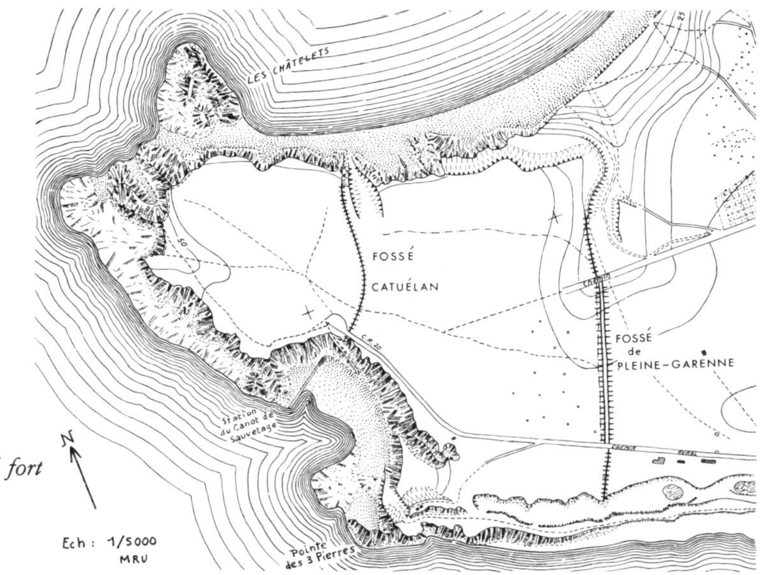

28 ***Cap D'Erquy****, Iron Age hill fort*

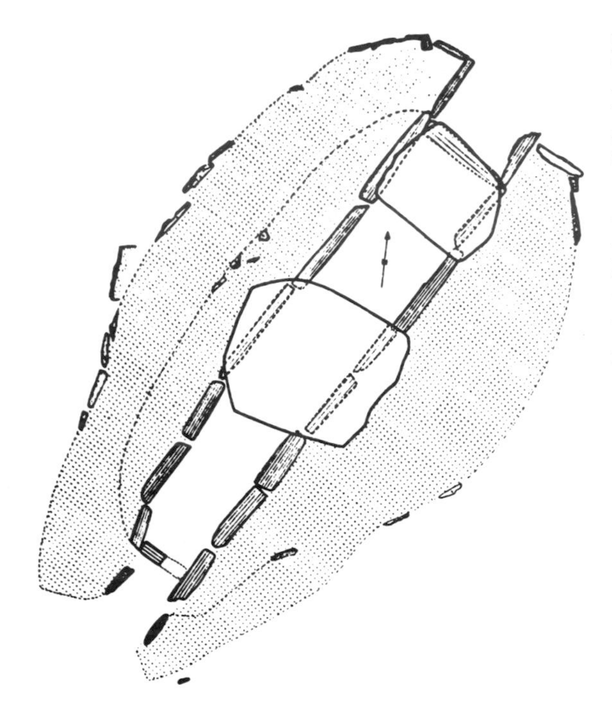

29 Liscuis I and II, Laniscat

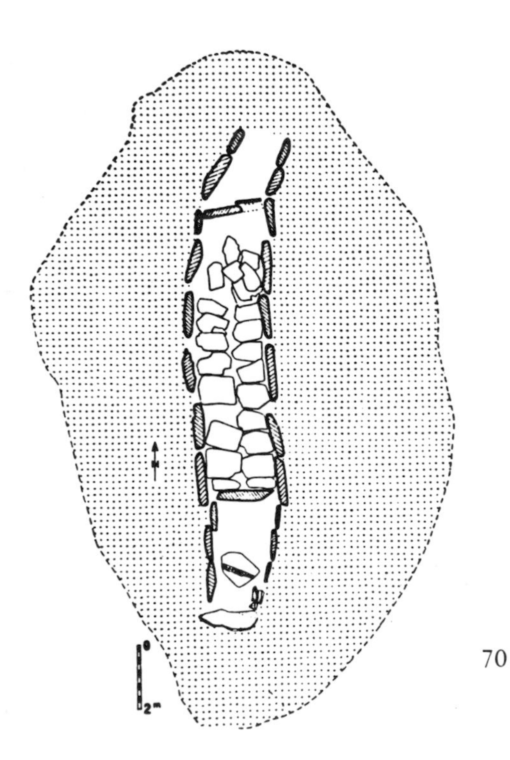

Laniscat

Liscuis 58/18
gallery graves Neolithic
(Figures 29–31) Pontivy 1–2
194,12/72,45

A marvellous site, untouched, unknown, on the high, bracken-covered schist outcrop of the Landes de Liscuis. Not, however, easy to find. In Laniscat take the D 76 south-west (→ Gouarec) and 150 m *before* the end-of-town placard (and 100 m after the Antar filling station on the right), take a small road left (wooden signpost → Gorges du Daoulas etc.). Almost immediately continue ahead on the R 47 (→ Canach' Léron). After 1.25 km at a T-junction, turn right, continue 500 m and take the first, small (unmarked) road to the left. Follow it as it bends right and continue to the end (200 m from the main road). Then walk up the sunken track left ('sentier piétonnier') and after 100 m, at the top of the hill, turn left onto a smaller grass track. Another 150 m takes you to a signpost (indicating Saint-Gelven to the left). Turn *right* (unmarked). Another 125 m, then ignore path to the left, and another 60 m brings you to the gallery graves.

The cairn of Liscuis II, orientated north/south, is a huge oval structure (22 × 12 m). There are traces of a megalithic revetment, and, perhaps, of an internal revetment. The cairn is built partly of quartzite blocks, partly of schist plaques. The chamber 8.5 m long and 2 to 2.3 m wide, is divided from a slightly angled antechamber, 2.5 m long, by a septal stone. There is a triangular opening between this stone and the wall of the chamber, and the small triangular stone found in front of this opening is probably the original 'door'. At the other end, the terminal cell, like the antechamber, is slightly angled. Both the terminal cell and the small cist that prolongs it are more roughly constructed than the chamber.

Recent excavations uncovered a very fine chamber floor made of shaped schist plaques on a footing of three rows of sandstone blocks.

The very fragmentary pottery seems to include both coarse Seine-Oise-Marne ware, and a finer carinated ware, including a sherd with vertical incisions, with definite Kerugou affinities. Four dolerite A axes and a fibrolite axe pendant were found in a cluster in the north-west part of the cairn, and another dolerite A axe, two quartzite pendants and some small flint blades and flakes were also found.

There are two carbon-14 dates for Liscuis II: the one from the antechamber is 2220 + − 110 bc (calibrated 2880 BC), the other, from the terminal cell, is 2500 + − 110 bc (calibrated 3245 BC).

Liscuis I lies 150 m further down the path. It has an egg-shaped mound edged with small plaques, one of which was roughly shaped to an anthropomorphic form. The internal structure of the cairn has been carefully examined during the recent excavations; blocking stones were found wedged up against the chamber uprights, followed by a couple of layers of quartzite slabs that sloped up against the blocking stones, topped with a central core of over-lapping schist plaques, and finally a rougher outer perimeter of both schist and quartzite blocks butted up against the schist plaque peristalith. This peristalith presents a more monumental façade at the east end. The very short antechamber, 1 × 0.8 m, is delimited by a transverse stone which leaves a narrow, triangular opening. The chamber is 12 m long and widens to 2 m at the back. The terminal cell is small, uncovered and open ended.

The grave contained coarse carinated fragments of four vases, somewhat similar to Late Neolithic Kerugou ware and very similar to the pots from the lateral entrance grave of Champ-Grosset, *Quessoy*, Côtes-du-Nord. There was also a small rough amphibolite axe and a steatite bead. A dolerite A axe roughout was found in the cairn.

For the third mound, Liscuis III, take the path running to the right of Liscuis I. This monument, orientated east/west, is well preserved, sub-quadrangular, and delimited by a façade of schist slabs at both ends and a dry-stone wall revetment, with isolated uprights, along both long sides. The total length of the antechamber, chamber and terminal cell is 14.5 m. A notched septal stone divides the antechamber from the chamber.

The few sherds found were all Seine-Oise-Marne in type. The carbon-14 date of the small hearth at the back of the chamber is 2250 + − 110 bc (calibrated 2910 BC).

This region is, or was, rich in megalithic monuments. *Saint-Giles-Vieux-Marché* and *Quillio* are included in this guide, but others, ruined or totally dismantled, such as the gallery graves of Bonnet-Rouge and Kerivoelen, Plélauff, the lateral-entrance grave of Coët-Correc, Mur de Bretagne, several menhirs and gallery graves between Caurel, Saint-Mayeux and Saint-Gilles-Vieux-Marché, are not. The great dolerite axe factory of Sélédin, *Plussulien* is only 6 km away.

30 Liscuis III, ***Laniscat***

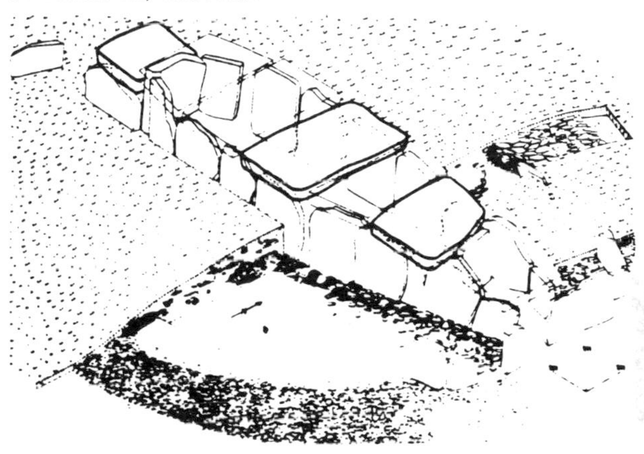

Lanleff

'Le Temple'
11th-century church 59/2
Marked on the Michelin. About 50 m north of the present church of Lanleff to the left of the road to Yvias.

Lovely ruin of an extraordinary circular church made of local pink granite. Only the lower part of the arcades of the central area, a part of the encircling collateral and one of the three original small semicircular apses remain. The carvings on the capitals are almost eroded away. It used to be thought that the building was Roman or tenth century, but in fact it is late eleventh century and the circular plan is similar to that of the Saint-Croix at *Quimperlé*, Finistère.

Lannion

1 Coz-Yaudet 58/7
Iron-Age and Gallo-Roman camp Iron Age/Gallo-Roman
Lannion 1–2
168,52/131,25
From Lannion take the D 786 south-west (→ Saint-Michel-en-Grève) for 4 km. Turn right on the D 88 (→ Ploulec'h). Continue through Ploulec'h and on to le Yaudet (4.5 km). The Iron Age rampart is still

visible behind the hotel, and a site-plan in the car-park indicates the Roman gate and wall which lie to the east of the car-park.

The rampart dates to the Iron Age La Tène. During the later Roman empire a defensive wall was added to the earthwork.

2 Church of Brélévenez — Church
One hundred and forty-two steps to the top of the hill, and a fine view. The church was built by the Templars in the twelfth century, but was largely rebuilt between the thirteenth and fifteenth centuries. The south doorway with its colonnettes and three stone pillars representing the Trinity, the apse—best viewed from the outside— and the crypt, are Romanesque.

Penvenan

Tossen-Keler — 58/1
tumulus — Neolithic
The stones that formed the peristalith of this tumulus have been moved to the quay at *Tréguier*.

Perros-Guirec

59/1
Perros-Guirec is a great tourist centre. One escape route is the Sentier des Douaniers west from the town along the cliff edge. Particularly dramatic in the morning when the seas are pounding in. It takes you to the Pointe de Squewel and then on to Ploumanac'h—passing a series of fantastical weather-sculpted pink granite rocks.

church — Church
A fine church, particularly inside. The nave and aisles are twelfth century and the cylindrical capitals have carvings of archaic figures in deep relief. An interesting font at the end of the nave is also carved with archaic figures. The fourteenth-century choir and transept are nondescript, whilst the tower is a curious seventeenth-century construction. There is a small Romanesque side-porch with a tympanum showing Christ flanked by the signs of the apostles.

31 Liscuis II, ***Laniscat***

Plédran

Camp de Péran — 59/13–3
or Camp Romain — Iron Age
plateau camp — Saint-Brieuc 5–6
221,80/97,15
Marked on the Michelin. Take the D 27 out of Plédran (→ Saint-Brieuc), then after 1.5 km turn left (→ la Ville Doyen, Péran). After 2 km there is a large plan of the camp, and about 100 m further up the road, to the left, is a fine exposure of the vitrified wall. There are two banks and ditches, approximately circular, enclosing an hectare. The inner rampart is about 3 m above the interior ground level, and 4 to 6 m above the present bottom of the ditch. The main bank is of heavily vitrified gneiss and one can still see the sockets of the former timbers. They are about 0.2 m in diameter and spaced at one metre intervals (Introduction page 53).

Plénée-Jugon

La Brousse — 59/14
gallery grave — Neolithic
Broons 5–6
248,20/80,40
In Plénée-Jugon take the D 59 south (→ Langourla) and after 1.5 km turn right onto the C 4 to Ville-Jéhan. Go through Ville-Jéhan and just after the village turn left (→ la Brousse). In la Brousse turn right (→ Gillaudière) and then take the first track to the left. 100 m before the track forks, to the right of the track and below an oak-tree, is a bramble-infested grave.

After all that, nothing special. A gallery grave with an antechamber and a terminal cell, both uncovered.

Plésidy

Menhir de Caïlouan — 59/2–12
Neolithic
Guingamp 5–6
194,20/95,12
Marked on the Michelin. In Plésidy take the D 5 south-west (→ Bourbriac, Saint-Nicolas-du-Pélem).

When the road forks continue towards Saint-Nicolas. The third road thereafter on the right is marked 'le Menhir'. Then the first track to the left, again marked. And then again the first track left—which leads to a fine menhir 7.4 m high (in all 4 km from Plésidy).

Pleslin

Champs des Roches 59/5
alignments Neolithic

In Pleslin at the church take the D 28 west (→ Corseul) and after 75 m the alignment is signposted on the left. Follow the road for 600 m and when it forks keep right. The road becomes a track and leads to the stones on the left.

There are about sixty-five stones in five lines. The largest is about 3.5 m high.

32 Christianised menhir of Saint-Duzec, ***Pleumeur***

Pleumeur-Bodou

59/1

Since you may want to come to these sites either from Trégastel-Plage or Trébeurden the inset map gives various means of access. The gallery grave of Prajou-Menhir, Trébeurden—well worth a visit—is so close to the Pleumeur-Bodou monuments that I have listed it here rather than under Trébeurden. The lateral entrance grave at Kergüntuil, *Trégastel* is also close by.

1 Saint-Duzec Neolithic
menhir Perros-Guirec 5–6
(Figure 32) 168,30/137,80

Marked on the Michelin (see inset map, Figure 33). Turn off the D 21 at the Café du Menhir. Continue for 500 m to a fork, keep left and the menhir is to the right of the road. This is a famous menhir; a massive stone which in 1674 was elaborately sculpted with the crucifixion and the signs of the apostles. Old postcards show a Christ figure painted below the signs.

34 Isometric drawing of the gallery grave of Prajou-Menhir, ***Trébeurden***

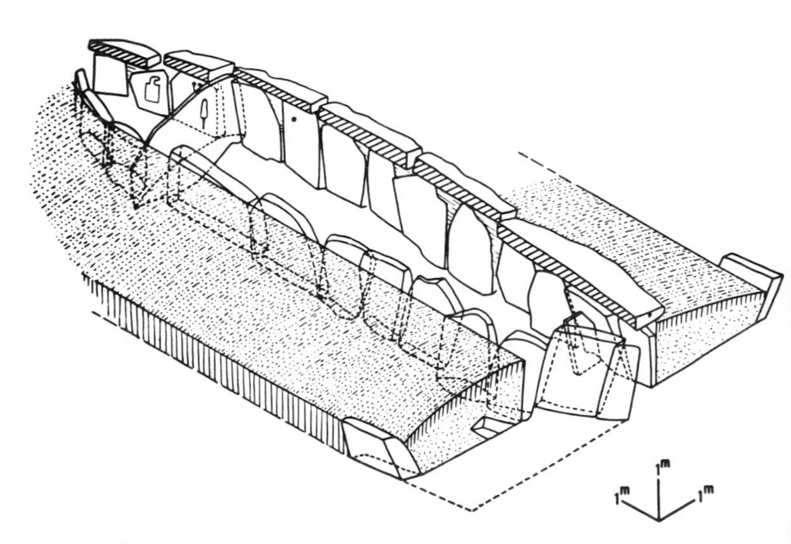

2 Prajou-Menhir — Neolithic
gallery grave — Perros-Guirec 5–6
(Figures 34 and 35) — 166,90/138,60
(actually in the commune
of Trébeurden)

See inset map, Figure 33. Once on the road to Ile Grande continue for 0.5 km and just after the road first touches the coast keep a sharp look out for a sign in the left-hand hedge to the 'allée couverte'.

It is difficult to distinguish the antechamber from the chamber, but there is a transverse pillar between the two. The antechamber is 1.75 m long and widens towards the chamber. The chamber, 9.5 m long, has two capstones.

It is hard work getting into the terminal cell, but once in, there is a fine array of breasts and daggers. On one upright there is a dagger, a pair of breasts and a necklace. On the stone next to it a square anthropomorph, on the stone opposite a cartouche with two pairs of breasts and on the stone between the terminal cell and the chamber there are two daggers and two square anthropomorphs.

The chamber is austere by comparison. Three uprights have single protuberances sculpted on them.

Relatively few grave-goods were found in the recent excavation, the grave had obviously been looted earlier. Fragments of coarse, flat-based ware may be of the Seine-Oise-Marne type. Fortunately two complete collared flasks and a fragment of a third were overlooked by the looters. One was found in the antechamber, the other, and the fragment, in the chamber. There was also a round, perforated quartz bead.

15 m from the entrance of the gallery grave is a small menhir, 1.4 m high.

3 Ile Grande — Neolithic
gallery grave — Perros-Guirec 5–6
166,40/139,50

Marked on the Michelin (see inset map, Figure 33). Once on the Ile Grande road continue for 1.2 km to the Hôtel des Rochers. Turn right, then first left, rue du Dolmen, and after 300 m the monument is to the left of the road.

This is a short gallery grave, 8.5 × 1.6 × 1.4 m, made of large granitic orthostats. The entrance to the grave is marked by an upright and a threshold stone; two large capstones are in place and the peristalith of the mound is still visible.

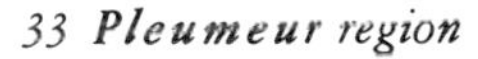

33 ***Pleumeur*** *region*

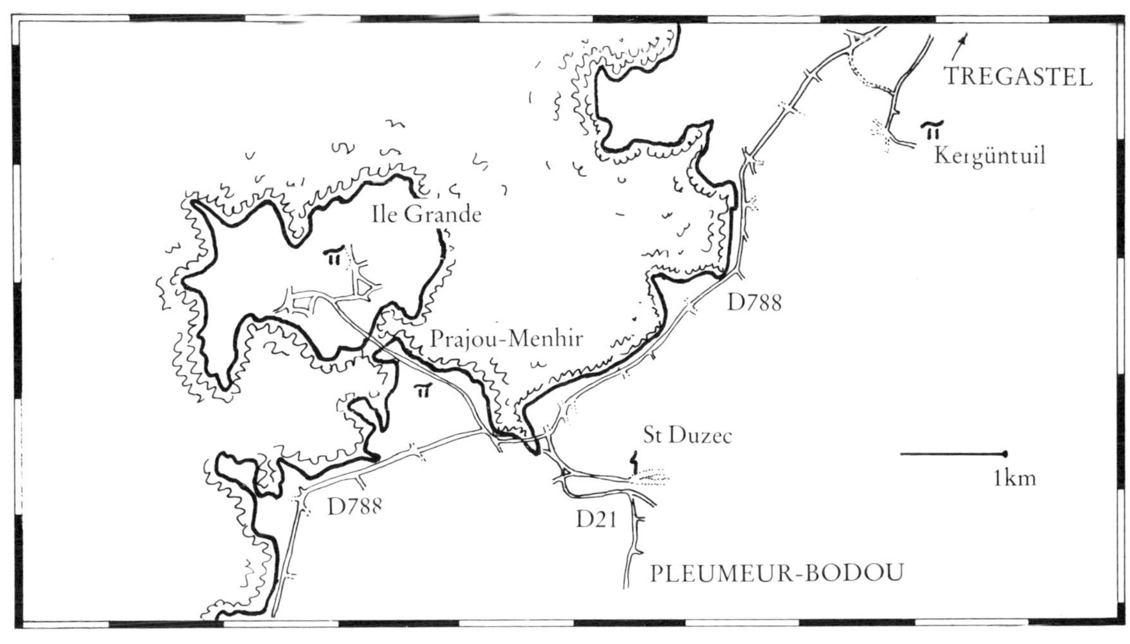

35 Bas-reliefs and engravings in the terminal cell of the gallery grave of Prajou-Menhir, ***Trébeurden***

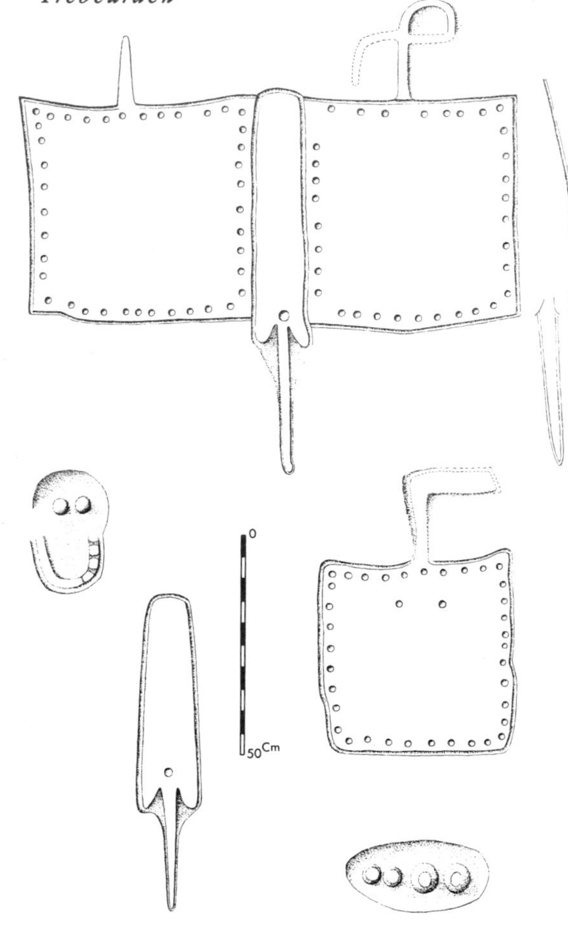

Pléven

tumulus 59/5
Bronze Age
Lamballe 7–8
256,45/97,75

Marked on the Michelin. Take the D 68 south out of Pléven (→ Plorec). Cross the bridge and one kilometre beyond take a small road left. After 250 m take the track, right, marked to the tumulus. Another 300 m and the track ends. The tumulus is to the left.

Ploubazlanec

Le Mélus 58/2
lateral-entrance grave Neolithic
Tréguier 5–6
203,10/138,15

Marked on the Michelin, but not easy to find. Directions start at Paimpol. Take the D 789 north (→ Ploubazlanec) and almost immediately turn left, north-west, on the D 15 (→ Loguivy). Continue down this road for 3 km. Once past the placard announcing Loguivy take the second paved lane, unmarked, to the left. From the top of this lane directions to the 'allée couverte le Mélus' are clear. From the final signpost there is a 300 m walk to the further edge of the field.

The chamber is 14.5 m long and roughly the same width and height throughout. The lateral entrance on the south side, closer to the east end, is surmounted by a lintel and preceded by two small stones—much obscured by brambles.

Grave-goods were found throughout the chamber with a high concentration towards the east end. There was a collared flask, many round-based pots, one large 'flower-pot', and sherds of Kerugou ware. There were also four polished dolerite axes, a flint axe, a Grand Pressigny dagger and blade, five flint blades and a scraper.

The tiny port of Loguivy would do for a non-megalithic pause, or still better, go to the Pointe de l'Arcouest a bit further to the west.

Ploufragan

1 Le Bourg 58/9
gallery grave Neolithic
Saint-Brieuc 5–6
221,10/100,32

Marked on the Michelin. From the church at Ploufragan take the D 45A south (→ Saint-Julien) and after 50 m, to the left, on the edge of a playing field, behind the parking lot, is the gallery grave.

Brambled, long, with two capstones in place and a possible terminal cell.

2 La Couette Neolithic
gallery grave

Directions as for le Bourg gallery grave (above), but

then continue on the D 45A (→ Saint-Julien) to the main road, the N 168. Turn left, then take the first road right (→ l'Argentel). Continue to a large new complex on the left, the Station de Paléologie Porcine, and, opposite the furthest building, take the track to the right. Continue for about 170 m and behold—a very brambly, long gallery grave all capstones intact.

3 Le Grand Argentel — Neolithic
gallery grave
Directions as for la Couette (above), but then continue past the Station de Paléologie Porcine for another 400 m, and there, just visible in the hedgerow to the left of the road, is yet another gallery grave.

It seems to be very well preserved, still partially imbedded in its mound, all capstones in place. Too bramble-infested for any view of the interior.

Plussulien

Sélédin — 58/18–19
dolerite A axe factory — Neolithic
(Figure 36) — Quintin 7–8
199,95/76,20

Not much to see but a very important site. Only discovered in 1964, it is the source of dolerite A of which 40% of all Breton polished stone axes are made. The centre of this 100-hectare work-floor is the outcrop of le Roc'h-Pol, south of Quelfénnec.

In Plussulien, in front of the church (and the war memorial) take the D 44 west (→ Laniscat), but then immediately take the first left (unmarked) and then left again (→ Kersouès, Kerohan, Quelfénnec). Continue over the first crossroads, and again, at the second crossroads, with Quelfénnec signposted to the right and Kerégan to the left, continue straight ahead. After 500 m there is a small stony track to the left. Follow it to the end (c. 200 m). Then, in line with the track, walk along the upper edge of a maize field for 200 m; deflect slightly through a gap into the second field and now take the lower edge. 25 m from the gap take the very small path leading off left through the bracken. Another 25 m, then sharp left and almost immediately you are at the rock outcrop. (If all this fails, return to the Quelfénnec crossing, and go through Quelfénnec and on a little way, to

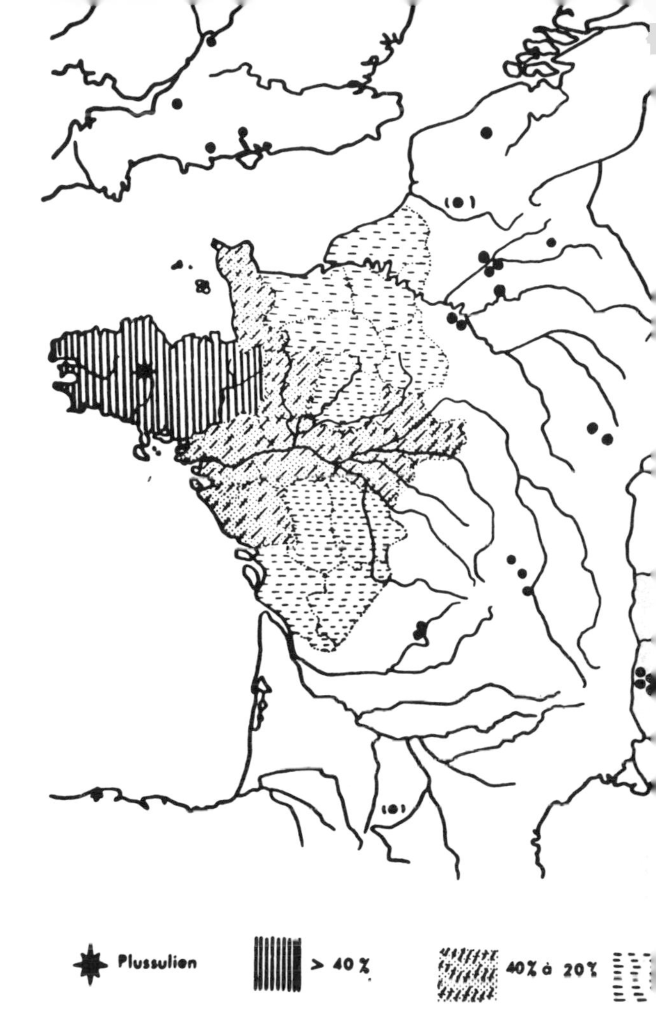

36 Distribution of dolerite A axes from the axe factory of Sélédin, ***Plussulien***

Kerohan, where, at the white farmhouse with the white fence, Monsieur Perennez can probably be persuaded to act as guide).

The work-floor extends along the northern flank of the anticline of Laniscat-Merléac and covers the whole outcrop and the slope down to the river. Careful excavation, including an area at the base of the outcrop where four floor levels were uncovered, and a long series of carbon-14 dates, allow a reconstruction of the development of the site. The earliest exploitation probably occurred between 4000 to 3600 bc (calibrated 4845 to 4450 BC), at a time when the interior was more or less deserted. Presumably people came up from the Morbihan coast, some 50 km away to obtain the dolerite. Transport would have been reasonably easy, using the rivers Blavet, Oust and

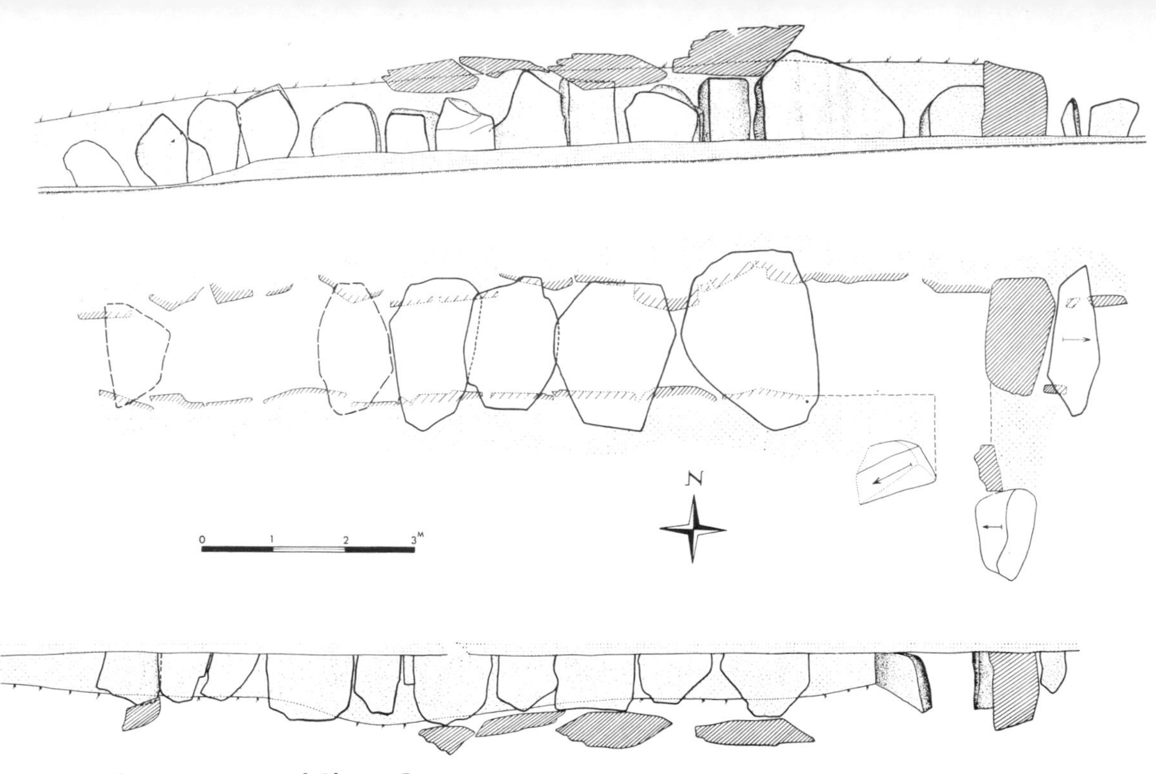

37 Lateral-entrance grave of Champ-Grosset, ***Quessoy***

Lower Vilaine. Concentrations of axes on the Carnac coast, at Er Lannic and Camp-de-Lizo may be connected with a further stage in the axe production, when the roughouts were trimmed and ground, prior to further distribution. The early exploitation at Sélédin seems to have been fairly limited and techniques were quite rudimentary, mainly involving the loosening of rocks that were already fractured. This method created large irregular pits, one, sometimes even two, metres deep. But even in this early phase some use was made of heavy hammer-stones.

In the next phase c. 3400 bc (calibrated 4250 BC) 'mining' with heavy polyhedric hammer-stones intensified, and huge rocks were moved in order to provide suitable work surfaces for roughing out the axes. A certain amount of grinding occurred on the spot, a few grinding hollows and striations have been found.

Around 3000 bc (calibrated 3785 BC) there seems to have been a partial abandonment of the site, followed, in the third phase, by a great revival. During the Late Neolithic, starting about 2300 bc (calibrated 2970 BC), an enormous quantity of dolerite was mined and new methods were introduced. Fire-setting was used and huge hearths, extending for almost 6 m, have been uncovered. By this time the upland region was beginning to be densely populated. We can assume that a rather different organization of mining, axe-preparation and trading occurred. Certainly the axes (in rough or polished form) were traded over a large area. A few reached southern England, others got as far as the Alps, Pyrenees and the Rhine (Introduction, page 26 and map, Figure 36).

Finally, c. 2000 bc (calibrated 2520 BC) the work-floors began to be abandoned, although some activity continued right through to the Early Bronze Age.

Quessoy

Champ-Grosset — 59/13
lateral-entrance grave — Neolithic
(Figure 37) — Saint-Brieuc 7–8
288,10/92,50

In Quessoy take the D 28 south-west (→ Saint-Carreuc). After one kilometre turn right (→ le Beau Frère). Another 1.25 km, through mixed oak and pine forest, and the grave is on the left, 30 m from the road, between the further edge of the forest and a cultivated field.

Another brambled monument, which makes it

hard to see the lateral entrance—apparently on the east end of the south side—or the interior septal stone that demarcates the open-ended cell at the east end. At any rate the chamber is 12.9 m long, the cell is 1 m long. The cairn, now almost ploughed out, was made of stones.

Most of the grave-goods were found close to the north wall. They include four flat-based carinated pots, related to Kerugou ware, two fragments of flat-based Seine-Oise-Marne ware, several round-based bowls, often with slightly rolled rims, and also three polished dolerite axes, five flaked stone discs—probably weights—a black schist pendant, and numerous flint blades including one honey-coloured one, probably made of Grand Pressigny flint.

There is a carbon-14 date of 1870 bc (calibrated 2335 BC).

A similar grave at la Roche Camio, Plédran is so totally blackberry-infested that it has not been included in the guide.

Quillio, le

long mound — *58/13*
Neolithic
Quintin 7–8
210,80/73,70

From le Quillio take the D 35 south-west (→ Mur-de-Bretagne). Almost immediately turn right onto the D 69 (→ Saint-Gilles-Vieux-Marché). At Notre-Dame-de-Lorette turn right to the church. Alongside the church is an impressive peristalith of twenty-nine large uprights that mark the vanished long mound of le Quillio. The mound was orientated east/west and was about 20 m long and 5–7 m wide. The two sides of the peristalith are rather different with massive stones on one side and thin plaques on the other.

Saint-Giles-Vieux-Marché

menhir — 59/12
Neolithic
Quintin 7–8
206,80/74,50

Marked on the Michelin map. Take the D 63 north-east (→ Saint-Martin-des-Prés), after 750 m branch onto the D 69 (→ le Quillio). The menhir is 400 m from the turning, signposted and to the left of the road.

Nothing special.

Saint-Michel-en-Grève

menhir — 58/7
Neolithic
Lannion 1–2
167,50/127,45

Marked on the Michelin. Go out of Saint-Michel on the N 786. The menhir is 250 m before the crossing with the D 88, on the left, behind a hedge. It is nearly 5 m high.

Not exciting.

Saint-Quay-Perros

Crec'h Quillé — 58/1
lateral-entrance grave — Neolithic
(Figures 38 and 39) — Lannion 1–2
175,50/135,25

Only discovered in 1955, it is hard to find, but well worth the search. Take the D 788 south from Saint-Quay-Perros (→ Lannion). After 1.5 km note the turning right to Saint-Méen but continue on the D 788. Then take the second turning left, unsignposted (1 km beyond the Saint-Méen turn-off). After 150 m turn left down a track. Another 100 m and the mound is to the left in a pine-tree grove.

Only the western and southern parts of the rectangular mound are intact. It has a central stone core, covered with a mound of loess bounded by orthostatic uprights (some of which have marks engraved on them, and one of which, on the north side, is shaped) and dry-stone walled panels. There was originally a menhir in the centre of the short west end.

The entrance passage, on the south side, off-centre to the length of the chamber, is delimited by an upright on either side and a sill-stone. The width and height of the chamber increases from east to west. At the east end it is 1 m wide and 1.2 m high, at the west end 1.8 m high and wide. The total length of the chamber is 15.2 m.

In the chamber, the upright opposite the entrance

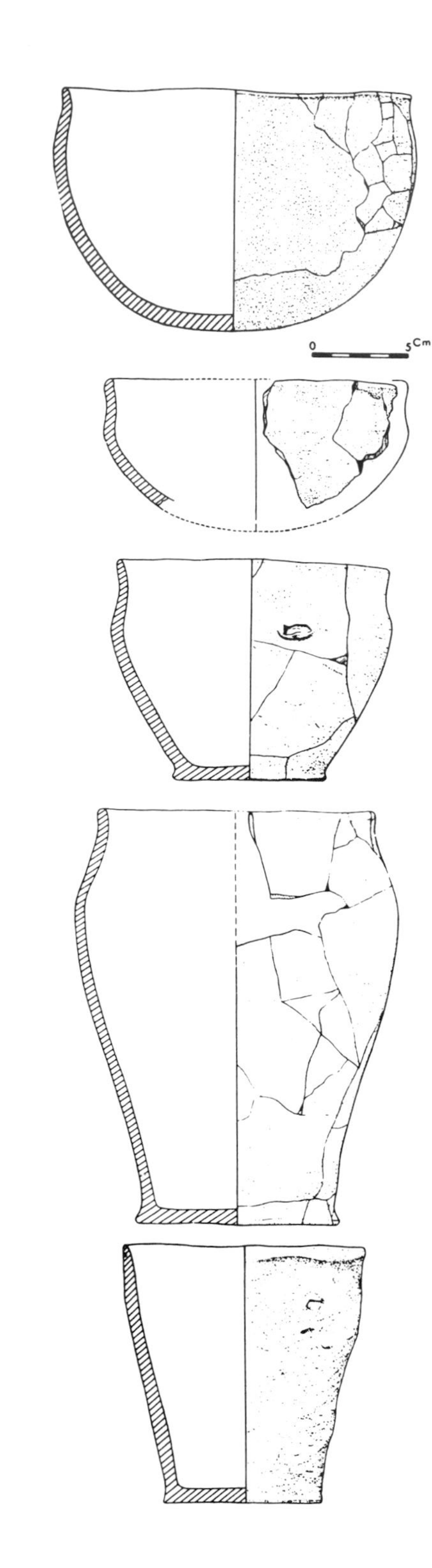

38 Plan and some of the contents of the lateral-entrance grave of Crec'h Quillé,
Saint-Quay-Perros

39 Bas-relief from Crec'h Quillé, ***Saint-Quay-Perros***

is roughly shaped to an anthropomorphic form and has sculpted breasts and a 'necklace' (not easy to see in the daylight). Opposite this stele, between the two stones marking the entrance to the chamber, a cist made of several stones was set into the floor. It contained five almost complete pots, both round- and flat-based, one of which held a stone pendant. This offering placed just opposite the anthromorph, allows a rare glimpse of some of the ritual that must have been associated with these monuments. There is also evidence that a fire was lit in the passage sometime before the final blocking occurred. The grave-goods consisted of two 'flower pots', two flat-based globular vessels, many flat bases, many round-based bowls with slight necks, fragments of carinated pottery and a fragment of a large collared vessel. There was also a dolerite axe, a flint axe-blade, three schist pendants, two flint blades and a few scrapers and flakes. The southern end of the chamber was remarkable for the number of whole pots and for an offering composed of a flat-based vase with a small bowl inside, placed close to a small dolerite axe.

Carbon-14 samples give dates of 1810 + − 120 bc (calibrated 2235 BC) and 1790 + − 200 bc (calibrated 2215 BC).

This lateral-entrance grave is one of a group concentrated in north Trégor, the others are Kergüntuil, *Trégastel*; le Mélus, *Ploubazlanec* and Coat Mez, Trévou-Tréguignec.

Saint-Samson-sur-Rance

Le Tremblais — 59/5–6
or Pierre Longue — Neolithic
menhir — Dinan 5–6
278,28/97,49

Take the D 57 east from Saint-Samson-sur-Rance (→ la Hisse). Shortly after Saint-Samson, cross the railway line and 700 m beyond and to the left of the road, the menhir is visible on the edge of a wood. A small 'menhir' sign indicates the footpath.

7 m high, with quartz veins running through the granite. Legend has it that if one can slide down the upper face without being lacerated one will find a husband or wife within the year. The upper face is smoothed and in certain lights engravings can be seen. There are five or six horizontal rows made up of juxtaposed squares often with internal cup-marks and sometimes with a projection on top. On the lateral faces of the stone are engravings of hafted axes and crooks. The motifs are somewhat similar to those at Prajou-Menhir, *Trébeurden*, Côtes-du-Nord.

Trébeurden

58/1

The fine gallery grave of Prajou-Menhir has been described under *Pleumeur-Bodou*.

Trégastel

58/1

Another centre from which to explore the marvellous pink granite coastal formations.

40 Bas-reliefs and engravings from the grave of Kergüntuil, Trégastel

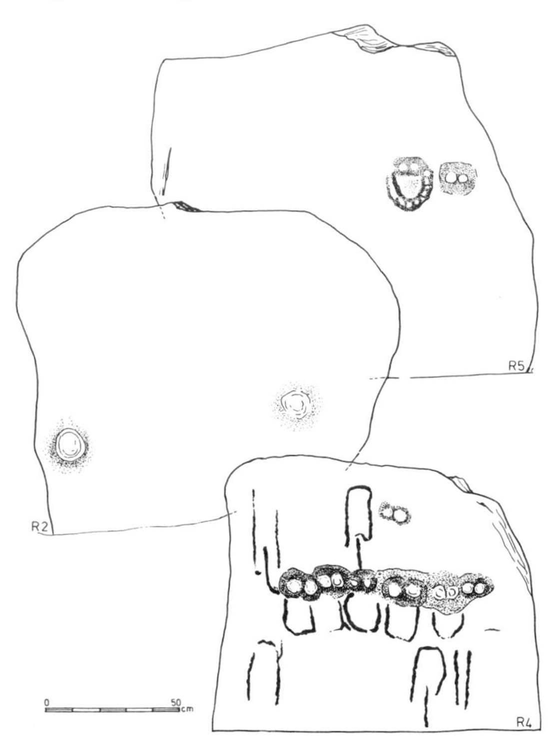

1 Musée Préhistorique, Sainte-Anne-Trégastel — Museum

100 m from the main quay of Sainte-Anne.

The name of the museum is a bit of a misnomer, but in among the tropical fish and other exotica are some chipped and polished stone tools, a few bronze objects, and, more important, the collared flask and Seine-Oise-Marne pottery from Kergüntuil.

Open 1 to 30 June from 2 to 6 p.m.; from 1 July to 1 September from 9 a.m. to 10 p.m., and from 2 to 15 September from 2 to 6 p.m.

2 Kergüntuil — Neolithic *(probable) lateral-entrance grave* — Perros-Guirec 5–6
(Figure 40) — 170,40/140,10

Marked on Michelin map (see inset map, Figure 33). Coming from Sainte-Anne-Trégastel take the D 788 (→ Trébeurden). After 1.5 km there is a small road to the left, marked to the 'dolmen'. Follow the signs.

There are two monuments. The first, close to the road, is small and heavily restored. The second, across the fields, is the fine monument of Kergüntuil. The chamber is 8.5 m long and orientated east-north-east/west-south-west. Like the one at Saint-Quay-Perros it increases in width and height from east to west. At the east end it is 1.4 m wide and 1 m high, at the west end 1.75 × 1.2 m. There are four capstones. The present entrance is at the west end of the north side but this is the result of an upright being removed; the original passage was probably at the extreme east end of the south side.

On the third upright from the entrance on the north side are eight pairs of breasts (seven in a row, one above), some mutilated, some with traces of 'necklaces' below them, and dagger motifs. On the preceding stone are two pairs of breasts and a necklace with small beads.

The grave-goods include at least two collared flasks, one 'flower pot', fragments of round and flat pot bases, five or six polished axes, and a Grand Pressigny dagger. Some of these objects are in the local museum (see above).

Trégon

La Ville-Hautière 59/5
gallery grave Neolithic
Lamballe 3–4
265,11/106,08

Marked on the Michelin map, From Trégon take the D 768 (→ Plancoët). After 0.6 km turn right on the D 786 (→ Matignon). Continue past a turning right (D 62 → Saint-Jacut) and then, at the second house (la Ville-Génouhan—1 km from the Matignon turn-off) take the track left for 200 m.

A fine grave with all its capstones intact.

Tréguier

Tossen-Keler 58/2
tumulus Neolithic

On the quay at Tréguier are the rather forlorn remains of a horseshoe setting of fifty-two granite stones. These originally stood at Tossen-Keler, Penvenan, where the stones, which included three with engravings, had been covered by two stone cairns and a great capping of loess, 38×32 m in diameter. There were no burials in the cairns, only two central hearths. It would seem to be a ritual or cult, rather than a funerary, monument. It is somewhat similar to the mound at Kermené, Guidel in Morbihan, which contained the broken stone fragments of a female deity.

Material from the hearths below the mound gave a carbon-14 date of 2550 + − 250 bc (calibrated 3310 BC).

Trémargat

Toul Goulic 58/8
promontory fort Iron Age
Carhaix-Plouguer 3–4
186,30/86,40

From Trémargat take the D 87 north-east (→ Saint-Antoine, Guiaudet). Continue for 2.5 km crossing the first bridge, passing a turning left to Peumerit-Quinton, and just before the second bridge, and before Saint-Antoine, take a track to the right. At the farm either ask Monsieur L. Salou to escort you, or get permission to walk through the farm and through the field with the race track. In the far left-hand corner, take the dirt track straight ahead. This track cuts through the rampart (much overgrown) and the deep ditch is visible to the right.

The site was intensively occupied during the Middle and Late Neolithic periods; flint tools, dolerite flakes and whole axes have been found. A Bronze Age palstave attests to later occupation and Late Bronze Age and Iron Age sherds were found in the earthen defences.

The Bronze Age/Iron Age defences enclose nearly five hectares, making it the largest camp in the Côtes-du-Nord. The single bank with traces of stone-facing on the exterior now stands to a maximum height of 3 m above the ground level. The bank follows the natural contours of the hillside and then cuts sharply across the ridge at both ends. There are traces of ditches across both ends, and of a counterscarp along the flanks. There is an entrance at both ends and a possible postern on the west side.

Yvias

Tossen-ar-Run 59/2
passage grave Neolithic
Pontreux 3–4
205,85/126,85

Go out of Yvias on the D 79, east, for 2 km, and just before the crossing with the D 7, to the right of the road, is the tumulus, crowned with a cross.

The passage is now blocked but originally it led to a corbelled chamber which contained a few Chassey-type sherds and a lot of Seine-Oise-Marne pottery, also some flint tools.

Yvignac

Church of Saint-Malo 59/15

A fine eleventh-century nave and a twelfth-century choir. The western porch has an interesting geometric decoration, reminiscent of the style found in Normandy.

Finistère

Berrien

58/6

Berrien, *Brennilis*, *Commana* and *Huelgoat* are in the high interior Monts d'Arrée area of western Brittany. A landscape of desolate moors and peat bogs, broken by jagged teeth of quartzitic rock. There are fine views from the Montagne Saint-Michel and from Roc-Trévezel.

Kérampeulven Neolithic
menhir Huelgoat 3–4
149,30/93,70

Marked on the Michelin. From Berrien take the D 14 south (→ Huelgoat). After 2.25 km turn right, marked 'le menhir de Kérampeulven'. In Kérampeulven continue 30 m beyond the menhir sign and turn left. The final signpost is then visible.

A respectable stone.

Beuzec-Cap-Sizun

58/14

You could use the monuments of *Beuzec-Cap-Sizun*, *Poullan-sur-Mer*, *Pont-Croix* and *Cléden-Cap-Sizun* as an excuse to explore this peninsula, particularly the precipitous, sea-lashed headlands of the Pointe du Raz and the Pointe du Van. Legend has it that between these two headlands, below the waters of the Baie des Trépassés, lies the city of Is, sixth-century seat of King Gradlon, and reputedly the most beautiful city in France. It was Gradlon's daughter who, having taken the devil as her lover, opened the protective dykes. The water surged in; her father escaping on his horse with his daughter up behind him was instructed by God to throw her into the torrent. He did, and she became a siren, luring sailors to their death upon the rocks.

1 Kerbalanec Neolithic
gallery grave Douarnenez 7–8
94,60/364,50

Marked on the Michelin. From Beuzec take the D 7 east (→ Poullan, Tréboul/Douarnenez). Continue for 4 km, passing the turning left to Pointe du Millier. Then take the small road left (→ Kerbalanec). At the end of the road the monument is signposted to the left.

A fine grave with all the capstones still in place. There is an antechamber, probably never covered, 1.5 m long, then a dividing stone with a triangular space to one side allowing access to the main chamber. Slight remains of the mound with a peristalith on one side can still be seen.

The grave-goods included three round-based pots—one with incised lines, an entire flat-based pot plus fragments of others, two 'Seine-Oise-Marne' pots, fragments of at least three Bell Beakers, a polished dolerite A axe with squared sides and a rectangular butt, a fragment of a polished fibrolite axe, flaked flints, blades and scrapers.

2 Castel-Coz Iron Age
cliff fort Douarnenez 5–6
(Figure 42) 89,70/365,75

In Beuzec take the D 507 north (→ Pointe du Château de Beuzec). The road eventually turns into a track. Continue along the track for 500 m. The three banks and ditches can then be seen just beyond the narrow point of the promontory.

The promontory was first occupied in Neolithic times. Wheeler suggests that the earthen or rubble bank between two lines of orthostats to the south of the Iron Age banks and ditches may date to this period. Then there is evidence of Bell Beaker occupation, and finally, in the Iron Age, probably during

41 Département of Finistère

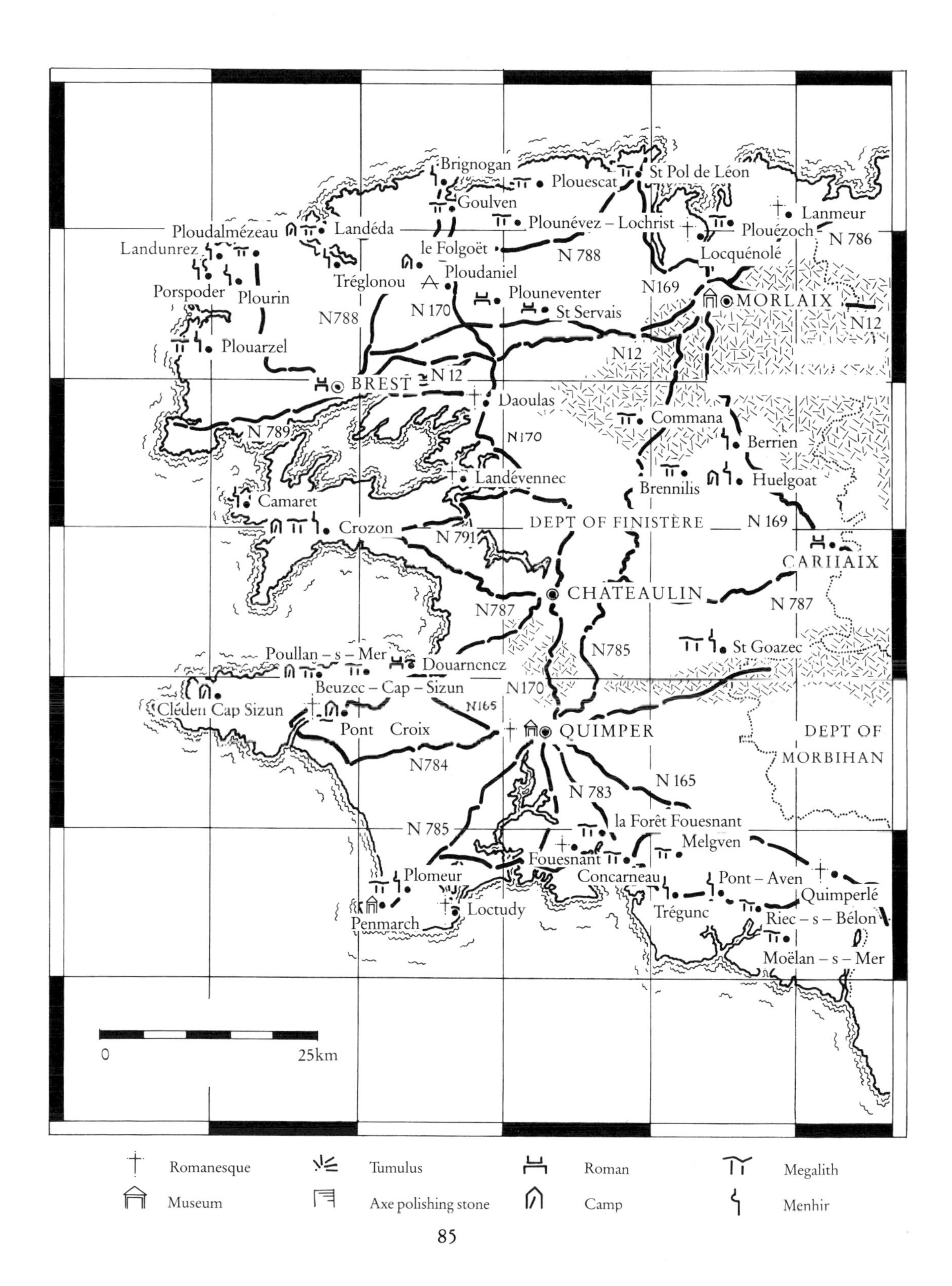
Brignogan
Plouescat
St Pol de Léon
Goulven
Lanmeur
Ploudalmézeau
Landéda
Plounévez – Lochrist
Plouézoch
N 786
Landunrez
le Folgoët
N 788
Locquénolé
Ploudaniel
Tréglonou
N169
Porspoder
Plourin
Plouneventer
MORLAIX
N788
N 170
St Servais
N12
Plouarzel
N12
BREST
N 12
Daoulas
Commana
N 789
N170
Berrien
Landévennec
Brennilis
Huelgoat
Camaret
Crozon
N 791
DEPT OF FINISTÈRE
N 169
CARHAIX
CHATEAULIN
N787
N 787
N785
St Goazec
Poullan – s – Mer
Douarnenez
Beuzec – Cap – Sizun
N170
N165
Cléden Cap Sizun
Pont Croix
QUIMPER
DEPT OF
MORBIHAN
N784
N 165
N 783
la Forêt Fouesnant
N 785
Melgven
Fouesnant
Concarneau
Pont – Aven
Quimperlé
Plomeur
Loctudy
Trégunc
Riec – s – Bélon
Penmarch
Moëlan – s – Mer
0
25km
Romanesque
Tumulus
Roman
Megalith
Museum
Axe polishing stone
Camp
Menhir

43 Gallery grave at Mougau-Bian, **Commana**

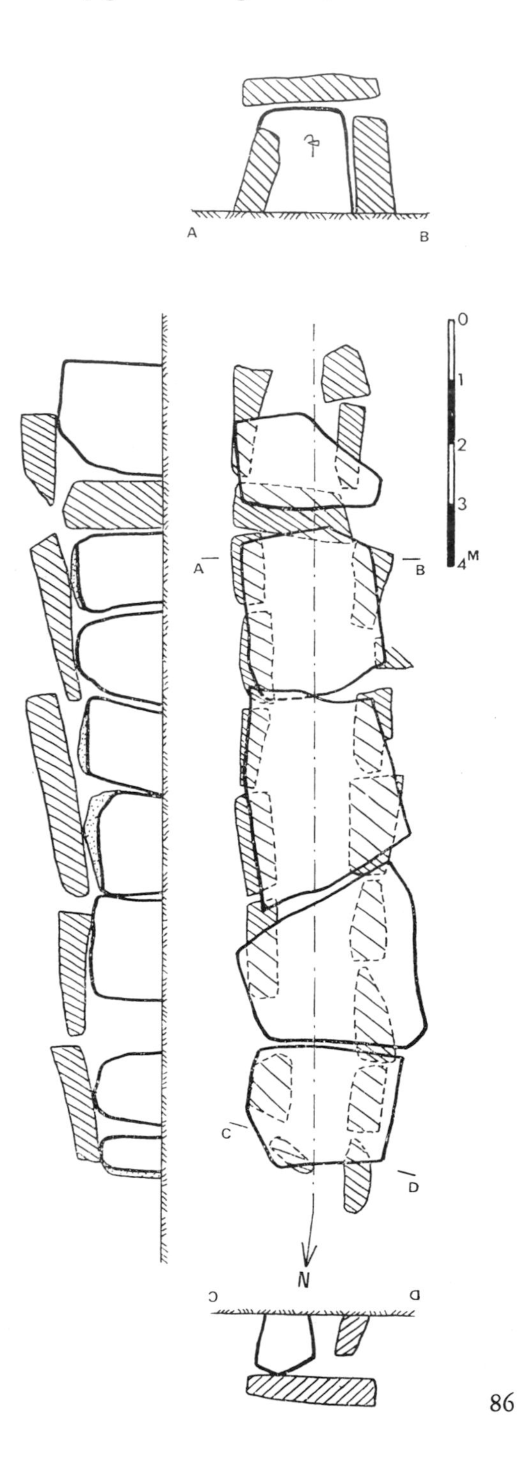

44 Engravings, Mougau-Bian, **Commana**

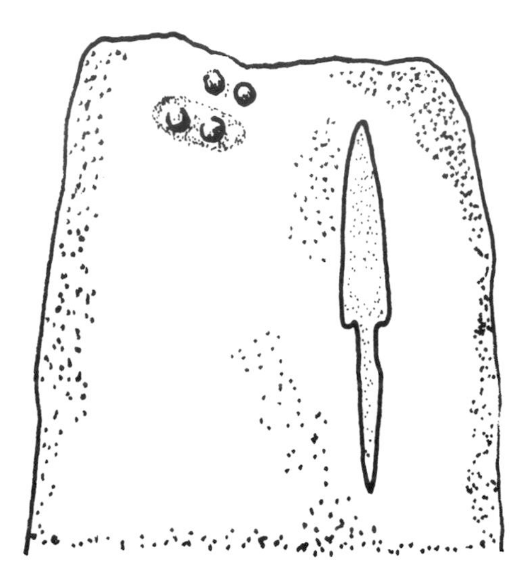

the La Tène III, the three banks and ditches were thrown up. These earthworks enclose about an hectare. The main bank (crowned by a medieval rampart) has an external dry-stone wall revetment. It continues as a low bank right round the promontory. The track goes through the original entrance. The small hollows within the camp may be Iron Age or medieval hut floors.

At the point where the promontory joins the main coastline Wheeler noted two further slight banks and some hollows, some of which contained medieval pottery.

The site was excavated in 1869 and the finds are in the *Penmarc'h* museum, Finistère. The pottery includes fragments of one or two Bell Beakers, bead-rimmed La Tène ware, probably La Tène III. There is a fragment of thick ware with a red haematite coating. The Iron Age pottery is mainly hand-made, with perhaps a few wheel-turned fragments. There are also coarse dishes and sherds, some with piecrust decoration, probably early medieval—ninth or tenth century AD. In addition there are saddle-back querns, a flat milling stone, clay spindle whorls, glass beads, polished stone axes, flint cores and flakes, part of a bronze sword, ten fragments of iron swords and over a hundred sling stones.

Brennilis

Ty-ar-Boudiguet 58/6
passage grave Neolithic
Huelgoat 1–2
142,20/92,30

Marked on the Michelin. On the north edge of Brennilis take the C 2 east (→ Plouénez, Penhars). After 200 m there is a small sign to the 'dolmen' on the right. Follow the footpath for 70 m.

A fine monument. One side of the passage and chamber form an almost straight line (partially destroyed towards the back of the chamber), whilst the other side of the chamber angles out before running parallel again. The total length of chamber and passage is 13.4 m and it gradually opens from 1 m at the passage entrance to 2.2 m at the back of the chamber. The chamber is built of large orthostats and is almost entirely covered by one enormous capstone and two smaller ones. In the middle of the chamber is an upright, free-standing stone.

The mound is oval and part of the large orthostatic peristalith is intact.

Brest

58/4

Brest was probably the site of the Gallo-Roman town of Gesocribate. At the end of the third century a series of fortifications was erected against the marauding Saxons. Part of the medieval castle rests on the Roman wall.

Brignogan

Men-Marz 58/4
menhir Neolithic
Plouguerneau 7–8
109,25/1129,50

Coming into Brignogan on the D 770 keep left (marked to the menhir). Go down to the quay and at the furthest point north, a small road, left, rue du Menhir (→ Plages du Phare, Chardons Bleus), takes you to the menhir.

9 m high, rough, surmounted by a small cross.

Camaret-sur-Mer

Lagatjar 58/3
alignments Neolithic
Brest 3–4
8560/8660

From Camaret take the D 8A towards Pointe de Penhir. The alignments are on the roadside, 1 km out of Camaret, to the right. Fine—especially if you see them *before* getting to Carnac.

Three lines, each with a different orientation, 140 stones in all. Restored between the two World Wars, they extend for 200 m but were originally three or four times as long.

Continue on to Pointe de Penhir, a wild headland, with terrific views.

Carhaix-Plouguer

58/17

The Jardin du Chapeau Rouge in the town centre contains some of the remains of the Gallo-Roman town. There are columns, part of the sewage system and stone coffins.

Cléden-Cap-Sizun

Castel Meur 58/13
promontory fort Iron Age
Pointe du Raz 3–4
76,95/363,95

Take the V 2 north-west (→ Pointe de Brézellec). After 750 m at the junction with the V 10 continue straight ahead to Meil-Kernot (3 km from Cléden). Then take the first turning right onto a small road to Kernot. Go through the hamlet, and onto the track beyond. When the track turns right, continue ahead on a grass track and after 400 m this track crosses the ramparts.

The earthworks stand out clear and true; the views are marvellous.

The hill fort, like Beuzec, was first inhabited in Neolithic times, then Bell Beaker people built a burial mound and later again during the Iron Age, a triple rampart was constructed to protect an area of about 2 hectares. There is an additional ditch with possible traces of a fourth bank or counterscarp. The track goes through the original entrance.

Brittany

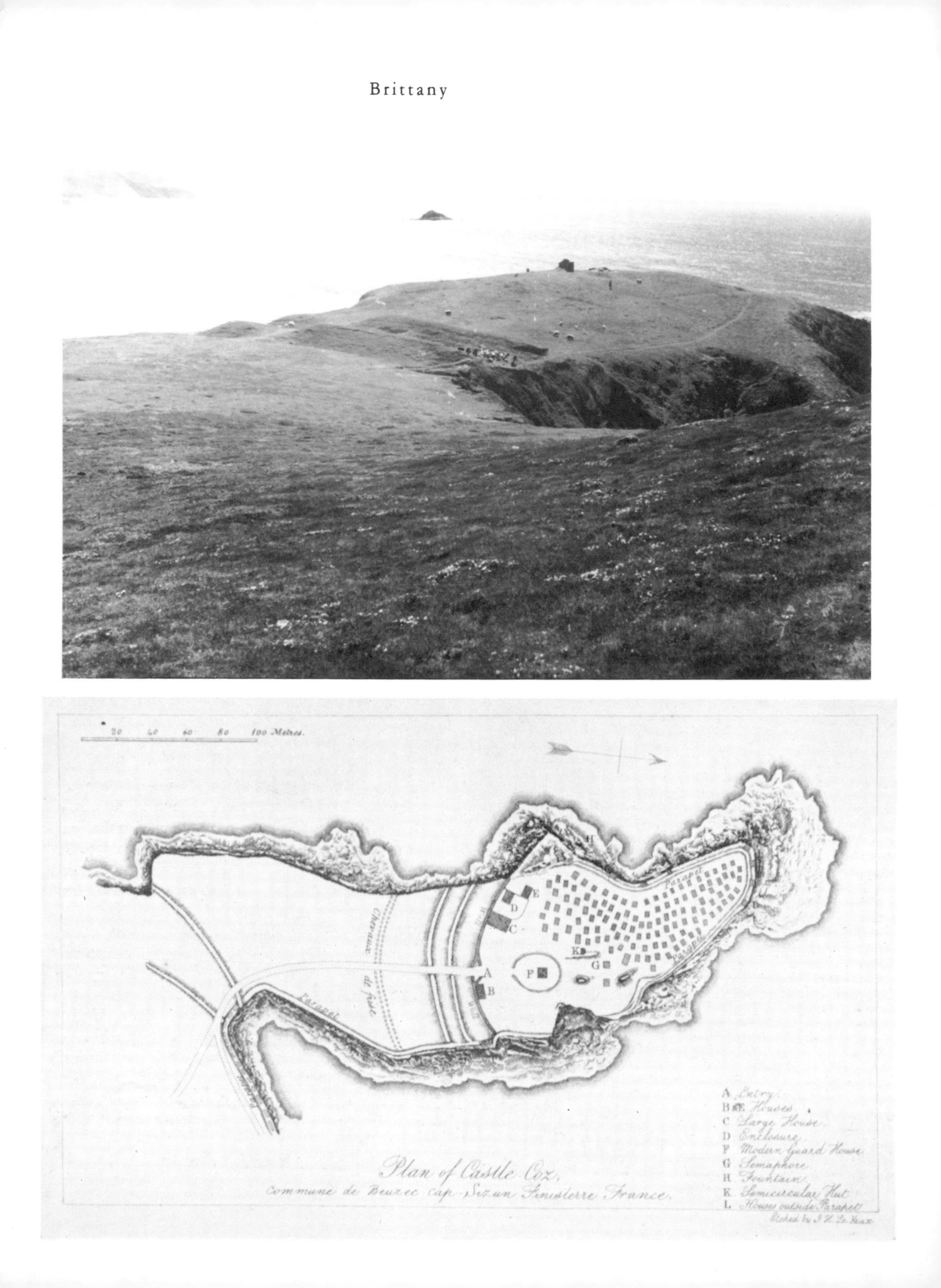

20 40 60 80 100 Metres.
Parapet
Parapet
Parapet
Wall
Wall
Chevaux de frise
A Entry
B E Houses
C Large House
D Enclosure
F Modern Guard House
G Semaphore
H Fountain
K Semicircular Hut
L Houses outside Parapet
Plan of Castle Coz,
Commune de Beuzec Cap-Sizun Finisterre France.
Etched by J. H. Le Keux

45 Hill fort of Lostmarc'h, ***Crozon***

In 1889 du Châtellier excavated the rectangular or oval hut depressions, which are still visible. There were ninety-five in all, ranging from 3.6 m square, to 7.6 × 4.6 m. The sides were revetted with dry-stone walling. They had apparently all been destroyed by fire.

The excavator found a lot of coarse pottery, spearheads, swords, daggers, an iron helmet, an iron ploughshare, sickles, blue glass beads, a fragment of a gold bracelet, grinding stones, sling stones and flint arrows. Some of the pottery was 'piecrust' medieval, similar to that from Beuzec. There were also a few sherds of finer ware. All this material is now in the museum of Saint-Germain-en-Laye near Paris.

Commana

Mougou-Bian — 58/6
gallery grave — Neolithic
(Figures 43 and 44) — Le Faou 3–4, 133,75/97,20

Marked on the Michelin. From Commana go south 400 m to the junction with the D 764 and cross onto the small road opposite, marked 'allée couverte Mougou-Bian'. The gallery grave is to the right, 1 km down the road, up against a hedge, and easy to drive straight past.

An interesting monument. The entrance is at the north end of the 11 m chamber (the 'lateral' entrance is simply a missing upright). The terminal cell at the south end is open to the sky.

There are some fine sculptings in the main chamber: a hafted axe on the north face of the divide between chamber and terminal cell; two pairs of breasts and a dagger, and three or four daggers respectively on two uprights on the west side and three daggers on one upright on the east side.

42 ***Beuzec-Cap-Sizun,*** *plan of the Iron Age promontory camp of Castel Coz, about 1869*

Concarneau

Keristin — 58/15
passage grave — Neolithic
Rosporden 5–6
430,55/2341,20

Nothing special. From the very interesting fourteenth-century fortified 'ville close' of Concarneau take the D 783 (→ Quimper). After crossing a railway line take the first small turning left to Keristin. Continue to Keristin farm (1.6 km from the turn-off) and the monument is to the left of the road in a small copse just before the new farmhouse.

A small, ruined, free-standing, orthostatic passage grave with no capstones.

Crozon

58/4

Stay awhile on the peninsula of the Cap de la Chèvre. It is still remote, and unbelievably beautiful. And on your way to or from the peninsula make a small detour off the N 78 to Menez Hom, the most westerly outlier of the Montagnes Noires. There are fine views in all directions.

1 Rostudel — Neolithic
passage grave — Douarnenez 1–2
89,70/77,20

Marked on the Michelin. From Morgat (south of Crozon) take the D 255 through Saint-Hernot and continue another 1.8 km to the turning right (→ Keravel, Keroux, and Kergonan). Then back-track down the D 255 to the fifth wooden telegraph pole and take a mini-footpath to the left for 25 m to a tidy mini-dolmen.

One capstone; three uprights.

2 Lostmarc'h — Neolithic
alignments

Directions as for Rostudel (above), but at Saint-Hernot turn right (→ Kerdreuz), then right again in front of the church of Saint-Hernot. Continue for 2 km and at a T-junction turn left and go through the hamlet of Lostmarc'h. On the edge of the hamlet, on the crest of the hill, there is a row of small uprights.

Originally there were at least three rows, and in 1902 fifteen uprights were still in place.

3 Lostmarc'h | Iron Age
hill fort | Douarnenez 1–2
(Figure 45) | 88,40/80,40

Directions as for the alignments. Continue through the hamlet of Lostmarc'h and onto the dirt track beyond. From the summit of the hill the tiny promontory protected by a short stretch of earthworks is clearly visible.

There were Neolithic people on the promontory long before the defences were set up. Wheeler mentions a possible ruined megalithic tomb at the highest point within the enclosed area; Giot mentions two.

The Iron Age earthworks consist of two banks, apparently dump constructed, and ditches, with an entrance 20 m from the south end. They protect an area of just under one hectare. There are some shallow depressions which may be hut floors.

A few early Iron Age sherds were found.

Daoulas

58/5
Church

A beautiful precinct with the remains of a fine twelfth-century cloister with a sculpted *lavatorium* in the centre. The church is heavily restored but has a twelfth-century west porch, and, in the cemetery, an ancient calvary. (See *Plomeur* for a list of some of the other calvaries.)

Douarnenez

58/14

During the Iron Age and then in the Gallo-Roman period there were important salt-works at Douarnenez. Salt was a highly valued commodity and was widely traded. Around the coast many of the workings were associated with fish-salting tanks and with tanks in which fish sauce, *garum*, was prepared (see General Introduction, page 56).

Plomarc'h | Iron Age/Gallo-Roman
salt-working site | Châteaulin 5–6
104, 90/364,60

Down on the beach of Douarnenez take the footpath, 'sentier pietonnier', running eastwards. It runs along the cliff top and close to the salt-workings. These have mainly been backfilled after excavation but the Roman wall between two salt-working units is still visible.

There are other sites scattered northwards along the Anse d'ar-Vechen and at the Anse de Caon near Telgruc-sur-Mer.

Folgoët, le

Castel Pen-Lédan or | 58/4
Castel Bras-Landivern or | Iron Age
Camp de César | Plabennec 3–4
hill fort | 107,60/1116,25

Take the D 788 (→ Brest) for 1.5 km, cross a bridge, and then turn onto a track to the left, marked to the Moulin du Folgoët. When the track branches keep left and continue past an almost dry mill-pond. The track starts to climb and then circles right round the base of the rampart.

The most massive earthwork in western Finistère—it may in fact be medieval rather than Iron Age. It encloses just under one hectare. The eastern line of the rampart cuts across the neck of the promontory and still stands nearly 7 m above the present bottom of the ditch and over 3 m above the interior ground level. The north, west and south sides of the rampart follow the natural contours. In the south-east corner, the eastern rampart turns at right angles inside the southern rampart to give an inturned entrance. There are traces of an outer dry-stone walled revetment.

Wheeler mentions that 70 m to the east of the eastern rampart are possible traces of a second rampart, now incorporated into a field boundary. A plan drawn up in 1900 suggests that it continues on from the bank of the main enclosure, and has an entrance to the south. *If* it really is ancient, it must have formed an outer enclosure.

Forêt-Fouesnant, la

Kerlevan 58/15
compartmented passage grave Neolithic
(Figures 46 and 47)
From la Forêt-Fouesnant take the D 44 (→ Pont Aven). After 1.5 km take the right turn to Kerlevan. At Kerlevan follow the signs to the 'Camping International Saint-Laurent'. Go into the camp ground and ask for a key at the reception. The monument lies behind the café.

There is a placard, in English, with a plan and a detailed description. Briefly: the sub-trapezoidal cairn was once much larger; the primary, western section which covered a passage grave (A) has been destroyed. The secondary eastern part contains two compartmented graves. These, and the destroyed one, all opened to the south-south-west. The grave to the east (C on the plan) has a roughly square chamber, 4 × 4 m, made of orthostats and dry-stone wall panelling, a passage 3.5 m long and, at the entrance to the passage, a notched stone with, alongside it, a small stone that may have been used as a plug. The western chamber (B) less intact, has a small cell on the north-east corner.

Neither chamber is roofed, both may have had low corbelled domes. The passages too are open to the sky and they probably had capstones. Both passages were purposefully blocked with large stones. Both chambers are compartmented by thin orthostats or by short sections of dry-stone walling.

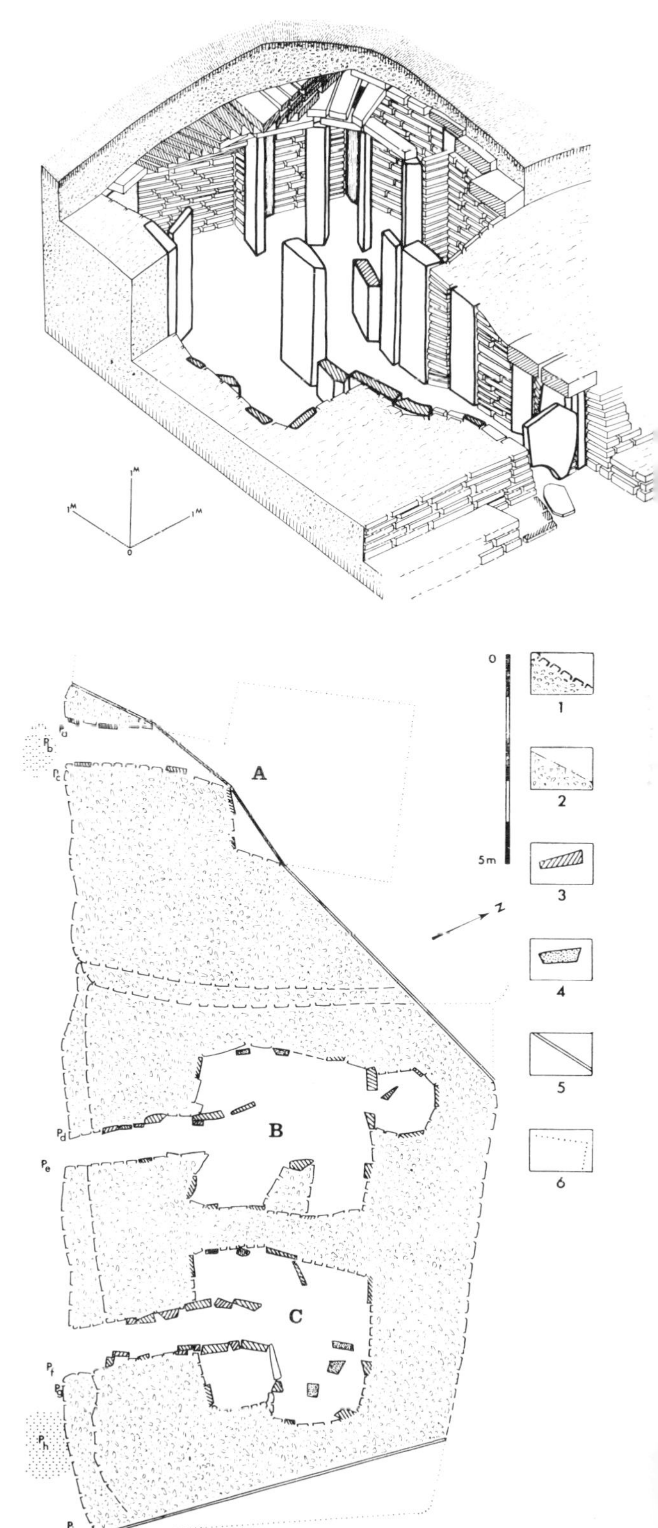

47 Isometric reconstruction of chamber C, La ***Forêt-Fouesnant***

46 Multi-chambered cairn at La ***Forêt-Fouesnant***

1 *Intact revetment walls*
2 *Reconstructed revetment walls*
3 *Intact uprights*
4 *Uprights placed during reconstruction*
5 *Limits of destroyed area*
6 *Reconstructed contours of destroyed sections*

A fragment of a decorated vase-support and numerous fine round-based bowls, often decorated with paired pastilles or with incised chevrons, were found in chamber A. They are Middle/Late Neolithic in style (Kervadel/le Souc'h types). There are also some rather coarse fragments, probably Kerugou ware, as well as a polished dolerite A axe, an axe fragment and some flint blades.

There is a carbon-14 date of 2875 + − 125 bc (calibrated 3660 BC) from chamber A, and a late date of 1950 + − 120 bc (calibrated 2455 BC).

Fouesnant

58/15
Church

The exterior of the twelfth-century church was largely reconstructed in the eighteenth century but the nave and transept have remained more or less untouched. There are some rather curious capitals in the nave, and some fine carved figures on the capitals in the transept.

Fouesnant is famous for its cider—reputedly the best in Brittany and definitely potent.

Goulven

Cosquer — 58/5
gallery grave — Neolithic
Saint-Pol-de-Léon 5–6
111,95/1123,80

Marked on the Michelin. From Goulven take the D 125 south (→ Lesneven). After 400 m turn left (→ Tréflez) and after another 600 m there is a small 'dolmen' sign on the right. Continue another 400 m and the gallery grave is to the left of the road.

It is open ended, and has an internal divide. Only one capstone is still in place. There is a row of large uprights parallel to the long side of the grave and possible traces of a second row; both probably served to consolidate the mound.

Huelgoat

58/6

Just east of Huelgoat is a great rock-strewn forest. The Camp d'Artus lies deep within it.

1 Le Cloître — Neolithic
menhir — Huelgoat 1–2
146,50/91,35

Marked on the Michelin. From Huelgoat take the D 764 west (→ Brest) and after 1.4 km turn left onto a small road marked to Kervinaouet and le Cloître. Continue another 2 km to a turning right (→ le Cloître): a good-sized menhir is then immediately visible to the right.

2 Camp d'Artus — Iron Age
hill fort — Huelgoat 3–4
(Figures 48 and 49) — 150,20/92,90

From Huelgoat take the D 764 east (→ Carhaix-Plouguer), and 1 km out of Huelgoat in the Forêt

PLATE II

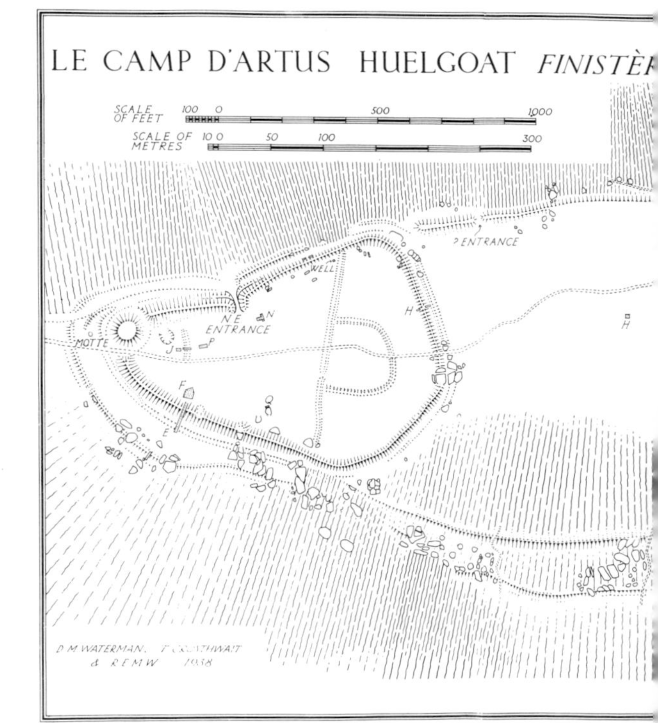

48 ***Huelgoat,*** *the Iron Age Camp d'Artus*

Dominiale there is a signpost left to the Camp d'Artus. It is about 1 km from here on foot following the signs, or, when they peter out, keeping straight on. Just as you are about to give up you will arrive at the dramatic entrance to the earthworks (southern end) set among huge boulders—'lumps of granite encumbering the scene like herds of elephants' (Wheeler 1957:23). A small path circles round the top of the rampart.

This site was carefully planned and partially excavated by Wheeler in 1938. He describes a huge outer enclosure covering 30 hectares, a reduced fortified area at the northern end, protecting 4 hectares, and a medieval motte (eleventh/twelfth century), once crowned by a stone tower, at the northern apex.

The excavations revealed that the larger enclosure was only very slightly earlier than the reduced structure and that all the banks conformed to the same *murus gallicus* construction. That is, they were made of earth and sand, with an internal wooden scaffolding kept in place with huge quantities of nails. A section through the rampart at the southern end of the large enclosure (A on the plan) revealed that it was originally 10 m wide and had an external dry-stone revetment. It was flanked by a wide berm and had a small external bank and ditch. Another section, taken through the north-west rampart within the reduced area, revealed that the original structure, 3.5 m high, had been topped with earth kept in place by a rough stone wall. In this section of the camp the land sloped rather gently, and a further earth bank had been thrown up outside the main rampart. The main entrance seems to have been in the north-east part of the reduced camp. The stone-faced inturned walls of the rampart, with additional stone curbs, form a passage way.

Wheeler argues convincingly that the occupation was short-lived. The defences were 'built on some occasion when, under exceptional stress, the tribesmen of a large area had momentarily assembled under central discipline'. The tribe was the Osismi and the occasion probably the Caesarian campaigns of 56 BC. (In many ways this sequence parallels the history of the *murus gallicus* camp at *le Petit-Celland*, Manche, Normandy.) The defensive measures were in vain. Or, at least, the south-east gateway shows signs

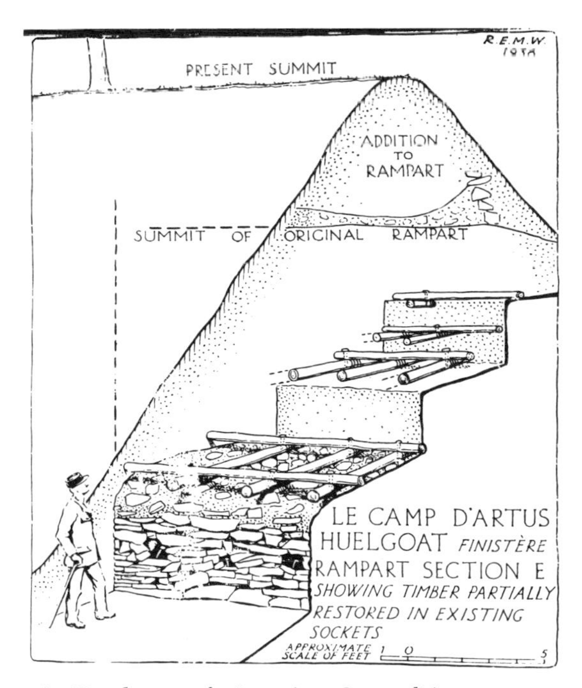

49 ***Huelgoat,*** *the Iron Age Camp d'Artus, section through the* murus gallicus

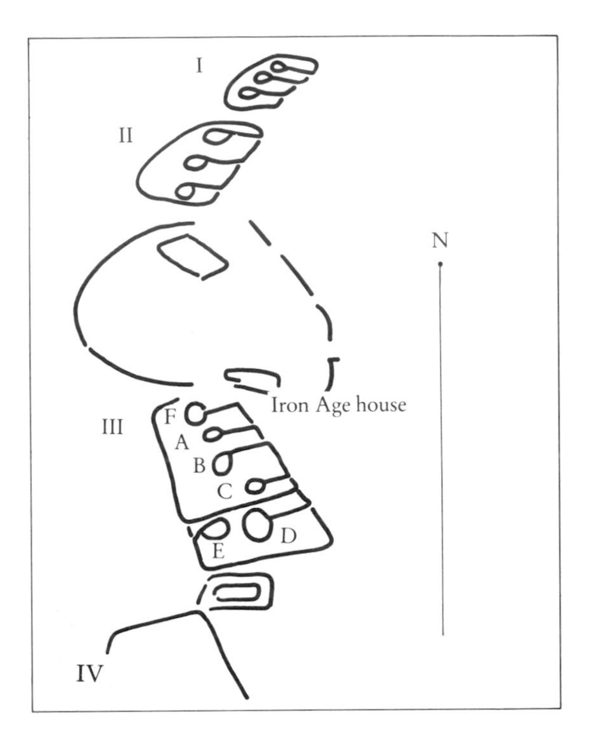

50 Plan of Ile Gaignog, ***Landéda****, taken from an aerial photograph*

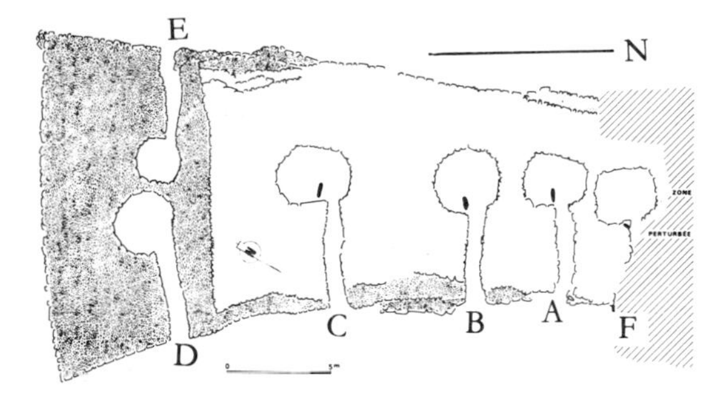

51 Cairn III, Ile Gaignog, ***Landéda****, showing primary and secondary cairns and the position of the stelae in chambers A, B and C*

of violent destruction.

The pottery found is very uniform, La Tène III, and very limited in quantity. It is mainly wheel-turned. Among the more notable finds were some graphite-coated ware, a fragment of lustrous black cordoned ware, and an example of counter-sunk handles—a trait found quite frequently on pottery from southern England. A Celtic coin is ascribed to the first half of the first century BC. The material is in the *Penmarc'h* museum, Finistère.

Landéda

Ile Gaignog or Guennoc	58/3–4
multi-chambered cairns;	Neolithic/Bronze/
Bronze and Iron Age	Iron Age
enclosures and hut	Plouguerneau 5–6
foundations	86,50/1123,80

(Figures 50 and 51)

Hard to get to but one of the most beautiful and interesting sites in Brittany. *To be protected at all costs!* In the main square of Landéda keep left (south) of the church on the C 3. Continue 250 m, then turn left (→ Passage Saint-Pabu and Streat-Glas). Go down to the sea at Beg Ar Vill. You can probably persuade the men who run the oystery to take you to the island in one of the oyster boats. The journey there and back takes an hour.

Ile Gaignog was inhabited from Mesolithic through to medieval times, and for most of that long period it formed part of the mainland. Now it is an island, inhabited only by rabbits and sea-gulls and dominated by three great cairns. Several scatters of microliths have been found under, and close to, cairn III and it may be that here, as at Dissignac, *Saint-Nazaire*, Loire-Atlantique, and doubtless many other parts of Brittany, indigenous gatherer-hunters gradually adopted farming.

Starting at the south end, the first cairn is cairn IV with two passage graves. Then, separated by an Iron Age hut floor, comes cairn III, which is an elongated, trapezoidal shape, 28 m long, 18 m at the south-south-east end, and 8 m at the north-north-west end. It covers four passage graves, all opening to the north-east. The most northerly one, chamber F, has a slightly different orientation from the other three (A, B, C) and may represent the first stage of building, or an addition. A later extension of the cairn to the south-south-east has a different orientation, and contains two more passage graves. D opens to the north-east; E, smaller, opens to the south-west. All six chambers are dry-stone walled and were originally corbelled.

In chambers C, B and A there are roughly shaped stelae to the left of the entrance. These are 0.5 to 0.6 m wide, a maximum of 0.25 m thick and 1 to 1.4 m high. The one in chamber C has a roughly shaped head and shoulders. In chamber E the grave-goods were sealed in. There were fragments of three or four pots including half a Carn bowl.

Chamber III C has a carbon-14 date of 3125 + − 140 bc (calibrated 3910 BC) and 3850 + − 300 bc (calibrated 4630 BC). Chamber III E (the later extension) has a date of 2250 + − 120 bc (calibrated 2910 BC).

The next cairn to the north, cairn II, contains three square orthostatic chambers. The capstones have gone. The two southerly ones (B and C) are asymmetrical with one wall lying on the same axis as the passage. In chamber II C U-signs and crooks were found—but they are not very visible.

The most northerly cairn (I) also has three chambers, this time with long passages and small dry-stone walled chambers, originally corbelled. Again the first and third chambers (a and c) are asymmetrical. Chamber Ic contained a pedestalled vase similar to those from Barnenez, *Plouézoc'h*, Finistère; Dissignac, *Saint-Nazaire*, Loire-Atlantique; and Larcuste, *Colpo*, Morbihan.

The island was reinhabited during the Late Bronze Age. The passage graves were reused and a circular enclosure 35 m in diameter was built between cairns III and II, overlapping the end of cairn III. Then, later, during the La Tène Iron Age, the passage graves were again reused, the enclosure was elaborated and numerous quadrangular houses were built, some within the enclosure, others close to the cairns but outside the enclosure; yet others, simpler in form, in the more exposed parts of the island. One hut, close to the north-east end of cairn III and butting up against the entrance to the passage of chamber F, measures 6 × 5 m on the outside, 2 × 4 m inside, has an entrance to the north-west, and foundations made of small stones set between large slabs. This house was reused in medieval times and a fine oven was built in the entrance of the passage grave. The La Tène people also built a bank around much of the island, parts of which can be seen to the south of cairn III.

Landévennec

Abbaye de Guénole — 58/4
Church

In the fifth century AD Saint Guénole founded a monastery on this site. Now all that remains are the ruins of the later, Romanesque church. The walls of the nave, transept and choir still stand quite high and the column bases with some minimal sculpting are intact.

The abbey is open from Monday to Saturday from 9 a.m. to 12 noon and 2 to 6 p.m., and on Sundays from 3 to 6 p.m.

Landunvez

Saint-Gonvanc'h — 58/3
menhir — Bronze Age
Plouarzel 3–4
79,90/2314,00

Go through the centre of Landunvez and out south to the T-junction. Turn left (→ Kergastel, Kernézoc etc.). After 1.6 km continue past the turning right to Kerhouézel. Then, through the second field-gap to the left, the menhir is visible 100 m from the road.

Set among strangely shaped high earth-walled fields, the menhir is 6 m high, carefully shaped, and probably Early or Middle Bronze Age in date.

From here go on to *Crozon* and *Camaret-sur-Mer*.

Lanmeur

58/6
Church

The church is modern but the crypt below the choir (entrance to the left of the altar) is pre-Romanesque, sixth century—the oldest in Brittany. It once contained the tomb of Saint Melard. There are eight great pillars, two with marvellous sculpted columns.

A signpost opposite the church points the way to the Chapel of Notre-Dame-de-Kernitron (350 m). The nave and part of the transept are Romanesque, as is the weather-beaten southern doorway with its sculpted tympanum showing Christ surrounded by the signs of the apostles.

Locquenole

58/6
Church

The four pillars at the transept crossing are Romanesque. The capitals have rather unusual carvings.

Loctudy

58/15
Church

The finest Romanesque church in Brittany. The front is disguised by an austere eighteenth-century façade, but once inside the twelfth-century structure has hardly been touched. The high nave with narrow aisles is covered with a wooden vault broken by double stone arches. The choir is flanked by narrow arches leading to the ambulatory. Capitals and often pillar-bases are richly carved with a multitude of geometric, floral and figurative motifs.

Out in the churchyard, behind the choir, is an Iron Age stele, 2 m high, firmly Christianized.

Melgven

1 Luzuen — 58/16
gallery grave — Neolithic
Rosporden 5–6
142,40/2339,95

From Melgven take the D 44 east (→ Pont Aven), then the D 24 south (→ Pont Aven). After 750 m turn left—marked to the 'dolmen'. Another 700 m then left again, also signposted. 650 m and another small sign on the left of the road. Once inside the field, left yet again!

A free-standing, rather ruined gallery grave with a fine terminal cell covered by an immense capstone.

2 Coat-Ménez-Guen — Neolithic
gallery grave — Rosporden 5–6
(Figure 52) — 142,60/2340,70

Directions as for Luzuen (above), but continue on past the Luzuen grave to the end of the small road. Take a fine wooded track straight ahead. Walk 200 m to the bottom of the valley, then follow the track as it swings left for another 200 m. Just after a field entrance to the right, a small path to the left goes up over the bank to the monument.

A bit overgrown but interesting. It is of the 'arc-boutés' type; the uprights that form the two sides of the grave slant inwards and meet in the middle. Three capstones are balanced on top. The chamber is 14 × 2 m. There is a notched entrance stone at the south end and another notched stone between antechamber and chamber. The mound is visible—now an amorphous oval, 35 × 32 m, but originally rectangular, 22 × 12 m, with a revetment of high stones.

Moëlan-sur-Mer

1 Kergonstance — 58/11–12
gallery grave — Neolithic
Concarneau 3–4
153,05/329,80

Take the D24 west from Moëlan, and 100 m after the sign announcing the end of the village, to the right and visible from the road, is the monument.

A fine large gallery grave with a small terminal cell, all capstones in place.

*52 **Melgven**, gallery grave* arc boutés *of Coat-Ménez-Guen*

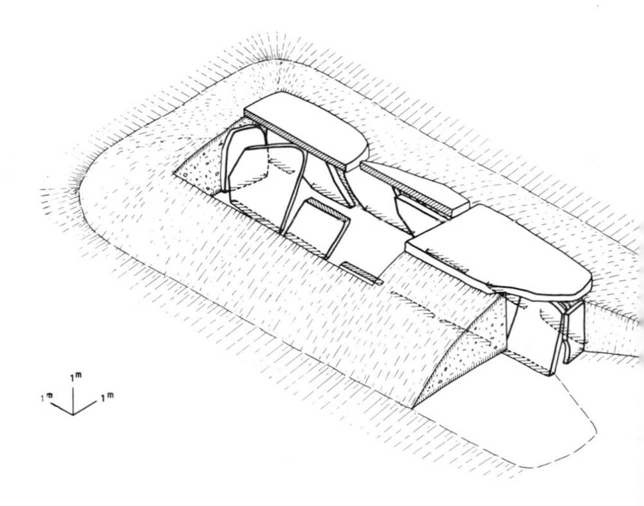

2 Kermeur-Bihan — Neolithic
gallery grave — Concarneau 3–4
148,30/330,15

From Moëlan take the D 116 south-west (→ Brigneau) then quickly turn right, still the D 116 (→ Kerfany). Continue for 6.5 km to Kergroës. Then take a very small road right (→ Kervigodès, Kersaux). After 0.75 km, at a stop sign, turn left (→ Kermeur-Bras, Kermeur-Bihan). Another 1.4 km, at the end of the road turn into the farmyard of Kermeur-Bihan. Take the track straight ahead and after 400 m the monument is to the right (about 70 m from the track).

A fine long gallery grave with capstones intact, a terminal cell, and an exterior row of orthostats to one side.

The grave-goods included three round-based pots (one with small lugs); one Seine-Oise-Marne pot with lug; one carinated pot similar to the Beaker 'Jersey bowl'; six polished axes (four dolerite, one quartz, one amphibolite)—some with squared sides and butts; many flaked flints, some points; a flint and a jadeite pendant and a tanged and slightly barbed arrowhead.

3 Kerandrègc (Kerandrèze) — Neolithic
gallery grave — Concarneau 3–4
151,20/328,00

Again the D 116 out of Moëlan but this time keep on towards Brigneau, ignoring the turning right to Kerfany. 2.8 km from Moëlan the 'mégalithe' is signposted and lies 50 m to the left of the road.

A small gallery grave with three capstones. The floor is paved with thin slabs and there is a sill-stone towards the back of the chamber.

It contained a thick-sided round-based bowl, a flat-based pot with elongated lugs, another flat-based vase with a circular neckband (perhaps a very degenerate collared flask), a Seine-Oise-Marne pot, Bell Beaker fragments, three pendants, five polished axes, two square-tanged and barbed arrowheads, a Grand Pressignian dagger, a wristguard, and many flint flakes and blades.

There is a menhir close by.

Morlaix

Musée municipal, — 58/6
rue des Vignes — Museum

A pleasant, old-fashioned museum with a bit of everything local. Four showcases cover the Neolithic to Roman periods and include some fine Bronze and Iron Age pottery.

Open from 9 a.m. to 12 noon, and 2 to 6 p.m. Closed on Mondays.

Penmarc'h

58/14

See *Plomeur* for details of this area and for other monuments in the vicinity.

Musée Préhistorique Finistèrien, — Museum
Porz-Carn, Saint-Guénole,
Penmarc'h

In Penmarc'h take the D 53 west (→ Saint-Guénole). After 1.5 km turn north on the V 11, signposted to the museum.

Two rooms full of interesting prehistoric material, mainly from Finistère. For a logical progression take in the Palaeolithic/Mesolithic showcases along the left side of room 1 then the Neolithic and Early/Middle Bronze in room 2, then return to room 1 for the Late Bronze and Iron Age. Note the showcases on the dolerite axe trade, the cast of the statue menhir from Laniscat, le Trévoux, the maps of Bronze Age finds, the axe hoards, the rich Early Bronze Age grave-goods—including the reconstruction of the grave of Kernonen, Plouvorn, and the reconstruction of Iron Age inhumations and cremations. You will also get some idea of what all the different pot styles mentioned in this book really look like.

In the forecourt is part of the curious double-passage grave of Run-Auour, originally sited in the commune of Plomeur. The reconstruction is less than accurate and the round dry-stone walled chamber has got lost. There is just the main orthostatic passage, open to the sky, 16.5 m long and 1.5 m wide, and, at right angles, 1.5 m before what would have been the chamber entrance, a secondary passage 12 m long and 2.1 m wide. Between the two is a threshold stone.

The grave-goods included three whole vases plus a lot of fragments, mainly Kerugou ware. Also an almost complete Bell Beaker and fragments of others, and a Seine-Oise-Marne pot. In addition there were polished flint, fibrolite and dolerite adzes, a few flint blades, some flint flakes, and a stone polisher.

Also in the forecourt are Bronze Age cists and Iron Age stelae. One stele, from Kerviltré, Saint-Jean-Trolimon comes from an early La Tène cemetery with eighty inhumations and half-a-dozen stelae, of which this one was the centrepiece.

The museum is open from 1 June to 30 September from 10 a.m. to 12 noon and 2 to 6 p.m. In winter it can be opened on request, but write beforehand.

Plomeur

58/14

This corner of Brittany, the old kingdom of Cornouaille, is a fine place to come to rest: a great sweep of sand along the Bay of Audierne (much of it deposited in Iron Age and medieval times); rocks just north of Saint-Guénole; seafood feasts. To the north of la Torche lies the earliest and, I think, most satisfying of the fifteenth/sixteenth-century calvaries. It stands, wind-swept, eroded, lichened, alongside the little church of Notre-Dame de Tronoën, on the site of an Iron Age camp. The calvaries and precincts, mainly clustered in western Brittany, are beyond the scope of this guide, but Plougonven (AD 1554, reconstructed AD 1896), Saint-Thégonnac (AD 1610), Guimiliau (AD 1581), Pleyben (AD 1550, reconstructed AD 1850) and Plougastel-Daoulas (AD 1601–4), all in Finistère, and Guenenno, Morbihan (AD 1550, reconstructed AD 1883), should on no account be missed.

1 Kerugou — Neolithic
passage grave — Pont-l'Abbé 1–2
103,10/337,35

From Plomeur take the D 785 south-west (→ Penmarc'h) and then, immediately outside Plomeur, turn right on the V 2 (→ Predela, Torche, Tronoën). 800 m from the junction take the unmarked road right leading to Kerugou. The monument lies just beyond Kerugou (also unsignposted) and 300 m before the village of Beuzec, to the left of the road.

The mound, 30 m in diameter, is still faintly visible. The passage, 6 m long, opens to the south-east. It continues through into the chamber, so that the chamber is divided into three sections. There are no capstones over the chamber and only one broken one over the passage. The floor was covered with thin paving stones laid on a bed of small pebbles, in turn resting on a layer of yellow earth. The grave was restored in 1938, with an ugly concrete plinth.

This monument has become the type site for a particular style of pottery – Kerugou ware—which comprises low carinated bowls with round bases, deeper flat-based carinated pots, both types sometimes decorated with three or four ribs running vertically between the rim and shoulder. The grave also contained polished fibrolite and dolerite axes, two fibrolite pendants and worked flints.

2 La Torche (Beg-an-Dorchenn) — Mesolithic/Neolithic
Mesolithic midden, passage grave — Pointe de Penmarc'h 3–4
99,75/336,60

Directions as for Kerugou (above) but continue on down the V 2 to the la Torche peninsula. On the narrow neck of the promontory, before the graves, the right-hand inlets have cut into a Mesolithic midden. With the eye of faith, or luck, flint microliths, bits of shell etc. are detectable in the section. On the left-hand side of the promontory there was a La Tène cemetery, but nothing remains to be seen.

On the end of the promontory a ruined gallery grave abuts against the passage of a rather derelict passage grave. This passage 3 m long, extends a further 5 m into the chamber, so that, like the one at Kerugou, the chamber is divided in three. The chamber being roughly octagonal, the two 'side-chambers' appear trapezoidal in shape.

The passage grave contained Chassey-style pottery, four schist beads, one fibrolite bead, Grand Pressigny flint, and gold wire. A le Souc'h vase was found close by, outside the chamber.

All the material—Mesolithic, Neolithic and Iron Age—is in the *Penmarc'h* museum.

3 Lestriguiou Neolithic
lateral-entrance grave Pont-l'Abbé 1–2
102,80/335,00

Take the D 785 south-west from Plomeur (→ Penmarc'h). After 2.5 km, just past a grove of cypresses on the left, take a small turning left (→ Kervéen). The monument is 75 m down the road to the right. The eastern part of the chamber has been destroyed. The capstones, with one exception, are gone, but at least the two uprights marking the entrance are intact!

The grave contained three Kerugou bowls, a flat-based carinated Kerugou pot, two polished dolerite axes (one with squared butt and sides mimicking a metal form), a small chloramelanite axe, a trapezoidal fibrolite pendant, a schist archer's wristguard, one large flint blade and some flakes.

There was once an important stone alignment between Lestriguiou and the chapel of la Madeleine. In 1865 there were five or six hundred stones in four or five parallel rows; in 1885 there were two hundred. Today there are none.

4 Grand menhir Neolithic
(actually in the commune of Penmarc'h) Pont-l'Abbé 1–2
102,50/333,20
menhir

Directions as for Lestriguiou (above) but continue down the D 785 (→ Penmarc'h). 200 m beyond the turn-off to Loctudy (D 53) and 100 m to the right of the main road is a 7 m menhir and nearby, another, 6 m long, fallen and hidden by vegetation.

From here go on to the museum at *Penmarc'h*.

Plouarzel

Kerloas 58/3
menhir Plabennec 5–6
81,50/1104,20

From Plouarzel take the D 5 east (→ Saint-Renan). After 2.5 km branch right, signposted to the 'menhir'.

One of the largest in Brittany, it is now almost 10 m high and was once higher, until struck by lightning in the eighteenth century. It weighs 150 tons and must have been transported at least 2.5 km. It has been shaped and near the base are two protuberances on opposite sides. There is a well-worn path to the menhir, and still today, after a respectable church wedding, the wife rubs herself against the knobs to ensure that she produces a male heir and that she rules the hearth.

Early and Middle Bronze Age pottery was found among the packing stones around the base.

Ploudalmézeau

Ile Carn 58/3
multiple passage grave Neolithic
(Figures 53 and 54) Plouarzel 3–4
82,10/1121,30

Well worth the slightly perilous journey. Marked on the Michelin. From Ploudalmézeau take the D 168 north-west (→ Bar-ar-Lan). 1.3 km out of town turn right onto the G 2 (→ Ridiny). Ignoring the crossroads continue straight on for 2.8 km and from the top of the dunes the cairn is visible. Only accessible at low tide, take care—or provisions—for the tide seems to creep back uncommonly fast.

The monument has recently been restored—and even more recently damaged by vandals—and one can examine the three-phase development. The central passage grave (a) seems to be the earliest, and was probably covered by a round cairn. Then the cairn was extended southwards to cover another grave (b), and then probably after a slightly longer time-lapse, it was extended northwards, with rather less care, to cover an odd double-chambered passage grave (c1, c2). Finally a huge cairn was built encasing all three structures.

The central grave (a) has a chamber that is asymmetric to its passage, a corbelled roof, and a floor with two levels of pavement. The southern grave (b) is also asymmetric and corbelled but has a longer passage.

The grave-goods from these two chambers (a, b) are very similar, and in particular, the material from chamber (a) is probably homogenous since the passage was sealed at both ends after use and there are no signs of later intrusions. In this chamber there were four round-based Primary Neolithic (Carn) pots, a few flint flakes, an unretouched flint blade and six rounded schist beads with biconical perforations.

Chamber (b) has a carbon-14 date of 3440 + − 150 bc (calibrated 4315 BC) and 2210 + − 120 bc (calibrated 2875 BC); chamber (a) has dates of 3280 + − 75 bc (calibrated 4070 BC) and

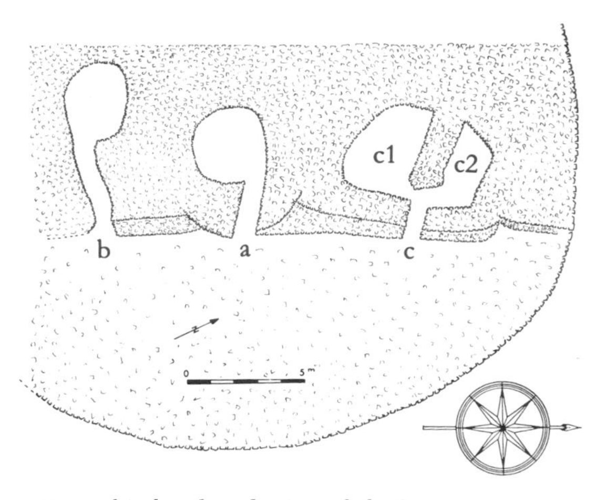

53 Multi-chambered cairn of Ile Carn, ***Ploudalmézeau***

54 Multi-chambered cairn at Ile Carn, ***Ploudalmézeau***

3390 + − 250 bc (calibrated 4235 BC).

The third structure (c1 and 2) is unusual. A short passage forks to two chambers, or rather to a large chamber with a double vault supported by a massive dry-stone wall divide.

The material from these chambers (c 1/2) is mainly Late Neolithic although a few Middle Neolithic sherds were also found. In the more northerly chamber (c 2) there were many transverse-tranchet arrowheads, two polished axes, a fragment of pumice, three small jet beads, coarse sherds and a collared flask. It looks as though the late Neolithic people finally sealed the whole monument by building a great semicircular revetment wall across the front of all the passages.

This chamber has a date of 2890 + − 150 bc (calibrated 3675 BC).

Ploudaniel

Ruat — 58/4
Iron Age stele — Iron Age
(Figure 19)

From Ploudaniel take the D 770 south (→ Landerneau) and just before the end of Ploudaniel turn right on the D 25 (→ Saint-Thonan, Guipavas). Continue for 1.5 km and at a small stone cross turn right and immediately right again (very small sign le Ruat). Another 150 m and the stone is just inside the courtyard of the farm on the left (visible from the road).

An enormous round stele.

Plouescat

Kernic — 58/5
gallery grave — Neolithic
(Figure 55) — Saint-Pol-de-Léon 5–6
118,00/1127,15

Not easy to find but worth the hunt. In Plouescat take the D 10 west (→ Goulven); then, before the end of Plouescat, turn right (north-west) onto the C 3 (→ Plage de Pors-Guen, Pors-Meur). At various unmarked junctions keep following the 'camping' signs. At the entrance to Pors-Guen/Pors-Meur turn left down the rue de Kernic, continue onto the sandy track and then take the first track left. Where the track branches, bear right. The track follows the line of the bay. The monument is within 30 m of the track, right down on the beach, and is regularly inundated by the sea. Indeed it provides good evidence of the post-Neolithic rise in sea-level. It is reckoned that since about 3000 bc (calibrated 3785 BC) the sea has risen 8 to 9 m. Kernic is not the only monument lapped by the sea, there is Er Lannic, *Larmor-Baden* in Morbihan, the ruined gallery grave of Lerric, Kerlouan, the Men Ozac'h menhir near Lilia, Plouguerneau, the Leuhan menhir at Treffiagat, the megalithic structure of Ezer at Loctudy, and another menhir at Pont l'Abbé. All these are in Finistère.

Kernic is a fine gallery grave, 9.5 × 1.5 m, with, at the seaward end, a triangular terminal cell 2 m long. The capstones have all disappeared. Originally a line of uprights on either side of the gallery helped to consolidate the mound, now only the north-west line is reasonably intact. These outer rows extend beyond the gallery entrance forming a sort of forecourt, roughly 6 m square.

Coarse flat-based Seine-Oise-Marne pottery, fragments of Bell Beakers, a fibrolite axe-pendant, three barbed and tanged arrowheads, a fragment of a thick retouched flint blade and flint scrapers and flakes were found.

55 Gallery grave at Kernic, **Plouescat**

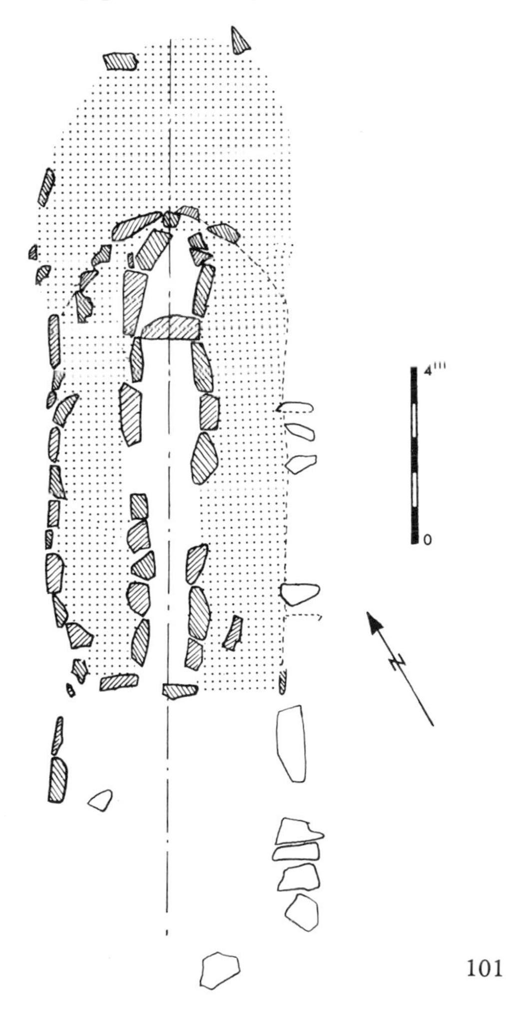

Plouézoc'h

Barnenez — 58/6
the most spectacular multi-chambered tomb in France — Neolithic
Plestin-les-Grèves 5–6
144,25/1126,20
(Figure 56)

Marked on the Michelin. Take the D 76 north from Plouézoc'h (→ Térénez). After 2.3 km, at Kergaradec, branch left to Kernéléhen, continue 300 m beyond this village and the cairn is signposted to the left.

Although I shall describe the monument in some detail, be warned that the chambers are sealed off, except those exposed by the quarry.

There are two phases of construction separated by perhaps two or three hundred years. The primary, eastern, cairn is sited on a flat surface just below the top of the promontory overlooking the valley of Morlaix. It takes the form of a narrow curved trapeze, 35 m long, 17.5 m wide at the east end, 21 m at the west end. There is a double revetment, strengthened in some places by contreforts, and, in part at least, the cairn is stepped. It is built mainly of local greenish dolerite, and it covers five passage graves opening to the south (G, G1, H, I, J).

The secondary cairn is appended to the west end. It lies on sloping ground which presents a considerable engineering problem. There is a complex system of revetments and shoring, particularly at the west end. Again it is trapezoidal in shape, with its short end up against the wider end of the primary cairn. The short end is 21.5 m wide, the longer end 29 m, the length 39 m. Primary and secondary cairns together total 74 m. The secondary cairn is built of different material. It is mainly granite, which comes from Ile Stérec, 2 km away. It contains six chambers, of which C, D, E and F are certainly contemporary. The chronological position of A and B at the west end is less clear.

There is a great deal of variation between the different chambers in both the primary and secondary cairns, putting paid once and for all to any neat evolutionary scheme of orthostatic construction preceding corbelling, or vice versa.

In the *primary cairn*, starting from the east the chambers of J and I were corbelled, though the roofs had already collapsed by the Iron Age. A capstone in the passage leading to chamber J has a single engraved anthropomorphic motif. This passage widens towards the exterior and it seems likely that the wide end remained open to the sky.

The central chamber of the primary cairn, H, must have held some particular significance for the constructors. It may even have served a different function from the rest. It has an antechamber bordered by granitic slabs and a corbelled roof, which is separated by two septal stones from a main orthostatic chamber covered by a great capstone. The western septal stone bears many deep engravings—one face has two triangular axes, the spine has an elongated arc-like sign, the other face has a triangular axe and a crook. There are other less carefully executed signs in the main chamber. The stone at the back has a large handled axe above undulating lines, with below, a triangular axe and U-signs. There are more undulating signs on an upright to the west, some U-signs on an upright to the east, while two other uprights to the east have poorly defined signs. Chamber H is remarkable not only for its construction and engravings but because of the presence of several small stelae. There are three to the right of the passage entrance and one to the left.

Moving west again, chambers G1 and G have long passages which narrow abruptly towards small corbelled chambers. It may well be that two phases of building are represented. In G there is a thin stele to the left of the entrance.

In the *secondary cairn*, F at the east end is a corbelled chamber, still intact. It has a passage that flares towards the exterior and a threshold stone between the narrow and flared sections, with two stelae set in front of it. The flared section, like that of the passages to J, D, C, and B, was probably never covered.

E had a corbelled chamber but the roof has collapsed. D and C were likewise corbelled and the roofs only tumbled in when the back of the monument was quarried in 1955—a monstrous demolition. B is a classic orthostatic grave with six uprights and a capstone. It is intact but exposed by the quarrying. Finally in chamber A the walls are a mixture of large orthostats and dry-stone wall panels and the roof is corbelled. The floor of this chamber was irregular and was filled in and then paved—unlike all the other chambers where depositions were placed directly on the ground surface and then covered with a layer of small stones. A, like H in the primary cairn, seems to be particularly important. It is the only one in the

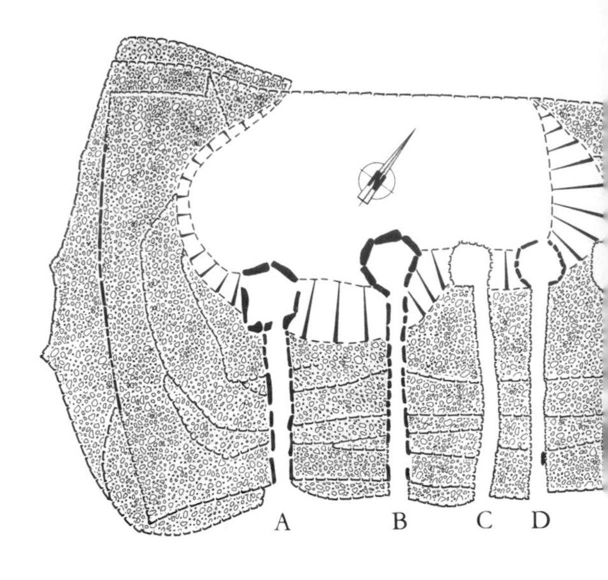

secondary cairn to have any engravings. There are seven U-signs on an upright on the right-hand side of the passage. Yet another particularity is the blocking stone, with a small artificial hole in the lower half, between the chamber and the passage.

The positioning of the engravings and the stelae in the chambers at each end of both the primary and secondary cairn, and in the central chamber of the primary cairn, reinforces the impression that the Neolithic builders had a clear overall vision of the layout of the monument and of the particular significance of each of the units within the total ensemble.

Given the massive nature of the undertaking, the general lack of grave-goods or offerings, particularly within the primary structure, comes as a surprise. Apart from a fragment of a small round-based Carn pot found in the passage to chamber H there was almost nothing in the primary cairn. There is a little more in the secondary cairn. A few flints and a lot of Early Neolithic pottery, some with lugs, in the passage to chamber A; a le Souc'h vase in the chamber itself; a few flints and a polished axe in the passage of chamber B; some Early Neolithic pottery in chamber D. Perhaps, rather than grave-goods placed within the grave, the emphasis was on offerings placed along the exterior façade of the monument. There is a considerable concentration of objects between the passage entrances to chambers C and D. These include

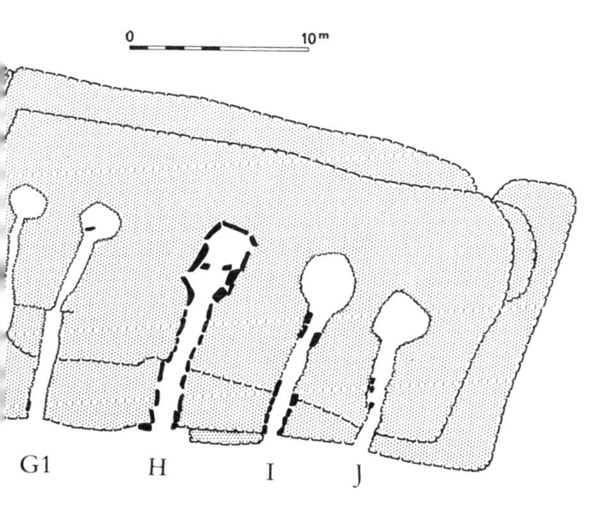

*56 Plan of the multi-passage grave mounds at Barnenez, **Plouézoc'h***

Primary Neolithic pottery; Chassey-type ware including fragments with incised laddered garlands and a vase-support, a fine pedestalled pot and a fragment of a second one, a lot of later Neolithic flat-based ware, even some Beaker ware, and flint blades and transverse-tranchet arrowheads.

In some of the chambers there is evidence of later reuse. For example, in chamber D there was Beaker ware separated from the Neolithic finds by a sterile level and, also in the upper level, a barbed-and-tanged arrowhead, some coarse Early Bronze Age pottery and dolerite axes. In chamber C there was a small copper dagger. Iron Age people reused some of the graves and in chambers I and J the position of their deposits shows that the corbelled roofs had already fallen in.

There are carbon-14 dates from chamber G in the primary cairn of 3800 + − 150bc (calibrated 4590 BC), from chamber F 3600 + − 150 bc and 3150 + − 140 bc (calibrated 4450 and 3935 BC), and from chamber A in the secondary cairn 3500 + − 150 bc (calibrated 4375 BC).

There used to be another cairn 100 m to the north on the plateau top. It was much smaller and contained at least one large passage grave.

Plounéventer

58/5

Plounéventer is the site of part of a small Gallo-Roman town. It was built in the first century AD. It was a small commercial centre—a considerable number of coins, imported pottery, amphorae and glass were found. But it was not rich, there were no baths and no mosaics. In the second century the town was rebuilt and included a theatre. In the third century it stagnated, and was eventually abandoned.

Roman theatre Gallo-Roman
Landerneau 3–4
115,10/1116,30

Take the D 29 north from Plounéventer for 4 km, then turn left on the D 32 (→ Saint-Méen). After 1.5 km turn left (→ Kergroas). At the T-junction at Kergroas turn right and after 100 m, on the next corner right, is a small Roman borne with a cross. Turn right onto the track at the borne, then after 50 m turn left and immediately duck into a field. Follow the upper edge of the field and in the copse are the remains of a Roman theatre.

Plounévez-Lochrist

Kermener 58/5
passage grave Neolithic

At Plounévez-Lochrist take the C 2 north-west to the hamlet of Lochrist. In Lochrist turn right (north-east) onto the D 110 and take the second small turning left—unmarked (400 m from Lochrist). After 600 m turn right to Bretouare Cour and ask first for Kermener farm, and then for the monument.

Brambles and nettles encase the large mound which is topped by a ruined building. It contains a sizeable chamber with low orthostatic uprights and a great capstone. The passage is very short.

Plourin-Ploudalmézeau

See Porspoder 58/3

Pont-Aven

58/3
58/11 (inset)

At the head of the estuary of the Aven. The river flows fast and Pont Aven was once renowned for its numerous windmills—'fourteen mills and fifteen houses'. In the late nineteenth century Gauguin settled in the town and the Pont-Aven group of artists became well known. There is a well-tramped walk up-river past the windmills and into Bois d'Armour.

1 Lesdomini — Neolithic
menhir

Marked on the Michelin. West out of Pont-Aven on the D 783 (→ Concarneau) for 0.5 km, then left onto the V 4 (→ le Hénant, Kerdruc). Shortly after the turning follow the signs to the menhir.

Better than many, with an engraved cross.

2 Luzuen — Neolithic
gallery grave

See *Melgven*

Pont Croix

See *Beuzec-Cap-Sizun* for a general description of the area.

1 Notre-Dame-de-Roscudon — 58/14
Church

A lovely church; the exterior fifteenth century, the interior mainly mid-twelfth to mid-thirteenth century. The roof is wooden, the nave and aisles, and four bays in front of the choir, and the double-aisle to the left of the sanctuary present a fine ensemble with their round arches, colonnaded pillars and decorated capitals.

2 Menei-Castel — Iron Age
promontory fort — Pont-Croix 1–2
88,10/359,70

Not exciting. From Pont-Croix take the D 765 west (→ Audierne) for 3 km. Immediately after crossing a bridge across a tributary of the Goyen take the first field-track to the right. After 100 m the banks are just visible below thick bracken.

The promontory is protected on the east side by the tributary, on the south by the estuary of the river Goyen, and on the west and north by a triple earthwork. The protected area covers less than half an hectare. According to Wheeler there is a centrally placed entrance, now damaged, but perhaps originally protected by the inturned ends of the main rampart. At the north-east end there seem to be traces of a possible fourth bank.

Porspoder

1 Ile Melon — 58/3
passage grave — Neolithic
Plouarzel 7–8
74, 90/1111,90

From Porspoder take the D 27 south 3.2 km to Melon. The island is close to the little harbour and only accessible at low tide.

The monument is a small, free-standing orthostatic passage grave. There was a very large menhir close by but this was destroyed during World War II.

2 Kerhouézel or Kerenneur — Bronze Age
menhir — Plouarzel 3–4
77,20/1114,55

Marked on the Michelin. In Porspoder take the C 3 south-east (→ Larret) and after 1.1 km the menhir can be seen to the left of the road.

It is 6.6 m high, shaped, probably Early or Middle Bronze Age.

3 Kergadiou — Bronze Age
menhirs — Plouarzel 7–8
78,80/1112,55

(Figure 57) (actually in the commune of Plourin-Ploudalmézeau)

Directions as for Kerhouézel (above), but continue on the C 3 to Larret. At the cross and chapel turn right. Continue for 2 km, the road becoming unsurfaced, to a small track to the right signposted to the 'menhirs Kergadiou'. The two menhirs are about 200 m further on. One stands, 8.8 m high and carefully shaped, the other lies, 10.5 m long.

4 Saint-Denec — Neolithic
menhirs — Plouarzel 7–8
76,95/1113,15

Going south in Porspoder on the D 27 take the second turning left after the church (→ Penfrat, Kerménou, Gorré). Continue for 1.5 km, ignoring roads in from left and right. Watch carefully for the menhirs on the right and stop at a triple field-entrance. The menhirs are in the right-hand field.

There are two standing menhirs and a fallen one. On the upper face of the fallen stone are relief carvings of two hafted axes.

57 *Menhirs at Kergadiou,* ***Porspoder***

Poullan-sur-Mer

Lesconil — 58/14
arc-boutés gallery grave — Neolithic
(Figure 58) — Douarnenez 7–8
100,25/365,00

Marked on the Michelin. From Poullan take the D 7 east (→ Douarnenez). Then the first turning left (→ Plages de Tréboul). At the fork keep right (→ Lesconil) and after 400 m the grave can be seen to the left, 70 m from the road.

A superb example of an 'arc-boutés' grave, the two sides slanting inwards and touching in the centre. The chamber is 14 m long, opens to the south-east, has a short antechamber delimited by a septal stone, and a small terminal cell. The remains of the peristalith that once demarcated the edge of the narrow mound can be seen, particularly in the south-east section.

During the 1895 excavation three polished axes and three fragmented pots were found.

Eight such arc-boutés structures are known in southern Finistère and Morbihan. One, now destroyed, lay quite close to Lesconil at Treota.

Quimper

58/15

Between AD 30 and 35 a small Gallo-Roman settlement was established on the left bank of the Odet, at the foot of Mont Frugy. There was a modest cemetery and, not far from the settlement, a large villa at Parc Ar Groas. The settlement was favourably placed on the wine route which extended from the Garonne (and ultimately Italy), along the Atlantic coast and finally across the channel to Britain, and in the second half of the first century, under the Flavian emperors, it grew in importance. There were local bronze and probably pottery industries. Then in the second century it apparently declined. It may be that the centre shifted to the other side of the river (see General Introduction page 57).

1 Musée Départemental
Breton, rue du Roi-Gradlon,
next to the imposing
thirteenth- to fifteenth-
century cathedral

In the courtyard is a stele with vertical grooves which

was found in Quimper. Within the museum is the so-called Menhir de Kernuz (actually it comes from Kervadel, Plobannalec), an Iron Age stele reused by the Gallo-Romans and carved with seven deities, including Mercury, Hercules and Mars. There are a few other Gallo-Roman exhibits. The museum is in process of reorganization and should eventually be much more informative.

Open 1 July to 15 September, 10 a.m. to 12 noon and 2 to 6 p.m.; 16 September to 1 November, 10 a.m. to 12 noon, 2 to 5 p.m., 2 November to 31 March 10 a.m. to 12 noon, 2 to 4.30 p.m.; 1 April to 30 June 10 a.m. to 12 noon, 2 to 5 p.m. Closed on Tuesdays.

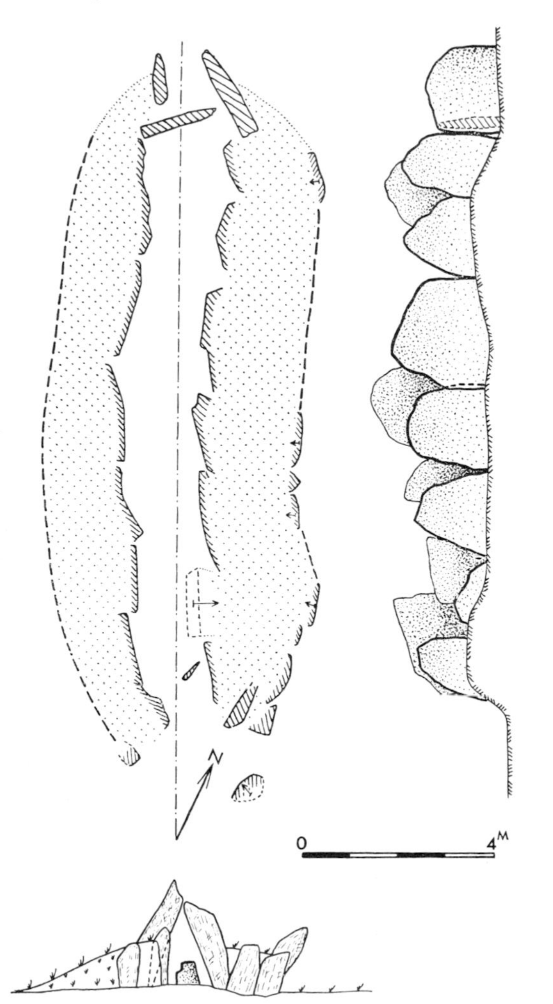

2 Notre-Dame-de-Locmaria Church
In Quimper take the D 34 south of the river (→ Bénodet). The road climbs up through the town and the church is near the top, to the right of the road.

A bit derelict, and very austere. The nave with its massive plain pillars is the earliest example of Romanesque architecture in Brittany and may date between AD 1025 and 1050. The choir, the transept and tower are twelfth century (the choir was restored in the nineteenth century). The transept has a few simply carved capitals. Part of the Romanesque cloisters still remain.

Quimperlé

Sainte-Croix 58/17
Church

The church, in the lower part of the town, is very large, very perfect and very cold. It was built in the eleventh century and destroyed—except for the apse and crypt—in the nineteenth century when the tower collapsed. It was then faithfully rebuilt. The circular plan is a copy of the Saint-Sepulchre in Jerusalem. Below the choir in the original vaulted crypt are some massive columns with fine, ornately carved capitals.

Riec-sur-Bélon

Goulet-Riec 58/11
gallery grave Neolithic
Pont-Aven (East) 3–4
146,30/(2)330,40

Marked on the Michelin. From Riec take the C 3 south-west (→ Bélon, Rosbras). After 1.25 km keep left on the V 10 (→ Bélon, Goulet-Riec). When the V 10 forks continue in the direction of Goulet-Riec. After another 0.75 km you will *pass* a small turning to the left (→ Kerlagathu). The monument is 175 m beyond the turning, 20 m to the right of the road, visible through a field entrance.

Very overgrown, but the arc-boutés construction is very clear.

58 Gallery grave, arc boutés *type, at Lesconil,* ***Poullan***

Saint-Goazec

Castel-Ruffel 58/16
menhir and gallery grave Neolithic
Gourin 7–8
145,43/1067,12

Menhir marked on the Michelin. From Saint-Goazec take the V 3 south-eastwards. After 3 km, at a T-junction, turn right onto the D 41. Then, after 2 km turn right down a track marked to Trimen. The menhir is to the right, and the grave is alongside it.

The grave is very ruined, has two huge capstones, and, according to L'Helgouach, is an example of the arc-boutés type.

Saint-Pol-de-Léon

Kerivin 58/6
gallery grave Neolithic
Plestin-les-Grèves 5–6
136,70/1125,58

Take the D 769 south from Saint-Pol (→ Morlaix), then, just beyond Saint-Pol the D 58 (→ Carantec). The 'dolmen' is then well signposted.

It is beautifully situated, on high ground overlooking the estuary of the Penzé. The orthostatic chamber is covered by two capstones. It is 4 m long and increases in height and width from north-east to south-west. The second upright from the narrow end, on the south-east side (towards the river) has a pair of sculpted breasts. The antechamber, 4.6 m long, opens to the south-east and is asymmetric to the chamber. This monument may once have been a lateral-entrance grave.

Another rather similar grave, not far to the north, at Keravel-la-Barrière, Saint-Pol-de-Léon, was destroyed at the end of the war.

Saint-Servais

Kroazteo 58/5
Gallo-Roman borne Gallo-Roman
Landerneau 1–2
119,49/1111,80

Originally found near Drevers on the Roman road from Carhaix to Aberwrac'h, it was moved slightly to the south when the airport was built. Take the D 32 west from Saint-Servais (→ Saint Méen). Continue for 1.6 km and as you come round the large bend it is to the left, beside the road, in the corner of a field.

The lower part of this cross started life as an Iron Age stele, was then reused as a Gallo-Roman borne, and was finally Christianized and received an additional stone.

Telgruc-sur-Mer

Anse du Caon 58/14
salt-working site Gallo-Roman
Douarnenez 3–4
101,50/79,50

From Telgruc take the D 208 south. After 1.5 km take the left fork to Penquer and le Caon. Continue down to the sea and turn left. Almost immediately, on the beach, just south of a small stream, is a much-eroded Roman salting tank.

Tréglonou

menhir 58/16
Bronze Age
Plabennec 1–2
89,55/1118,00

Marked on the Michelin. Take the D 28 west from Tréglonou (→ Ploudalmézeau). Just over 4 km beyond Tréglonou take a left turn (marked 'menhir'). At a fork keep to the lower track, at the crossroads turn left and then right (marked 'menhir'). In all about 1.5 km from the left turn.

Not too exciting, but over 5 m high.

Trégunc

menhir 58/16
Neolithic
Concarneau 3–4
137,70/(2)336,13

Marked on the Michelin. From Trégunc take the V 3 north (→ Melgven). After 0.5 km, just beyond the café du Menhir, take a track right for 50 m. The menhir, an imposing 7.4 m, with a cross on top, lies 50 m to the right.

Ille-et-Vilaine

Dol

Champ-Dolent 59/6
menhir (Figure 60) Neolithic/Bronze Age
Dol-de-Bretagne (West) 1–2
299,12/1100,85

Marked on the Michelin. Take the D 795 south from Dol (→ Combourg). Well signposted all the way.

Very large, 9.5 m and very impressive. The stone must have been hauled overland for at least four kilometres. 'Champ-Dolent' means the field of sorrow, so named after a legendary battle.

Do not miss the cathedral at Dol.

Essé

Roche-aux-Fées 63/7
enormous portalled gallery grave Neolithic
(Figures 61 and 62) La Guerche-de-Bretagne (West) 5–6
320,55/2333,00

Marked on the Michelin. Take the D 99 south from Essé (→ Theil-de-Bretagne). After 1 km turn left onto the D 341. Another kilometre and the monument is to the left of the road.

Truly monumental—for sheer size the Roche-aux-Fées dwarfs everything else in Brittany. The total length is 19.5 m. A great trilithon forms the entrance and gives onto a relatively low passage 3.5 × 2.8 × 1.1 m, covered by a large capstone. Then there is the chamber which is 14 m long, 4 m wide and 2 m high and is covered by six great capstones (some of which are 18 m square and weigh 38 tons). Three septal stones perpendicular to the west wall divide the chamber into four sections. All these massive stones are of Cambrian schist, and the nearest outcrop is at least four kilometres away.

The distribution of this type of grave, with a portal entrance, is centred on the Loire valley around Saumur. Scattered examples are found in the Vienne, Indres-et-Loire, Deux-Sèvres, Vendée and Charente regions. Essé is an isolated north-west outlier and there are a couple more in Morbihan (les Tablettes, *Cournon*; la Maison Trouvée, *la Chapelle-Caro*). No grave-goods were found at Essé, and this, in conjunction with its size, has led to speculations that it was a ritual or cult house rather than a tomb.

60 The menhir of Champ-Dolent, ***Dol***

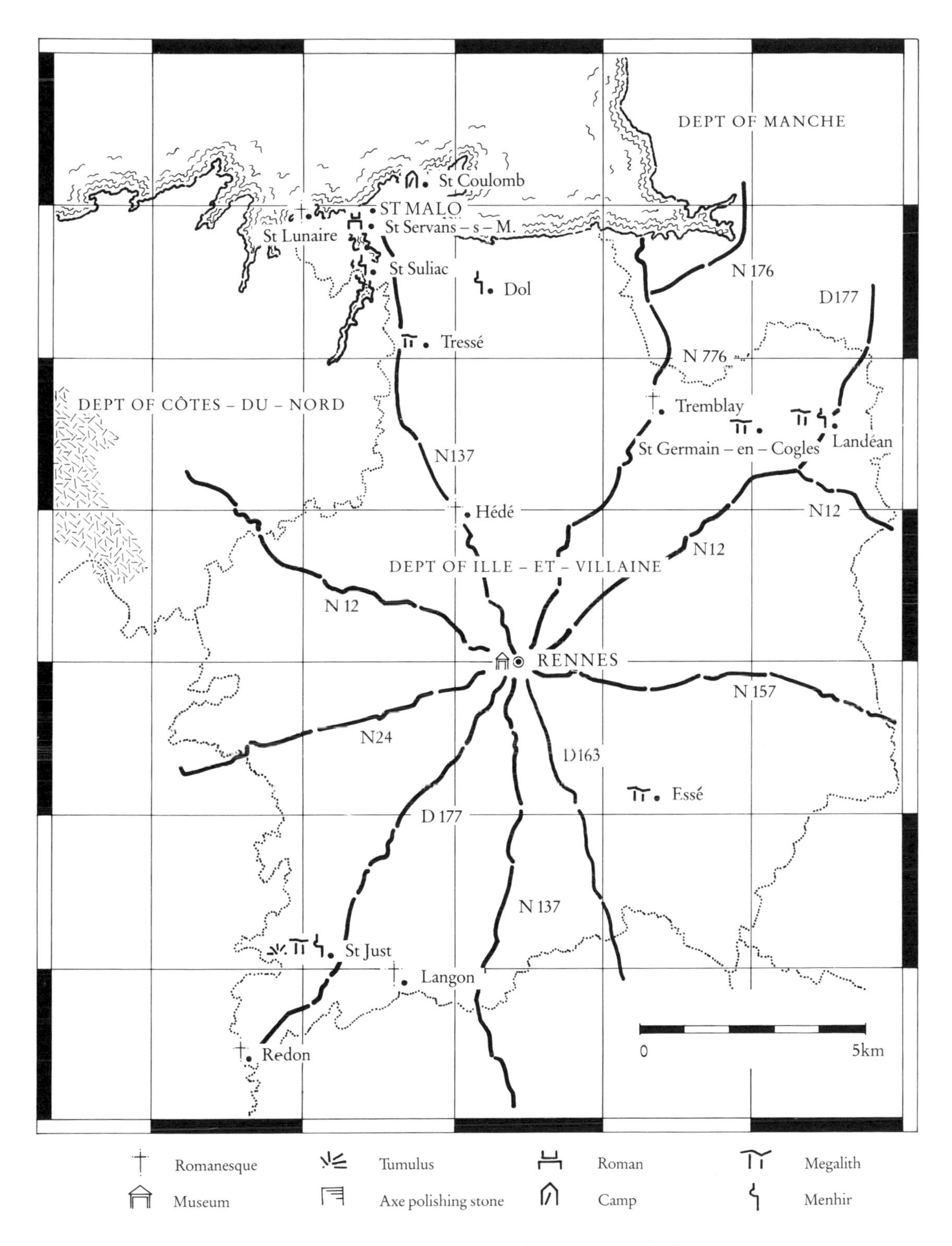

59 Département of Ille-et-Vilaine

61 *The great gallery grave at la Roche-aux-Fées,* **Essé**

62 *La Roche-aux-Fées,* **Essé**

Hédé

59/16
Church

From the outside the early twelfth-century village church looks untouched, with a fine Romanesque western façade and a massive square tower. But inside it has been completely transformed, with false Gothic vaulting in the nave and platform ceilings in the aisles. The lower part of the granite font is Romanesque. There is a grand view from the church.

Landéan

59/18

To the south of Landéan lies the forest of Fougères. Several monuments are found within it. They are not spectacular but they give purpose (if required) to pleasant walks. It is simplest to set out from Fougères.

1 La Pierre Courcoulée — Neolithic
gallery grave — Fougères (East) 3–4
339,37/1083,37

Marked on the Michelin. Take the D 177 north-east from Fougères (→ Vire, Landéan). Just outside Fougères turn left on the D 108 (signposted to the Pierre Courcoulée). After 1.3 km at the crossroads—where one track is marked 'Route Forestière de la Tendraye'—turn right onto a track with a placard 'Zone de Silence'. Continue 400 m and the grave is to the right.

It is small, 7.3 m long, and not very well preserved. There are two capstones, the remains of a mound and a peristalith.

2 Cordon des Druides — Neolithic
alignment — Fougères (East) 3–4
341,60/1082,80

Marked on the Michelin. From Fougères take the D 177 north-east (→ Vire, Landéan). After 2.5 km, in the forest of Fougères, take a road right marked to the 'Cordon des Druides'. After 0.7 km there is a footpath signposted to the left.

A sinuous line of eighty low, rough, quartzite stones, extends for 300 m among the birch trees. The highest is 2 m.

3 La Pierre du Trésor — Neolithic
dolmen — Fougères (East) 3–4
341,13/1083,30

Directions as for the Cordon des Druides (above), but continue on the D 177 for another 500 m to a small rough lay-by on the right. A footpath, right, leads to the dolmen, 150 m away.

Very ruined. One capstone in place. The remains of a mound still visible.

Langon

1 Chapelle de Sainte-Agathe — 63/6
Gallo-Roman
Church

Opposite the church of Langon (which has a Romanesque apse, two archaic sculptures and a fresco of Christ) is a very interesting chapel. It started as a Gallo-Roman shrine, probably to Venus. The walls consist of a core of mortared rubble faced with small blocks and alternating red brick courses. In 1839 a fresco was uncovered inside. It seems to depict Venus Anadyomene rising from the waves, with a winged cupid riding on a dolphin by her side. The shrine was Christianized, probably by Saint Melven, and in the twelfth century the chapel was enlarged. Finally in the seventeenth century the church was re-dedicated to Sainte Agathe and became a centre of pilgrimage for nursing mothers.

2 Demoiselles de Langon — Neolithic
alignment — Pipriac (East) 7–8
285,72/2310,78

Marked on the Michelin. In Langon take the D 56 north (→ Guipry) and immediately take the first turning left marked to 'les Demoiselles'. Take a right turn by the new houses and the menhirs are 100 m further on, to the right of the road. There are thirty-seven stones in two rows.

Redon

Church of Saint-Sauveur — 63/5
Church

The church was originally part of a Benedictine abbey, in turn built on the site of a ninth-century monastery that had been destroyed by the Normans. The most impressive feature is the massive square tower with three arcaded levels. The nave, eleventh and twelfth centuries, was partially destroyed by a fire in the eighteenth century and was restored in a rather heavy fashion with a sombre wooden vault that cuts out much of the light. Some of the lower parts of the nave are pre-Romanesque in date. The capitals in the transept-crossing are worth looking at. A fresco of Christ, below the vault of the tower, has recently been rediscovered; it dates to the thirteenth century.

Rennes

Musée de Bretagne, 59/17
20 quai Emile-Zola Museum

This museum has a first-rate archaeological section. It makes an excellent starting point for any tour of Brittany—or, maybe, a finishing point to clear up any confusions that beset you. It begins with a multi-lingual push-button map that illustrates the geography and the cultural development of Brittany. Then the history, or prehistory, from the Palaeolithic onwards, unfolds, with maps, mock-ups, casts and material. It is invidious to select but there are models of different types of Neolithic tombs, fine Bronze Age gold-work, Iron Age stelae and reconstructions of the salt-making industry, Gallo-Roman inscriptions and bornes, and some marvellous medieval sculptures with accompanying music.

Open every day except Tuesday, from 10 a.m. to 12 noon and 2 to 6 p.m.

Rennes is the administrative capital of Brittany. It was almost entirely rebuilt in the eighteenth century, after a terrible fire that lasted seven days had more or less destroyed the entire town. The style is classical, the layout formal, the general aspect sober. Only a few of the older houses remain, clustered around the cathedral.

Saint-Coulomb

Pointe du Meinga 59/6
or Ville des Mues Iron Age
promontory camp Saint-Malo 3–4
285,75/120,10

In Saint-Coulomb, in front of the church, take the D 74 northwards (→ la Guimorais) and immediately take the first small road left, C 4 (→ Camping des Chevrets). After 2 km, at the junction with the D 201, turn right (→ Cancale). Another 250 m and turn left (→ Camping la Rafale). The road quickly becomes a track, continues out onto the Pointe du Meinga and as you come onto the neck of the promontory the high bramble-covered bank stretches to the left. This wide, rough, beach-stone wall backed by earth reaches 3 m in height and cuts off 16 hectares. It is probably a *murus gallicus* construction with an internal structure of horizontal wooden beams held in place by thousands of nails. It may be the work of the Ambibari tribe.

Saint-Germain-en-Cogles

Le Rocher Jacquot 59/18
gallery grave Neolithic

Directions from Fougères. Take the D 155 north-west (→ Antrain) and just out of the town turn right onto the D 17 (→ Saint-Germain-en-Cogles). Continue for 5 km; cross the railway line and then take the second surfaced small road to the left—it is marked to the 'Rocher Jacuou' but the sign is not visible coming from this direction. After 700 m the grave is in a field to the right, just before some pigsties.

A very ruined gallery grave. A copper dagger (Bell Beaker type) was found inside it.

Saint-Just

63/5–6

There is a fine collection of megaliths on a rock-strewn heath of bracken and pine with, close by, an almost deserted slate-roofed hamlet. See inset map, Figure 63.

1 Demoiselles de Cojoux Neolithic
menhirs Pipriac 5–6
275,80/2316,20

Marked on the Michelin. Saint-Just lies just east of the D 177, 16 km north of Redon. In Saint-Just take a small road east, the V 3 (→ Sixt-sur-Aff) for 1.5 km. Then turn right on a track marked Landes de Cojoux (the sign is hard to see). It is best to walk from here. At the T-junction turn left and continue for 0.75 km

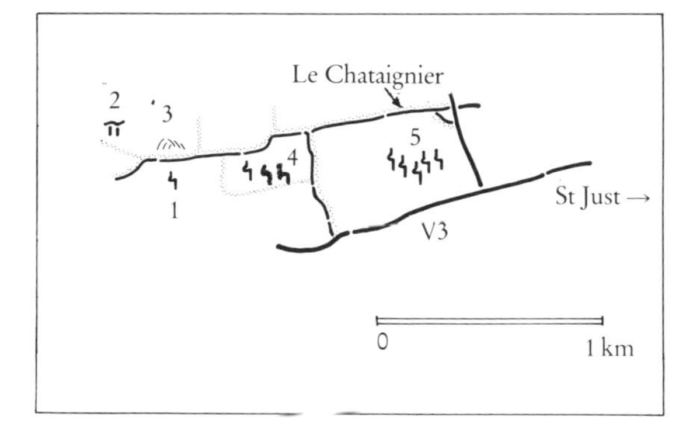

63 ***Saint-Just***
1 Demoiselles de Cojoux, menhirs
2 Four-Sarrazin, lateral-entrance grave
3 Croix-Saint-Pierre, long mound
4 Butte de Hu, tumulus and menhirs
5 Le Moulin de Cojoux, alignment

ignoring tracks to the right and left. The menhirs can then be seen to the left of the track, in amongst the pine and gorse.

A lovely setting for a half-circle of nine glinting quartzitic stones, the highest about 1.7 m.

2 Four-Sarrazin
lateral entrance grave (probably) Neolithic
Directions as for the Demoiselles de Cojoux (above), but continue down the track for another 50 m. Where the track bends left, take the track right. The grave is then 30 m away, on the right. Very ruined; orientated south-east/north-west. It is made of thin schist slabs. The entrance passage seems to have been on the south side, close to the east end. The rectangular mound and some of the peristalith is still intact. The edge of the cliff lies 300 m to the west of the grave, with a lovely view of the valley of Canut de Renac.

3 Croix-Saint-Pierre Neolithic
long mound, tumulus Bronze Age
Directions as for the Demoiselles de Cojoux (above), but now back-track 60 m from the menhirs, and then, to the left, and not easy to see, there is a long low mound with a fine peristalith. The mound is 20 m long and orientated east-west. The peristalith is made of small uprights and has a menhir 1.3 m high in the short west end. Some post-holes were found below the west end of the mound suggesting that there had once been a wooden structure. Some Chassey-type sherds were also found.

Such long mounds are rare, widely scattered, and ill dated. They are found, for example, at *le Quillio*, Côtes-du-Nord, at Manio, *Carnac*, Morbihan and also in south Finistère, the Loire-Atlantique, and Calvados in Normandy.

Croix-Saint-Pierre has a carbon-14 date of 2308 + − 120 bc (calibrated 2980 BC).

A round mound lies just to the north of the long mound. There are apparently six more round mounds in the vicinity.

4 Butte de Hu or Château-Bû Neolithic
tumulus/stone circle Pipriac 5–6
276,22/2316,20
Having turned back from the Demoiselles de Cojoux, and having passed the long mound and the round mound on the left, stop at the first field-track on the right and take the small footpath that lies between the track and the field-track. This leads up onto a large mound (25 m diameter) topped with a circle of seven stones. There are two more standing stones to the south, and another fallen one.

5 Le Moulin de Cojoux Neolithic
alignments Pipriac (East) 7–8
(Figure 64) 277,10/2316,15
Directions as for the Demoiselles de Cojoux (above), but instead of turning left at the T-junction, *turn right*. The track goes through the extraordinary, almost deserted hamlet of Châtaignier and then reaches the road. Turn right, take the first track right and one row of the alignment lies to the right; soon after, a second row appears to the left. This line goes over the top of a tumulus.

There are actually three lines containing about thirty stones. Some very large, but most have fallen. Some are of schist, most are of quartzite. The largest still upright is 1.9 m.

A recent excavation uncovered the remains of a

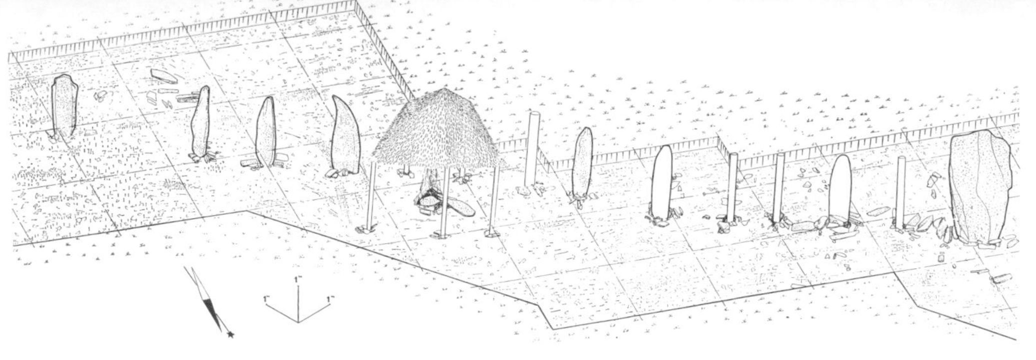

64 *The southern alignment at le Moulin de Cojoux,* ***Saint-Just***

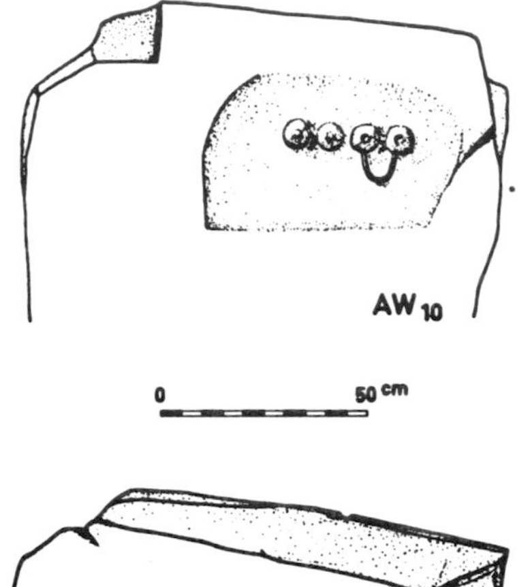

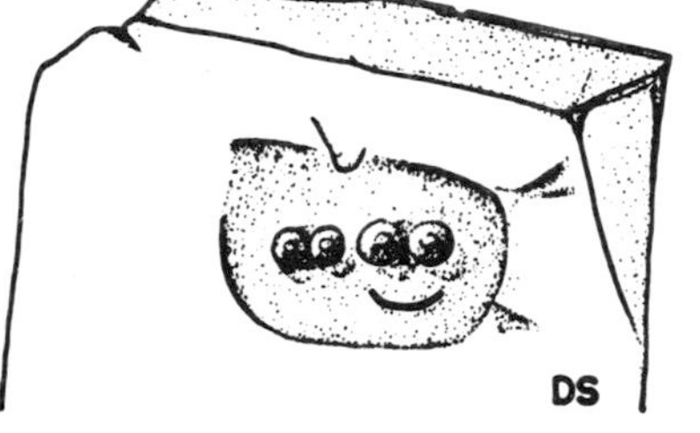

66 *Sculpted breasts on the uprights of the terminal cell of the* ***Tressé*** *gallery grave*

small cairn containing two cists. A reused menhir formed the base of the cairn. The cairn probably dates to the Bronze Age. During the excavation of the southern line of stones a number of post-holes for stone and timber uprights were uncovered at the east end. There were also five post-holes surrounding a hearth just outside the south alignment. This was probably a small roofed structure. In the central part of the southern line much larger stones were uncovered, some of which were grounded in a large stone cairn, 50 × 4.5 m, in part covered by an earthen mound. A series of small hearths were found below this cairn. These are carbon-14 dated between 3600 and 3800 bc. The cairn is undated but seems to have continued in use till Beaker and Early Bronze Age times—the remains of at least four fine beakers were found. There are some interesting parallels to be made between these various structures and those recently uncovered at les Fouaillages, *Vale*, Guernsey.

If you continue on down the road you come back to the V 3. You can turn left to Saint-Just, or if ready for more, turn right to Tréal.

6 Tréal or Grotte aux Fées — Neolithic
lateral-entrance grave — Pipriac 5–6
275,00/2317,40

Take the V 3 from Saint-Just (see directions for the Demoiselle de Cojoux, above) and continue for 4.5 km, passing great rock-strewn slopes, a water-mill etc., and just before the crossing with D 67 take the small road to the right (→ Bocadève, le Val—the sign is hard to see). Continue 3 km to a cross, then turn left (→ Tréal—again hard to see). After 0.5 km continue past the small road right to Tréal and 100 m further on take a tiny footpath up the steep slope to the right (almost opposite a barn). Skirt the natural rock outcrop, and on the summit, slightly to the left, is the grave.

13 m long, 1.2 m wide, made of rather thin schist slabs. The entrance seems to be close to the east end of the south side. Most of the capstones have slipped off.

Saint-Lunaire

59/5

Behind the modern seaside resort (good beaches; fine views of the 'emerald coast' from the Pointe du Décollé) is the old town. And in the old town is a fine church. The nave still has its eleventh-century arches surmounted by small blind windows; the apse and transept are seventeenth century. The lower part of the tomb of Saint-Lunaire is Romanesque, the figure is fourteenth century.

Saint-Servan-sur-Mer

Cité d'Alet 59/6
(Figure 65) Gallo-Roman
Saint-Malo 5–6
279,05/112,80

Iron Age Alet was a thriving port, dealing with much of the seaborne trade with Hengistbury Head in southern England. By AD 20 the town, and the trade, had declined. Eventually the town was fired, perhaps as a result of a local uprising against the Romans. Then in the third century AD, as the barbarian threats intensified, it was incorporated into a second line of defence, behind the *litus saxonicum*. It was surrounded by a wall 1800 m long and between 1.5 and 1.95 m thick. The line followed the contours of the peninsula and may have included ten towers and two gates. In the fourth century another fortification was built on the rocky outcrop to the south-east of the main defence.

In Saint-Servan follow the sign for the Tour Solidor and/or 'Camping d'Alet'. The tower is just in front of the camp site, and the foundations of part of the Cité d'Alet are alongside it.

65 *Cité d'Alet, Saint-Servan-sur-Mer*

Saint-Suliac

menhir 59/6
Neolithic
Dinan 3–4
283,50/105,10

Marked on the Michelin. From Saint-Suliac at the church take the road towards Châteauneuf and after 1.9 km turn left on the D 7 (towards Saint-Suliac again). After 500 m the menhir stands to the left, 30 m from the road.

Tremblay

59/17
Church

Parts of the church date to the eleventh and twelfth century, although there was a lot of restoration in the sixteenth century. There is only one aisle. A heavy square tower surmounts the transept-crossing.

Tressé

Maison-ès(des)-Feins or 59/16
Bois-du-Mesnil Neolithic
gallery grave Dinan 7–8
(Figure 66) 288,70/95,85

Marked on the Michelin. From Tressé take the D 9 east (→ le Tronchet) and after 0.75 km the 'dolmen' is signposted to the left and lies 300 m from the road.

A very fine gallery grave, 14 m long, orientated north-north-west/south-south-east. The terminal cell is now uncovered and open-ended, but according to the excavation reports it was originally blocked by a large orthostat. All the capstones are in place. On the septal stone, terminal cell side, is a cartouche with two pairs of breasts, one pair larger than the other, and this motif is repeated on the upright on the western side of the cell. A recent re-examination of these carvings has shown that in both cases a 'necklace' was sculpted below the right-hand pair of breasts. The parallels with Crec'h Quillé, *Saint-Quay-Perros* and Prajou-Menhir, *Trébeurden*, both in the Côtes-du-Nord, are very close indeed.

The grave was excavated by Miss Collum in 1931 and despite finding numerous flints, including three transverse-tranchet arrowheads and a fine Grand Pressigny blade, and a mass of coarse Seine-Oise-Marne pottery, the excavator was convinced that the tomb was a degenerate form built in Late Iron Age or Gallo-Roman times to house the single crouched inhumation which she found, complete with Iron Age and Gallo-Roman pottery, a dagger, bits of iron and beads. With hindsight it is clear that this burial was simply a secondary reutilization.

The material is at Saint-Germain-en-Laye, near Paris.

Loire-Atlantique

Ancenis

La Pierre Couvretière 63/18
dolmen Neolithic

The Route de la Marne runs close to the river. Coming east from the castle up the Route de la Marne the dolmen is signposted to the left down a small street just beyond the Braud factory.

The dolmen is now below the level of the Loire—good evidence of the rise in sea-level since Neolithic times. The small dolmen contained the remains of at least ten individuals placed on a thin level of sand and covered with stones. Carbon-14 dates suggest that these burials are secondary and belong to the Late Bronze Age. Items found in the dolmen include a barbed-and-tanged arrowhead, a copper chisel, a perforated gold plaque, and sherds with *pointillé* impressions and finger-nail indentations. Most of these are probably Bell Beaker.

Batz-sur-Mer

63/14

From Neolithic times and through to the Gallo-Roman period, Batz was sited on a narrow elongated island cut off from the mainland by a wide sea-channel. In the third millennium the channel silted up and formed a great marsh, and later a sand spit developed between the east end of the island and the mainland.

Menhir de Pierre Longue Neolithic
Saint-Nazaire 1–2
235,75/263,80

From La Baule take the D 45 south-west to Batz-sur-Mer. In the village turn left down to the small port. The menhir is to the left on the rocks. It is worth the trip—for the scenery if not the stone. From here you could continue on to *le Croisic*, a pleasant drive, another menhir.

Bourgneuf-en-Retz

Musée du Pays de Retz 67/2
Museum

A small museum with a bit of everything: rural crafts, costumes, tableaux of peasant interiors, plus a lot of Iron Age material from the site of Fougerais. Worth a visit.

Open 1 June to 30 September from 10 a.m. to 12 noon and 2 to 5 p.m., every day except Tuesday. 1 October to 31 May open Wednesday, Thursday, Saturday and Sunday 10 a.m. to 12 noon, 2 to 6 p.m.

Clion-sur-Mer

Pré d'Air, la Boutinardière 67/1–3
transepted passage grave Neolithic
Machecoul 1–2
265,95/242,50

A marvellous walk; a moderate grave. Take the D 13 south-east out of Pornic (→ Bourgneuf). After 3 km turn right to Boutinardière Plage. At the beach take the steps up the cliff to the right (→ la Fontaine-Breton) and continue along the cliff-walk overlooking a series of decaying wooden tuna-fishing jetties for about one kilometre. The grave is then just visible to the right, 300 m beyond the end of the fine stone wall of a large estate.

It is very ruined but the form and part of the round mound are still discernible. It has two lateral chambers, one either side of the passage, and a small terminal cell covered by an enormous stone. The grave-goods included two fine Grand Pressigny daggers, the butt of a battle-axe and a fine fibrolite pendant.

There is another similar grave, though with a larger terminal cell, not far away at la Joselière but it is in an even worse state of preservation and has not

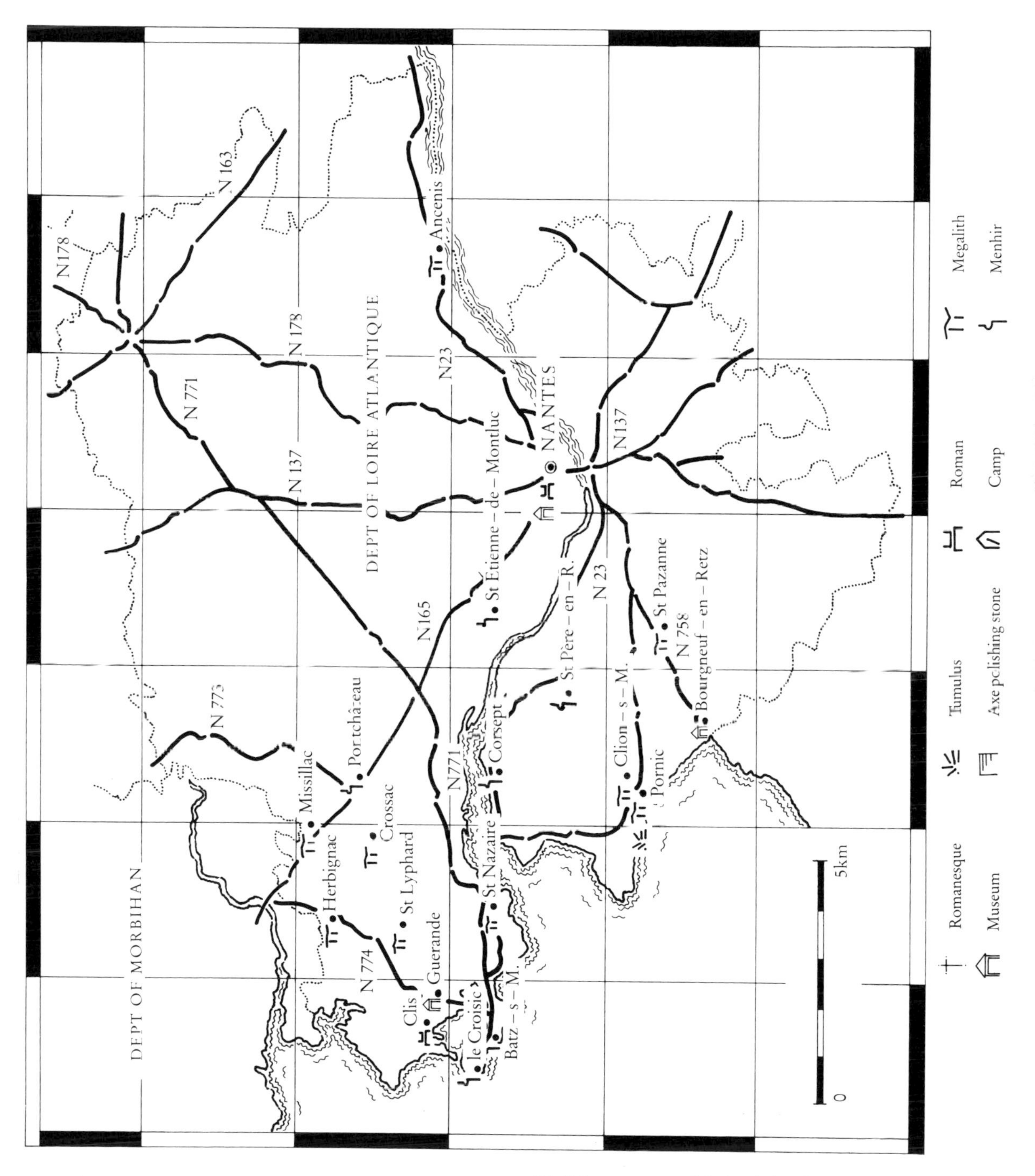

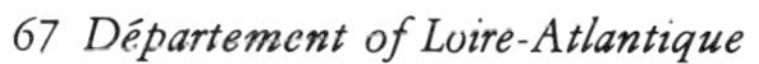

67 *Département of Loire-Atlantique*

therefore been included. There are other transepted graves at *Pornic* and *Herbignac*.

Clis

63/14
Gallo-Roman
Saint-Nazaire 1–2
237,10/270,50

Not much to look at, just a touch of a Gallo-Roman wall. In Clis take the small road south alongside the church. Continue past the last house of the hamlet of Ruguerre to a small turning right marked to Petit Bois. Take the footpath opposite and the wall on the left-hand side of the path was once part of a small Gallo-Roman villa.

Clis lies on a scarp formed by a small fault line. It is a warm and sheltered spot, much sought after from Mesolithic times onwards. It overlooks the great marsh flats that stretch south towards Batz. Until Gallo-Roman times this area formed a sea embayment. Then a local drop in sea-level of about 15 m resulted in the formation of a vast marsh, still, however, regularly inundated by the sea coming in through a narrow gap betwen Pebron and le Croisic. The marsh flats became—and remains to the present day—an important source of salt. The considerable concentrations of Gallo-Roman pottery found in the fields to the south of the Clis villa may mark the site of a small port associated with the salt trade. A Gallo-Roman funerary pit has also been found in the vicinity.

Corsept

Champs-Cassis 67/1
menhir Neolithic
Paimboeuf 5–6
265,40/257,30

Marked on the Michelin. Take the D 96 from Corsept south-west (→ Saint-Brevin-l'Océan). After 4 km, just beyond the 'mile-stone', the large menhir rears up to the left.

Croisic, le

Vigie la Romaine 63/13
menhir Neolithic
Hoëdic 3–4
232,090/265,570

Take the D 45 or the N 171 out of la Baule (→ le Croisic). One kilometre before le Croisic turn left (→ Port Lin, le Pointe Croisic). In Port Lin turn west along the coast road and continue almost to the tip of the peninsula. The menhir is to the left of the road.

The stone is not very big, nor is it in its original position—but it is a fine drive.

Crossac

63/15

See *Saint-Nazaire* for a general description of the Grande Brière and an itinerary of sites in the area.

La Barbière Neolithic
passage grave Savenay 5–6
(Figure 68) 260,85/277,20

Crossac lies south of the D 33 between Herbignac and Pontchâteau. In Crossac take the D 4 south-east (→ Donges). About 200 m after the sign that marks the end of Crossac a miniscule, almost entirely eroded sign points the way to the dolmen which lies about 75 m to the left of the road.

There are two monuments. The one to the south-west is clearly a large very ruined passage grave. It has one capstone supported by three uprights, the remains of a passage with two displaced capstones and some indication of a mound. The stones to the north-east may be part of another passage grave. Of these, the long fallen stone has some curious markings, with several rows of triple cup-marks separated by grooves. Incidentally an account written in 1836 mentions that at the beginning of the nineteenth century, an old woman lived in the dolmen.

68 Passage grave(s) at la Barbière, ***Crossac***

Guérande

Musée Régional, 63/14
Porte-Saint-Michel Museum
The couple of exhibits of Neolithic tools and Roman Samian ware are not in themselves worth a visit, but they are housed in a fine fifteenth-century tower (part of the town ramparts) and there are some marvellous exhibits of Breton furniture and costumes.

Open from Easter to 30 September, every day from 9 a.m. to 1 p.m. and 2 to 7 p.m.

Herbignac

63/14
See *Saint-Nazaire* for a general description of the Grande Brière.

Le Rihalo Neolithic
transepted passage grave La Roche Bernard 3–4
253,35/283,75
From Herbignac take the D 33 east (→ Pontchâteau) and after 1.25 km turn left (→ Sapilon Langâtre, Sapin Vert). Another 2.5 km, to a T-junction, and turn right. Continue past the first turning (1.2 km) on the left, and 100 m beyond, just visible 30 m from the road, is the grave.

Not in very good condition, but the transepted form can just about be made out. There is a lateral chamber either side of the passage and the remains of a small terminal cell. Such transepted graves are a local speciality. There are similar ones at *Pornic* and *le Clion*. There seems to be a strong link between these monuments and the Severn-Cotswold series along the Bristol Channel.

Missillac

63/15

See *Saint-Nazaire* for a description of the Grande Brière.

Roche aux Loups — Neolithic
dolmen — La Roche Bernard 3–4
256,90/282,90

Directions from Herbignac. Take the D 33 east from Herbignac (→ Pontchâteau). After 5 km at la Chapelle-des-Marais, turn left onto the D 50. At l'Anglo-Bertho turn right onto the D 4 (→ Saint-Reine-de-Bretagne). After 1.25 km, in the first hamlet, turn right (→ la Gravelais; le Bas Bergon). Take the first field-track right and the dolmen is 550 m further on.

Only three uprights, a couple of smaller stones, and a capstone remain.

Nantes

63/17

There was a thriving Gallo-Roman port at Condevicnum, but little remains. In the third century AD a rampart with towers was erected. Some sections can be seen near the cathedral and the lower courses of the Porte-Saint-Pierre are still visible.

1 Musée Dobrée, — Museum
place Jean V

The prehistoric and Gallo-Roman exhibits (for example, from the Gallo-Roman towns of Ratiatum—Rezé—and Mauves, and from the port of Condevicnum at Nantes) are royally but unimaginatively displayed in the new building. There are a great number of objects, several maps but no description. There is also some fine twelfth-century sculpture in the nineteenth-century building.

2 The Musée d'Histoire — Museum
Naturelle is just down the road

The museum has Palaeolithic exhibits, including explanations of flint-tool manufacture, and some fine Bronze Age material.

Open on Tuesday, Thursday, Saturday and Sunday from 2 to 6 p.m., on Wednesday from 10 a.m. to 12 noon and 2 to 6 p.m. Closed on Mondays and Fridays.

Pontchâteau

Le Fuseau de la Madeleine — 63/17
menhir — Neolithic
Savenay 1–2
262,90/280,30

On the Michelin map. Take the D 33 from Pontchâteau west (→ Herbignac) for 3 km to la Calvaire. Turn left at the large statue of Christ and continue for another 600 m. Then turn left (→ la Viauderie) and after 150 m there is a fine upstanding menhir.

Pornic

1 Les Mousseaux or — 67/1
la Motte-Sainte-Marie — Neolithic
passage graves — Machecoul 1–2
(Figures 69 and 70) — 262,35/244,80

In Pornic take the road west along the north bank of the river to the old port, then the road right (→ Nouveau Port de Pornic). At the T-junction turn right (→ Sainte-Marie-sur-Mer, le Bourg), and then again take the first turning right (chemin de la Motte). Les Mousseaux is then visible; *Les Trois Squelettes* is further down the road (plan, Figure 71).

Les Mousseaux was first excavated in 1840, and then again quite recently. A large trapezoidal mound (18 m long on the south-east side, 14 m on the north-west, and 11 and 12 m respectively on the two shorter sides) with three dry-stone wall revetments, contains two transepted passage graves both opening to the south-east.

In structure A there is a 4.5 m stretch of passage, then the passage passes between the two lateral cells, then another 2 m stretch until finally the large terminal cell is reached. Each of the lateral cells is 2 × 2.3 × 1.5 m, and is covered by a capstone. These do not sit directly on the uprights but on an intermediate level of large stones. The capstone that spans the passage between the cells rests on the capstones of the lateral cells.

Chamber B is similar except that it has only one

lateral chamber to the north-east, and the terminal chamber is asymmetric.

In front of the façade, on a rough paving, numerous sherds were found, including some Carn ware. At the base of the south-west revetment wall were fragments of an Er Lannic vase-support.

Close by, at Hautes Folies, were two more transepted graves but they have been destroyed. Pornic seems to be the centre of this transepted form which also extends southwards to the Ile d'Yeu and Noirmoutier, both in the Vendée.

69 Transepted passage graves at les Mousseaux, ***Pornic***

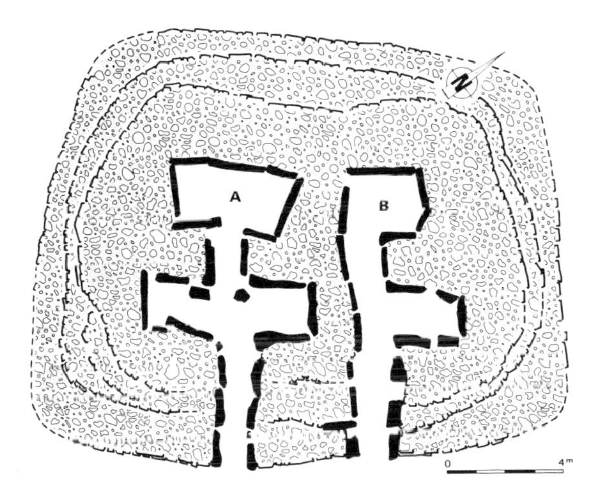

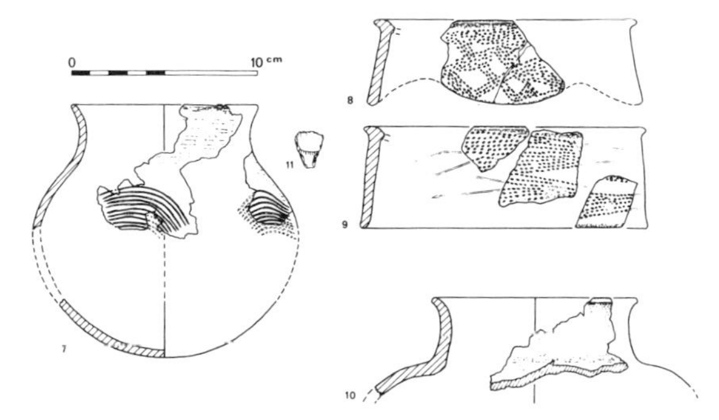

70 Some of the Chassey-type pottery found at the foot of the retainer walls of the cairn at les Mousseaux, ***Pornic***

2 La Motte — Neolithic
mound
(plan, Figure 71)
The large mound is just visible down the lane between les Mousseaux and Trois Squelettes, through the gate of the house to the right of the white house at the bend of the lane.

3 Trois Squelettes — Neolithic
passage graves,
transepted grave
(plan, Figure 71)
As for les Mousseaux and la Motte but continue on to the end of the lane.

These graves were excavated in 1873. The three graves seem to have been covered by one large mound. Two are passage graves and one (the dolmen de la Croiz) is transepted. A Souc'h vase with a band of zigzag decoration and a gold tubular bead were found. They are in the museum at *Nantes.*

Saint-Etienne-de-Montluc

Menhir de la Laiterie — 63/15
Neolithic
Paimboeuf 3–4
285,400/261,100
Marked on the Michelin. At Saint-Etienne-de-Montluc take the D 93 south-west (→ Cordemais). After 1.5 km take the turning left to la Haute Roche. The menhir, 4 m high, is in a courtyard.

Saint-Lyphard

63/14
See *Saint-Nazaire* for a description of the Grande Brière and a round trip of the area.

Ile de la Motte — Neolithic
passage grave — La Roche Bernard 5–6
245,30/273,25
From Saint-Lyphard take the D 51 south-west (→ Guérande). After 5 km turn left—near two windmills—(→ Kervernet, Pierres Druidiques de Kerbourg). After 250 m turn right onto a field-track. Another 200 m and the monument is to the right.

71 Plan of the various monuments at les Mousseaux, ***Pornic***

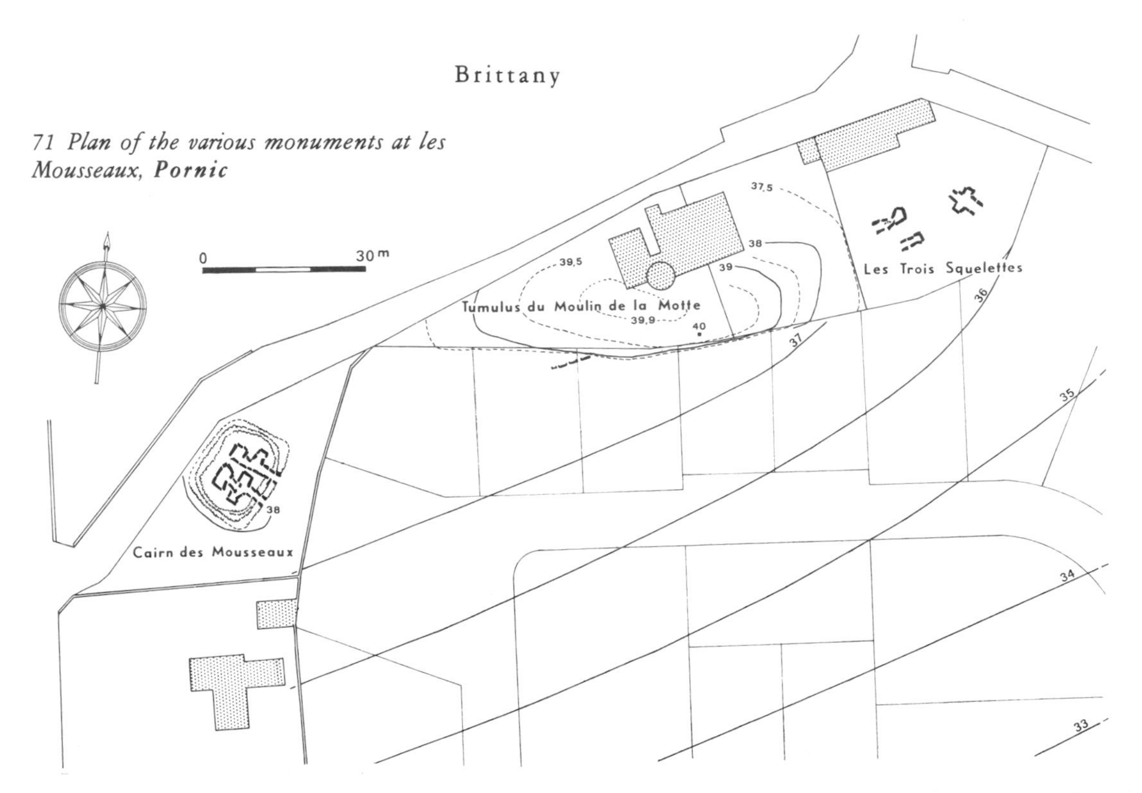

A fine passage grave: a large capstone over the chamber, three over the passage. The paved chamber is approached by an angled passage which was perhaps built in two stages. It opens to the south-east.

Saint-Nazaire

63/14

The area to the north and west of Saint-Nazaire is not well known—except to naturalists and anglers—and can be explored quite peacefully even in the middle of summer. It centres on the Grande Brière, an area of swamp, marsh and thick peat deposits, criss-crossed with canals. Small hamlets of whitewashed, thatched houses huddle on the granite hillocks and are protected by dykes. Much of the transport is still by flat-bottomed boat.

In Neolithic times it was not so marshy. It was not until the third millennium that the level of the Loire rose and the small river Brivet was dammed back to form a great lake that gradually silted up. Menhirs within the Grande Brière, such as la Pierre Blanche and Saint-Malo-de-Guersac, are now partially covered by later deposition. All this, and more, is explained with maps and photos, in the Maison de la Brière, Ile de Fédrun.

At Saint-Joachim on the Ile Butte-aux-Pierres in the middle of the Grande Briére a huge Neolithic habitation site has been uncovered. It is not open to the public. It includes a rare Neolithic hut structure—an oval setting of post-holes, 8 m in length. The occupation seems to have been long-lived, and two levels, separated by a sterile deposit, have been found. The upper level has Chassey ware, including vase-supports, apparently associated with a microlithic flint industry. This would seem to suggest that there was some continuity between the Mesolithic and Neolithic occupation of the area (see also Dissignac, *Saint-Nazaire*) but the picture is somewhat confused since the lower level seems to contain undecorated ware and no microliths.

A large, low cairn was found close by and was probably associated with the upper Chassey level. It contains numerous pits with fragments of bone, burnt flint and Chassey pottery.

A fine round trip of the area should include the monuments of *Saint-Nazaire*, *Batz-sur-Mer*, *le Croisic*, *Guérande*, *Clis*, *Saint-Lyphard*, *Herbignac*, *Missillac*, *Pontchâteau* and *Crossac*.

1 Dolmen Neolithic
Saint-Nazaire 3–4
256,55/263,25

In Saint-Nazaire, place du Dolmen, near the port, is a 'dolmen' comprising two uprights and a capstone, and a menhir. The latter is not in its original position. The capstone, like some of those at Dissignac, is of amphibolite-pyroxenite which probably comes from the coast.

2 Dissignac Neolithic
passage graves Saint-Nazaire 3–4
(Figures 72 and 73) 250,95/262,60

Marked on the Michelin. In Dissignac take the N 171 west (→ la Baule) and continue for 1.25 km to a sign to the 'tumulus' on the right side of the road. At present Dissignac can only be viewed through the wire netting, but it will soon be opened to the public.

This site has recently been excavated and produced some very interesting information. There were two stages of construction. In the first stage a stepped cairn was constructed, delimited by a fine dry-stone wall (doubled in the section to the right of the passage to chamber B). This cairn was covered with a thick layer of clay again demarcated by a circle of large granite and quartzite stones surmounted by smaller pebbles and stones. This circle formed the original (primary) façade of the mound which, at this stage, had a diameter of 16–17 m. Within it were two passage graves. In both cases the chamber was asymmetric to the long (7 m) passage. But while chamber B is a neat oblong, chamber A is a smaller, squarer edifice preceded by a slight antechamber. The roof of chamber A has fallen in. It was probably similar to chamber B, in which the relatively small chamber uprights supported a level of large stones surmounted by a corbelled structure of large slabs. The maximum height from bedrock to roof is 3 m. One of the roof slabs of chamber A has engraved crooks and handled axes, very similar to those found in the Carnac area at Mané Rethual, Kercado and Mané-er-Hroeck.

The second phase of construction followed quite quickly. The passages were extended another 4 m, another mass of clay was added, covering the primary façade, and a new façade of small granite blocks was built between the passage entrances. The edge of the rest of the clay mound was contained by a small dry-stone wall. This peristalith was then immediately masked by yet another capping of clay and another dry-stone wall revetment. It would seem that the clay cappings rose in tiers and that the surface of the clay was covered with flat stones. By the end of the second phase the mound was 30 m in diameter and probably 4 m high.

Many of the stones, including the large slabs of amphibolite-pyroxenite, came from the coast.

Pollen samples taken from the soil that underlies the mound suggest that the site had been cleared of trees and the area had probably been grazed. A typical pasture spectrum of pollen was found, and in addition a few wheat grains, beans and hazelnuts.

73a First phase of construction at Dissignac, ***Saint-Nazaire***

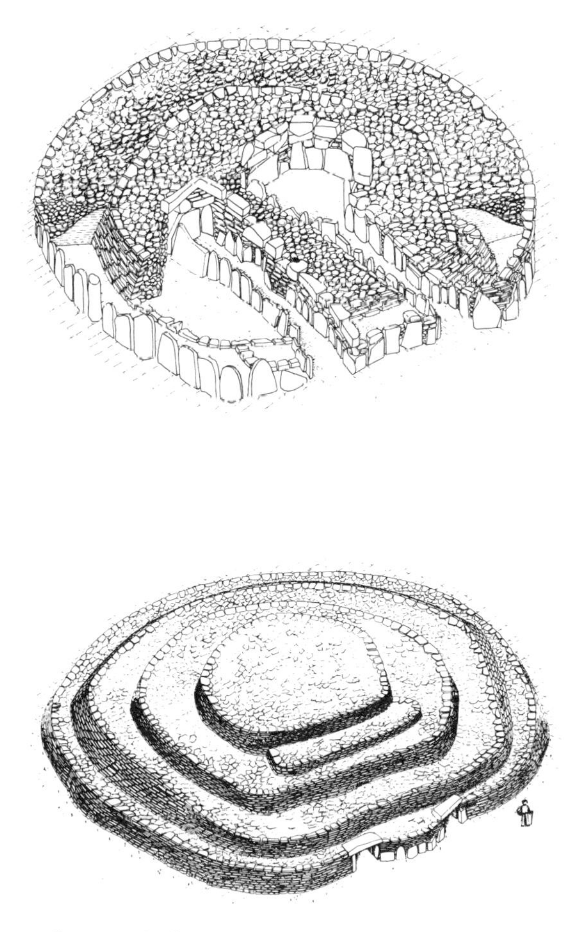

73b Second phase of construction at Dissignac, ***Saint-Nazaire***

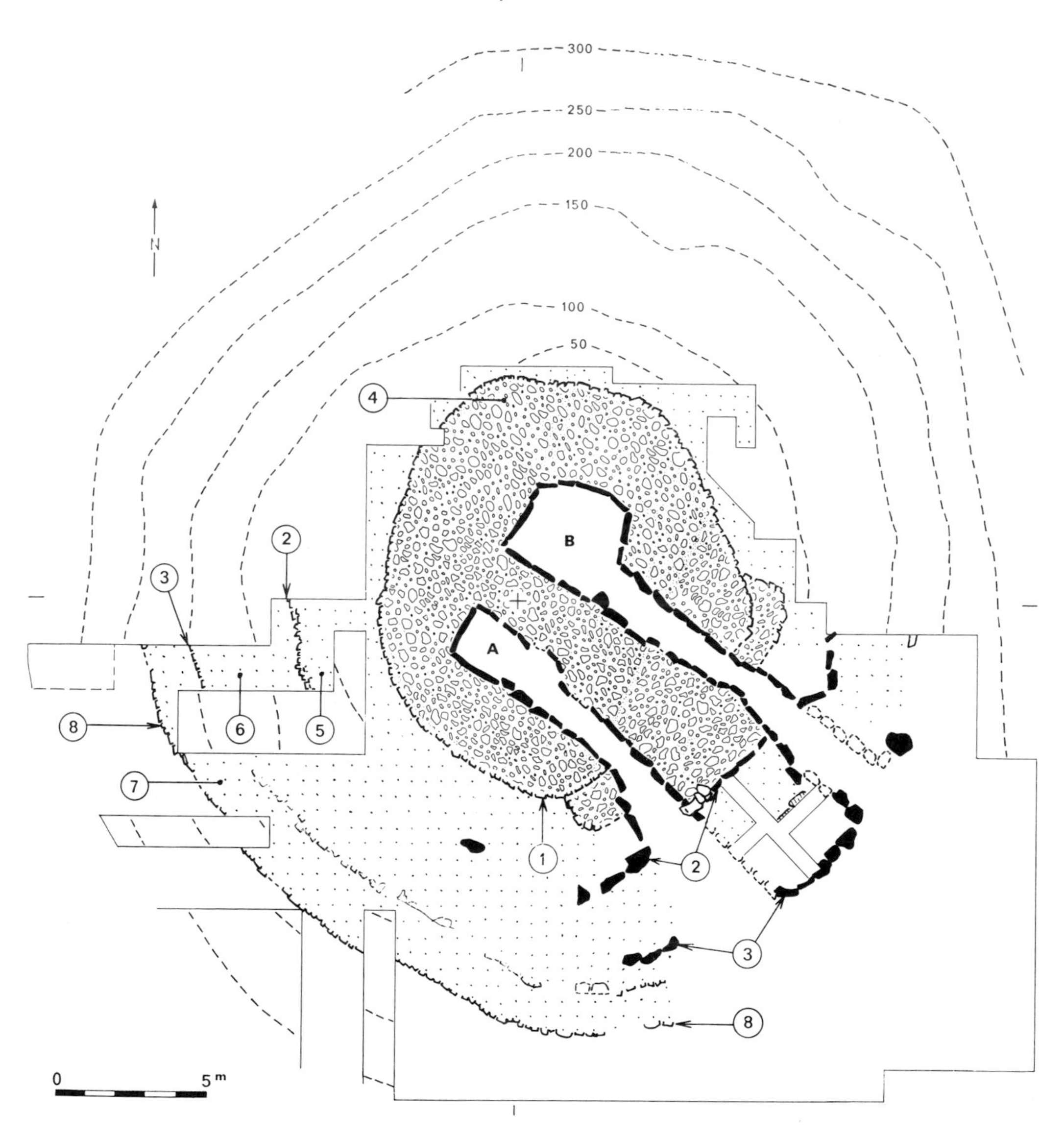

72 Passage graves of Dissignac, ***Saint-Nazaire****.*
Results of L'Helgouach's excavations
A and B Passage graves
1 Central dry-stone wall
2 Megalithic peristalith
3 and 8 Secondary phase dry-stone walls
4 Central cairn
5, 6 and 7 Compacted clay capping

Apart from the pottery placed within the chambers, there was a heavy concentration in front of the secondary façade. Among the offerings was a pedestalled bowl similar to the two found at Barnenez, *Plouezoc'h*, Finistère, and others found at *Colpo*, Morbihan.

One of the unusual features of the site was the juxtaposition of Neolithic pottery with microlithic flint tools. In the fill from chamber A which had been thrown out during the original 1873–4 excavation, there were many Middle Tardenoisian-type microliths associated with a wide range of Neolithic pottery. These tiny flint instruments are usually assumed to pre-date the Neolithic and it could be of course that they had been left on the land-surface long before the monument was constructed. But this does not seem likely, for they are also found in front of the primary façade below a rough paving. Here they are associated with a quantity of undecorated, rather poor quality pottery and this seems to represent a relatively uncontaminated primary assemblage. So there may well be continuity between the indigenous gatherer-hunters and the farming population that built the tombs.

Three carbon-14 dates for the primary phase are 3830 + − 150 bc (calibrated 4615 BC), 3990 + − 150 bc (calibrated 4830 BC) and 4570 + 150 bc (calibrated 5435 BC); while the second phase has a date of 2990 + − 140 bc (calibrated 3775 BC).

3 *passage graves* Neolithic
Saint-Nazaire 7–8
249,70/259,90

Take the D 92 south-west from Saint-Nazaire (→ Pornichet, la Baule). Turn left on the D 26 (→ Saint-Marc-sur-Mer, Sainte-Marguerite); continue for 1.75 km and just before the first major cross-roads there is a sign to the 'cromlech'.

Ruined; forms undistinguishable; probably two passage graves.

Sainte-Pazanne

La Port Faissant 67/2
dolmen Neolithic
(Figure 74) Saint-Philibert-de-Grand-Lieu 1–2
286,70/239,30

From Sainte-Pazanne take the N 758 east (→ Port-Saint-Père) then turn right onto the D 95 (→ Machecoul); then left onto the D 61 (→ Saint-Philibert). Another 0.5 km and just before the bridge, to the left of the road, is a fine trilithon—two uprights and a capstone.

Saint-Père-en-Retz

La Caillerie 67/2
five menhirs Neolithic
Paimboeuf 5–6
269,90/250,95

Take the D 5 south-east out of Saint-Père-en-Retz (→ Arthon) and 2.25 km beyond the intersection with the D 58 turn right (→ la Caillerie, la Pierre-le-Matz). Continue to la Pierre-le-Matz (1.25 km) and take the first field-track left beyond the houses. There is a large menhir about 60 m to the left of the track. Return to the road and continue. Just after the sign announcing the hamlet of Croterie and before the first house take a field-track to the right and at the summit of the hill, to the left of the track, are three very large fallen stones, one of which has a couple of smaller stones below it. Return to the road, go through the hamlet and just beyond the last house, on the roadside, is another very large menhir, with a large stone lying alongside it.

74 ***Sainte-Pazanne**, la Port Faissant*

Morbihan

Arzon

1 Er Lannic
stone circles
See *Larmour-Baden*

2 Grah-Niaul — 63/12
passage grave — Neolithic
Auray 7–8
206,80/296,90

In Arzon ask for the rue de Graniol (running north-east). Follow it out of the village past the Ecole Notre-Dame. Shortly afterwards the road becomes a track. The grave is 60 m down the track, to the left.

A dilapidated monument comprising a long orthostatic passage, a small ruined chamber propped up by concrete posts, and a large lateral cell. Several of the uprights have engravings. All the capstones are in place and the mound is still visible.

Finds of round-based Primary Neolithic pottery, stone axes, variscite beads and a gold bead are recorded.

3 Petit-Mont — Neolithic
passage grave — Auray 7–8
205,90/295,05

Marked on the Michelin. From Arzon take the D 780 (→ Vannes) and 0.5 km out of Arzon take a small road signposted to Petit Mont. The road peters out just in front of the mound. It is a gigantic stone mound, defaced by German bunkers which cut down into the megalithic grave. Recent excavations have rediscovered the long passage and small 4 m-square chamber, and rather faint engravings on some of the stones including a fine hafted axe, an anthropomorph and a disc with lines radiating out from the centre. However one fine stone with crooks, anthropomorphs and a pair of 'footprints' has disappeared.

Grave-goods included a fragment of a vase-support, variscite beads and—evidence of a later intrusion—fragments of Bell Beaker.

There probably were, or are, other passage graves within this mound.

4 Butte de César or — Neolithic
Tumulus de Tumiac — Vannes 5–6
mound — 208,20/295,40

Marked on the Michelin, signposted and clearly visible from the road (a rare combination), the mound lies 200 m north of the D 780, 1.5 km east of Arzon. It is a large mound, 200 m in circumference and 15 m high. Excavations in 1853 uncovered a small closed chamber on the eastern side of the central stone cairn, part megalithic, part dry-stone walled, which contained thirty polished stone axes, three necklaces of variscite beads, and some human bones.

There is a fine view from the top. Legend has it that Caesar stood here to watch Brutus lead the Roman galleys to victory in their great naval battle against the Veneti.

Belz

1 Er Mané (Kerhuen) — 63/1
passage grave — Neolithic
Auray 1–2
186,60/312,50

In Belz at the church take the road north-west to Kerhuen. In Kerhuen turn west (→ Moulin des Oies) and continue for 200 m, bearing right. The monument is to the left of the road and marked by a 'Zone de protection' placard. See map, page 157, Figure 100.

The mound contains three passage graves. The first, a large, well-preserved, orthostatic monument, is now free-standing on the edge of the mound. The second and third—reached by continuing down the

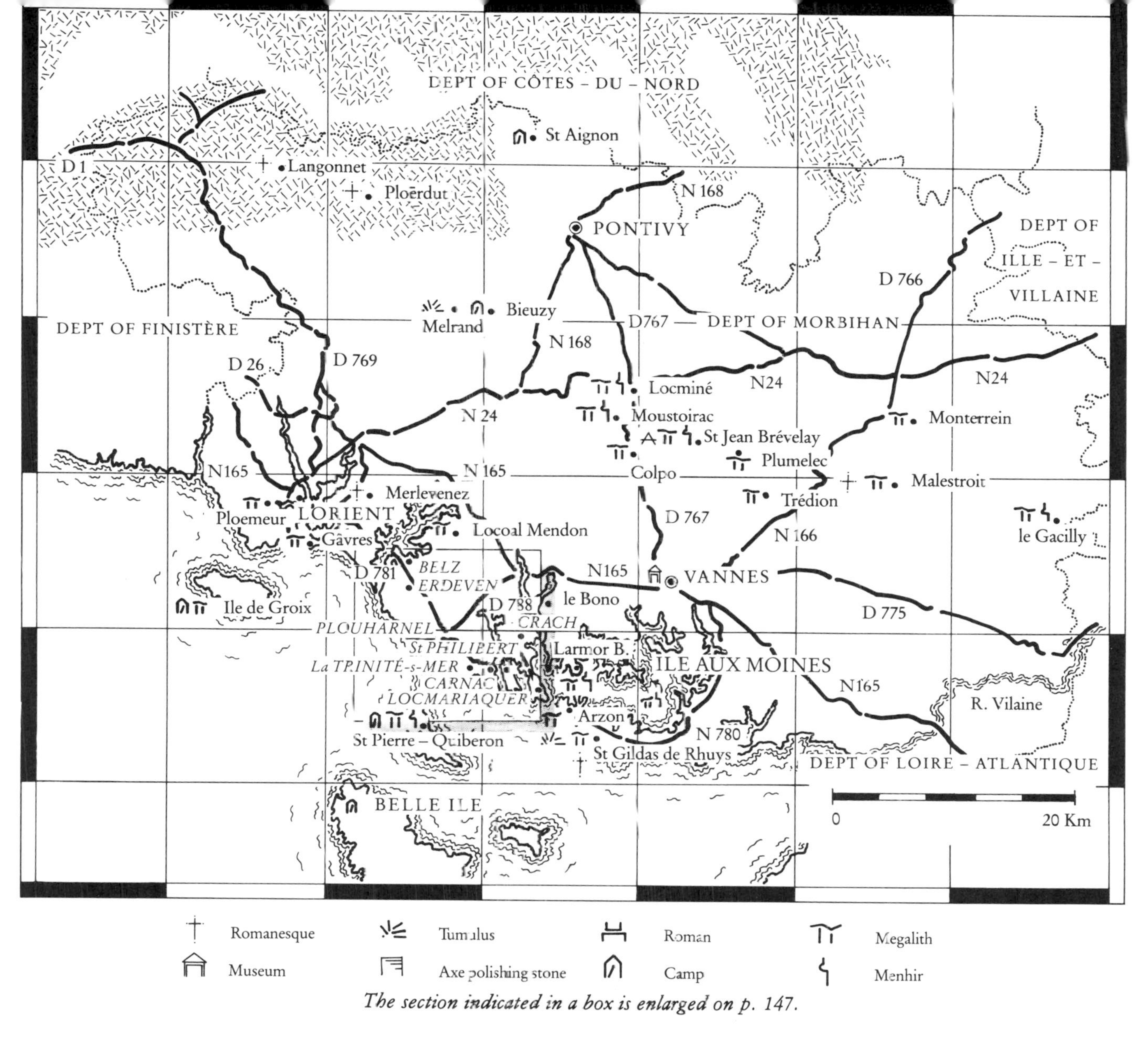

The section indicated in a box is enlarged on p. 147.

75 *Département of Morbihan*

small road that runs in front of the first passage grave—are very ruined.

2 *Passage grave* Neolithic
Auray 1–2
185,99/311,70

For enthusiasts only. Marked on the Michelin. From Belz take the D 9 (→ Lorient) for about 1 km, then, opposite the turn-off to the Chapelle de Saint-Cado, take the track south for about 170 m and then a track west for 30 m. The monument lies directly to the left of this track. See map, page 157, Figure 100.

Very ruined, the passage embedded in brambles. The chamber, built of orthostats and dry-stone walling, is covered by a large capstone.

Bieuzy

Castennec 63/2
hill fort Iron Age
Bubry 3–4
198,50/345,10

The 'Site de Castennec' is marked on the Michelin and signposted on the D1 between Castennec and Saint-Nicolas-des Eaux. Coming from Saint-Nicolas take the steep winding road above the river, past the first sign to the 'Site de Castennec' and on to the second sign and the look-out point. Continue another 100 m to the small chapel of Sainte-Trinité on the left, and after another 50 m the low rampart and shallow ditch—all smothered in brambles—are visible to the right. Then if you take the track to the left of the road, the bank and ditch, looking somewhat more impressive, reappear between the houses.

The site is on a peninsula formed by a meander of the river Blavet. The bank, just over 1.5 m high, encloses an area of about 6 to 8 hectares.

Bignan

See *Locminé* 63/3

Bohal

See *Malestroit* 63/4

Bono, le

1 Le Rocher 63/2
angled passage grave Neolithic
(Figure 76) Auray 3–4
202,45/306,10

Marked on the Michelin. Take the D 101 from Auray towards Baden (first stopping awhile among the old houses and cobbled streets of Auray lower town, around the place Saint-Goustan). After 4 km make a small detour to see the tiny Renaissance chapel of Sainte-Avoye, then continue on the Baden road. Cross the suspension bridge—with a fine view down to the small fishing port—into le Bono. Here take the first turning to the right, and after 700 m, on reaching a large tarmacked area, keep left for another 100 m. Beyond the last house of the village take a footpath to the right for 250 m, through gorse, bracken and pine-trees.

Well worth seeing. The angled passage grave opens to the south-east within an oval mound 21 × 28 m in diameter. The first section of the passage, 11 m long, runs in a south-east/north-west direction, then it abruptly changes course and the second 8 m runs north-east/south-west. Finally the passage splays out to form the chamber. Both passage and chamber are finely constructed of orthostats and dry-stone panelling. There are fairly cursory engravings, in particular anthropomorphs on an upright to the right of the passage, beyond the angle.

The grave-goods included a Kerugou vase, an Upper Conguel pot, a fragment of Bell Beaker, a leaf-shaped arrowhead, a Grand Pressigny blade and a polished chloromelanite axe.

2 Le Rocher Iron Age
Iron Age mounds

Same access as above, but on reaching the footpath turn right immediately. A small path leads to five Iron Age mounds.

These are small and round, made of earth and defined by sloping stone revetments. Each one has a small central cist in which an urn containing ashes was found. The urns were of pottery, with the exception of one iron-banded situla. The richest burial however was not a cremation but an inhumation, with twenty-four bronze and two iron bracelets placed alongside the body.

The material is all Late Hallstatt/Early La Tène, post 500 BC, and is now in the museum of *Carnac*.

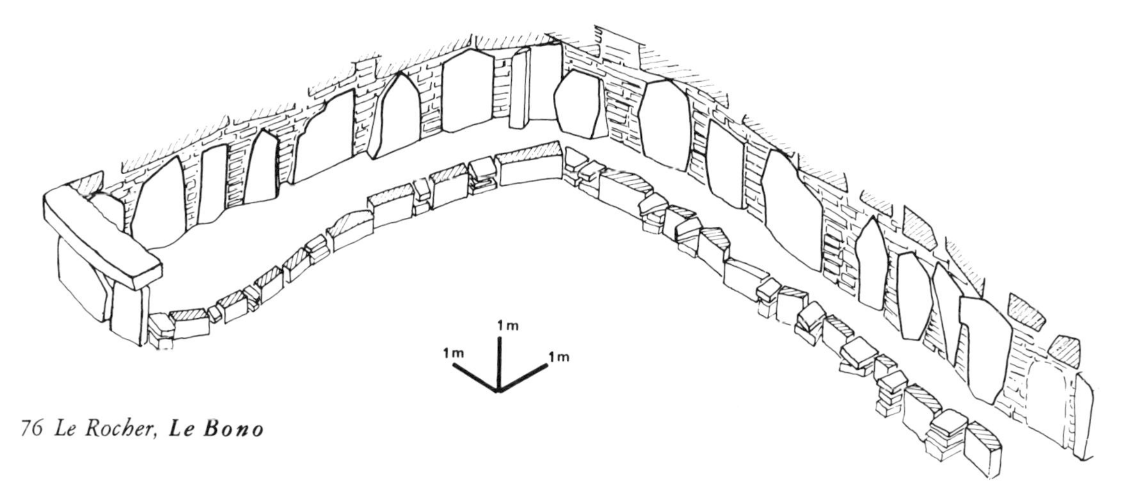

76 Le Rocher, ***Le Bono***

Carnac

63/12–2

The name Carnac may derive from the Latin *carnacium*—'an ossuary or charnel house'—or from the Celtic *carnacon*—'a mound of stones, an area filled with cairns'. Both are appropriate, for in this region of roughly 20 by 15 km there is a greater concentration of megaliths than in any other part of Europe. Even now after millennia of destruction there are about a hundred megaliths in the Quiberon-Carnac area alone. True, the coastal soils were fertile, and the rivers and sea bounteous, the climate mild, but these factors alone cannot explain the concentration. Like Salisbury Plain in southern England this area must have had a particular religious and ceremonial significance. Le Rouzic may not have been far wrong when he suggested in 1897 that 'without a doubt, this region was a religious centre to which one came on pilgrimage from far distant places, or brought the bodies of rich and powerful, military or religious, leaders—a sort of Champs-Elysées ... an intellectual centre, and a trading centre between people from the North and South ... Iberia ... northern Europe ... Ireland.'

Le Rouzic also expounds on the legend of Carnac, apparently introduced by Irish monks. Saint Cornély, so it is said, was a pope at Rome. He was chased out by pagan soldiers and he marched ahead of them accompanied by two bulls who carried his baggage and sometimes the saint himself. One day he arrived at the village of le Moustoir; he wanted to stay, but on hearing a young girl insult her mother, he continued and came to a small mountain village. Before him lay the sea, behind lay the soldiers ranged in battle formation. He stopped, turned and 'petrified' the army—turned them to stone—and so the alignments came into being. The legend continues that Carnac became a holy place, a place to ask Saint Cornély to save sick animals. The pilgrims who came made their way through the stones—the men carried small stones, the women earth, and they left them on a mountain near Carnac—and so the mound of Saint-Michel grew up.

Until very recent times a fertility cult lingered on. After a marriage ceremony the couple would go and press themselves against one of the great stones of the alignment. A barren woman would do likewise.

But enough of the moonshine. Carnac is now a popular seaside resort. Unless you like crowds it is best avoided in August. May is a fine month, when the gorse blooms among the stones, or early September when the heather is out.

The Carnac monuments have been listed in such a way as to permit a grand round trip, but obviously, and preferably, this may be broken up into a number of excursions (see map, Figure 77).

With Carnac as a centre you can fan out to take in the monuments to the west and north-west: *Plouharnel* and *Erdeven*, *Belz* and *Locoal Menden*; to the east: *la Trinité*, *Crach*, *Saint-Philibert* and *Locmariaquer*; and, further afield, Saint-Avoye, *le Bono* and *Larmor-Baden*. In each area the monuments are listed to form an itinerary.

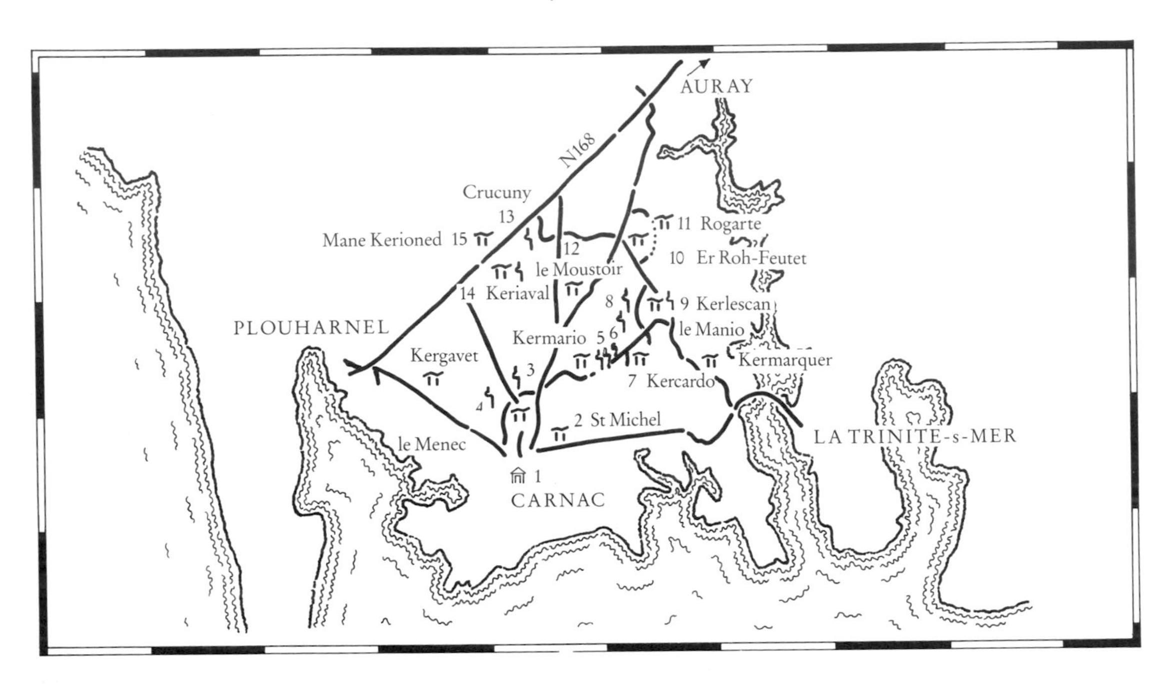

77 *Carnac – la Trinité-Sur-Mer region (numbers refer to the text)*

1 Musée de Carnac, Museum
10 place de la Chapelle
A very interesting collection of mainly local material, much of it donated by Le Rouzic. There are small mock-ups of some of the local chamber tombs and alignments, and full-size casts of some of the grave art.

Open from Easter to 1 October every day from 10 a.m. to 12 noon and 2 to 6.30 p.m. From 2 October to Easter closed on Tuesdays, otherwise open from 10 a.m. to 12 noon and 2 to 5 p.m.

2 Saint-Michel Neolithic
mound Auray 5–6
(Figure 78) 193,40/301,60
In Carnac follow the sign for the Hôtel de Tumulus. Ask at the hotel for a guided tour of the mound.

This is an enormous rectangular mound (124 × 60 × 10 m) containing both closed chambers and a passage grave (very similar to the set-up at Mané-Lud, *Locmariaquer*). The spine of the mound is constructed of stones within a retaining wall that circumscribes an area roughly 98 × 10 × 5.6 m. This, in turn is covered by a thick deposit of clayey soil.

A modern passage has been built to allow access to the interior and much restoration has occurred, so that it is hard to separate fact from fiction. But within the stony spine eleven small rough cists were found concentrated around one more carefully made and larger chamber. This central chamber, paved with small stones and covered with a large capstone was about 2.4 × 1.8 × 1 m. A little to the south of the main chamber and beyond the stone spine was another chamber with a short passage. Other cists found in the east end of the mound are probably secondary.

The rough cists seemed to have contained very little—a few animal bones perhaps represented meat offerings. The wealth is concentrated in the main chamber. There was a little pottery and a few burnt bones, but then also thirty-nine finely polished stone axes, some of which had apparently been placed blade upwards. Some of the axes were of fibrolite, and some were huge, with splayed blades and squared-off cross-sections. There was also a deposit of

135 variscite beads.

The other large mounds of this type are le Moustoir, *Carnac*; Mané-Lud and Mané-er-Hroëck, *Locmariaquer*; and Tumiac, *Arzon*.

3 The alignments — Neolithic
(Figure 79) — Auray 5–6 192,80/302,20
Auray 7–8 195,40/302,30

Best to walk the whole length, about 3 km, if possible when no one else is around. Start at the south-west end (out of Carnac on the Plouharnel road, D 781, then turn north onto the D 196), with the Ménec alignments (Figure 80).

First there is a discontinuous oval (more precisely Professor Thom's megalithic egg) of seventy close-set stones, off-centre to the main alignment. Very few of these are in their original positions—the ones that Le Rouzic replaced are marked with little inset squares of pink concrete. Eleven lines of uprights (1099 in all), 4 to 0.6 m high, fan eastwards from the oval, covering an area roughly 100 m wide and 1167 m long. At a certain point along the way they change direction and then decrease in size towards the east. Again many of these stones have been reset by Le Rouzic. The eastern section is cut by the D 119. (You could at this point take a quick look at the Ménec dolmen and then return to the alignments.)

The Ménec alignments peter out. Thom has found a number of close-set stones at the east end that may be the remains of another oval setting. There is then an open space, c. 250 m long, which may have contained the oval setting marking the beginning of the Kermario alignments. Within this space lies the Kermario passage grave. Thom, in his careful mapping of these alignments suggests that there are seven main rows, plus several ancillary rows on the southern border, and he plots three bends in the orientation. He suggests that towards the east end—that is the sections on either side of the ravine—there are two overlapping systems in operation. In all, the Kermario alignments consist of 1029 stones, and cover an area 100 m by 1120 m. The stones pass over the top of the Manio long barrow. Excavations at the base of the stones revealed foundation offerings—flints, pottery and ash.

390 m beyond the Manio barrow is the oval setting (again running over a low long barrow) that marks the west end of the third stretch of alignments, the Kerlescan group. 594 uprights in all, of which thirty-nine form part of the oval. The rest make up thirteen lines, about 139 m wide and 880 m long.

Finally several lines straggle on further to the east, beyond the hamlet of Kerlescan, at a different orientation. This is the Petit-Ménec alignment.

North of the Kerlescan alignments are the remains of a large stone circle (thirty-six stones still upright, six fallen), and there is also, to the east of this circle, the fine lateral entrance grave of Kerlescan (see below).

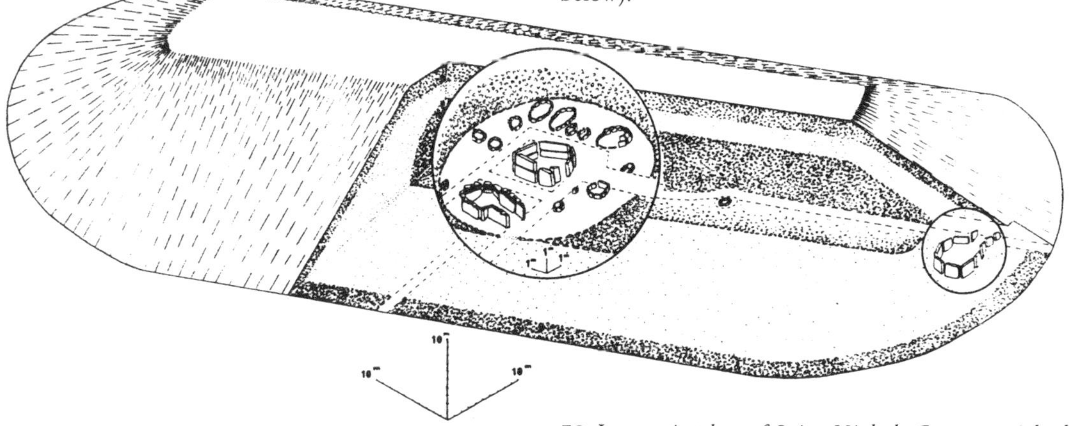

78 Isometric plan of Saint-Michel, ***Carnac*** *with the central section and the eastern passage grave enlarged.*

It is hard to put a precise date on the alignments: they are later than the unchambered long barrows at Manio since they override them; probably later than the passage grave at Kermario. They are probably Late Neolithic.

There are other alignments in the region, at *Erdeven*, *Plouharnal*, *Saint-Pierre-Quiberon*, and there are two oval settings at *Larmor-Baden* (Er Lannic) and the remains of a circle on *Ile-aux-Moines*. Le Rouzic, who had an unparalleled knowledge of the area, suggested that the original alignments extended still further, eastwards to the river Crach, westwards to the river Sainte-Barbe, in all more than 8 km.

Numerous 'explanations' of the alignments have been offered. Thom has an elaborate hypothesis that the Ménec and Kermario alignments formed part of a gigantic lunar observatory, probably set up to permit the prediction of eclipses. The 'observatory' centres on the huge menhir of Er Grah at *Locmariaquer*, which was the universal lunar foresight for use in several directions, in particular to the eight main positions corresponding to the rising and setting of the moon at the standstills. Thom reckons to have established the position of several of these backsights, and he suggests that the alignments of le Ménec and Kermario were placed so as to make it possible to obtain the extrapolation distance for the backsights in the western sector, at Kerran, Kervilor, Quiberon and *Saint-Pierre-Quiberon*.

There are obviously real problems involved in proving such a theory, not least the inaccuracies that occurred in the resetting of the stone alignments by Le Rouzic and others. One might also wonder at the feasibility of sightings involving distances of the order of 15 km and of the possibility of the sort of accuracy that Thom's model requires. Nor is it clear that the Great Menhir remained upright for any length of time. It might be more reasonable simply to accept that the oval settings were set out with care, that the alignments do often point in the direction of standstill points of the sun and moon, and that there was some sort of fairly accurate measurement—a megalithic 'pace' rather than Thom's megalithic 'yard'. But even if one queries the specifics of Thom's work it is important because it emphasizes, rightly, that Neolithic people were not intellectual 'pygmies', and also because it involves one of the first attempts at really accurate surveying of the alignments. For more on Thom's theories see A. and A.S. Thom, *Megalithic Remains in Britain and Brittany*, 1978, Clarendon Press, Oxford.

Another thesis, which need not contradict the notion that some of the stones were used in astronomical sightings, is that the oval enclosures and the pathways between the stones were the setting for tribal ceremonies, and that the actual erection of the stones was part of the ceremony, so that different sections, different lines of stones may have been placed at different moments in time. The changes in orientation, the straggling outliers etc. seem to support this notion of physical renewal.

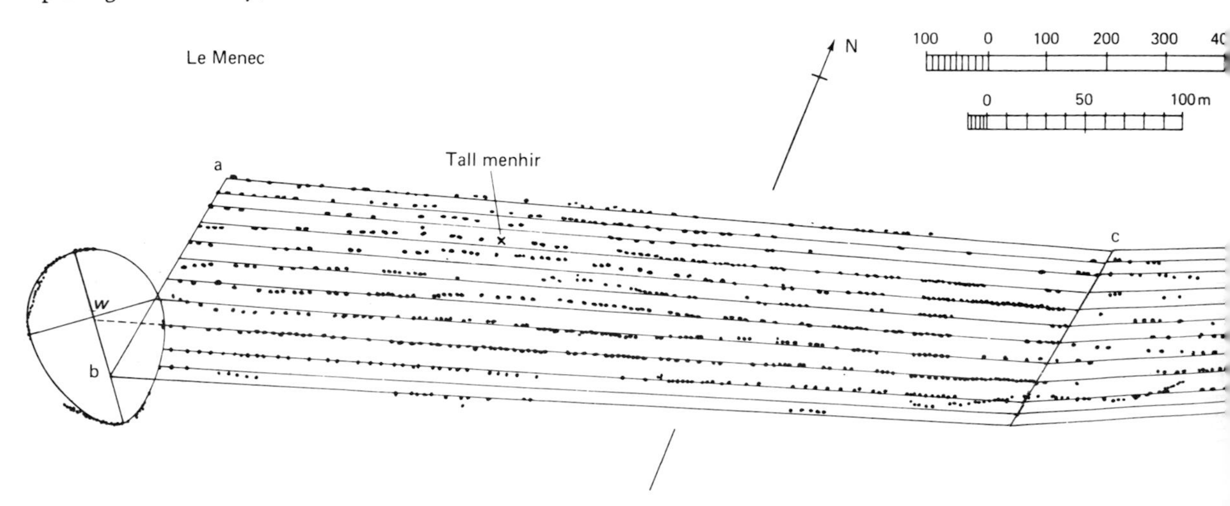

79 ***Carnac***, *plan of alignments of le Ménec*

4 Ménec | Neolithic
passage grave | Auray 5–6
192,90/301,70

Half way down the Ménec alignments turn south on a small road to Carnac (the southerly continuation of the C 4). After 400 m, beyond the seventh house on the right and visible from the road, is a small orthostatic chamber crowned with a cross. The passage has long since been destroyed.

5 Kermario | Neolithic
passage grave | Auray 5–6
193,95/302,45

Directions as for the alignments. On the D 196, just at the beginning of the Kermario alignments, to the north of the road, is a passage grave with no mound.

The monument is heavily restored. The original plan is less than certain, but according to Lukis (1854) there was a large trapezoidal chamber 5 × 2.5 × 3.5 m. It is oddly placed, west of the Kermario alignments in an area that may originally have been within the oval setting that marked the beginning of the alignment.

6 Manio | Neolithic
long mound and menhir | Auray 7–8
194,77/302,82

Directions as for Kermario (above); continue east on the D 196, almost to the end of the Kermario alignments. Beyond the small lake, and 200 m before the discreet entrance left to the Château de Kercado, one taller stone stands out within the alignments. This is the 4 m menhir that marked the end of a now invisible long mound. There are five wavy lines engraved near the base of the stone and these can be seen by peering through the hole broken into a flat stone alongside the menhir. Le Rouzic excavated the long mound in 1922. He found five polished stone axes (four of dolerite, one of fibrolite), placed blade-upwards, and, nearby, a quartzite pendant. Close to the menhir a stone engraved with a hafted axe may have covered a cist. The mound itself was some 35 m long, 11 m wide at the west end, 16 at the east, and was surrounded by a revetment of small stones, doubled and trebled at the north-west end. Both within the mound, and beyond the north end, were fifty small cists and hearths. Some of these comprised four upright stones with a covering of flat stones angled towards each other. They contained a few Chassey-type sherds, a few flaked flints and a little charcoal. Below the centre of the mound was a rectangular pit 3.2 × 0.8 m surrounded by upright stones. Again it contained minimal material.

Since the alignment passes over the mound, the mound must be earlier in date.

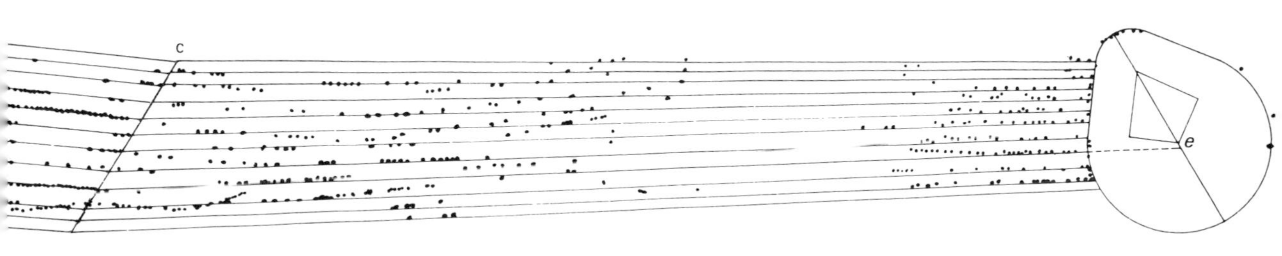

80 Alignments at le Ménec, Carnac

7 Kercado — Neolithic
passage grave — Auray 7–8
194,90/302,35

Marked on the Michelin. Directions as for the alignments and the Manio long mound. Continue on the D 196 and at the end of the Kermario alignments take a small road right marked to the Château de Kercado. At the château ring (and ring again!) and get the key to the monument.

A very fine, apparently early, passage grave still imbedded in a great round mound. Both the passage—which lies slightly off-centre with regard to the chamber—and the square chamber are built of orthostats topped with a level of dry-stone walling and surmounted by capstones. There are a few non-descript engravings, including one hafted axe on the underside of the chamber capstone. A very rough anthropomorphic stele forms part of the wall of the chamber, to the right of the chamber entrance. 6 m beyond the mound is an exterior circle of small uprights.

The grave contained a fragment of a Chassey vase-support, Kerugou, Late Conguel and Bell Beaker ware, as well as Grand Pressigny flint, 154 variscite beads and pendants, and a Bell Beaker-type gold plaque with rolled edges. There is a carbon-14 date of 3890 +/- 300 bc (calibrated 4670 BC).

8 Quadrilatère de Manio and Grand Menhir — Neolithic
Auray 7–8
194,80/303,30

Continue on the D 196 past the Château de Kercado entrance and 350 m beyond the entrance take the path left with a discreet sign to the Manio Quadrilatère. Continue on the track to a further sign pointing left (in all about 500 m from the road). The 'quadrilatère' is to the right of the path; the Grand Menhir to the left.

9 Kerlescan Neolithic
lateral-entrance grave Auray 7–8
195,45/303,50

This fine grave is marked on the Michelin but is not easy to find and is very overgrown. Directions as for Kercado and Manio, but continue east on the D 196. Stop at the end of the Kerlescan alignments just before the hamlet of Kerlescan and turn left on a small paved road. After 100 m take the track left along the north edge of the alignments. Continue for 150 m and at a fork keep right, along the right-hand edge of a field. After 75 m this path goes into a fir-copse; take the right-hand track through the copse for 100 m, almost to the far end, and there is a tiny path left for 30 m to the megalith.

The sub-rectangular mound is 40 m long and 6.7/8.5 m wide and is delimited by uprights. The entrance is off-centre on the south side. The passage, the two notched stones that used to form the 'port-hole' between the passage and chamber and two more notched stones that originally divided the chamber into two sections, have all gone. The western section, 9 m long, is built of orthostats with dry-stone wall panelling; the eastern part, 8 m long, is made of dry-stone walling. The width and height of the grave remain the same throughout, and the entire floor is paved with flat stones. Only one capstone remains.

The grave-goods included a Kerugou bowl, a Bell Beaker plus fragments, a coarse beaker with finger-nail impressions, a pot with a decorated handle, a fibrolite axe, four stone pendants, two barbed-and-tanged arrowheads and flaked flints.

From Kerlescan you could continue to the passage grave of Kermarquer, *la Trinité-sur-Mer*.

10 Er-Roh-Feutet, la Madeleine — Neolithic — Auray 3–4
pasage grave — 195,20/305,00

Directions as for Kerlescan (above) but continue on to the end of the D 196 and then turn north on the D 186 (→ Kergroix). At the crossing with the road to Carnac, continue north-east towards Kergroix (still on the D 186) for 70 m. There is then a 'zone de protection d'un monument préhistorique' placard close to a track to the right of the road. Follow the track and when it divides bear left, then after 20 m, take the track to the right and after another 15 m the monument is just visible 70 m to the left across the field.

There is a short, low passage with one capstone, and a square orthostatic chamber with two capstones. Bell Beaker ware was found in the chamber.

11 Rogarte, la Madeleine — Neolithic
passage grave — Auray 3–4
195,55/305,10

Directions as for Er-Roh-Feutet (above), but continue on the D 186 (→ Kergroix) and take the first road to the right, the R 19, to Kergueno. Just before the first house of the hamlet is a 'zone de protection' sign on the right. Follow the track and when it begins to curve right the dolmen can be seen—though only with difficulty when the maize is ripe—50 m to the left.

Very ruined—a small asymmetrical orthostatic and dry-stone walled chamber with one large tilted capstone, and the remains of a passage.

Primary Neolithic, Kerugou and Bell Beaker ware were found. Also some variscite beads.

12 Le Moustoir — Neolithic
mound and menhir — Auray 3–4
194,50/304,40

Marked on the Michelin. Directions as for Er-Roh-Feutet and Rogarte (above), but this time, at the crossing of the D 186 and the road to Carnac, turn towards Carnac. Go through le Moustoir. Beyond the next corner is a 'zone de protection' sign on a track to the right. There is a small menhir immediately to the left of the track, and an impressive mound 90 × 40 m to the right. A path leads round the base of the mound to the entrance to a small orthostatic chamber.

As well as the chamber visible on the west side, which contained bones and an interesting vase-support, there are two cists on the east side, both of which are reported to have contained human bones. In the centre of the mound a setting of small stones contained a mass of ash and animal bones and a fine, large pot.

The mound, like the ones at Saint-Michel, *Carnac* and Tumiac, *Arzon*, consists of a central mass of stones covered with a thick layer of clayey soil.

13 Crucuny — Neolithic
mound and menhir — Auray 1–2
193,60/305,10

Marked on the Michelin. Again, directions as for Er-Roh-Feutet, but at the crossing of the D 186 and the road to Carnac go west on the C 10 (→ restaurant Stirwen). Just beyond Stirwen there is a 'zone de protection' placard on the right which marks a passage grave with a round chamber, 20 m from the road. This is *not* Crucuny!

Continue on the C 10, then over the crossroads onto the C 123 (→ Crucuny), through the village of Crucuny, and another 'zone de protection' sign to the left signals a large mound and menhir.

14 Keriaval — Neolithic
passage grave with lateral cells — Auray 1–2
192,90/304,70

Marked on the Michelin. Coming from Crucuny, continue north from the village on the C 123 to the junction with the D 768, and turn left (south-west) on the D 768 (→ Plouharnel). (Alternatively, coming straight from Carnac, go north on the D 119, turn left on the C 123 to Crucuny and continue as above.) 1.1 km down the D 768, just before the C 202 turn-off right to Quelvezin and Quéric la Lande, there is a 'zone de protection' placard to the left of the road. A small path leads to the monument (100 m from the road) and then continues to a group of menhirs.

A fine orthostatic monument which has lost its mound. The chamber at the east end is not very clearly divided from the passage. Two lateral cells each covered with a large capstone, give onto the north side of the chamber. There were also two on the south side but one of them has been destroyed.

Rich grave-goods were found, including a Chassey vase, much Middle Neolithic ware, variscite beads and red clay spindle-whorls. These are at the *Vannes* museum.

This type of grave is a regional south-coast type; it is found again at cairn II, Larcuste, *Colpo*, at

Cruguellic, *Ploemeur*, both in Morbihan and at *Crossac* in the Loire-Atlantique.

15 Mané-Kérioned | Neolithic
passage graves | Auray 1–2
(Figures 81 and 82) | 192,65/304,70

Marked on the Michelin. Directions as for Keriaval but continue on the D 768 (→ Plouharnel) and to the right of the road, 50 m beyond the junction with the C 202, the monument is signalled by a 'zone de protection' placard. *Do not forget a torch.*

One of the most interesting and well-preserved monuments in this region. There are three passage graves.

Chamber C is the westerly one. Both chamber and passage splay out, widening towards the back, and there is no sharp break between the 5 m passage and the small chamber. However, the height increases from 1.25 m in the passage to 2 m at the back of the chamber. The floor is paved with pebbles and a layer of rough paving.

To the east and approached by a small path close to the road and stone steps, is chamber B. It is still deep within its mound, only the chamber capstones are visible on the surface. Again, passage and chamber are trapezoidal in shape: the passage, 5.5 m long, increases in width from 1.1 m at the outside entrance to 1.5 m at the chamber entrance, and then the chamber widens from 1.7 to 3.5 m. Again, the division between passage and chamber is not clearly marked.

The orthostats of both passage and chamber are surmounted by large stones that carry the capstones, and the roof gradually increases in height from 1.6 m at the beginning of the passage to 2 m at the back of the chamber. As in chamber C the floor is covered with pebbles and rough paving.

Six of the uprights in this passage grave have a fine series of engravings, four others are more minimally decorated. On one of the uprights on the right-hand side of the chamber (R 11) the entire surface has been worked, an engraved line delimits the edge to form an anthropomorph and this is filled with a variety of signs including 'crooks'. A stone found within the mound has two engraved hafted axes on it.

Chamber A lies between the two, and at right angles to them. It is a classic small passage grave and is certainly earlier than the other two, for they completely block its access. It is not clear whether all three graves were once covered by a single mound.

81 Mané-Kérioned, ***Carnac*** *1 Chamber B, 2 Chamber C*

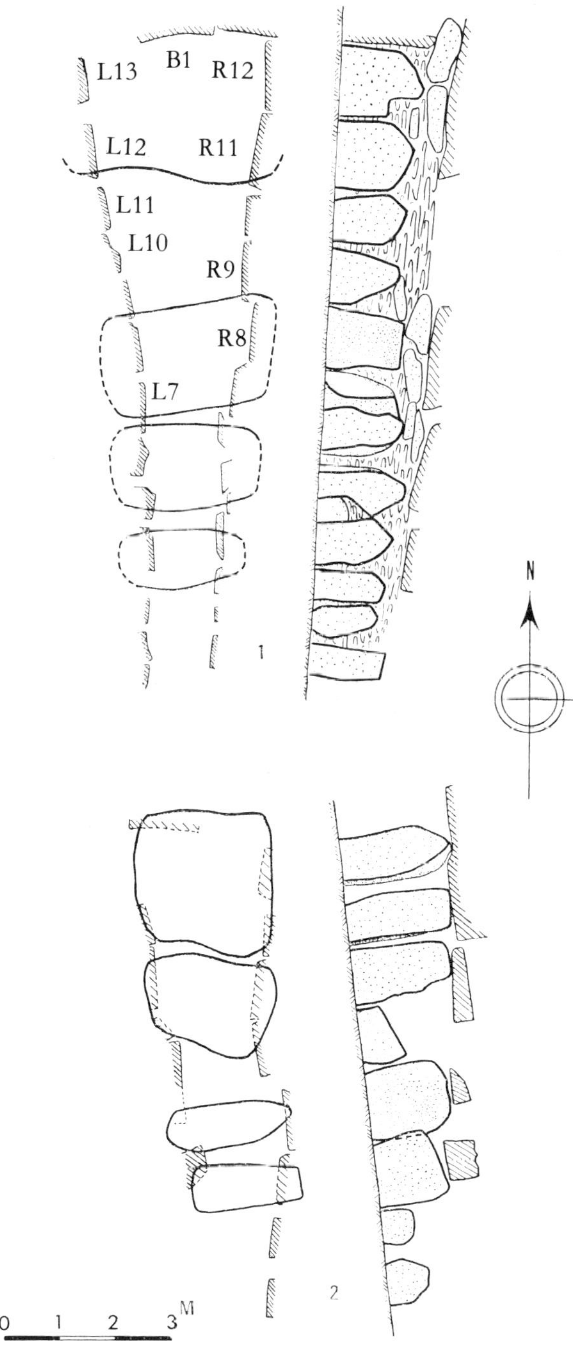

82 *Mané-Kérioned B,* ***Carnac****, stone R 11 on the plan*

16 Er-Mané (Quéric-la-Lande) — Neolithic
passage graves — Auray 1–2 — 192,85/306,85
(Figure 83)

Directions as for Keriaval (above), but turn north off the D 768 onto the C 202 (→ Quelvezin, Quéric-la-Lande). Go through Quelvezin (c. 1.5 km) and continue another 0.5 km to the isolated farm of Quéric-la-Lande—to the right of the road, just before a sharp bend. Turn into the farmyard and the rather neglected-looking monuments can be seen in the field to the left.

The more southerly one is a small passage grave with traces of a round mound. The orthostatic chamber has lost its capstone and the short passage is covered by two stones.

40 m to the north is another small orthostatic five-sided passage grave with one capstone over the chamber. The top of one of the passage uprights looks as though it has been used as a grinding surface.

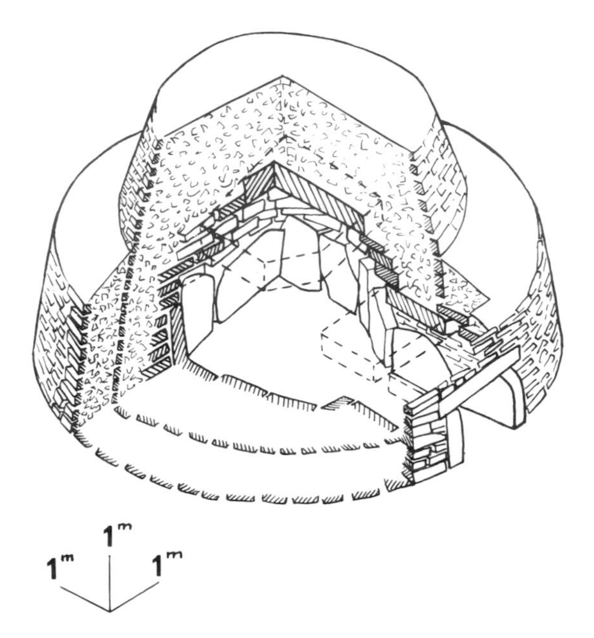

83 *Quéric-la-Lande,* ***Carnac***

Chapelle-Caro, la

See *Monterrein* 63/4

Colpo

63/3

The uplands to the north of the Morbihan coast remain unspoilt and unvisited. There is a fine tour to be made through the rugged, rock-strewn scenery that marks the granitic Lanvaux outcrop, and that harbours a large number of megalithic monuments. Rivers run down to the Morbihan coast and early Neolithic contacts were primarily with that region. Then, later, towards the end of the Neolithic, there were also contacts with the north. A visit to Colpo should be combined with the Kermarquer menhir at *Moustoirac*, the gallery graves of *Plaudren* and *Saint-Jean-Brévelay* and (perhaps) with the passage grave at *Bohal*.

86 Larcuste, ***Colpo****, cairn II*

Larcuste — Neolithic
passage graves — Elven 1–2
(Figures 84–6) — 215,10/(2)324,30

At Colpo take the D 767 south (→ Vannes), and after 700 m turn left on the C 104 (→ Plaudren). Almost immediately turn right to Larcuste. Go to the highest house in the village and ask for directions and the key.

Therc were four monuments at Colpo, two (le Champ de la Motte and Min Goh Ru) have been destroyed, two have been rediscovered, re-excavated (1968–72) and reconstructed.

Cairn I, the northern one, is an oval stone-built mound, 30 × 20/22 m, with two or three dry-stone wall revetments. It covers two passage graves, both made of orthostatic uprights topped with dry-stone walling. The passages, 4 and 5 m long, run almost parallel; the chambers are small and oval. The northern one is covered by a single large granite capstone resting on the dry-stone walling. The southern one is open to the sky—either the capstone has gone, or perhaps the dry-stone walling continued upwards to form a corbelled dome.

On the right-hand side of the southern chamber are some fairly invisible engravings, U signs, 'crooks', serpentine forms. On the back-stone of the northern chamber is a somewhat better preserved U sign.

The two passages open to the south-east, onto a slightly concave façade, and between the passage entrances is a fine 2 m stretch of dry-stone walling. It was at the foot of the wall, close to the north entrance, that a fine and rare pedestal vase with *pointillé* decoration and two small double buttons was found. Undoubtedly the vase had originally been placed on top of the wall. (Other similar vases are two from Barnenez, *Plouézoc'h*, Finistère, and some fragments from Lizo, Morbihan, Gaignog, *Landéda*, Finistère, and Dissignac, *Saint-Nazaire*, Loire-Atlantique.)

The contents of the southern chamber were found more or less intact (the northern one had been robbed). On the rough paving were some burnt flint flakes and fragments of a large Primary Neolithic pot. A Bronze Age cordoned urn was found placed within the already tumbled chamber walls.

The façade of cairn II is aligned with cairn I. The stone mound had only a single revetment wall. The grave takes a more complicated form. An 8 m long dry-stone walled passage leads to six small chambers, each with an entrance sill, each made of dry-stone walling, each covered with a single capstone and blocked with a dry-stone wall after the final depositions.

There was no pottery in the chambers but in the passage and in front of the entrance the remains of eighteen pots with affinities to Middle Neolithic Chassey ware were found. These may well indicate reuse of the passage *after* the small chambers had been blocked up.

Cairn II has carbon-14 dates of 2660 + – 110 bc (calibrated 3440 BC), 2030 + – 110 bc (calibrated 2560 BC)—both rather low, and another of 3540 + – 120 bc (calibrated 4400 BC)—which is perhaps a bit high.

84 Isometric plan of cairn I at Larcuste, **Colpo**

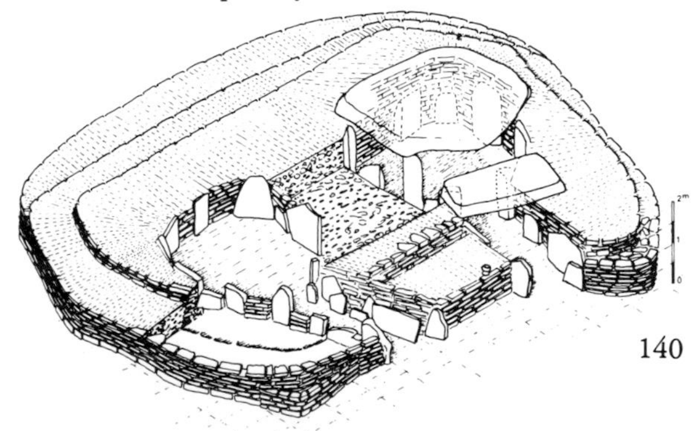

85 Isometric plan of cairn II at Larcuste, **Colpo**

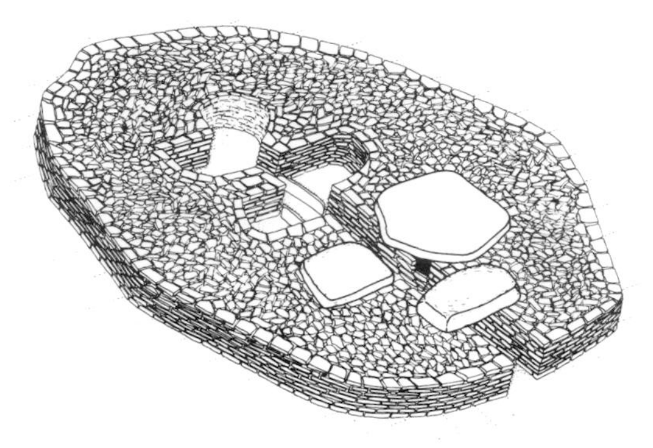

Cournon

See *Gacilly, la* 63/5

Crach

63/2

None of the monuments around Crach are easy to find, and two of the three are less than spectacular, but they are in lovely unfrequented settings (see map, page 147, Figure 92).

1 Beudrec — Neolithic
angled grave — Auray 3–4
198,60/304,00

In Crach ask for the C 204 (→ Luffang). About 650 m beyond Crach turn left on a small road to Beudrec. Continue to the end of the road and ask for directions at the house. Even with directions the grave is hard to find.

It seems to be an angled passage grave with a small terminal chamber. Three capstones are still in place.

2 Parc-Guren — Neolithic
passage graves — Auray 3–4
(Figure 87) — 197,85/304,50

Directions as for Beudrec (above), but continue on the C 204 (→ Luffang). 0.75 km out of Crach (just beyond the Beudrec turn-off) cross onto the R 14 (→ Luffang). On the right, 250 m beyond the crossing, is a small pine-forest. At the further end of the forest turn right off the road onto the forest track (see plan). 10 m before the forest gives way to a field, on the left

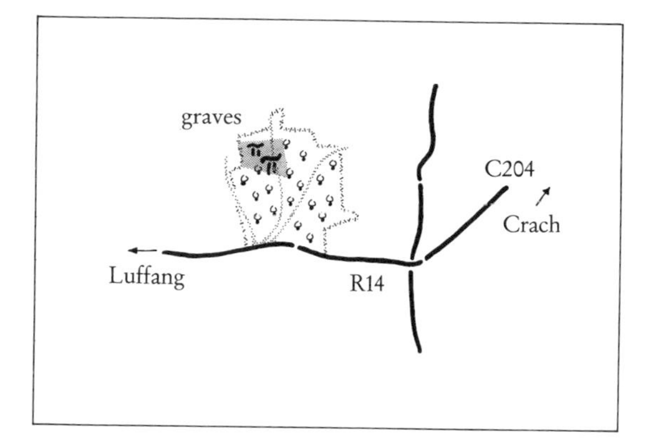

87 Plan of access to Parc-Guren passage graves, ***Crach***

of the track, and not easy to see, is a ruined passage grave (Parc Guren II). The large circular chamber is open to the sky and may originally have had a corbelled roof; the passage—asymmetric to the chamber—still has one capstone. There is an isolated U engraving. Bell Beaker fragments were found in the grave, and in either this grave or Parc Guren I, Le Rouzic found a 'faience' bead.

Go back down the track c. 30 m and on the same side is another passage grave (Parc Guren I), only recently uncovered, or rather rediscovered. It is equally difficult to find. This one has a passage with three capstones, an orthostat blocking the entrance to the passage, and a very small chamber. It had—perhaps has—a 'menhir' lying within the passage.

3 Luffang — Neolithic
angled grave — Auray 3–4
197,35/304,15

Directions as for Parc-Guren (above): the C 204, then the R 14, to and through Luffang, and continue down to the sea. Before the road reaches the sea, there are three trackways going off to the right. *Opposite* the second of these is a small path (thus south of the road) going up through the trees to the grave, which is about 20 m from the road.

The grave is immensely long. The antechamber, which opens to the south and is orientated south/north is c. 8 m long; the chamber which makes a right angle, is c. 18 m long. There are no capstones. The uprights are covered with moss so that the engravings are invisible, but they include the anthropomorphic motif. One engraved stone has been removed to the museum of *Carnac*.

The grave-goods included a fragment of Kerugou ware, eight tanged arrows, some with well-defined barbs. Four of these are certainly a Bell Beaker type, the others may belong to the Seine-Oise-Marne inventory. There was also a Grand Pressigny dagger, polished stone axes and ten variscite beads (both tubular and discoidal).

There was another angled grave nearby at Pointe de Vide Bouteille (Crach). Apart from the one at Beudrec, just mentioned, there are two more in the Morbihan district—le Rocher at *le Bono* and les Pierres Plates at *Locmariaquer*. A little further west, at *Gâvres* is a particularly interesting one which has tentatively been interpreted by L'Helgouach as a chief's tomb combined with a long ceremonial antechamber.

Erdeven

63/1

1 Kerzerho — Neolithic
alignments — Auray 1–2
188,45/307,15

Marked on the Michelin. The D 781 from Plouharnel (→ Erdeven) cuts across the alignments just before Erdeven (see map, page 157, Figure 100).

The main part of the alignment has 1129 stones set in six lines. They extend for 2 km, changing orientation *en route*.

2 Mané Groh or Mané Groc'h
compartmented passage grave
See *Plouharnel*

Gacilly, la

63/5

1 Le tablette de Cournon — Neolithic
gallery grave — Pipriac 5–6
(actually in the commune of Cournon) — 265,70/2315,95

For fanatics only—though the little town of la Gacilly is pretty.

Marked on the Michelin. In la Gacilly take the N 773 south (→ Redon). After crossing the bridge, continue past the N 777 turn-off left, and almost immediately take the small road left (marked 'dolmen des Tablettes'—but difficult to see). The monument is again signposted to the right at the top of the hill.

Originally, before being virtually destroyed, this monument may have been similar to the great chamber at *Essé*, Ille-et-Vilaine. But all that remains are two enormous broken and cemented capstones perched on concrete posts. One curious feature about this grave is that it is made of four different types of rock—Cambrian puddingstone, sandstone, quartz and Tertiary puddingstone, all of which are locally available.

2 Roche Piquée | Neolithic
menhir | Pipriac 5–6
264,70/2316,70

Marked on the Michelin. In la Gacilly take the N 777 south-west (→ Saint-Martin). Just before the placard announcing the end of la Gacilly the menhir is signposted and visible to the right. It is large, and has a fallen stone beside it.

Gâvres

Anse de Goërem | 63/1
angled grave | Neolithic
(Figures 88 and 89) | Ile-de-Groix 3–4
173,20/315,30

A fine grave, but rather at the end of nowhere, with military establishments strung out along the peninsula. For access see inset map, Figure 88. *Take a torch.*

This well-preserved grave lay below the dunes close to the beach of Goërem and was discovered and excavated between 1964 and 1967.

The mound is composed of a mass of stones and then a compact covering of earth. The passage, 9 m long, opens to the south, then a long chamber runs at right angles, east/west. The entrance to the chamber is demarcated by two closely set uprights and the chamber itself is divided into four compartments. The first three are intercommunicating, and marked off by pairs of uprights, while the fourth and end one is entirely sealed off by two transverse stones and dry-stone walling. The walls of the chamber are made of alternating orthostats and dry-stone wall panels. After the Late Neolithic construction and use, the entrance between the passage and chamber was sealed off with a large orthostat and a heap of stones, and the outside

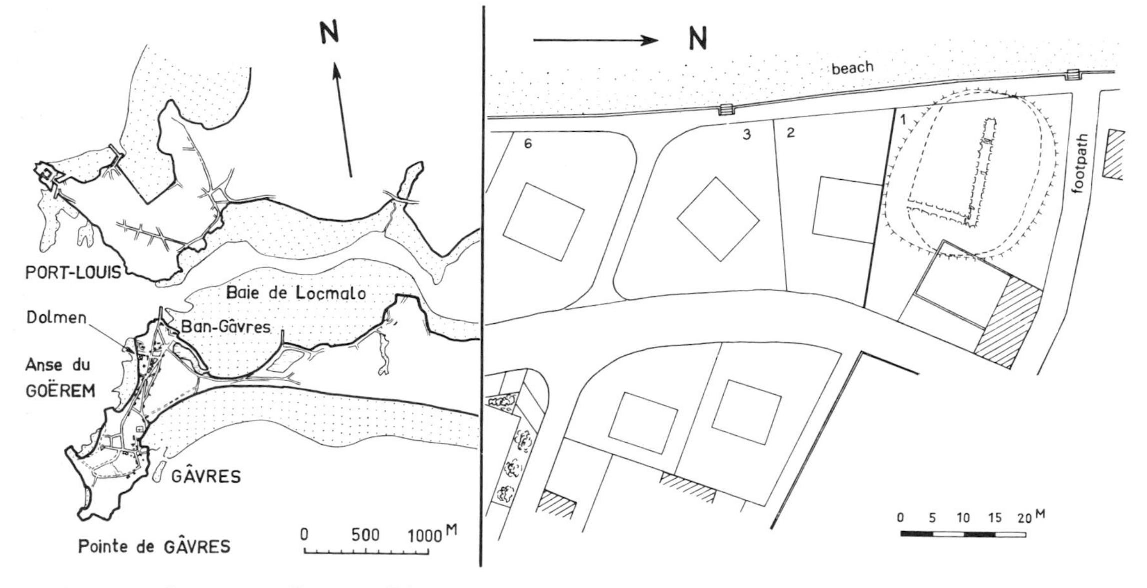

88 Access to the grave at Goërem, ***Gâvres***

entrance to the passage was likewise sealed off with stones.

There are engravings, but they are not easy to see: some signs on the two uprights flanking the passage entrance, on one upright in the first compartment, on four uprights in the second, and on one in the third. They include the anthropomorph motif.

Complete Kerugou pots were found in the terminal compartment. Some time after the grave had been closed up, Bell Beaker people reutilized this terminal compartment and deposited two beakers, a copper awl, two arrowheads and four gold plaques. The Conguel pot found in the passage is probably also contemporary with the Beaker intrusion.

There is a carbon-14 date of 2480 + − 140 bc (calibrated 3225 BC).

Although very similar to other angled graves, such as le Rocher, *le Bono*; les Pierres Plates, *Locmariaquer* or Luffang, *Crach* (all in Morbihan), this is the first one where a terminal compartment is clearly demarcated and where there is evidence that it was sealed off almost instantly. L'Helgouach has suggested that perhaps only this terminal cell was used as a grave, for an important chief or leader, and that the rest of the monument, in which the engravings were found, was part of a ritual complex.

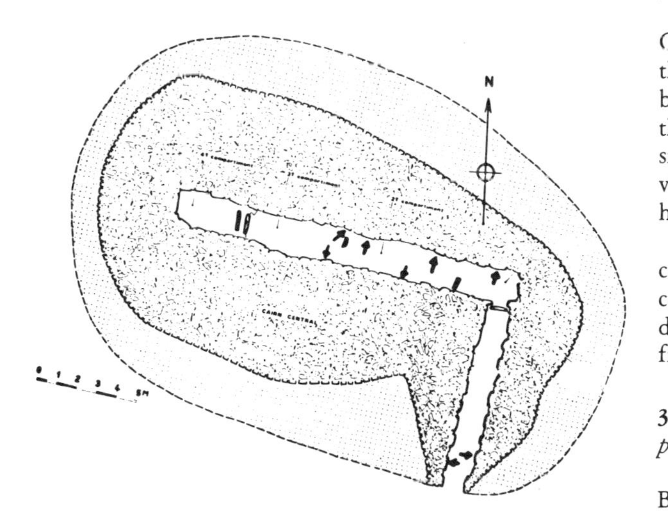

*89 Angled passage grave, Goërem, **Gâvres***
(→ indicates stones with engravings)

Ile-aux-Moines

63/12

Boats set out from Port Blanc (5.5 km south-east of Baden) every half hour from 7 a.m. to 9 p.m. during the summer (June to September) and from 7 a.m. to 8.30 p.m. during the rest of the year. Foot-passengers only, although cars can be taken by arrangement.

The farmers have left the island, the second-homers have taken over, so in late autumn and winter it is almost empty. But even in summer the southern end remains uncolonized and is a fine, though rather sad, place.

1 Kergonan — Neolithic
stone circle — Vannes 5–6
210,10/300,75

The village of Kergonan lies a third of the way down the island on the main, very small, road. The villages tend to drift into each other, so Kergonan is most easily recognized by the telephone box. Just after the house with the telephone box take the small track, right, for 30 m and the remains of an oval setting of uprights lie to the right again.

2 Penhap-Boglieux — Neolithic
passage grave — Vannes 5–6
209,45/298,68

Continue south down the main road to Penhap—near the south end of the island. The road makes a sharp bend at a calvary. At the further end of the bend take the track right (marked 'dolmen') for 125 m and the small orthostatic passage grave is to the left and visible from the track. If you reach a small white house you have gone too far.

There is a small chamber covered by one large capstone and an asymmetric passage with only one capstone in place. There are some minimal axe and U decorations on the small left-hand upright at the front of the chamber.

3 Pen-Nioul — Neolithic
passage grave — Vannes 5–6
209,30/297,50

Back to the main road and continue till the road gives out. Then on again along the track till that too ends. Then, if undaunted by the 'proprieté privée' sign, continue ahead down a small path to the end of the island and the dolmen (800 m in all from the road).

A very ruined passage grave with one inclined, and a couple of fallen, capstones.

Ile-de-Groix

58/12

From 21 June to 7 September there are at least six crossings daily from Lorient to Port-Tudy on the Ile-de-Groix. During the rest of the year there are at least three. The journey takes 45 minutes.

Camp de César — Iron Age
hill fort — Ile-de-Groix 1–2
161,50/309,70

Take the road west from Groix (→ Kervédan). After 4 km turn left to Kervédan. The camp lies about 600 m to the south-east on the coast.

This small but impressive cliff-castle defends less than an hectare of land. On the west side, the site is protected by cliffs; on the east by a marshy valley, and on the north, across the neck of the promontory, by a complex of banks and ditches. Excavations in 1939 showed a three-phase construction. In the first phase the innermost rampart, now standing 2.5 m above the ground surface, was erected. It was made of clay, rubble and turves with an interior and exterior revetment of dry-stone walling. It was associated with a rock-cut ditch, and beyond the ditch were more small dump-constructed banks and five shallow ditches. There was a central entrance across the whole complex. In the second phase the outer shallow ditches partially filled up, an oblique approach cut across them, and other small modifications occurred. And in the third phase the outer shallow ditch was covered over by a large bank, associated with a well-cut, flat-bottomed ditch with a counterscarp.

Within and adjacent to the innermost bank was a roughly circular stone-walled hut with four post-holes. It was built on top of the debris from the bank and is therefore later in date. On the hut floor were fragments of pottery including a sherd of a grooved urn, probably wheel-turned, possibly dating between 100 and 50 BC.

Langonnet

58/17
Church

Much of this church was reconstructed in the fifteenth and sixteenth centuries, but parts of the nave are Romanesque. There are very plain columns with simple capitals, and a couple of interesting rather archaic sculpted figures.

Larmor-Baden

1 Gavrinis — 63/12
an exceptional passage grave with marvellous engravings — Neolithic
Auray 7–8
206,40/298,95
(Figures 90 and 91)

Between 1 May and 15 September small boats regularly make the short journey from the little port of Larmor-Baden across the island-studded and oyster-studded bay of Morbihan to Gavrinis. In prehistoric times the bay would mainly have been land, only the deepest channels would have been invaded by the sea. Gavrinis would have been on a hill rising above the coastal plain. The boat passes close to the island of *Er Lannic* and you can see quite clearly how the rising sea-levels have covered the lower of the two stone circles. It is estimated that the sea-level has risen at least 5 if not 7 or 8 m since Neolithic times. The coastal area would have been one of the most fertile parts of Brittany, where riverine and marine fishing could easily be combined with agriculture. The rich graves, and industrial workshops like *Er Lannic*, allow glimpses of the well-organized and flourishing societies of fourth and third millennia Brittany.

On the island of Gavrinis a small footpath winds up to the grave entrance. *Don't forget a torch.*

Inside the great mound, a passage, the longest in Brittany, stretches for 13.8 m. It is paved with eleven wide stones: the fifth forms a sill, and the eleventh, with decoration on the three visible faces, forms the threshold to the chamber. In the relatively small chamber (2.5 × 2.7 m) both floor and roof are made from single huge slabs.

Almost all the uprights, one capstone and two paving stones are carefully engraved with panels of decoration. Many of the panels are divided by vertical

90 Engraved stones from the passage grave of Gavrinis, ***Larmor-Baden***

or horizontal lines. The eighth upright on the right of the passage has a lower panel with clearly defined axes and serpentine forms, and a middle panel with an anthropomorph and 'crook'; another, close to the chamber, on the left, has eighteen engraved axes. Some of these have splayed blades while on another stone the axes show perforations. They are obviously very similar to the beautiful jadeite axes found at Saint-Michel, *Carnac*. The anthropomorph motif is repeated over and over again, and, very recently, it has been recognized that the rows of upside down Vs that look rather like heads of grain are, in fact, rows of arrowheads with on occasion the bow depicted alongside.

Within the small chamber the decoration of the stones on each side of the chamber was clearly visualized as a unit with each pair of stones showing linked motifs. The holes bored on the left-hand side of the chamber may have been made by the nuns who sought refuge on the island.

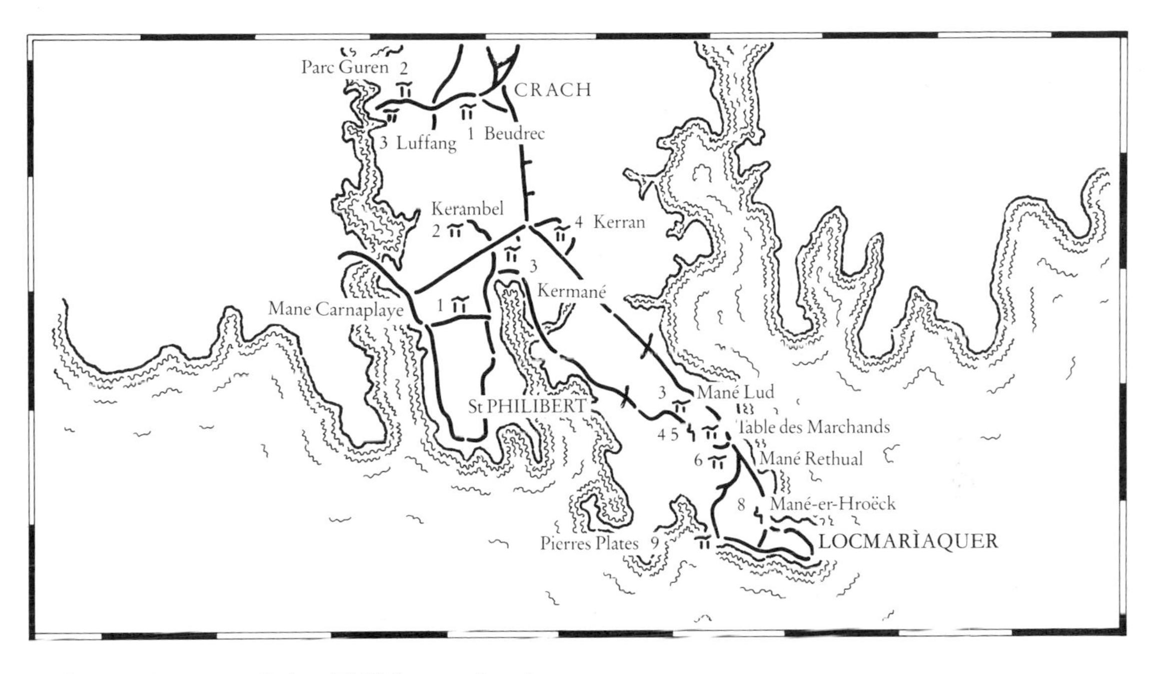

92 ***Locmariaquer – Saint-Philibert – Crach*** *region*

Gavrinis is being re-excavated and restored. The revetment wall on either side of the passage entrance stands 5 m tall, and the cairn appears to be quadrangular in shape. The excavator has discovered that some of the uprights within the passage and chamber also had 'bas-reliefs' on the side that faced away from the chamber—signs that would have been invisible once the mound had been erected. Thus the one at the back of the chamber, to the right, has on its reverse side two handled axes. The most exciting of these new discoveries is an upright that was once free-standing. On its reverse it has a handled axe and part of an ox and plough. The other part of this engraving is on the underside of the capstone of la Table des Marchands at *Locmariaquer*!

This recent excavation also uncovered a shaped stone on the top of the mound, with two sets of concentric half-circles. This may be a fragment of a statue menhir, somewhat similar to the fragments found at le Trévoux, Finistère and Guidel, Morbihan.

91 Engraved stone from the passage grave of Gavrinis, ***Larmor-Baden***

2 Er Lannic — Neolithic
stone circles — Auray 7–8
206,55/298,50

The boatmen going from Larmor-Baden to Gavrinis can usually be persuaded to detour for a closer look at the island of Er Lannic.

There are two stone circles (actually ovals), one with thirty stones more or less submerged, the other with forty-nine stones stretching up the beach. They have been heavily, and certainly inaccurately, restored, so that the fact that a hypothetical line from the centre of the Er Lannic monument to the centre of the oval on Ile-aux-Moines coincides with the rising sun at the summer solstice need not be of great significance.

Apparently pottery was found at the base of each upright in small cists. It is possible that the circles originally formed the edge of two large mounds, and that these are later in date than the main Neolithic occupation of the island.

The island is also the site of an important stone axe industry. The inhabitants worked in fibrolite which came from Port Navalo across the bay, and dolerite A from the interior, probably from *Plusulien*, Côtes-du-Nord. Many polishers and roughouts have been found. It is also famous for producing the greatest number and variety of 'vase-supports' in Brittany—there are at least 160 different examples. Many are in the museum at *Carnac* (and some are in the British Museum). There is also much Conguel ware and some Beaker ware.

Locmariaquer

63/12

Coming in from the north you can potter along from megalith to megalith, starting with the modest Kercadoret, ending with the fine angled grave of 'les Pierres Plates'. This itinerary could also be combined with the nearby *Saint-Philibert* site. See map, Figure 92.

1 Kercadoret — Neolithic
passage grave — Auray 7–8
(Figure 93) — 200,60/301,30

From Crach take the D 28 south, then the D 781 (→ Locmariaquer). (Or, from la Trinité, go north to join the D 781, then dip south-east, still on the D 781 and watch out for the junction with the road from Crach.) 1.25 km after the junction, still on the D 781, just before a left turning to Kercadoret, take either of two small paths going off to the right. The monument is 50 m away in a field.

The passage and mound have disappeared, only a small orthostatic chamber with one capstone remains. The floor was covered with pebbles.

There were rich Late Neolithic and Beaker grave-goods associated with this monument: barbed arrowheads, a copper point, eight fine barbed-and-tanged arrowheads, Bell Beakers.

2 Kervéresse — Neolithic
passage grave — Auray 7–8
(Figure 95) — 201,65/300,40

Directions as for Kercadoret (above), but follow the D 781 for another 1.5 km. Continue past the junction with the road left to Kerouarc'h, and the monument is in the second field, to the left of the D 781.

The passage has gone, but there is a fine chamber covered with a large capstone, and there are a few engraved 'crooks' etc. on three of the uprights, and a mass of cup-marks on the underside of the large capstone.

A Primary Neolithic shouldered vase and a fragment of a stone battle-axe were found in the grave.

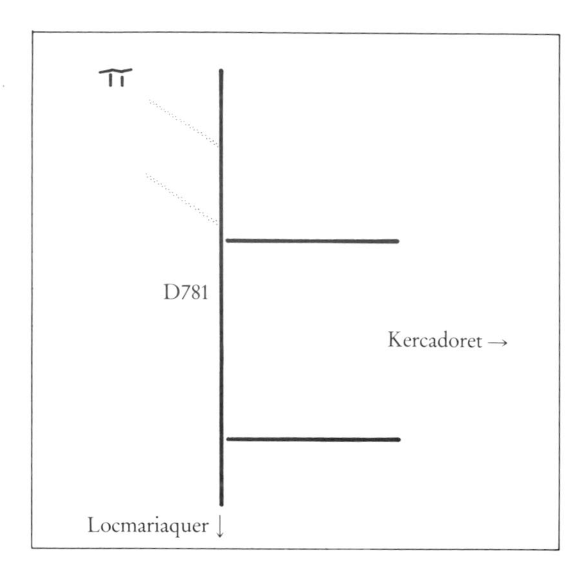

93 Access to Kercadoret passage grave, ***Locmariaquer***

3 Mané-Lud — Neolithic
large mound — Auray 7–8
and passage grave — 202,50/299,45
(Figures 94 and 95)

Marked on the Michelin. Continue on down the D 781 and just after the placard announcing Locmariaquer, a signposted path on the right leads up to the grave. *Torch.*

The path leads over the top of the huge, roughly rectangular mound which is about 125 × 60 m and 10 m high. The passage grave is in the western side and the vast broken capstone protrudes above the surface. (It is possible that the passage was there before the mound was constructed; the set-up is very similar to Saint-Michel, *Carnac*.)

The long passage and chamber are made of orthostats with dry-stone walling in the interstices. The floor of the chamber is paved with great slabs below which is a layer of imported soil and small stones.

There are many isolated and quite roughly executed engraved signs on eight of the uprights in the passage and chamber. One upright on the left-hand side of the passage has a dozen U signs, one in the chamber has both U signs and 'crook' signs, while the last upright on the right side of the passage (just before the chamber), has a fine cross-section—an anthropomorph, a U, schematic axes, dotted circles. Finally on the back-stone of the chamber the natural relief has been picked out and added to, to make a double-U motif.

Below the paving stones numerous variscite beads were found.

Within the large mound, according to Le Rouzic, excavations at the end of the nineteenth and beginning of the twentieth century uncovered a circle of low uprights at the east end. These were associated with horses' skulls. A small corbelled chamber in the middle of the circle contained burnt human bones.

94 Passage grave, Mané-Lud, ***Locmariaquer***
(→ indicates stones with engravings)

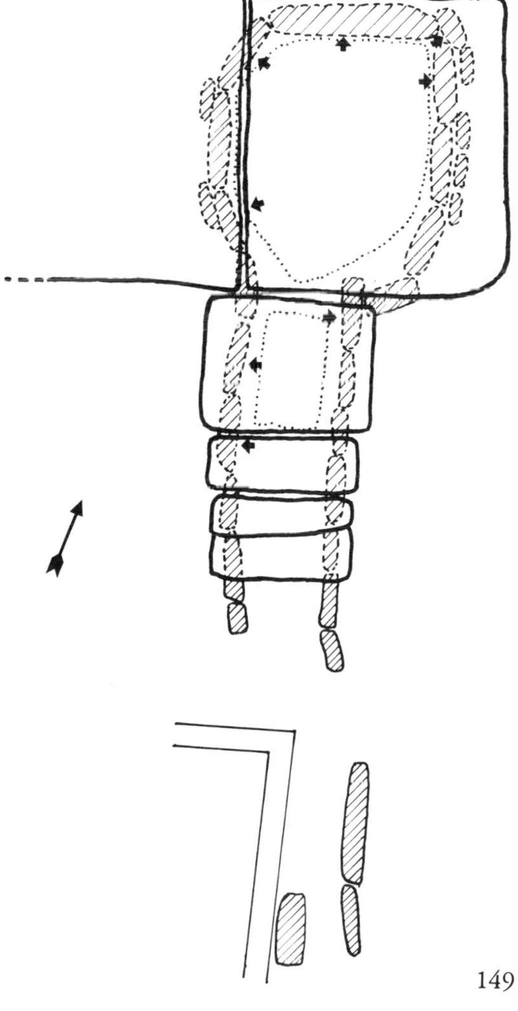

95 Engraved passage grave uprights,
Locmariaquer
1 and 2 Mané-Lud
3 Kervéresse

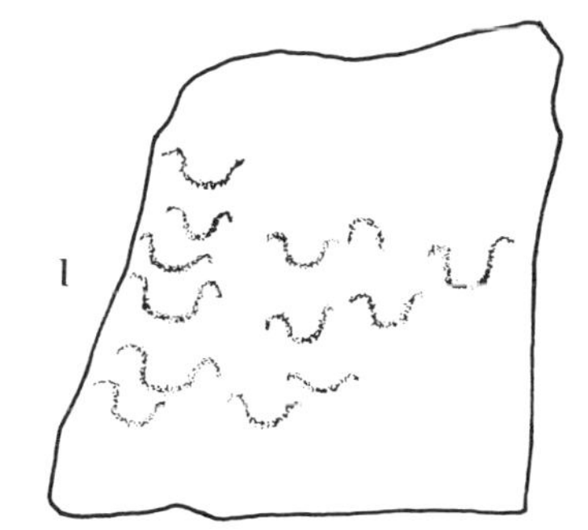

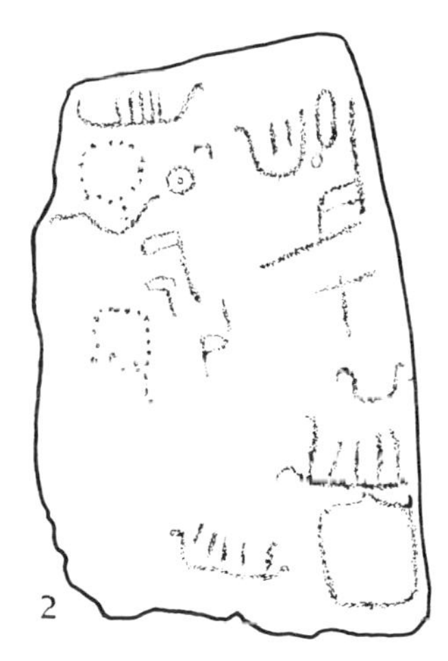

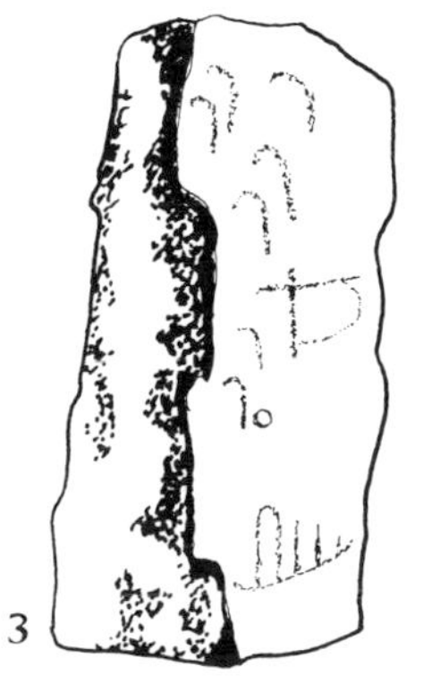

4 Table des Marchands Neolithic
passage grave Auray 7–8
(Figure 96) 202,60/299,20
Marked on the Michelin. On again, another 400 m and one of the best-known monuments is signposted to the right. (Visits are often enlivened by blood-curdling explanations offered by small local boys—for a price.) *Torch*.

The grave has been heavily restored. It is mainly remarkable for its huge capstone (8 × 4 m, and weighing 50 tons), and for the fine relief-carved back-stone which is shaped into the ogival form of an anthropomorph and then has four rows of 'crooks' sculpted on it. Below these are another series of engravings but these are now below the ground-surface. On the back of the stone are the two engraved semicircles which frequently form part of the anthropomorph motif. This back-stone, unlike the rest of the monument, is made of Tertiary sandstone, and, freshly carved, it would have gleamed in a quite spectacular way. It was probably originally free-standing and was only later incorporated into the grave. The great chamber capstone was also, like the one at Mané-Rethual (see below), free-standing. Indeed it now seems that it was part of an enormous stone of which one part was incorporated into the passage grave of Gavrinis, *Larmor-Baden*. The capstone at la Table des Marchands has a large engraving of an axe with a handle, and another which seems to be part of an ox and plough.

5 Men-er-Hroëk Neolithic
menhir Auray 7–8
Next to la Table des Marchands. 202,55/299,15

The largest menhir in France. It has fallen and broken into four pieces. The base fell one way, the rest the other (one small piece is missing). In all it is 22 m long and when placed upright would have stood 16 or 17 m above the ground. It must weigh about 350 tons and has been shaped. On the upper surface of the second largest fragment is an almost obliterated relief-carved axe. Legend has it that it fell when blasted by lightning, or during an earthquake – or it may have fallen while being hoisted into position.

The menhir is central to Professor Thom's 'lunar observatory' theory, and was, supposedly, an artificial foresight to provide very accurate long-distance alignments to the extreme risings and settings of the moon (see alignments, *Carnac*, page 131 for details).

The menhir is at the southern end of a long, low, mound (most of which was destroyed when the car-park was constructed) which contained a small chamber in its northern section.

Within the church cemetery which lies close to the menhir and la Table des Marchands is the site of a small Roman theatre—it would seem that Locmariaquer was quite an important Gallo-Roman settlement. There are no visible remains.

6 Mané-Rethual (Rutual) Neolithic
passage grave Auray 7–8
202,70/298,90
Turn off the D 781 as for la Table des Marchands, but immediately take a road left and continue for 150 m to a footpath, right, marked 'Dolmen de Mané Rethual'. When after 100 m, the footpath forks, keep left.

A fine passage grave still partially imbedded in its mound. There is a long passage, then an antechamber 2.3 m square, and then the chamber 3.7 × 3.4 m. (The 'chamber' right at the back was created by excavators.) It is built of orthostats and dry-stone walling and the entire chamber and part of the antechamber is covered by a huge, broken capstone 10 × 4 m. This capstone is very interesting, for on the underside is a large, engraved anthropomorph. It can hardly be seen and it seems likely that this capstone originally stood upright—thus it was a 'statue menhir'. Another small capstone over the ante-chamber has a hafted axe engraving, as does the right-hand divider between antechamber and chamber. There are also a couple of 'crooks' on the orthostat next to the divider, within the antechamber.

7 Church Church
The small church of Locmariaquer has suffered some heavy-handed restoration. The choir and transept are eleventh and twelfth century. There are fine capitals in the transept-crossing.

96 Back-stone in la Table des Marchands, ***Locmariaquer***

8 Mané-er-Hroëck Neolithic
large mound Auray 7–8
(Figure 97) 203,35/298,15

Marked on the Michelin. The mound is signposted south of Locmariaquer on the C 4. Take the footpath to the right for c. 50 m. This mound, rather overgrown and tumbled, still stands 10 m high and has a diameter of 100 × 60 m. It contained a number of closed cists (the passage is a quite recent construction). The largest, central cist, 4 × 3 m, made of coarse stonework and covered with two stones, contained a grandiose offering: more than ninety small fibrolite axes, a dozen jadeite axes, including one perfect specimen 35 cm long, and quantities of variscite beads and pendants. All were found below the chamber floor except for one polished stone axe, placed on the paving next to a flat perforated serpentine disc. Among the blocking stones of this cist were the fragments of an engraved menhir, which, on reconstruction, showed a central anthropomorph motif, within which was a U sign and two opposed 'crooks'. Above and below were many hafted-axe signs. L'Helgouach has recently suggested that the U and 'crook' signs are closely related to the anthropomorph motif, and when found alone, may represent a shorthand rendition.

Mané-er-Hroëck forms one of a series of large Neolithic mounds in the Gulf of Morbihan area. The others are Mané-Lud, *Locmariaquer*; Er Grah, Locmariaquer (now destroyed); Saint-Michel and le Moustoir, both at *Carnac*; and Tumiac, *Arzon*.

97 Stele found within the mound of Mané-er-Hroëck, ***Locmariaquer****, 1.7 m high*

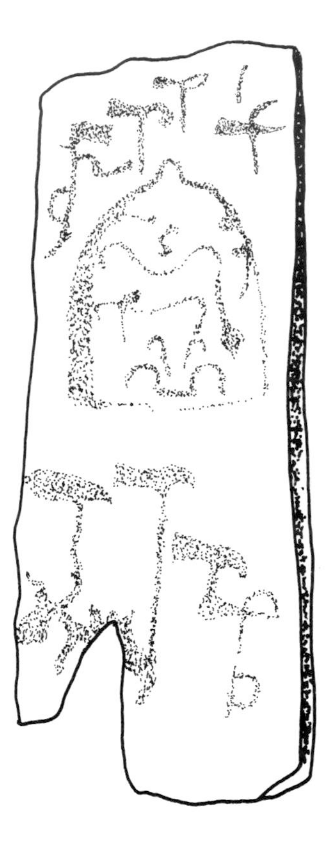

9 Les Pierres Plates Neolithic
angled passage grave Auray 7–8
202,35/297,50

From the Mané-er-Hroëck mound continue south on the C 4 till you reach the beach, then turn right for a kilometre. Les Pierres Plates lies directly to the right of the road. *Torch.*

The entrance opens to the south. The first part of the passage is 7.5 m long. It then makes an angle of 135° and continues a further 13.5 m. At the angle is a small cell. The terminal chamber, only 1.7 m long, is marked off by a septal stone. Both the height and width of the passage and chamber increase from the entrance to the back.

Fourteen of the uprights have fine engravings, including a number of anthropomorph motifs. There are three particularly fine examples in the chamber, and another on the fourth upright on the right of the passage, beyond the angle. In each case the outline is doubled or even trebled, the motif is divided vertically, and each side contains different signs.

These angled graves (Gâvres; le Bono; Luffang etc.) seem to be quite late in date—they may be contemporary with the more northerly gallery graves (Introduction page 34).

Locminé

1 Gallery grave (actually in the commune of Bignan)
63/3
Neolithic
Elven 1–2
216,50/(2)332,32

From Locminé take the D 767 south (→ Vannes) for 2 km. Then turn east onto the V 7 (Saint-Just). Go through the hamlet of Saint-Just and just beyond is a small road, right (south), marked to Kergonfalz. On the corner of the junction is a small moss-encrusted gallery grave with three capstones at various odd angles.

2 Bignan-Moustoirac
Neolithic
passage grave
Elven 1–2
216,40/(2)332,40

An excuse for exploration rather than an end in itself.

From the gallery grave (above), back-track 20 m down the road towards Saint-Just and take the track slanting off to the right (north) just beyond a great chestnut-tree. Walk another 20 m then leave the track and go right, straight up the pathless hillside through bracken and prickly gorse for about 40 m. The passage grave is below a large pine-tree.

There is not much sign of the passage, and the chamber is small and covered with one capstone. The grave is still imbedded in its mound.

Locoal-Mendon

1 Mané-Bras du Mané-er-Hloh
63/2
passage grave
Neolithic
Auray 1–2
191,00/313,30

Not easy to find. From Belz take the D 16 (→ Locoal-Mendon). After 5 km turn right (south) onto the C 6 (→ Kerdelam, Loqueltas). Continue for 300 m (passing a quarry) and turn onto a forest-track to the right. This quickly becomes rather narrow. Another 175 m brings you to a clearing; take an even smaller path to the left and then bear slightly right to the monument.

There is a fine long passage and a big, almost round, chamber (3.9 m diameter) covered with a huge capstone (4.3 × 2.3 m) which is further supported by two uprights within the chamber. One of these, the larger, southern one has a few faint engravings on the side facing the passage.

2 Mané-Bihan de Mané-er-Hloh
Neolithic
angled passage grave
Auray 1–2
190,850/313,00

Directions as for Mané-Bras (above). Then continue another 375 m. Just before a small turning left, take a small path to the right of the C 6. Continue for 150 m and the angled grave is to the right and 75 m from the path. The mound is 28 × 25 m. The angled passage opens to the south onto a straight façade made of small stones and dry-stone walling. The first 5.5 m of the passage runs south/north, then it angles south-east/north-west and continues another 4.5 m, then it angles yet again and runs east/west for 7.5 m. The roof of the passage is at different heights in the different sections, but rises from 1 m at the entrance of the passage to almost 2 m at the entrance to the chamber.

A fragment of a Chassey pot, a carinated Kerugou pot with vertical ribs, fragments of at least three Bell Beakers, a tanged arrowhead and a Grand Pressigny blade were found.

3 Loqueltas
Neolithic
passage grave
Auray 1–2
191,05/311,05

Directions as for Mané-Bras and Mané-Bihan (above), but continue on the C 6 to Loqueltas. In Loqueltas take the first—unmarked—right turn (at a chapel) and at the furthest house strike out left of the road around the field. The monument is just visible in front of a copse, 200 m from the road.

A well-preserved grave: passage 3.7 × 0.9 m, chamber 2.6 × 2.2 m with two lateral chambers. Only a couple of capstones in place.

Malestroit

1 Saint-Gilles
63/4
Church

A fine mixture of twelfth- and sixteenth-century styles. There is a double nave, one side of which has a Romanesque transept-crossing, southern transept-arm and tower.

2 Hardys Béhélec Neolithic
passage graves Malestroit 1–2
(actually in the commune 242,75/2322,05
of Bohan)

Fanatics only! From Malestroit take the D 776 south-west (→ Vannes), after 1.5 km turn right (west) onto the D 321 to Saint-Marcel. In Saint-Marcel continue straight ahead on the V 6 for 1 km, watch carefully for the modest pillared entrance to the farm of Hardys Béhélec on the left. Go up the drive to the farm and ask for directions.

In the trackless forest are the ruins of two, perhaps more, passage graves.

Melrand

Saint-Fiacre 63/2
mound Bronze Age
Bubry 1–2
194,90/347,30

From Melrand take the D 2 north (→ Pontivy). Continue for 2 km. The mound lies to the left of the D 2 between a left turn, D 159, and a left turn to Saint-Fiacre. It is clearly visible from the road.

Many of the grave-goods that were found within the central wooden coffin are now in the Ashmolean Museum at Oxford. There is a carbon-14 date for the coffin of 1950 + – 135 bc (calibrated 2455 BC).

Merlevenez

church 63/1
Church

The church was originally part of the twelfth-century monastery, and the church foundations, three exterior doorways and north-west and eastern contreforts date to this period. The south doorway is particularly fine. Inside, the pillars and sculpted capitals are also of this date, surmounted by fifteenth-century arches. Well worth a visit.

Monterrein

1 Les Chambrettes 63/4
gallery grave Neolithic
(actually in the commune
of Chapelle Caro)

From Monterrein take the D 8 south (→ Rouffiac, la Gacilly) and 2.5 km south of the village a small sign 'dolmen' on the right indicates the footpath.

Fairly ruined and well hidden by bracken. There is a small uncovered terminal cell, now open-ended but with traces suggesting that it was originally closed.

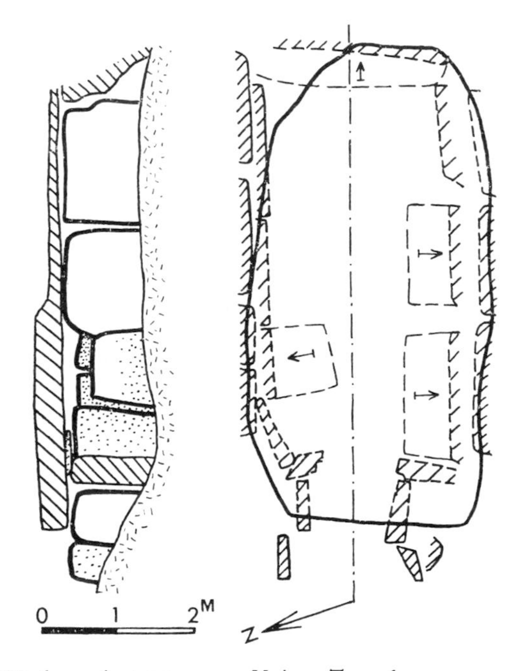

98 Angevin-type grave, Maison Trouvée, ***Monterrein*** *(Chapelle Caro)*

2 La Maison Trouvée Neolithic
portal gallery grave Ploërmel 5–6
(Figure 98) 247,60/331,40

Marked on the Michelin. At Monterrein take the small road west (→ la Ville-au-Voyer). At the first crossroads (1.5 km from Monterrein) turn right to Ville-au-Voyer. After the hamlet, when the road swings right, take the track left. The dolmen is signposted. Continue for 400 m, past the wood, to a fork where the track deteriorates. Then strike out left around the field to a copse of oak-trees.

Not immediately impressive, but closer examination reveals an enormous capstone covering a narrow entrance passage and a large rectangular chamber 4.3 × 2 m. Several of the uprights in the chamber have fallen. There are the remains of a round mound.

This portal gallery grave is an outlier—like the ones at Cournon, *la Gacilly*; and *Essé*, Ille-et-Vilaine—of a type that is more massively concentrated in the Saumur region of the Loire.

Moustoir, le

See *Saint-Jean-Brévelay* 63/3

Moustoirac

Kermarquer 63/3
menhir Neolithic

There is a route called the Circuit des Mégalithes et Menhirs—more or less a misnomer and frustrating if your mind is set on viewing authentic prehistoric remains. But if you are not such a purist it is a fine tour through crags and pine-forests—with just the occasional megalith.

From Locminé take the D 767 south, then the V 1 west to Moustoirac. Follow the signs—'menhirs' and 'mégalithes'. After 3 km 'no. 1' is a small dolmen to the right of the road. There follows a plethora of signs. When eventually you reach no. 8 you have got the real McCoy—the menhir of Kermarquer. It is 6.72 m high, shaped and has some not immediately apparent engravings on three faces: two 'crooks' low down on the south-west face, two less well-defined opposed 'crooks' low down on the south-east face and three 'crooks' on the north-east face (plus two less clearly defined markings). All are relief carved—which means that the surrounding area had to be pecked away, more work than simple engravings.

If you do not want the preamble and simply want megalith 8—the menhir of Kermarquer—you can go out of Moustoirac on the V 2 (→ Kerhéro and Auray). Then after 1 km branch left onto the V 5 (→ Croix-de-Bois). Another 3 km take a right at Kermarquer la Lande and the first field-track to the left leads to megalith 8.

If you do not go right, but continue on towards Croix-de-Bois, 300 m from the Kermarquer turn-off, to the right in the wood, is another, modest, menhir (Kerara menhir).

Locminé; *Colpo*; *Saint-Jean-Brévelay* are all close at hand.

Plaudren

See *Saint-Jean-Brévelay* 63/3

Ploemeur

58/12

Cruguellic Neolithic
passage grave with lateral cells
(Figure 99) Lorient 5–6
63,69/320,20

From Ploemeur take the road west (→ Fort Bloqué). After 4.75 km (c. 0.75 km *before* Fort Bloqué) take the small road right (→ Cruguellic). After 100 m, at a fork, the dolmen is signposted to the right. Follow the road, which, after the houses, becomes a track, for 275 m to an open space. The passage grave is immediately to the right.

This grave, partially destroyed during and after World War II, has been restored. The passage opens to the south-west, in the long side of a now flattened sub-rectangular mound, 20 × 12 m, with a dry-stone revetment wall, doubled and sometimes trebled in places. The 3 m long passage prolongs as a corridor for a further 5 m, flanked by five orthostatic cells—two on either side, one at the end. Each cell is 2 to 3 m square. Only two of the cells and the corridor are reasonably well preserved. Two of the uprights in the corridor have anthropomorph engravings, though these are hard to see.

Among the grave-goods were some fine Middle Neolithic ware (Chassey type, sometimes with decoration). In the corridor and south-east cell were the remains of two flat-based Seine-Oise-Marne type pots and two collared flasks. In the north-west cell were

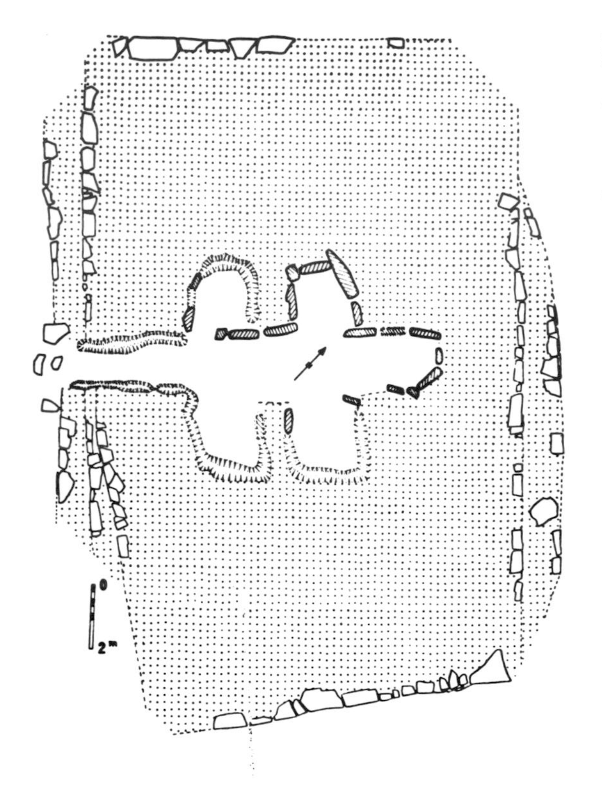

99 *Cruguellic passage grave at* ***Ploemeur***

fragments of a fine Bell Beaker. There was also a lot of lithic material: two dolerite A axes, a rough fibrolite adze, a tiny ecologite axe, two pendants, thirteen steatite beads and some small flints including geometric microliths (the latter particularly concentrated outside the entrance).

The grave is similar to the ones at Keriaval, *Carnac*, and Larcuste, *Colpo*, both in Morbihan, and further afield, to some of the English Severn-Cotswold group.

Ploërdut

church 58/18

The nave and aisles of the church are eleventh and twelfth century and there is an interesting and relatively rare alternation of plain and buttressed pillars. The capitals are decorated with geometric motifs.

Plouharnel

(See map, Figure 100)

1 Kergavat 63/2–12
passage grave Neolithic
Auray 5–6
190,95/302,70

From Carnac take the D 781 (→ Plouharnel). The monument is 200 m before the placard signalling Plouharnel, on the right.

Fairly ruined. The passage opens to the south-east, the chamber is covered by a large capstone. A fine Bell Beaker was found in the lateral cell.

2 Rondossec Neolithic
passage graves Auray 5–6
190,30/303,10

Marked on the Michelin. In Plouharnel take the D 781 (→ Erdeven), and, still within Plouharnel, the 'dolmens de Rondossec' are signposted down a road to the left.

A very impressive monument. The more northerly passage grave (nearest the road) opens to the south-east, has an 11 m long passage and a squarish chamber 3.5 × 2.5 m. To one side of the chamber is a small lateral cell, 1.2 × 1.8 m, its entrance partially closed by two uprights. This lateral cell is covered by a capstone which is blocked below two of the capstones of the main chamber.

The second passage grave has a similar orientation, a slightly shorter, 7.5 m passage, an even larger and finer chamber, 6 × 2.5 m, and no lateral cell.

The third, southern grave is not orientated at quite the same angle and is much smaller: the passage is 4.7 m long, the asymmetrical chamber 3 × 1.8 m. The latter is composed of small uprights surmounted by dry-stone walling. It seems to be planned in order to permit the construction of a large circular mound (c.20 m diameter) covering all three structures. This mound is still partially intact.

The grave-goods found in 1849 have disappeared; some fibrolite axes, a barbed-and-tanged arrowhead and nine quartz beads found in 1920 are in the museum at *Carnac*. A unique find, a vase containing two finely decorated gold bracelets is now at Paris in the Musée des Antiquités Nationales. These bracelets and vase are clearly an intrusive offering. They were

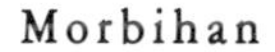

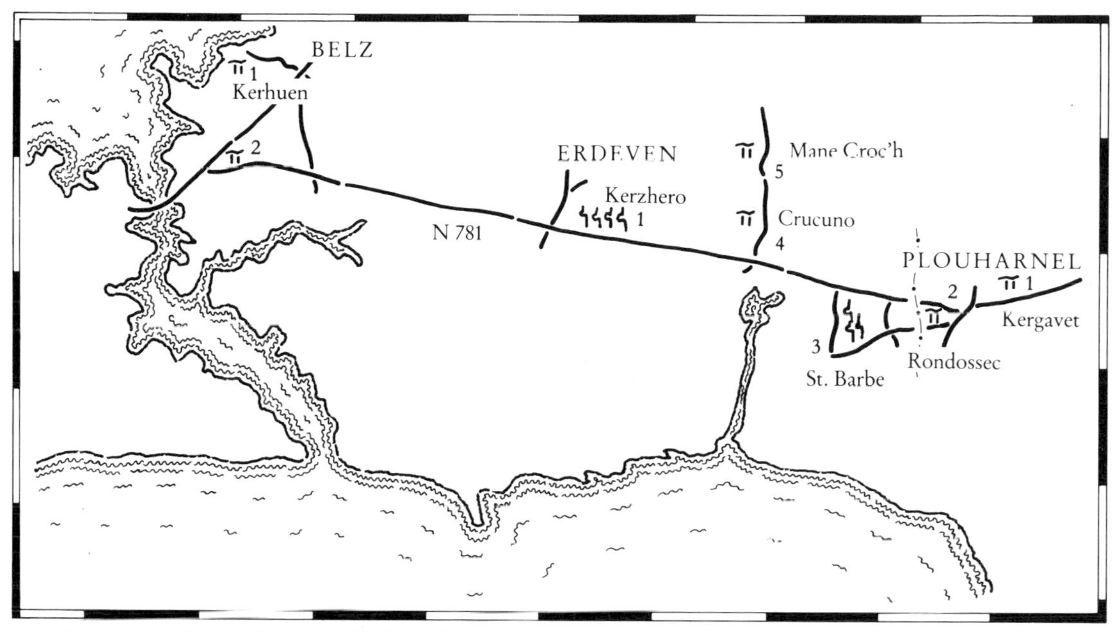

100 ***Plouharnel – Erdeven – Belz*** *region*

placed within a small dry-stone walled structure in the centre of the northern chamber. They are very similar to examples from western Iberia which are found in association with Palmella points and date to the Early Bronze Age, or even a little earlier.

3 Sainte-Barbe — Neolithic
alignment — Auray 5–6
189,20/303,20

Marked on the Michelin. Directions as for Rondossec (above), but continue on the D 781 (→ Erdeven), and after 2 km turn left (→ Sainte-Barbe). The alignments are to the left of the road, just before the village.

There are several closely set stones, probably part of an oval setting, and at least two long rows of stones. According to Le Rouzic there were at least fifty stones but many have fallen and are half buried.

4 Crucuno — Neolithic
passage grave — Auray 1–2
189,70/305,90

Marked on the Michelin. Directions as for Sainte-Barbe (above), but continue on the D 781 for another 900 m after the Sainte-Barbe turn-off (or 2.5 km from Plouharnel), to a turning right to Crucuno. The chamber is on the further side of the Crucuno village green.

The passage—which according to early accounts was very long—has been destroyed; only the large orthostatic chamber covered with a huge capstone, and a smaller capstone marking the junction between passage and chamber, remain.

The grave, free-standing since records have been kept, has been used variously as a place to brake hemp, a bandstand for village festivities and as a prison for the village idiot. It was saved just as it was about to serve its ultimate function—as building stone for the villagers.

5 Mané-Groh or Mané-Groc'h — Neolithic
compartmented passage grave — Auray 1–2
(actually in the commune of Erdeven) — 190,20/306,35

As for Crucuno, then take the road north-east out of Crucuno (→ Saint-Laurent). After 700 m there is a 'zone de protection' sign to the left of the road. Another 30 m and the passage grave is to the left of the road.

Within a long mound, c. 22 × 10 m, is a compartmented passage grave and a small closed cist. The passage, opening to the south-east, is 6 m long. It debouches into a large chamber, 3 m long, and runs as a corridor between two pairs of cells. These are boxed off by uprights, and each one, 1.5 m square, is covered by a capstone. The capstone(s) that originally covered the corridor probably rested on top of these.

A similar grave at Mané-Bras just over 1 km to the north-west is very ruined. It lies alongside two passage graves.

Plumelec

63/3

Could be combined with *Trédion*, *Saint-Jean-Brévelay* and *Locminé*, or with the fifteenth-century calvary at Guéhenno, 6.5 km north of Plumelec.

La Migourdy — Neolithic
passage grave — Elven 3–4
227,30/(2)324,63

In Plumelec take the D 1 south (→ Trédion). After 3.2 km turn right on the V 8 (→ Cadoudal). Then the first left, marked 'Le Tiernan (sans issue)'. Continue over the bridge nearly to the end of the road. Where the road finally swings left to the farm, continue ahead up a track. Near the summit of the hill stop at the first field on the right. Go into the field and there is a bosky copse about 100 m to the right. In front of it is a neat, small passage grave with a large capstone and the remains of a mound.

Saint-Aignan

Castel Finans — 58/19
hill fort — Iron Age
Pontivy 3–4
201,65/68,95

From Saint-Aignan take the D 31 north-west (→ Barrage Guerlédan). Continue past a turn-off left to Bon Repos (1.5 km from Saint-Aignan), and just beyond the road takes a big bend. On the further side of the bend take the second stony trackway to the left (500 m from the Bon Repos turn-off). This goes up parallel to, and then across, a great cascade of stones which forms part of the Iron Age rampart—at this point running south-west/north-east. The stone track becomes a dirt track and reaches a T-junction. To the right is a small chapel. To the left, after 50 m, there is a fine view of the bank swinging to the north-west.

Wheeler and Richardson (1967:104) describe Castel Finans as follows: a great cascade of stones with a gap on the south end with an inturned entrance; at the west end there is an outer line of rampart extending 50 m beyond the inner line and between these two are traces of two smaller banks with a ditch between them. A central gap through the western system may mark another entrance. The ramparts enclose about 25 hectares.

Saint-Gildas-de-Rhuys

1 Le Net — 63/12
gallery grave and menhir — Neolithic
Vannes 5–6
210,10/294,10

Turn south off the D 780 at the hamlet of le Net (3.25 km east of Arzon), onto the D 198 (→ Saint-Gildas-de-Rhuys), and 150 m down the road, opposite a white gate, go left into the field. The menhir, 50 m from the gallery grave and 20 m from the field entrance, is visible from the road.

The gallery grave is somewhat obscured by brambles but consists of a very long chamber, 15.2 m, and then, separated by two transverse stones, a terminal cell 6.3 m long.

Coarse pottery and Bell Beaker ware, one barbed-and-tanged arrowhead, two stone pendants, a dagger of Grand Pressigny flint, and a few other stone tools were found.

2 Church — Church

The church of Saint-Gildas-de-Rhuys is a large sober edifice with a fine eleventh- and twelfth-century transept, choir, ambulatory (with carved capitals) and side-chapels. Four of the capitals have been reused as holy-water stoups. There are interesting medallions and three bas-reliefs on the outside walls of the choir.

The village of Saint-Gildas began as a sixth-century monastery. In the twelfth-century Abelard became the abbot and wrote to Heloise: 'I live in a barbaric country whose language is unknown to me and horrible; I only have contact with savage people, my walks are along the inaccessible edge of a violent sea.' The monks eventually tried to poison him—he just managed to escape.

The monuments at *Arzon* are only a few kilometres away.

Saint-Jean-Brévelay

63/3

Could be combined with *Locminé*, *Colpo*, *Moustoirac*, or, going eastwards, *Plumelec* and *Trédion*. For a general description of the area see *Colpo*.

1 Keramel — Neolithic
menhir — Elven 5–6
220,80/(2)325,82

Take the D 778 from Saint-Jean-Brévelay south (→ Vannes). After 3 km the menhir can be seen to the left of the road.

2 Roh Coh Coët — Neolithic
gallery grave — Elven 5–6
219,72/(2)325,32

Directions as for Keramel (above), but continue for another 700 m (3.7 km from Saint-Jean-Brévelay) and then turn right (west) onto the V 3 (→ Kerguillerme—the signpost is hard to see; it is just before the turn-off to Le Moustoir). After 0.5 km the dolmen is clearly signposted. The last 150–200 m involves a pleasant walk through a wood.

A very large gallery grave, partly built up against a great granite outcrop. There seems to be a terminal cell. Three capstones remain—one is immense.

3 Le Moustoir — Iron Age
stele

Directions as for Roh Coh Coët (above), but continue on the D 778 for another 200 m and take the next turning west, to le Moustoir. In the hamlet, behind the small church, is an Iron Age stele with a cross engraved on one face.

4 Men Goarec — Neolithic
gallery grave — Elven 5–6
(actually in the commune of Plaudren) — 220,20/(2)323,07

Marked on the Michelin. Directions as above but continue on the D 778 (→ Vannes) for another 2 km after the le Moustoir turn-off. Then turn right onto the small road to Colpo. Another 0.5 km and then, to the left, a small menhir, la Tête du Lion, is visible. The gallery grave is to the left of this and further from the road (250 m). Neglected and brambly.

The mound and elliptical setting of revetment stones are visible. The passage opens to the east and is 5.7 m long and 1.4 to 1.6 m wide. There is only one capstone in place. On the external side (west face) of the back-stone of the chamber is a pair of sculpted breasts—a symbol frequently found in more northerly gallery graves such as Prajou-Menhir, *Trébeurden*, Côtes-du-Nord, or to the east, in the great gallery grave of *Tressé*, Ille-et-Vilaine.

A satisfactory inventory of grave-goods includes Seine-Oise-Marne ware, fragments of collared flasks (again found in the northern graves), thinner ware (with a heavy filler) including a carinated round-based bowl similar to Kerugou ware; sherds of harder, fine-tempered beige ware, probably Middle Neolithic, and fragments of Bell Beaker.

At Kérallant, 200 m north of Men Goarec there was another small gallery grave. This had a cartouche with a handled axe—now in the Musée de Bretagne, *Rennes*, Ille-et-Vilaine. There was also a passage grave.

5 Coléo — Neolithic
menhir — Elven 5–6
219,15/(2)323,40

As for Men Goarec. Continue on the road to Colpo and 1.5 km beyond the Men Goarec gallery grave, to the right and visible from the road, is the large menhir of Coléo.

Saint-Philibert

63/12

A visit to these monuments could well be combined with those in the *Locmariaquer* area (see map, page 147, Figure 92).

1 Mané Carnaplaye — Neolithic
passage grave — Auray 7–8
198,45/301,40

From Carnac, take the D 781 to la Trinité-sur-Mer and on towards Locmariaquer, then right, onto the D 28 to Saint-Philibert. In Saint-Philibert take the C 2 west (→ la Trinité). After 500 m, just past the turning left (south) to Kermouroux and Kercadoret, take a small path to the right of the road. 350 m further on, just within a fine forest, and on the left, is the grave.

A very pleasant walk, especially in the blackberry season. However the grave is not spectacular: a small chamber, the remains of a passage and one capstone.

2 Petit-Kerambel (Mané-Han) — Neolithic
passage grave — Auray 7–8
198,60/302,38

From Saint-Philibert take the D 28 north to the junction with the D 781 and continue across onto the small road to Kerambel. (Alternatively, from Carnac, take the D 781 to la Trinité-sur-Mer and then continue in the direction of Locmariaquer. 3 km beyond la Trinité-sur-Mer take the small turning left to Kerambel.) Then the first turning left (just beyond Kerambel) and continue until the road ends at a small, very pretty farmstead. The monument is 30 m behind, and to the right of the house.

The chamber was originally built of low orthostats surmounted by dry-stone walling on which the massive capstone rested. Now the dry-stone walling has gone and the capstone has settled onto the orthostats. There are three capstones still in place over the low passage.

3 Kermané (Roch-Vras) — Neolithic
passage grave — Auray 7–8
199,40/301,99

Directions as for Petit-Kerambel (above) but do not turn off the D 781. Continue in the direction of Locmariaquer and 250 m beyond the turn-off to Kerambel (250 m *before* the junction with the D 28) take the very small road to the right. When the road peters out, the monument is on the left.

A free-standing orthostatic structure. The mound has entirely disappeared.

4 Kerran — Neolithic
passage graves — Auray 7–8
199,00/302,31

Directions as for Petit-Kerambel and Kermané (above), but continue on the D 781 (→ Locmariaquer) and just beyond the junction with the D 28 (→ Crach) turn left (→ Kerran). In the second field on the right, in a mass of gorse, are the remains of three very ruined passage graves.

Saint-Pierre-Quiberon

63/11

Quiberon, once an island, is now joined to the mainland by a narrow strip of Holocene sands. Not one of my favourite areas, having become a rather endless tourist resort, but still, there is a fine walk along the wild western cliffs particularly from Pontivy to Vivier, and here and there a few monuments remain.

1 Le Moulin — Neolithic
alignment — Quiberon 1–2
188,70/294,00

In Saint-Pierre-Quiberon take the small C 2 road to the east of the main D 768. Just before the end of the town, the alignments are signalled to the right of the road with a 'zone de protection' placard.

About twenty not-too-large stones are still in place. Some extend east-south-east below the high-tide mark.

2 Roh-en-Aud — Neolithic
passage grave — Auray 5–6
188,20/294,85

The grave is in the rue du Dolmen, Saint-Pierre-Quiberon. Go into Saint-Pierre-Quiberon on the D 768 and turn right, west, onto the Route du Roch (→ Portivy, Côte Sauvage, Pointe du Percho). The rue du Dolmen goes off to the right just before the edge of the town.

There is a large (3.9 × 4 m), almost square, free-standing chamber and a very short passage. The chamber is built of orthostats surmounted by large flat stones which originally supported the roof. Only two small capstones are still in place.

3 Beg-en-Aud — Iron Age
Iron Age camp — Auray 5–6
186,35/295,55

A great walk, and a great view. Directions as for Roh-en-Aud (above), but continue down the Route du Roch through Portivy to the Côte Sauvage. Then follow the coast round southward for about 1 km to the first really large peninsula. The bank and ditch are clearly visible. The peninsula drops sheer to the sea on three sides. The neck was protected by a bank and ditch c. 50 m long.

Early Iron Age sherds were found on the surface of the camp, some are in the museum at *Vannes*.

4 Croh-Colle — Neolithic
Neolithic camp — Quiberon 1–2
187,00/292,95

If you are walking from Portivy, continue on past Beg-en-Aud, down the coast to 'Poste no.10, lieu-dit Portstang'. Or direct from Saint-Pierre-Quiberon, take the west coast-road, the D 186 (→ Quiberon) and having gone past the turning left to Portivy continue to Poste no.10.

Not much to see, except a fine seascape. A semicircle of very small stones across the neck of the spur demarcates the extent of the Neolithic camp. It is a bit like le Pinacle on Jersey. Some early Conguel pottery was found on the site.

5 Pointe de Conguel — Neolithic
menhir de Goulvarh — Quiberon 1–2
190,73/289,25

From Quiberon take the D 200 east for c.1.5 km. At the Hôtel Sofitel take the footpath north from the car-park for 250 m.

A fine menhir, which Thom considered as a possible sight-line for the Grand Menhir of *Locmariaquer*.

6 Belle-Ile

Belle-Ile is very flat, but there is a great line of cliffs, particularly on the north-west corner, interspersed with small sandy coves. So the medieval/Iron Age ramparts can be combined with fine walks.

The ferry for Belle-Ile sets off from Port Maria, south of Quiberon. There are frequent crossings and it takes 45 minutes.

Pointe de Vieux Château, Sauzon — Iron Age
hill fort — Quiberon 5–6
177,95/278,45

Starting from the small port of Sauzon (which looks a nice place to stay), at the church take the road to l'Apothicairerie. Follow the signs.

At l'Apothicairerie, rock-cut steps lead down the cliff and round under a natural sea-cut arch. Fine rocks and swirling seas.

From the car-park if you run your eye along the far cliff horizon to the north you can see the low protuberance of the Vieux Château ramparts. You can get there along the cliff top, but the paths bifurcate alarmingly. A foolproof way is to go back down the road for 800 m and take the first track left (c. 200 m before the houses of Kerguec'h). The track continues for 750 m down to a small sandy creek with a low stone wall across it. Either take the small path through the bracken following the left edge of the creek, which after 250 m brings you onto the ramparts, or take the small path through the bracken following the right edge and after 250 m watch for a fine view, left, of the ramparts. This path leads up to a sandy track which takes you down to the next somewhat larger cove.

The Vieux Château promontory is dominated by a medieval motte and a large bank and ditch that cut off an area of five hectares. Below the bank are traces of an earlier bank and an inturned entrance, while outside these earthworks are three small banks and ditches. The earlier bank and these external earthworks are presumably Early Iron Age. A few sherds, possibly first century BC, and slingstones have been found.

7 Hoëdic — Mesolithic

A somewhat arduous journey from Port Maria to Houat and then on to Hoëdic. There are usually only two boats a day. There is little visible prehistory, but this little island is important as the site of a Mesolithic cemetery within which certain inhumations were singled out and were associated with depositions of antler. A similar set-up was found on another small island, Téviec, which lies to the west of the narrow strip of sand that joins Quiberon to the mainland. Here some of the burials, also with antler depositions,

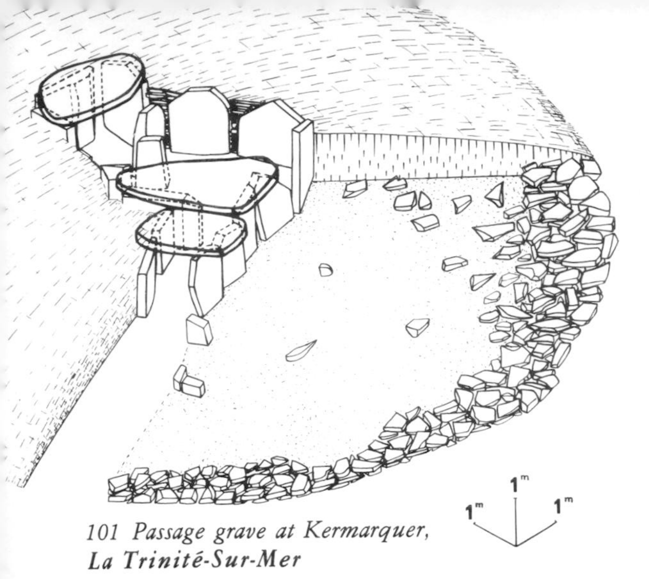

101 Passage grave at Kermarquer, La Trinité-Sur-Mer

were placed in quite substantial stone-built graves—possible forerunners of the megalithic tombs (Introduction page 24).

Trédion

Kerfily — 63/3
gallery grave — Neolithic
Elven 7–8
230,82/(2)319,13

Take the D 1 south from Trédion for 3 km to the turn-off right to les Princes Saint-Germain, then back-track 400 m to the first house on the right. Then ask. The grave is about 250 m from the road, but hidden in the Bois de Kerfily.

A small rather curiously constructed gallery grave. There are two outer long walls of orthostats, two inner walls that slant inwards and meet in the centre (*arc boutés*), and a large capstone that covers both inner and outer walls. Remains of the mound can be seen.

Trinité-sur-Mer, la

Kermarquer — 63/12
passage grave — Neolithic
(Figure 101) — Auray 7–8
195,95/302,50

From la Trinité-sur-Mer take the D 186 north (→ Auray) for 0.25 km (past the turning right to Kerispert) and in the hamlet of Kermarquer take the unmarked right turn and immediately walk up the field-track to the left. After 160 m the monument is to the left.

The chamber is almost square and has a lateral cell on the west side, the entrance partially blocked by an upright. The short passage opens to the south-east and there are the remains of a circular mound, which has a dry-stone revetment. The three capstones were replaced in 1927.

There is a fine inventory of grave-goods: Middle Neolithic pottery, fragments of Bell Beaker, pots with finger-nail impressions, barbed-and-tanged arrowheads, and two gold objects.

Vannes

63/3

A pleasant small town, now administrative centre of Morbihan and once chief city of the Celtic Veneti. It was this tribe that Caesar defeated in a great naval battle in 56 BC, probably in the Gulf of Morbihan (Introduction page 53). In 27 BC it became a *civitas*, Darioritum. During the third century troubles a circuit wall with U-shaped towers was built and enclosed 5 hectares. Glimpses of this can be seen in the base of the great medieval rampart with its fifteenth-century crenellations.

The cathedral retains the twelfth-century plan and tower-base.

Musée de la Société Polymathique du Morbihan, Château Gaillard, 2 rue Noé — Museum

This fifteenth-century parliamentary building houses a large collection of local prehistoric material. There are maps, photos, plans, not much explanation, but a lot of interesting material from local sites, mainly Neolithic and Bronze Age and some Roman.

Open 1 July to 14 September from 9.30 a.m. to 12 noon, and 2 to 7 p.m. From 15 September to 30 June from 9.30 a.m. to 12 noon, and 2 to 6 p.m. Closed on Sundays.

Normandy

Calvados

The plain of Caen is flat, fertile and rather monotonous. Rich argicultural lands go hand-in-hand with fine large churches. Southwards the plain gives way to the more rugged, more isolated, more beautiful hills of the Suisse Normande.

Auvillars

church 54/17

The church has a nice twelfth-century doorway decorated with a sculpted arch of flattened heads, surmounted by a chevron arch.

Bayeux

54/15

Although nothing remains to be seen of the Iron Age settlement, Bayeux takes its name from the Baiocasses, a Celtic tribe. This was their capital. Later it became Augustodurum, centre of a Gallo-Roman *civitas*. Part of the town was fortified during the third century against the northern pirates.

1 Notre-Dame cathedral

The cathedral lies almost directly above a Gallo-Roman temple. It is a fine church largely rebuilt in the Gothic style; the only Romanesque features are the façade towers (1077), reinforced in the thirteenth century with heavy contreforts, the nave dating to the late twelfth century, and the eleventh-century crypt below the choir. The extensive decoration of the nave, particularly the low-relief wall decoration and the carved spandrels are rare for this period.

2 Bayeux tapestry
(Figure 103)

To the south of the cathedral on the other side of the rue le Forestier is the Musée de la Reine Mathilde.

This houses the Bayeux tapestry, over 70 m long, recounting in vivid detail episodes associated with the Norman conquest. It does not, in fact, have much to do with Queen Mathilde, for it was almost certainly commissioned by Odon of Conteville, bishop of Bayeux, at the end of the twelfth century, to adorn Bayeux cathedral after he had rebuilt it.

Open from 15 March to 15 October from 9 a.m. to 12 noon and 2 to 6.30 p.m., and during the rest of the year from 9.30 a.m. to 12 noon and 2 to 5 p.m. An English commentary on headphones is available.

3 Musée de Peinture Museum

The museum is to the north of the church, on the place Cour des Tribunaux. It houses a few local objects, Neolithic, Bronze and Roman.

Opening times as for the Bayeux tapestry, and entrance on the same ticket.

Bény-sur-Mer

menhir 54/15
Neolithic

Just south of Bény on the D 79 turn right at the calvary towards the hamlet of Bracqueville. Go through the hamlet to the end of the road. Bracqueville farm then lies to the left. Take the track right, in front of the farm and after 350 m the track left. The menhir is 200 m down this track to the left. It is 1.4 m high.

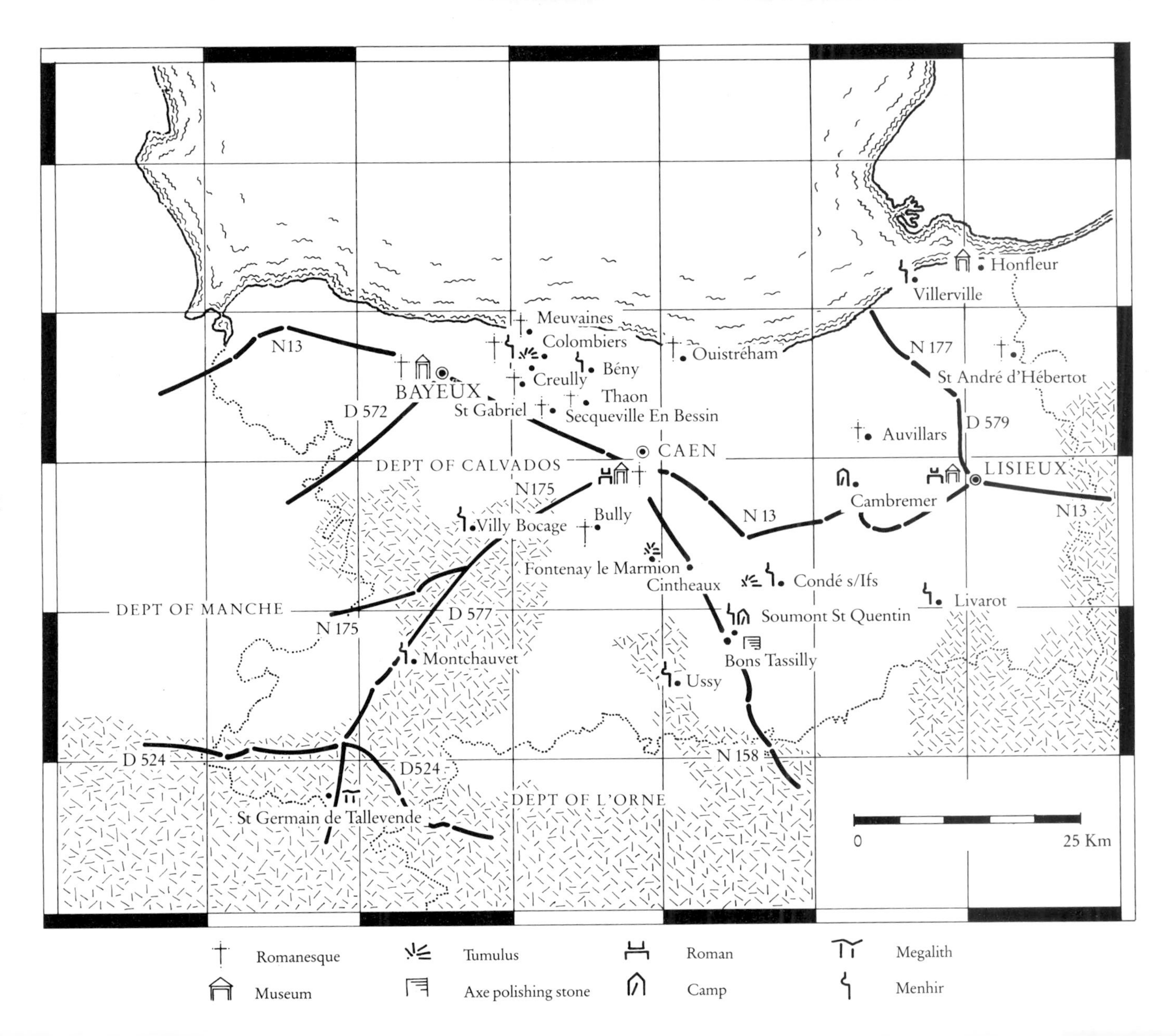

Honfleur
Villerville
Meuvaines
Colombiers
Bény
Creully
Thaon
Ouistréham
N 177
St André d'Hébertot
N13
BAYEUX
D 572
St Gabriel
Secqueville En Bessin
D 579
Auvillars
CAEN
DEPT OF CALVADOS
LISIEUX
N175
Cambremer
N 13
N13
Bully
Villy Bocage
Fontenay le Marmion
Cintheaux
Condé s/Ifs
Livarot
DEPT OF MANCHE
D 577
Soumont St Quentin
N 175
Montchauvet
Bons Tassilly
Ussy
D 524
N 158
D524
DEPT OF L'ORNE
St Germain de Tallevende
0
25 Km
Romanesque
Museum
Tumulus
Axe polishing stone
Roman
Camp
Megalith
Menhir

Bons Tassilly

two stone-axe polishers 55/12
See *Soumont-Saint-Quentin*

Bully

Saint-Martin 54/15–16
Church
The only noteworthy feature is the tympanum over the door with oriental motifs that may represent Daniel among the lions.

Caen

54/16
See the Michelin Green Guide to Normandy for an excellent street plan and more architectural detail.

1 Musée de Normandie Museum
Lies within the ramparts of the castle at the centre of Caen.

In among the local enthnography and Norman furniture is the Seine-Oise-Marne material from the trench grave at Bardouville in the Eure and a reconstruction of the Iron Age grave from Ifs.

Open from 10 a.m. to 12 noon and 2 to 6 p.m. every day except Tuesday.

2 There are various items on view at the University of Caen.

In the hall of the Faculté des Lettres is an interesting statue of a female deity, probably Gallo-Roman, found at Saint-Aubin-sur-Mer.

In the Faculté de Droit, on the fourth floor, there is a fine marble pedestal found at Vieux, south of Caen, in 1580. The stone, which suffered many vicissitudes before arriving in the law department, has a long inscription. It originally carried the statue of Titus Sennius Solemnis, priest to Mercury, Mars and Diana and the inscription recounts his many virtues and his many patrons—it includes 'letters of recommendation' from the latter.

102 Département of Calvados

3 Saint-Etienne or Abbaye aux Hommes Church
Rue Guillaume le Conquérant and place Monseigneur des Hameaux (next to the fine eighteenth-century town hall, once also an abbey building).

The abbey was founded by William the Conqueror, c. 1062–6, part of a penance imposed by Lanfranc when he lifted the excommunication incurred when William married his cousin, Mathilde. The church was consecrated in 1077 and ten years later William was buried there.

The austere western façade with its two slender towers was finished in 1080. (The spires are a later, Gothic, addition.) The nave is eleventh century except for the sexpartite vaulting erected in the twelfth century.

The abbey was much battered during the sixteenth-century Wars of Religion and was then restored in the seventeenth century.

4 La Trinité or Abbaye aux Dames, place Reine Mathilde Church
This nunnery, the counterpart of Saint-Etienne and part of the same penance, was founded by Queen Mathilde in 1060. It took seventy years (1060–1130) to build and shows a wider variety of styles than Saint-Etienne. The nave is very long, with nine bays and three levels, while the transept is very wide. The Romanesque chapels lead off from the north transept.

From the south transept there are stairs down to the fine crypt (1090) where groin-vaulting rests on sixteen columns, some with interesting decorated capitals. The chancel is of the same date and again has fine groin-vaulting, while the apse is a little later. Mathilde was buried in the abbey and the black marble tomb-slab of 1083 can still be seen near the choir entrance.

5 Saint-Nicolas, rue Saint-Nicolas Church
A lovely Romanesque church constructed in 1083 by the Benedictine monks from the Abbaye aux Hommes for their tenant-farmers. It has hardly been touched since, except for the addition of a fifteenth-century tower flanking the façade.

A gently melancholic graveyard encircles it. Unfortunately both graveyard and church are rarely open.

103 The ***Bayeux*** *tapestry*

6 The Castle
Within the ramparts, the exchequer, a great building of which the ceiling and roof have been restored since the last war, is a rare example of twelfth-century civil architecture.

Cambremer

Château des Anglais — 54/17
Iron Age camp — Iron Age
Lisieux 5–6
430,60/163,35

Take the D 101 southwards from Cambremer to join the D 50 and turn right on the latter (→ Caen). Continue for 4 km to the Carrefour Saint-Jean, then turn right on the D 16 (→ Pont-l'Evêque). Take the second road right at the Chapelle Pontfol. Follow this rough road up to the crossroads at the top of the hill and then bear right for a third of a kilometre and there is the camp.

The camp, on the summit of Mount Argis, overlooks the valley of the Auge. It has natural defences on two sides while the third, the east side, is protected by a bank and ditch. The bank rises 5 m above the interior of the camp and 10 above the present bottom of the ditch. The ditch is 20 m wide. The defended area is about 24 hectares.

Cintheaux

54/16
Church

The large twelfth-century church has fine external decoration on the archivolts of the windows and door.

Colombiers-sur-Seulles

1 Long barrow — 54/15
(Figure 104) — Neolithic

Coming west from Reviers on the D 176 (→ Colombiers-sur-Seulles, Bayeux), continue for 2 km and the mound lies within a copse to the left of the

road on the plateau.

First excavated and partially destroyed in 1825–6 by Caumont. More destruction in 1900. Then partially re-excavated by Lagnel in 1969–71.

The barrow is 50 m long, the west end is 5 m, the east end 16 m wide. Caumont found a central chamber (1.46 m in diameter) and another chamber at the west end, both containing bones, many of which had been burnt. A bronze bracelet was found but its original position was uncertain. Lagnel refound the central chamber and discovered a narrow passage leading into it from the north. He also found a series of internal revetment walls, and an outer revetment wall at the west end of the mound which contained two menhirs.

Such long barrows have a wide but sparse distribution stretching west through Brittany. Recently a long barrow was found at Vierville, Manche, alongside a round mound containing a passage grave. *If* these structures are contemporary then the long barrow should date to the Early or Middle Neolithic, for the pottery from the round mound had affinities with the Breton Carn and Castellic ware and also contained Chassey ware similar to that from la Hogue and la Hoguette, *Fontenay-le-Marmion*, Calvados.

2 La Pierre Debout — Neolithic
menhir — Bayeux 3–4
393,20/1181,35

300 m further down the road, beyond the long barrow (above), on the far side of the next small crossing and to the left of the road is a carefully shaped oolitic limestone menhir, 2.12 m high with a small hole near the summit. It has been re-placed on a concrete base. Several graves were found nearby with bracelets and Roman medallions and indeed the road that crosses the D 176 is the old Roman road from Veys to Bac du Port.

3 Colombiers — Church
small twelfth-century church

Condé-sur-Ifs

La Pierre Cornue — 54/16
menhir — Neolithic
(Figure 105) — Mézidon 7–8
419,85/1152,10

In Condé travelling south on the D 88, turn right 200 m beyond the church on the CV no. 2. The menhir is 25 m to the right of this road, and 120 m from the D 88 turn-off.

A fine 4.2 m menhir of local calcareous conglomerate.

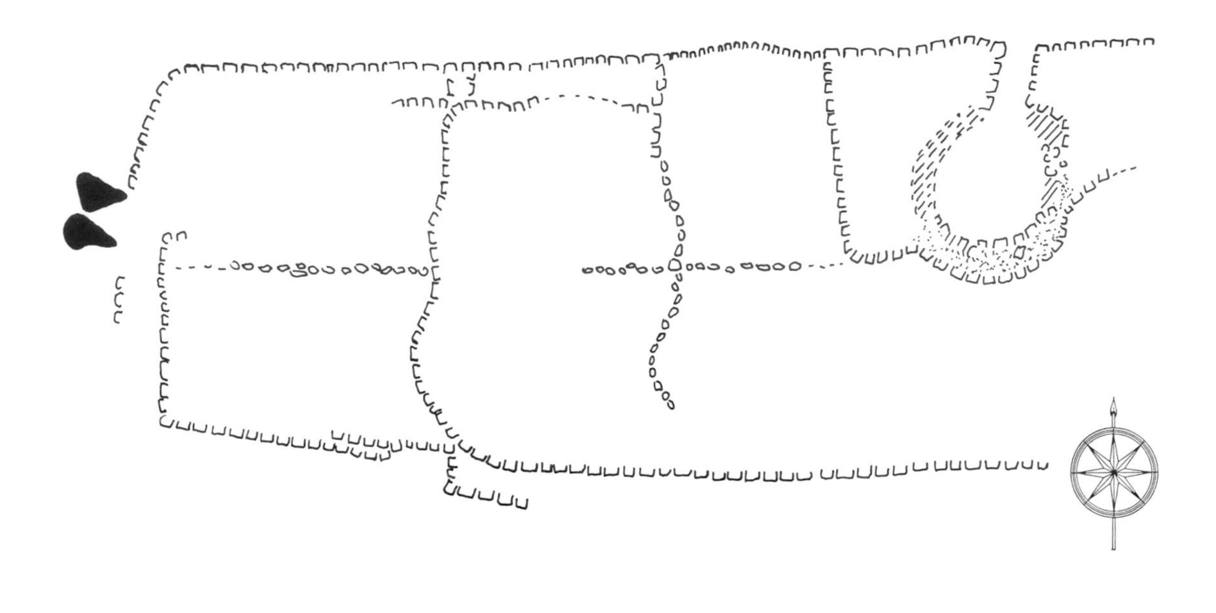

104 The long mound of ***Colombiers-sur-Seulles***

105 La Pierre Cornue, ***Condé-sur-Ifs***

106 Multiple passage grave, la Hogue, ***Fontenay-le-Marmion***

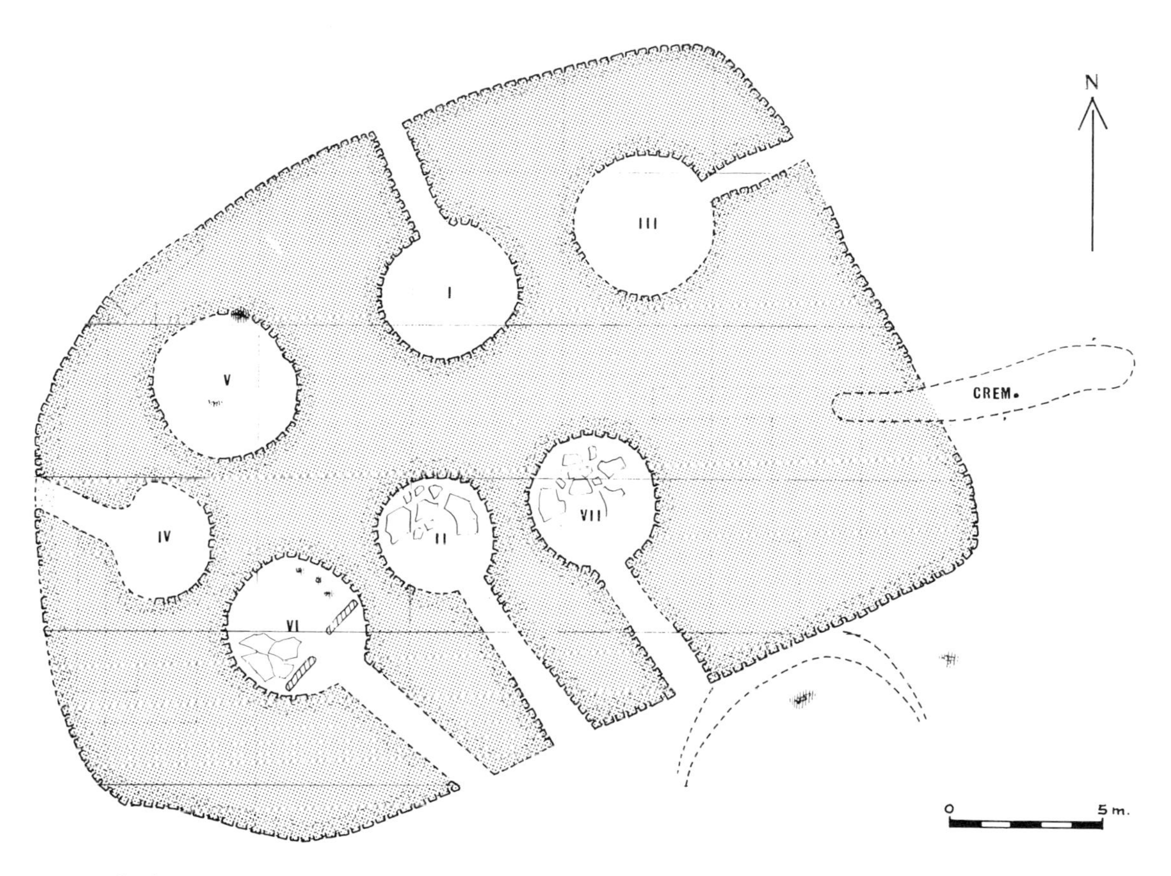

*107 Multiple passage grave, la Hoguette, **Fontenay-le-Marmion**, with the Seine-Oise-Marne crematorium alongside it. This monument is no longer visible*

Creully

church 54/15

Although rather heavily restored in the nineteenth century this church provides an interesting example of the late Romanesque style. Both inside and out there is cautious use of ogival arches.

Fontenay-le-Marmion

La Hogue 54/16
multiple passage grave Neolithic
(Figure 106) Mézidon 1–2
402,95/1158,60

Go out of Fontenay-le-Marmion north-west on the D 41B (→ May-sur-Orne). At the fork keep right and just beyond the village, and 50 m to the right of the road, is the large mound. The guardian lives in the house next to the mound.

The mound was first excavated in 1829 but the main excavation, by Coutil, was between 1904 and 1917. It has recently been restored and in part, re-excavated.

The mound, 49 m long from north to south and 37 m from east to west, is made of chalk fragments. It covers twelve chambers, set in two rows of six, five with passages going off to the east, five to the west, one to the south and one to the north (the northern one was destroyed by early quarrying). The passages are all made of dry-stone walling and roofed with capstones. The chambers are dry-stone walled and were originally corbelled. Some of them have internal features. For example, within the largest chamber (M on the plan) there is a capstone placed on two uprights, as well as some small uprights to the south. Whilst within chamber N, a rectangular area against the south wall is delimited by small slabs, 40–50 cm high, and has a fine paving.

108 *Bandkeramik sherds from la Hoguette,* ***Fontenay-le-Marmion***

109 *Chassey pot from chamber P, la Hogue,* ***Fontenay-le-Marmion***

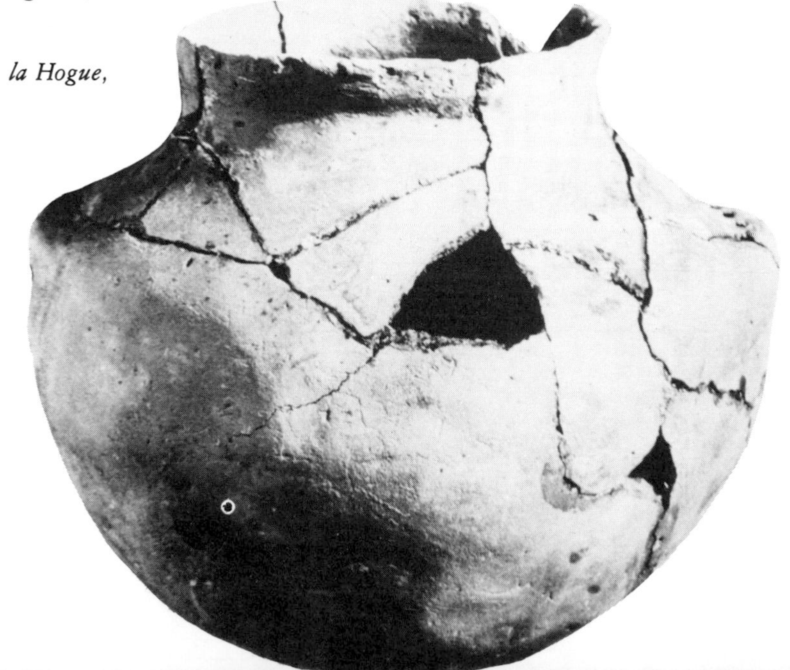

Bones, burnt and unburnt, were found in all the chambers. In chamber P a small cist made of four inclined stones contained a skull minus its lower jawbone. Close by an upturned pot was found within another small cist (Figure 109). This same chamber had more human bones placed below the paving and a concentrated mass of shells. In the south-west angle of chamber M (the large chamber), below a carefully placed layer of slabs, were two sets of human vertebrae, children's skulls, the lower jawbone of an elderly man, a canine tooth, the skull and bones of a crow, skulls of water-rats and weasel, a bovid humerus and a fox's skull. In other parts of the chamber were more human bones and many small rodent bones. And so it goes on in all the chambers, with finds also of flints and sherds, and, in chamber S, another pot which contained a small polished hard-stone axe and many rodent bones.

High in the mound a solitary Roman burial was found with four or five coins.

Although no longer visible a similar, very interesting, multiple passage grave mound was found 500 m from la Hogue in the direction of the church at Fontenay (Figure 107). La Hoguette was excavated quite recently and thus provides much more information than la Hogue. La Hoguette had a sub-rectangular mound, 31 m north-east/south-west and 21 m north-west/south-east, made of chalk. Below lay a paving which extended beyond the mound. There were eight passage graves in two parallel rows. The roofs had originally been corbelled. One chamber had an internal division. In many of the chambers flexed burials were found, varying in number from five to fifteen. Two chambers had been disturbed and the skulls had been buried separately. There were very few grave-goods, but a little Chassey pot was found on the paving outside the mound, while below the paving in one chamber and around the periphery of the mound were some fine Band-keramik sherds—probably contemporaneous with the construction of the mound (Figure 108).

A unique feature at la Hoguette was a crematorium, placed up against, and breaking into, the east side of the mound. This was an area, 8 × 1.5 m, that contained burnt calcareous stone, ash and charcoal and the burnt bones of at least sixteen individuals. There were also a few retouched flints, two perforated stone beads, one hundred and fifty shell beads below a skull, one collared flask and fragments of another. Clearly this structure is later than the mound and was constructed by Seine-Oise-Marne people.

Honfleur

54/8

The museum is not particularly special, but the small port is worth a big detour. It is on the estuary of the Seine and the quays are lined with tall seventeenth-century houses. In the place Sainte-Catherine is a wooden church with a double boat-shaped nave built to celebrate the departure of the English at the end of the Hundred Years' War. It was at Honfleur that the Impressionists first met, and many worked here.

Musée du Vieux Honfleur — Museum
Quai Saint-Etienne (partly in the church of Saint-Etienne).

There are a few local La Tène and Roman exhibits (and some much more interesting paintings by Boudin!).

From April to October the museum opens every day, from 10 a.m. to 12 noon and 3 to 6.30 p.m. From November to 14 January it closes on Friday, and from 15 January to 15 February it is closed altogether.

Lisieux

54/18

Lisieux was a centre for the Celtic tribe of the Lexovii—who threw up *murus gallicus* defences against Caesar on the nearby Castelier site. It became a Gallo-Roman commercial centre and port, Noviomagus Lexoviorum. The artisans' quarters were in the heart of modern Lisieux; the residential quarters, including an amphitheatre, to the west in the commune of Saint-Désir.

In the first half of the third century the town was probably sacked by the Saxons. It was rebuilt and part of the town was fortified. But it was sacked yet again between AD 368 and 370 and the suburbs were destroyed. The survivors retreated to the defended area and patched up the damaged walls.

1 Column Gallo-Roman
In a small square at the junction of rue Pont Mortain and place de la République is a third-century AD column and a small section of a first- or second-century Roman road.

2 Baths Gallo-Roman
The grand public baths and some of the surrounding houses have only recently been excavated.

There were separate baths for men and women, and the women's bath included a particularly fine fresco with a pastoral scene on the upper part, and imitation marble panels below.

The men's bath had a fine portico.

The baths were built in the late first century and early second century AD, were modified in the mid second century, and were destroyed by burning in the late third century, at the time of the Nordic invasions.

South of the baths, one particularly fine house was built over an earlier building. The corridor and at least one of the rooms were decorated with frescos. The house was gradually abandoned, pillaged and camped in, and finally torn down sometime before the late third-century invasions.

3 Musée du Vieux Lisieux, Museum
38 boulevard Pasteur
One room has some local Neolithic, Bronze and Roman material.

Open from 2 to 6 p.m. every day except Tuesday.

Livarot

La Pierre Tournante or 54/17
Tourneresse Neolithic
menhir Livarot (West) 7–8
(Figure 110) 441,75/1148,40
From Livarot take the D 4 east (→ Orbec) and at the cemetery on the outskirts of Livarot turn left onto the D 149. Continue past the first crossing and after 140 m there is a small forest-track to the left. 4 m before this track, to the left of the D 149, a tiny path goes over the field bank and leads to the menhir, only 7 m from the road but hard to see because of the trees.

The menhir is of puddingstone and stands 2 m high.

Meuvaines

church 54/15
A little Romanesque church, very simple, On the north wall is a rare sculpting of the Last Supper.

Montchauvet

slightly dubious alignment 59/10
Neolithic
Condé-sur-Noireau 1–2
377,10/1141,75
From Montchauvet take the D 298 east, then immediately take a small road right (→ la Bruyère). On reaching the D 55 turn left. Almost immediately, in the hamlet of la Plumaudière take a track right almost opposite a farm-building. 130 m down the track turn right into a field. In the field beyond is the alignment.

There is a scattering of quartzite stones with three still upright. An excavation showed that at least the largest upright was not just a rock outcrop but had been set up in a layer of yellow clay. This one, the menhir du Hu, is 3.2 m high.

Ouistreham

church 54/16
A twelfth-century Romanesque church, the interior heavily refurbished in the nineteenth century. The western doorway has four archivolts and is surmounted by a façade with three levels of blind arcades. The buttressed belfry is late twelfth century. Inside, the nave has two levels, with an ambulatory below the high windows. The chancel is a good example of thirteenth-century Norman Gothic.

Saint-André d'Hébertot

church 54/18
A small parish church with a Romanesque belfry and inside, in the chancel, a primitive ogival arch.

In the valley below the church is a fine moated castle with a seventeenth-century corbelled tower and eighteenth-century façade. It is not open to the public.

110 La Pierre Tournante, Livarot

Saint-Gabriel-Brécy

church 54/15

The remains of a lovely Romanesque priory surrounded by fine buildings are now part of the horticultural college of Saint-Gabriel-Brécy.

The priory was founded in 1058 by the monks of Fécamp. In 1749 two-thirds of the building was pulled down. Only the very large choir remains. The chancel has a square bay and a minor apse on each side, a three-storey elevation and is roofed, like la Trinité at Caen, with false sexpartite vaulting. The main apse has unfortunately been pierced with a late Gothic window. The extraordinary feature is the amount of delicate carving—miniature sculptings, fretted capitals and friezes. It has been called the 'ultimate stage of an evolution'.

A few kilometres south of Saint-Gabriel-Brécy is the small parish church of Rucqueville with some very fine capitals below the transept arches. Four of them have scenes from the life of Christ, one the Salvation of the Soul, one the Adoration of the Magi, and one has Doubting Thomas.

The church has not been used since the Revolution. The keys are kept in the house next door.

Saint-Germain de Tallevende

La Loge aux Sarazins 59/9
or Dolmen du Mont Savarin Neolithic
dolmen Vire 7–8
(Figure 111) 364,20/1126,20

From Saint-Germain take the D 577 north (→ Vire) then after 1.75 km turn right on the D 282 to the Cross at la Chaudronnière. Continue another 300 m down the D 282 then go through the further of the two field gates on the left. The dolmen is 150 m from the road.

The stones are all of granite. There is a capstone—originally larger but broken in 1780—and five uprights. The one in the south-west corner was moved and broken in 1820.

It was dug by treasure-seekers in 1825 who may have found a pot. A polished flint axe and a polished hardstone axe were found near by.

Secqueville en Bessin

54/15
Church

A fine eleventh-century Romanesque church; the western façade was rebuilt in the fifteenth century and the choir in the sixteenth century. The interior is very simple and has some remarkably fine carved capitals on the southern pillars of the nave. The exterior, particularly the south side, is more elaborately decorated, while the three-storey belfry is a very typical Romanesque form. It is surmounted by a thirteenth-century Gothic spire—the original spire having been fired in 1105 when Robert Fitzhamon, henchman of Henry I of England took refuge in the church from the soldiers of Robert, duke of Normandy.

111 La Loge aux Sarazins,
Saint-Germain-de-Tallevende

Soumont-Saint-Quentin

54/16

Menhirs, polishers and earthworks. A nice collection especially when combined with a walk through the gorge of the Brèche au Diable.

1 Menhirs Neolithic
(Figure 112) Mézidon 5–6 413,90/1144,20
Go eastwards out of Soumont-Saint-Quentin on the D 261 towards Mont-Joly. Continue 1.75 km to a T-junction. Turn right. 50 m before the small turning right to the Auberge du Mont-Joly, look to the left and the menhirs are visible 500 m from the road at the further end of a large field.

One of the stones has fallen, the other is still upright and stands 3.65 m high.

In the fields of this plateau below Mont-Joly there are great spreads of flint tools and waste. It is a large-sized industry and forms an extension of the great flint work-floors of Olendon further to the east.

2 Mont-Joly Neolithic/Iron Age
promontory site
Directions as for the menhirs but then continue for 50 m and take the small turning right to the Auberge Mont-Joly.

The water-tower south-west of the auberge is right next to the only remnant of the prehistoric rampart. The road swings round the auberge and church, and a track leads across the promontory to the tomb of Marie Joly—a very romantic ensemble concocted by Fouquet-Dolomboy, husband of the singer Marie Joly, in 1798.

The quartzitic sandstone promontory is protected to the south, west and north by the river Laizon flowing in the Brèche au Diable gorge. The eastern side is protected by a bank and ditch possibly of Middle or Late Bronze Age date. The protected area was about three hectares.

This is the only *visible* prehistoric feature on the promontory but there is a great deal of prehistory underfoot (indeed almost every molehill seems to bring up flints and sherds). A few Middle Palaeolithic Mousterian bifacial points have been found, and, in a lower level of a rock shelter on the west side of the promontory, some Upper Palaeolithic Solutrean tools. There is even more Neolithic material. Some

112 One of the menhirs at ***Soumont-Saint-Quentin***

was found in the upper levels of the rock shelter. Some was found by Fouquet-Dolomboy—while burying his wife he uncovered some much earlier burials. Some, still intact, had polished stone axes placed below the skull or arm bones, others were burnt or fragmented. In the 1950s and 60s a Chassey site was excavated on the promontory and hearths, pottery, occasional beads and a fine small-size flint industry was uncovered. Examples of similar lithic material collected on the surface can be seen in the museums of *Evreux* and *Rouen*. The Iron Age is represented by a gold coin, and graves at the foot of the promontory; the Gallo-Roman period by fibulae and sculpted stones; and, finally, Merovingian graves have been found in the field alongside the auberge.

3 Polishers (actually in the commune of Bons-Tassilly) (Figure 113) — Neolithic
Mézidon 5–6
412,60/1144,20

From the little church next to the auberge take the narrow path down into the gorge. In the gorge turn right and follow the wire-netting fence. Where it ends take an even smaller path towards the river and the polisher is almost immediately visible to the right. (There is another one on the other side of the fence.)

Both are of quartzitic rock and have well-marked hollows and grooves made in the process of grinding and polishing hardstone axes.

For a lovely walk, continue down the path to the gorge.

Thaon

Thaon old church (Saint-Pierre) — 54/15
Church

On no account to be missed. Coming into Thaon from the south (the D 170) go through the village and after 500 m take the small road right (Chemin de la Vieille Eglise) down into the valley of the Mue. At the end of the road is a house where the key to the church is kept. The church is just beyond, to the left.

A deserted, pure Romanesque church of the eleventh and twelfth century. The aisles of the nave have been amputated and the arcades filled in. These arcades are surmounted by a blind arcade with geometric decoration and a cornice. The doorway has a decorated archivolt, and the belfry, with a pyramid roof and deep, wide bays, is unique. Inside, the capitals are sculpted with animals and godrons.

Ussy

Pierre de Hoberie — 55/12
menhir — Neolithic
Falaise (West) 1–2
407,25/1141,02

Take the D 43 going south-west out of Ussy (→ Saint-Germain-Langot). At the hamlet of Pôt take the track to Hoberie farm and the menhir is in the field downhill from the farm.

A fine sandstone schist menhir, 3.1 m high.

113 Two axe polishers from Bons-Tassilly, at Soumont-Saint-Quentin

Villerville

Pierre de la Bergerie — 54/7
or la Grosse Pierre — Neolithic
or even la Pierre Grise
menhir

Set off from Trouville-sur-Mer (54/17) north-eastwards on the D 74 (→ airfield) and after 4 km, at the crossroads of la Croix-Sonnet, turn left on the D 62 (→ Villerville). Take the second track left to the farm de la Bergerie and the menhir is about 100 m west of the farm-buildings.

It is made of puddingstone and stands 2.95 m high. The nearest outcrop of this stone is 800 m away. At the end of the nineteenth century there were other large stones close by, but they have been knocked down and buried.

Villy-Bocage

Pierre Lée or Laye — 54/15
menhir — Neolithic
Villers-Bocage 1–2
381,45/1160,25

From Villers-Bocage take the D 33 northwards (→ Saint-Louet-sur-Seulles). 20 m before the sign announcing this village, at a bend in the road from which the church spire of Saint-Louet is visible, take a narrow tarmacked track right. The track ends after one kilometre and to the right is the beginning of a small valley. The menhir is on the left bank of the stream—go through the field alongside the stream for 400 m.

The calcareous stone is available further up the hillside. The menhir is 2.6 m high.

Eure

The departement of the Eure lies mainly within the chalk-lands south of the Seine. There are gentle hills, fine half-timbered buildings standing in large fields and orchards. Sometimes there are steep thatched roofs with a line of reeds along the pitch. It is a rich countryside and its prehistoric monuments are tucked away in odd less fertile corners, or hidden below ground, or are viewable only at second remove in the ample museums of the large country towns.

Aizier

Saint-Pierre 55/5
Church

The church of Saint-Pierre is pleasantly sited close to the Seine and forest of Brotonne. The fine five-storey tower and the choir date to the last part of the eleventh century. The nave was largely rebuilt in the sixteenth century.

Baux-Sainte-Croix

alignment 55/16
Neolithic
Saint-André-de-l'Eure 1–2
509,60/139,50

Baux-Sainte-Croix is on the northern edge of the forest of Evreux. Take the very small road south-west (→ Bruyères); the alignment is in a field to the right of, and 150 m from, the road. It is 250 m north of Bruyères.

Three puddingstone menhirs lie on a north-west/south-east axis. The northern stone is 1.5 m high, the middle one 1.7 m and the southern one, fallen, is 2.9 m long.

The base of all three stones has been excavated and the blocking stones have been found.

The dolmen of la Pierre Courcoulée, *les Ventes*, lies 2.4 km to the south-west, the Hôtel-Dieux dolmen, *les Ventes*, 3 km to the north-west.

Bernay

1 Musée Abbatiale 55/5
Museum

The museum is in the seventeenth-century abbot's residence, next door to the abbey of Notre-Dame, place de l'Hôtel de Ville. There is another entrance through a most ornamental public garden just down the rue Gambetta.

China, furniture, and, on the second floor, some prehistoric and Gallo-Roman material.

Open from 10 a.m. to 12.30 p.m. and 3 to 7 p.m. Closed Tuesdays.

2 Abbey of Notre-Dame, Church
place de l'Hôtel de Ville

At present closed for restoration. The outside with its hideous façade and excrescence of buildings slapped up against the choir disguises one of the earliest Romanesque churches in Normandy.

Founded by Judith of Brittany, wife of Duke Richard II, the church was probably built in two stages. Between 1017 and 1028 the nave was built, probably in part under the direction of Guillaume de Volpiano. Then, between 1060 and 1072, the transept and choir were completed. There followed much tampering and many vicissitudes. In the fifteenth and sixteenth centuries the north aisle was rebuilt in the Gothic style. In the seventeenth century cupolas were added to the south aisles, and two bays of the nave were removed. Then, in the nineteenth century, the north arm of the transept was destroyed, the choir was mutilated, and the church was used for grain-storage and workshops.

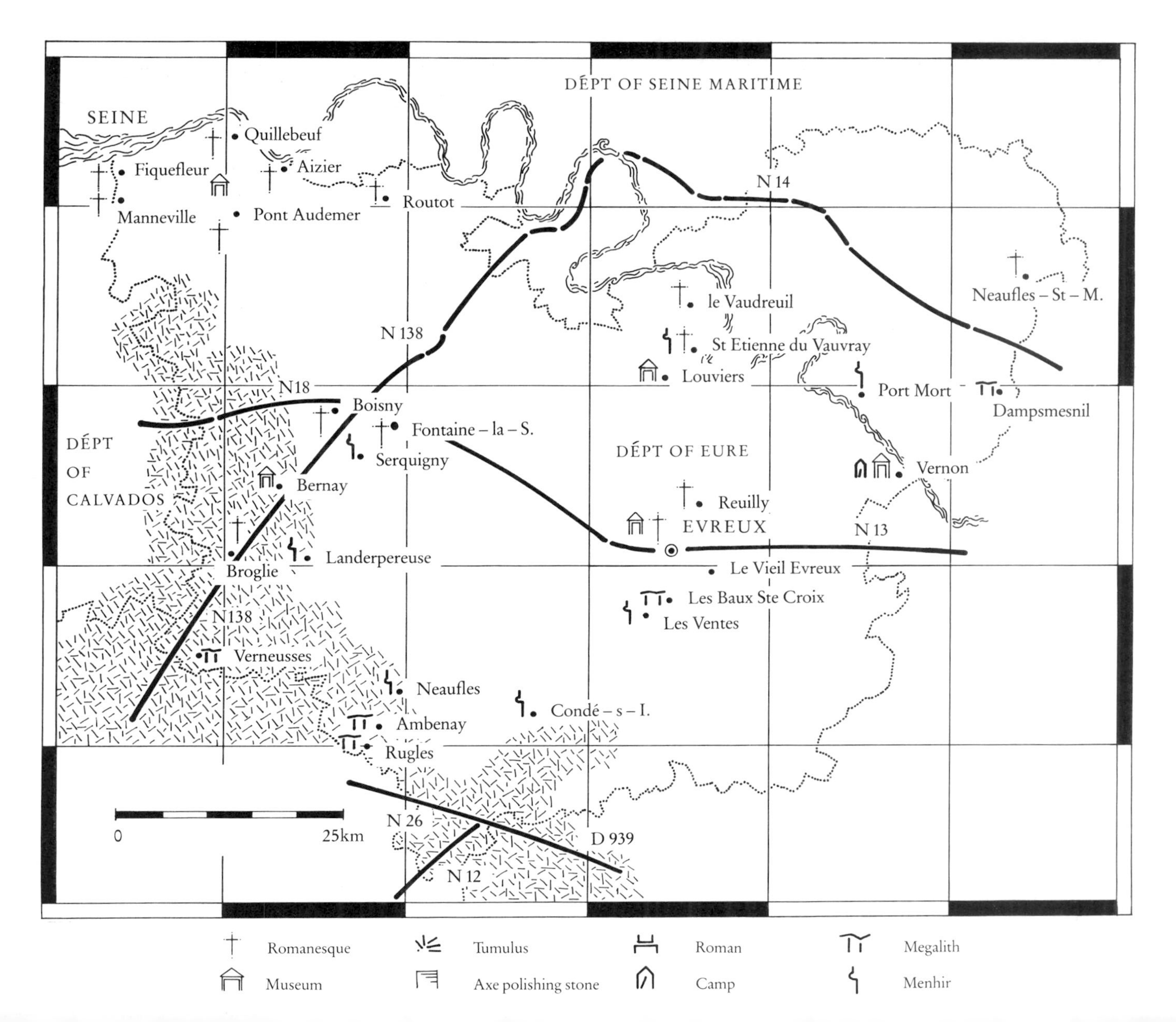

DÉPT OF SEINE MARITIME
SEINE
Quillebeuf
Fiquefleur
Aizier
Routot
Manneville
Pont Audemer
N 14
le Vaudreuil
Neaufles – St – M.
N 138
St Etienne du Vauvray
Louviers
Port Mort
Dampsmesnil
N18
Boisny
Fontaine – la – S.
Serquigny
DÉPT
OF
CALVADOS
DÉPT OF EURE
Vernon
Bernay
Reuilly
EVREUX
N 13
Landerpereuse
Broglie
Le Vieil Evreux
Les Baux Ste Croix
Les Ventes
N138
Verneusses
Neaufles
Condé – s – I.
Ambenay
Rugles
0
25km
N 26
D 939
N 12
Romanesque
Museum
Tumulus
Axe polishing stone
Roman
Camp
Megalith
Menhir

The five great bays of the nave remain, with almost square piles supporting undecorated arches. In the level below the windows a series of arched recesses probably once held painted decoration, like the round recesses at Saint-Pierre, *Jumièges*, Seine-Maritime. The capitals have sculpted decoration, though often mutilated. Those in the north aisle of the choir include a palmette motif. Finally there is a fine capital and plaque in the south arm of the transept with sculpted figures.

Boisney

Saint-Aubin 55/15
Church

It is worth a detour off the Route Nationale 13 to this small church with its cemetery and two great yew-trees. The exterior of the nave has been rebuilt but the interior remains a fine example of a rather archaic Romanesque style with wide arches carried on square pillars flanked by pilasters and half-columns. The eastern part of the church seems to be later in date, probably late twelfth century; the arches supporting the tower are beginning to be more angular and the trilobe denticulated corniche above the central arch of the south crossing and again above the chancel window begin to look more Gothic.

Broglie

Saint-Martin 55/14
Church

The church of Saint-Martin was built in the late eleventh century. There is a fine contrast between the red ironstone conglomerate used for the original church, seen for example in the façade, the lower part of the north side of the nave, the choir and the lower part of the belfry, and the white calcareous stone used for the late Romanesque decoration of the façade gable and the first two storeys of the north side of the nave. There was an ambulatory but this was destroyed in the fifteenth century. The south side of the nave and the aisles are sixteenth and even seventeenth century.

114 Département of Eure

Condé-sur-Iton

Pierre de la Gour or l'Agour or Pierre de Gargantua 60/6
menhir
Neolithic
Breteuil-sur-Iton 7–8
499,21/1124,00

Take the D23 south-east from Condé-sur-Iton (→ Tillières-sur-Avre). After 0.5 km turn right (→ Saint-Ouen-d'Attez). Continue towards Saint-Ouen and having ignored the left fork to Nuisement take the next small, unmarked, road to the right. Another 100 m, over a small bridge, and, just beyond a copse to the left, is the menhir, 100 m from the road and near the river.

The stone is 3.76 m high and has a bifurcated top. It is made of ferruginous sandstone. Flint tools, including some fine triangular and lozenge-shaped arrowheads, polished axes, one of diorite, have been found close by.

Dampsmesnil

trench gallery grave 55/18
(Figure 115)
Neolithic
Gisors 7–8
50,15/164,15

Very hard to find but worth the hunt. From Dampsmesnil take the D 119 west (→ Aveny) and after 1 km turn left on the D 170 (→ Fours, marked Allée couverte de Dampsmesnil). After another kilometre there is a sign to the right of the road to the Allée couverte. Lulled into a false sense of security start up the path—to find no further indications. However, follow the main path up through the forest bearing left if in doubt, and after 400 m take the first well-defined path left (near the top of the hill). Go 45 m and then take the small, almost concealed, path left. Another 45 m brings you to the grave. (If you go too far you will find the main path divides into a network over a more open tract with young saplings. Retrace your steps!).

The grave is in a 2 m deep trench opening to the south-west. It is 8.3 m long and 1.75 m high. The sides are lined with orthostats reinforced with dry-stone walling, and there are five capstones. The two most remarkable features are the sculpted pair of breasts (one almost obliterated) surmounted by a triple necklace on the first upright on the left side of

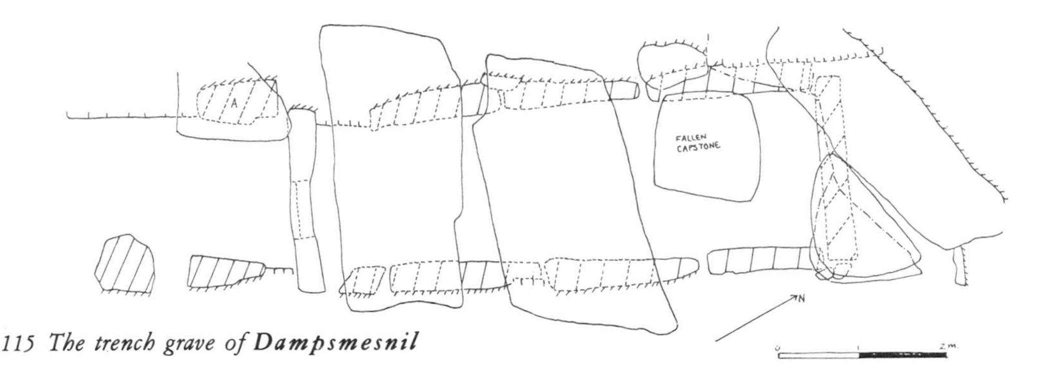

115 The trench grave of ***Dampsmesnil***

the grave, and the remains of the port-hole stone which once separated the antechamber from the chamber. Only the lower part of this remains, almost imbedded in the floor of the grave, just beyond the sculpted upright, but it shows part of the carefully worked hole with a lip.

The Romans seem to have been the first to rob the grave leaving behind Roman tiles and a possible Roman bronze. The grave was further excavated and destroyed before the Revolution and again in 1820, 1875, 1894 and 1895. Of the prehistoric contents all that is recorded are three barbed-and-tanged arrowheads, a few flint blades, a perforated bone bead, two flint tranchets, a hammerstone, two stone axes, sherds from a dozen 'Neolithic' pots (one or two of the Seine-Oise-Marne type), hundreds of human teeth, a bear's tooth, a wolf or dog canine and a horse's tooth.

Evreux

55/16–17

A Gallo-Roman town was established at Evreux in the mid first century and it rapidly pre-empted the administrative and economic functions of Vieil Evreux. It was a route-centre, a small port and a flourishing industrial centre. Ravaged in the late third century, it was quickly rebuilt with a *castrum* that enclosed about 10 hectares. Fine sections of this wall still rise above the river Iton.

1 Musée municipal — Museum

The museum is in the fine fifteenth-century bishop's palace, next to the cathedral.

Particularly strong on medieval and Gallo-Roman material. Most of the Gallo-Roman finds from *Vieil Evreux* are here, including the statue of Jupiter, much glass, pottery and bronze. There are also some interesting aerial photographs of the Roman baths, amphitheatre, temple etc.

There is one room with a well-presented but rather select collection of prehistoric material (and some beautiful faience upstairs).

Open Tuesday to Saturday from 10 a.m. to 12 noon and 2 to 5 p.m. On Sunday open from 2 to 6 p.m. Closed Mondays.

2 Cathedral of Notre-Dame — Church

Only the twelfth-century nave of the original Romanesque church remains, the rest is Gothic or later.

3 Saint-Taurin — Church

On the site where the fifth-century bishop Taurin was buried, Duke Richard I established, five centuries later, an important monastery. Very little remains of the Romanesque structure but it is worth looking at the exterior of the north aisle where there is a fine frieze of large arches, mainly blind, with decorated archivolts and within each is a coloured, oblique diamond patterning of white, red and blue segments. Such decoration is more frequently found on twelfth-century English and Scottish churches than in Normandy.

Fiquefleur

Saint-Georges 55/4
Church

A small, late eleventh-century church, made smaller by the eighteenth-century destruction of the façade and part of the nave when the Beuzeville-Honfleur road was widened. And long before that there were a series of additions and subtractions, the aisles were removed, the tower base strengthened and the height of the roof modified.

There are some quite interesting sculpted plaques, two on the piers of the triumphal arch, two outside on either side of the north door of the nave and three—hard to see—high on the east gable of the apse.

Fontaine-la-Soret

Saint-Lambert-de-Malassis, more commonly known as Saint-Eloi 55/15
Church

Marked on the Michelin. The church is on the D 46 between Fontaine-la-Soret and Serquigny. The beautiful setting as well as the chapel make it worth a visit.

Of the church founded in 1126 by William of Thibouville, only the chancel remains, the rest was destroyed in the nineteenth century when the façade was constructed—reusing several earlier elements.

Church or chapel, it has for many centuries been a place of pilgrimage and the spring rising below the chapel is considered to have healing powers. It has often been suggested that there was a pre-Christian cult at this site. Gallo-Roman finds have been made.

The sixteenth-century house next to the chapel contains a Romanesque structure—two bays, with massive pillars and groin-vaulting. The function of this building is unknown but there is no good reason to believe (despite the view still current in the Michelin Green Guide) that this is an early *martyrium*. This notion derives from the nineteenth-century romantic pseudo-archaeological writings of François Lenormant, the great-nephew of Mme Récamier, who, with her family, took refuge at Saint-Eloi during the Revolution.

Landepéreuse

La Longue Pierre 55/15
menhir Neolithic

Does *not* merit a detour

In Landepéreuse take the small road west towards Broglie, la Roussière etc. At the water-tower keep right (→ la Roussière etc.). After 2 km passing many stone outcrops along the way, ignore the road right to Jonquerets de Livet, and in the angle of the next small road right is the menhir.

A nondescript 2.25 m. When excavated in 1910 it was found to extend 1.2 m below the ground and to be wedged with small stones. A flint axe and fragments of pyrites were found at the base.

Louviers

Musée municipal, in the town hall, place E. Thorel 55/16–17
Museum

Mainly faience and pictures but there is a small room of local prehistory, and photographs of the Upper Palaeolithic engravings from the cave of Gouy (Introduction, page 22).

Open from 2 to 6.30 p.m. Closed on Tuesdays.

Manneville-la-Raoult

Saint-Germain 55/4
Church

Saint-Germain has a pleasant west façade and interesting choir. The latter dates to the second quarter of the twelfth century and has primitive ogival vaulting. The faint fresco on the north side of the choir is fifteenth century.

Neaufles-Auvergny

Pierre Gargantua 55/15
menhir Neolithic
Breteuil-sur-Iton 5–6
482,10/1130,80

Go west out of the village towards the river and the menhir can be seen in a huge field to the right just before the bridge. It is 175 m from the road.

A reasonable 3.9 m, made of sandstone.

Neaufles-Saint-Martin

Cross (one of the very few known in Normandy) 55/8

Take the D 10 east from Neaufles (→ Gisors) and the Romanesque cross is near the roadside to the left, just before the level crossing.

It is an interesting cross, sculpted on all faces and quite well preserved. It may date to the end of the eleventh century.

Pont-Audemer

Saint-Germain-Village, in the western suburb of Pont-Audemer 55/4 Church

This large and austere church has been much tampered with. During the Restoration three bays of the nave disappeared, and there were other modifications at the beginning of this century including botching up the western façade. The large nave and transept date to the last quarter of the eleventh century, and there is some restrained decoration on the capitals. The eastern part is probably a little later.

On the outside, along the nave, aisles and transept, are a fine series of figured plaques supporting a chequered tablet. The heavy Romanesque base of the tower is surmounted by an elegant fourteenth-century structure.

Port-Mort

Gravois de Gargantua 55/17
menhir Neolithic
Les Andelys 7–8
531,50/164,10

Marked on the Michelin map. Just north of Port-Mort on the D 313 (→ les Andelys), to the right of the road. It was moved to this site during the straightening of the N 313, and in the process lost a metre. It is now 3.5 m high.

Quillebeuf-sur-Seine

Notre-Dame-de-Bon-Port 55/4 Church

A rather tatty church with iron stains on the fine twelfth-century doorway, patched-up aisles built in 1786 and a sixteenth-century choir, all surmounted by an interesting but incomplete Romanesque tower. Inside, the nave is very simple Romanesque, dating to the first third of the twelfth century and has some austerely decorated capitals.

Reuilly

Saint-Christophe 55/17 Church

The church, outside the village, on the edge of a small valley, is a fine example of very simple, rural Romanesque architecture. It dates to the mid-eleventh century and consists basically of two rectangles—the larger being the nave, the smaller the choir. It is built with herring-bone masonry set in heavy mortar and only the angles are of dressed stone. The high gable of the façade is decorated with a series of perforated stones.

Routot

Saint-Ouen 55/5 Church

The most interesting feature of this church is the elegant tall tower crowned with a high wooden spire. Above the massive lower storey is a level with blind intersecting arches followed by a third, still more highly decorated level. It dates to the third quarter of the twelfth century and is already beginning to show some Gothic features.

Rugles

Dolmen de la Forge 55/15
Neolithic
Rugles 7–8
480,85/1127,30

Coming into Rugles from the north on the D 830 (→

l'Aigle) take the second small turning right after the church (small sign, Dolmen de la Forge 1.5 km). Follow the signs to la Forge, go through the hamlet and 250 m on, in a field to the right and visible from the road, is the dolmen. It seems, however, to be on well-defended 'Propriété Privée' and has a very private flowerbed all round the base.

All the stones are puddingstone with a capstone balanced on four uprights, another capstone lying to the west and two more uprights. The floor was paved with flints and covered with alluvium.

Saint-Etienne-du-Vauvray

1 Menhir 55/17
Neolithic
Les Andelys 1–2
516,60/171,55

In Saint-Etienne take the D 313 west (→ Louviers). Cross the D 77, pass under the motorway and the menhir is 250 m beyond, to the left of the road.

Made of chalk with flint nodules, 3.3 m high. It was moved during the construction of the railway, and was found to extend 1.3 m below the ground.

14 m from the original position was a trench gallery grave—like *Dampsmesnil*—with three levels of paving and six skeletons on each of the lower and middle levels. The skulls rested on stones, and the inhumations were accompanied by a fine antler axe-mount and mace, both in the museum of *Louviers*.

2 Church

Completely transformed by nineteenth-century restoration but dates to the eleventh century. The central arcade of the choir in the south side has a sculpted keystone.

Vaudreuil, le

Notre-Dame 55/7
Church

The main interest lies in the twelfth-century transept and choir, and, in particular, in the curious carvings on the capitals of the transept-crossing.

Ventes, les

1 La Pierre Courcoulée 55/16
dolmen Neolithic
Breteuil-sur-Iton 3–4
507,551/138,72

Marked on the Michelin map. In les Ventes take the road west in front of the church, at right angles to the Avrilly/le Plessis-Grohan road. Pass to the left of the war memorial and continue to the T-junction—then follow the plan (Figure 116).

A craggy puddingstone monument with a vast capstone (4.25 × 2 × 1 m) resting on four uprights with two other uprights alongside. It was dug in 1820 by Rever but someone had got there first.

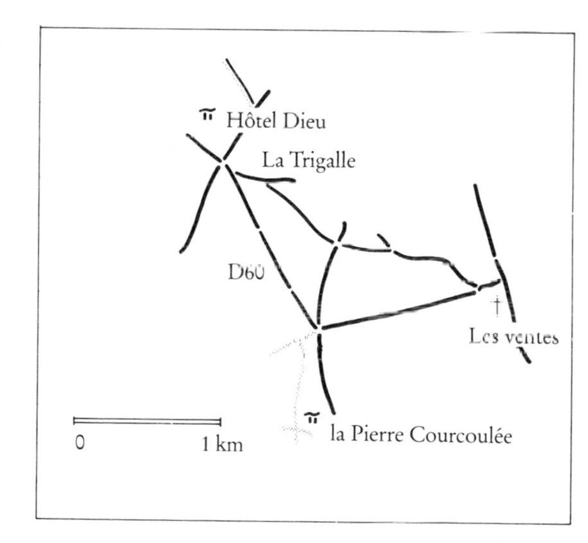

*116 **Les Ventes**, access to la Pierre Courcoulée and Hôtel Dieu*

2 Dolmen Hôtel-Dieu Neolithic
Beaumont-le-Roger 7–8
507,00/141,05

Directions as for la Pierre Courcoulée but at the T-junction turn right on the D 60 to la Trigalle. At the crossroads in la Trigalle turn right on the D 55 (→ Evreux) and 500 m from the crossroads the dolmen can be seen in the field to the left of the road (near a telegraph pole and 500 m from the road).

Fairly similar to la Pierre Courcoulée, *les Ventes* and to the Dolmen de la Forge, *Rugles*. Again, of puddingstone with a large capstone (2.6 × 2.1 × 0.8 m) resting on three uprights, plus another three uprights and one that has fallen.

Excavation in 1967 uncovered a floor made of carefully placed and sometimes dressed flint slabs. Part of a polished flint axe, a partially polished stone chisel, a hammer-stone, a blade possibly made from a fragment of a Grand Pressigny dagger, eight transverse-tranchet arrowheads and a dozen backed flint knives were found; also two quartz beads (certainly not of local origin), a shell (again, the source at least 80 km away), a large number of small sherds of Seine-Oise-Marne type and an equally large number of tiny bone fragments. This excavation at last makes it possible to establish the Late Neolithic context of this series of small 'dolmens'.

Verneusses

La Pierre Couplée or Grosse Pierre 55/14
dolmen Neolithic
Rugles 1–2
461,95/1135,30

In Verneusses, at the church, take the D 45 east (→ Notre-Dame-du-Hamel), then the first road left (→ Saint-Aquilin-d'Augerons) and the dolmen is 30 m further on, to the right of the road.

Again, rather similar to those at *Rugles* and *les Ventes*. The dolmen was overturned in 1820 but was restored, none too accurately, by Coutil. The capstone is a curious formation, the upper part is sandstone, the lower puddingstone. It is 4 × 3.45 × 0.6 m and rests on five uprights (four of sandstone, one of puddingstone). Coutil mentions that the cairn was made of siliceous nodules and that he found nothing in the chamber.

Vernon

1 Musée municipal 55/18
Museum

Recently reopened, but the prehistoric material is not yet on display.

2 Camp de César or Camp Romain or Camp de Mortagne Iron Age
Mantes-la-Jolie 1–2
539,40/155,20

You can examine the general layout and have a fine walk with a comprehensive view of the Seine, but alas, the camp has never been better defended, for it lies behind massive military wire. If undeterred—take the Paris road (N 181) north from Vernon across the river to Vernonnet, then the N 313 to the right (→ Gasny). This immediately climbs a steep hill and three-quarters of the way up there is an even steeper track to the right (marked 'Voie sans issue, escalade interdite, danger'). This track winds round the perimeter of the camp.

According to Wheeler, a rampart bounds the north-east side of the promontory and, at the east end rises 5 m above the interior of the camp and 8 m above the flat-bottomed ditch. It belongs to the Fécamp series; the two north-east entrances have strongly inturned flanks. There is a third entrance, marked by an overlap, close to the Gasny road.

A few Iron Age sherds are in the museum at *Vernon*.

Vieil-Evreux

55/17
Gallo-Roman

A very important site though not a great deal remains to be seen (Figure 117).

Vieil-Evreux is on a clay-with-flint promontory. There was an Iron Age settlement belonging to the Aulerci Eburovices, Cenomanni and Diablintes tribes, and then from the first century AD it became a Gallo-Roman town, Gisacum. The outline of the town formed a quadrilateral, the east side about 950 m long, the north 1650 m, the west 1250 m and the south 1200 m. A sanctuary and a theatre were aligned along the south side, which was backed by magnificently decorated baths. The sanctuary consisted of three temples linked by rooms and galleries. They seem to have been richly decorated—a sheet bronze mask, statues to Jupiter and Apollo and a fragment of a bronze tablet with an inscripton in Latin and Gallic were found (museum of *Evreux*). There was also in this area, a large building, the Champ des Dés, with important mosaics. The

117 Aerial photograph of le Moulin, Vieil-Evreux

residential areas were separated from this public quarter. An aqueduct carried water from the river Iton, nearly thirty kilometres away. Ancient roads from Evreux, Lisieux, Rouen, Amiens, Paris, Sens, Chartres, le Mans and Tours all met at Vieil-Evreux.

But its importance was relatively short-lived. Already in the late first century, the administrative centre was moved some seven kilometres to what is now Evreux on the banks of the Iton. It may be that the old site suffered from water shortages, certainly the new site offered port facilities and room for industrial growth. The new site had already been occupied in pre-Roman times, now it became Mediolanum Aulercorum. Vieil-Evreux gradually declined, the sanctuary was burnt down, probably at the end of the first century and never rebuilt. Nonetheless it seems to have remained a cult and pilgrimage centre. It was finally destroyed during the great northern invasion of AD 276.

Of the complex shown on the general plan only the baths and the amphitheatre can be visited.

1 The baths — Evreux 5–6
518,95/145,10

Take the D 67 south-east from Saint-Aubin-du-Vieil-Evreux (→ Garennes, le Val David) for 1 km to the junction at le Vieil Evreux (with a chapel on the left). Bear right, still on the D 67, and after 200 m there is a small track right, marked Thermes Romaines.

2 The amphitheatre — Evreux 5–6
(Figure 118) — 519,70/145,55

Much overgrown but parts of the perimeter wall can still be seen. Directions as for the baths but at the junction bear left (unmarked) for 400 m to a calvary. The wall of the amphitheatre can be seen just behind.

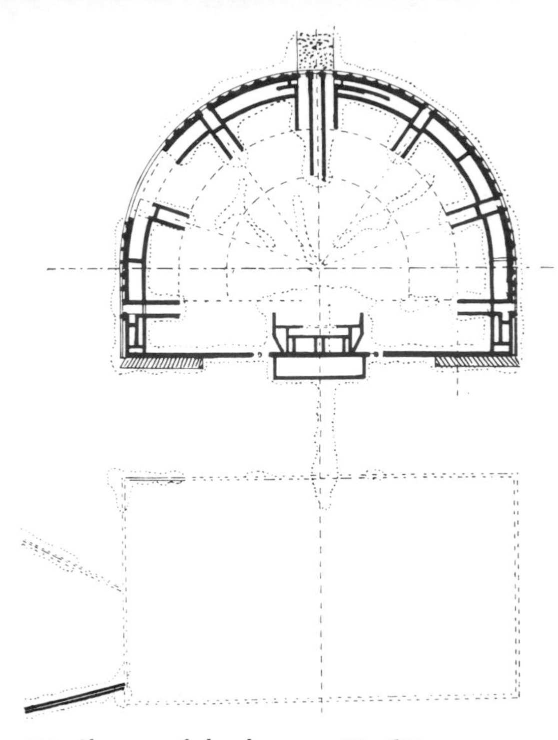

118 Close-up of the theatre at ***Vieil-Evreux***

3 Cracouville — Evreux 5–6

sanctuary — 518,40/143,95

(Figure 119)

Two kilometres from Vieil-Evreux is the sanctuary of Cracouville, close to a spring. Directions as for the baths but continue on down the D 67 to le Val David. Then turn right on the C 107 to la Trinité and in la Trinité turn right to the D 671 (→ Evreux). Just before the railway bridge before Cracouville there is a rough mounded area to the right of the road. The base of the walls of the square *fanum* set in a sacred enclosure can easily be distinguished.

The *fanum* was a fine construction made of small regular flint blocks with dressed calcareous blocks on the corners and on the eastern façade. The exterior walls of the gallery and *pronaos* had a thick coat of mortar and then plaster painted and polished red. The walls of the cella were painted with black, red, ochre and green bands and were decorated with green leaves on a red ground. Many precious small bronze objects were found—surgeons' instruments, perfume equipment, and offerings, including a gold and jade necklace and a gold bracelet. The coins found date to the first and second century.

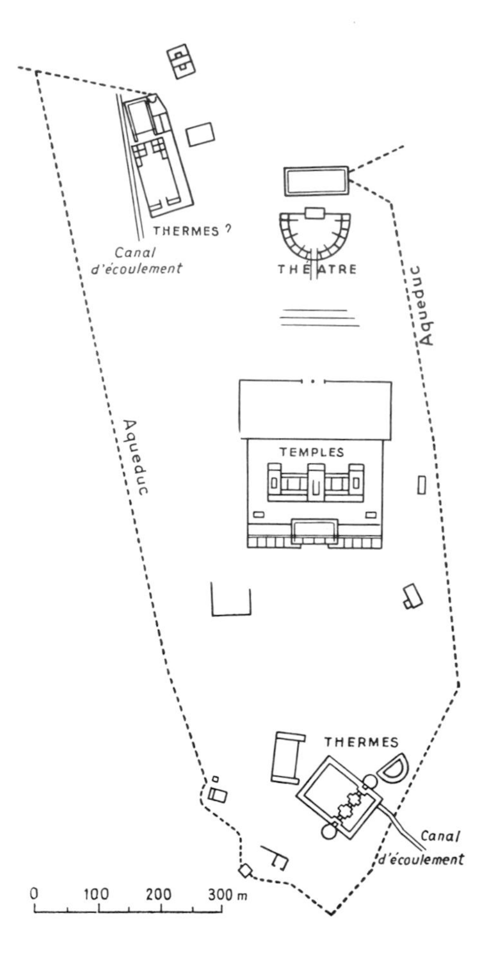

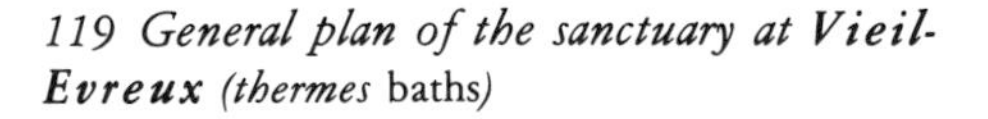

119 General plan of the sanctuary at ***Vieil-Evreux*** *(thermes* baths*)*

Below this construction lies an earlier, smaller, less well-built temple. In this temple the cella had paintings of iris leaves. It contained many bronze bracelets and rings, fibulae and Celtic coins dating to the last century BC.

Just to the east were the foundations of two basins. There were numerous fragments of sculpted chalk, fruit and flowers from the basins themselves, which must have been about 2.5 m in diameter. Further east again, the large rectangular structure, 22.3 × 8.9 m, was probably the bath house.

Manche

Barneville-Carteret

54/1
Church

A twelfth-century church with a fifteenth-century fortified tower. Inside there are some fine decorated arches and capitals with sculpted animals.

Beaumont-Hague

Hague-Dick 54/1
earthworks Bronze Age/Viking
Les Pieux 3–4
298,50/227,55

A long high bank and ditch once cut off the Hague peninsula. Much of it has been destroyed but a reasonably good section can be seen by taking the D 245 north from Beaumont (→ Digulleville). After 1 km the bank is visible among the brambles to the left of the road.

The earthwork once extended for some 2,700 m and enclosed an area of 3.5 hectares. The original entrance was probably at the point where the D 45, the old Roman road from Omanville-la-Rogue to Port-Bail, cuts through.

Excavations have shown that the bank to the west of the Beaumont-Digulleville road, which is about 4 m high, is made of layers of earth with a dry-stone wall revetment on the outer surface. This side is flanked by a ditch.

To the east of the Beaumont-Digulleville road the natural escarpment of the Sabine afforded protection but was heavily reinforced by a ditch, bank and palissaded platform.

Very little material was found but carbon-14 dating of charcoal found in the western bank suggests that the western defences were first erected in the Late Bronze Age. The eastern defences are almost certainly ninth century AD, and were probably constructed by the Viking invaders.

Bouillon

La Pierre du Diable or 59/7
Pierre Levée Neolithic
menhir Mont-Saint-Michel 3–4
315,70/126,45

Take the D 21 north from Saint-Michel-des-Loups (→ Bouillon) and after 800 m turn right. The menhir is to the left of the road.

Granite, quite small (2.45 m), and quite ordinary. It was once taller but the top was broken off in 1820.

Bretteville-en-Saire

La Forge or Clos-ès-Pierre 54/2
gallery grave or Neolithic
lateral-entrance grave Cherbourg 3–4
(Figures 121 and 122) 322,40/223,45

Marked on the Michelin. In Cherbourg take the D 901 east (→ Saint-Pierre-Eglise), then after 6 km turn left onto the D 320 (→ Bretteville, marked 'allée couverte 0.5 km'). The monument is to the right of the road.

The grave is 17.7 m long, 0.85 m wide and 0.8 m high. There are nine uprights on the north-east side, ten on the south-west, seven capstones in place and two lying to the south-west. Recent excavations suggest that this grave may have had a lateral entrance.

The north-east end was ransacked by treasure-seekers in 1872 but apparently nothing was found. During the recent excavations a carinated bowl, fragments of pottery, perforated beads (including one of quartz) and some chipped flints were found.

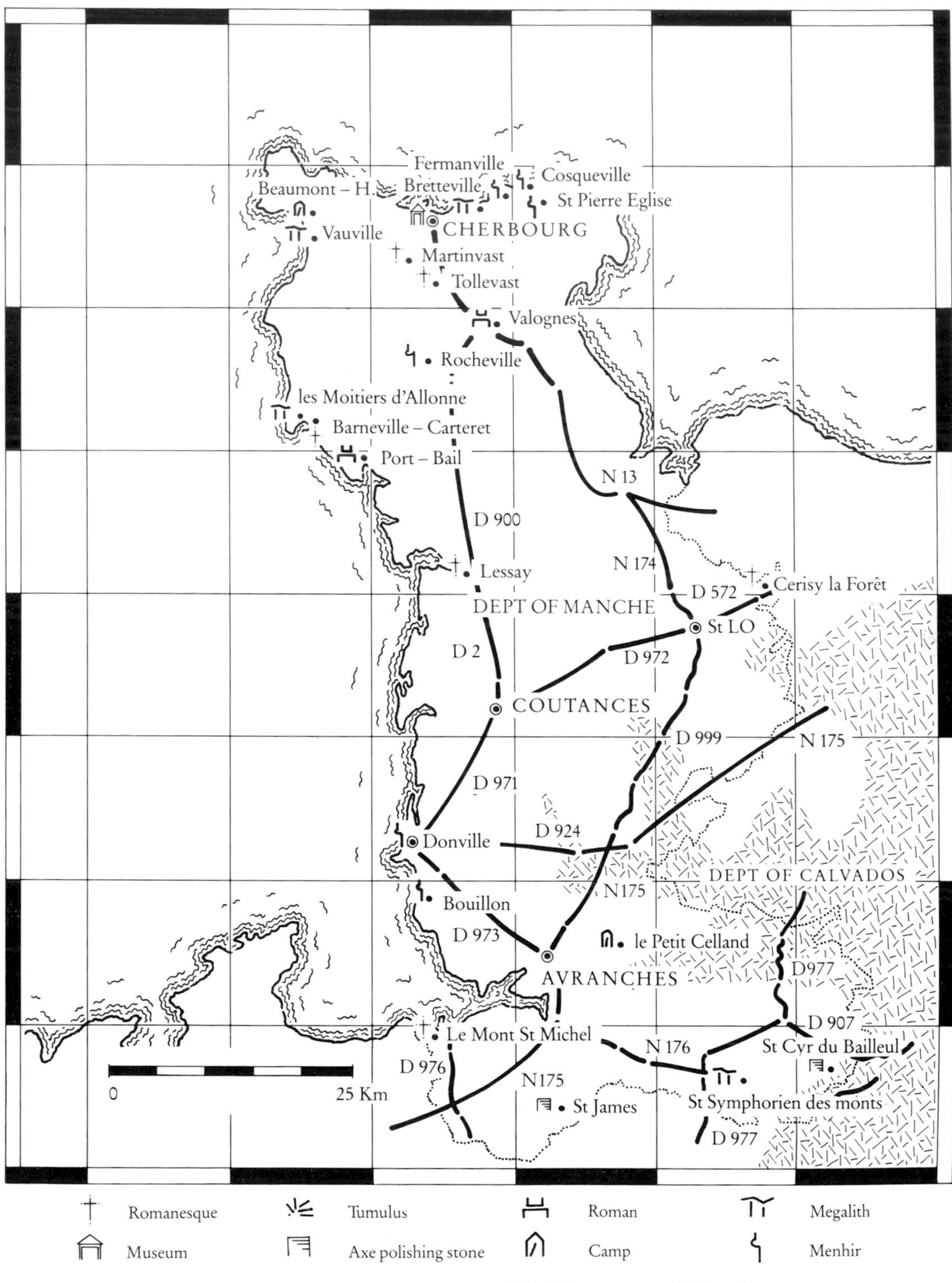

120 Département of Manche

122 La Forge gallery grave, ***Bretteville-en-Saire***

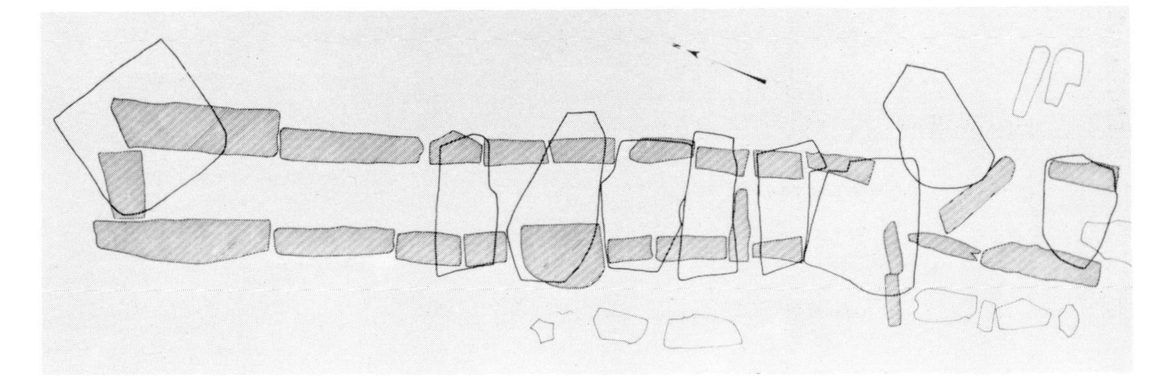

121 Plan of gallery grave of la Forge,
Bretteville-en-Saire

Cerisy-la-Forêt

54/14
Church

This very fine abbey, 'skilfull, generous and majestic' (Musset, 1967), was built by Robert the Magnificent, father of William the Conqueror. It conformed to the normal Benedictine layout, found, for example, at *Lessay*, Manche, and at Winchester and Peterborough in England. However in 1747 a wall was built across the nave separating off the last five bays. The choir and upper part of the nave were used by the monks, the lower part became the parish church. Then alas, in 1811, when the monks departed, the lower part was demolished. The remaining three great arches are surmounted by a triforium and then by a clerestory. These three levels are repeated in the choir and apse. The apse has fourteenth-century Gothic vaulting while the original roof of the nave was covered in 1872 by a false vaulting of wood and plaster.

There is a small museum in the thirteenth-century abbots' chapel on the north side of the forecourt which is open from July to 15 September from 10 a.m. to 12 noon and 2.30 to 7 p.m. The rest of the year it is open on Sundays and Mondays from 2.30 to 7 p.m. From 14 July to 31 August there is a *son et lumière* performance, at 10 p.m. in July, and 9.30 p.m. in August.

Cherbourg

54/2

Cherbourg was a Roman town in the fourth and fifth centuries AD, but there are no visible remains. There was also a fine medieval castle, built on Roman foundations, but that was destroyed in the late seventeenth century. Now it is a pleasant small port.

1 Musée des Sciences Naturelles — Museum

The museum is at the crossroads of the rue Emmanuel Liais and rue de l'Abbaye.

A small museum with a bit of everything including local prehistory.

Open from 1 May to 14 September from 10 a.m. to 12 noon and 2 to 5 p.m.; from 15 September to 30 April from 2 to 5 p.m. Closed Tuesdays.

2 Chapel Saint-Germain, Querqueville — Church

Querqueville is 7 km west of Cherbourg, on the D 801 (→ Beaumont).

Alongside the parish church at the top of the hill—with a vast view over Cherbourg port—is a tiny primitive chapel. Apparently built sometime between the sixth and eighth centuries it is one of the oldest religious structures in western France. It has a trefoil plan and herring-bone masonry.

123 La Pierre Plantée menhir, ***Cosqueville***

Cosquevelle

1 Le Grand Manoir *menhir* — 54/2
Neolithic
Pointe de Barfleur 5–6
330,15/228,10

This menhir and the two at Saint-Pierre-Eglise used to be known as the Marriage of the Three Princesses.

Take the D 116 east out of Cosqueville for 400 m, then turn right onto the D 26 (→ Saint-Pierre-Eglise). Continue 300 m and the menhir is on the right-hand side by a hedge in the first field beyond Cosqueville farm.

A fine upstanding menhir. Granite, 2.83 m high with seven natural grooves on the west face. Fourteen socketed bronze axes were found close to the base of the menhir.

One of the other Three Princesses is further down this road, see *Saint-Pierre-Eglise*.

2 La Pierre Plantée — Neolithic
menhir — Pointe de Barfleur 5–6
(Figure 123) — 330,40/228,15

At Cosqueville take the D 116 east (→ Barfleur). The menhir is signposted to the right, 200 m beyond the crossing with the D 26. Go through the gate marked 'Chasse interdite' and the menhir is in the second field.

Quite respectable, 1.77 m high with natural grooves on the south east face.

Donville-les-Bains

La Pierre Aigüe — 59/7
or la Pierre Hu — Neolithic
menhir

Just north of Donville on the D 971, at the water-tower, turn east on the D 114 (→ Longueville). After 600 m, to the left, in someone's front garden, with roses trailing over it, is the menhir.

It is 3.05 m high, has lost its south-west corner and is made of siliceous sandstone.

Fermanville

menhir — 54/2
Neolithic

From Fermanville take the D 116 east (→ Cosqueville). After 3 km the road bends and the menhir is visible to the left.

Not very impressive. 1.6 m high.

Lessay

54/12
Church

This austere abbey was founded in 1056 but the building was not dedicated until 1178. The exact date of the construction is not certain—either the end of the eleventh century, or the beginning of the twelfth. Either way it is the first large Romanesque building to take complete vaulting. The main body of the church is covered with diagonal ribbed vaulting, while the side-aisles have groin-vaulting.

At the time of the Revolution the abbey became the parish church. In 1944 it was badly damaged but has since been painstakingly restored.

Martinvast

54/1
Church

The choir and apse are twelfth-century rural Romanesque. Some of the capitals are sculpted but are not as fine as those at *Tollevast*. The nave and transept were rebuilt in the nineteenth century.

Moitiers-d'Allone

Dolmen du Breuil — 54/1
gallery grave — Neolithic
(Figure 124) — Bricquebec 5–6
303,80/198,90

Not so easy to find but the monument is quite interesting. From Barneville-Carteret take the N 802 north-east (→ Bricquebec) for 2 km. Continue *past* the tarmacked road on the left marked to les Moitiers-d'Allone and take the second track beyond it to the left. The monument is visible through the second gateway to the left.

One end of the grave is covered with brambles. The chamber is 20 m long, has ten capstones and is apparently blocked at both ends.

124 Grand Breuil gallery grave at ***Les Moitiers-d'Allone***

Mont-Saint-Michel

59/7
Church

Early in the eighth century AD, after the forest of Scissy had been covered by the sea, a large sandy bay formed from which protruded the rocky island of Mont Tombe. Here, tradition maintains, the archangel Michael appeared to Aubert, bishop of Avranches. The bishop was slow to respond but after the divine finger had penetrated his skull he hastily built an oratory on the island, soon to be replaced by a Carolingian abbey. Mont-Saint-Michel became a centre of pilgrimage and a considerable commercial success. Now it is a major tourist centre and horrendously commercialized. When the crowds depart it regains some of its power.

Most of the abbey and its defences are Gothic and cannot be described here (there is a very adequate account, with plans, in the Michelin Green Guide). But at the east end of the Notre-Dame-sous-Terre crypt is part of the first Carolingian abbey. On top of it a fine Romanesque church was built between 1017 and 1114. Additional crypts (the Aquilon crypt) were also built at this time to support the transept and choir. The chancel, however, collapsed and was replaced by a Gothic building between 1446 and 1521. Finally in 1780 the three western arches of the Romanesque nave and the western façade were destroyed.

The abbey is open from 9 to 11.30 a.m. and 1.30 to 4 p.m. (6 p.m. between 16 May and 30 September).

Petit-Celland

Camp de Châtelier 59/8
hill fort Iron Age
(Figures 125 and 126) Avranches 3–4
337,20/116,80

The camp is all right but the drive and the walk are even better. From the church at Petit-Celland take the small road west (→ la Brunière, le Bois Châtelier). After 1.25 km continue over the crossroads. The road shortly becomes a track. After 700 m continue alongside the lake and at the further end leave the car and take the track off to the right. After 200 m the track crosses the Iron Age bank, somewhat obscured and considerably enhanced by silver birch (see Figure 125: X marks where the path crosses the rampart).

The camp is on a steep-sided promontory. A single bank and ditch, with a short double bank and ditch (at C) encloses an area of 19.5 hectares.

Trenches were put down by Mortimer Wheeler in 1938, and showed that the main bank was a *murus gallicus* construction with an outer dry-stone wall revetment and a bonding of nailed timbers. In front of the bank was a 2 m berm and then a wide, shallow ditch. The external bank and ditch at (C) was less elaborate and had never been completed. The main

126 Section through the bank and ditch just south of the main entrance (B) of ***Le Petit-Celland,*** *showing the* murus gallicus *construction*

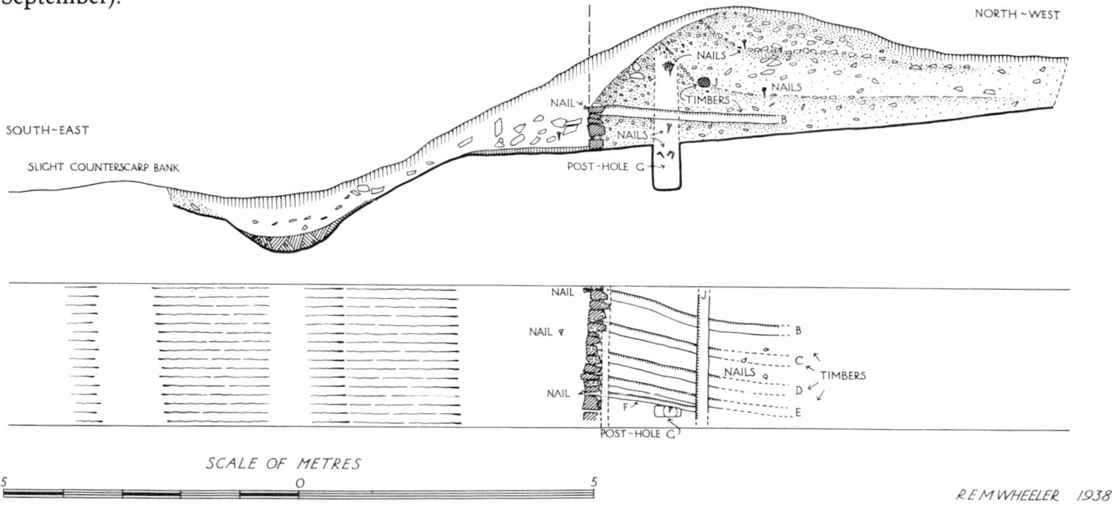

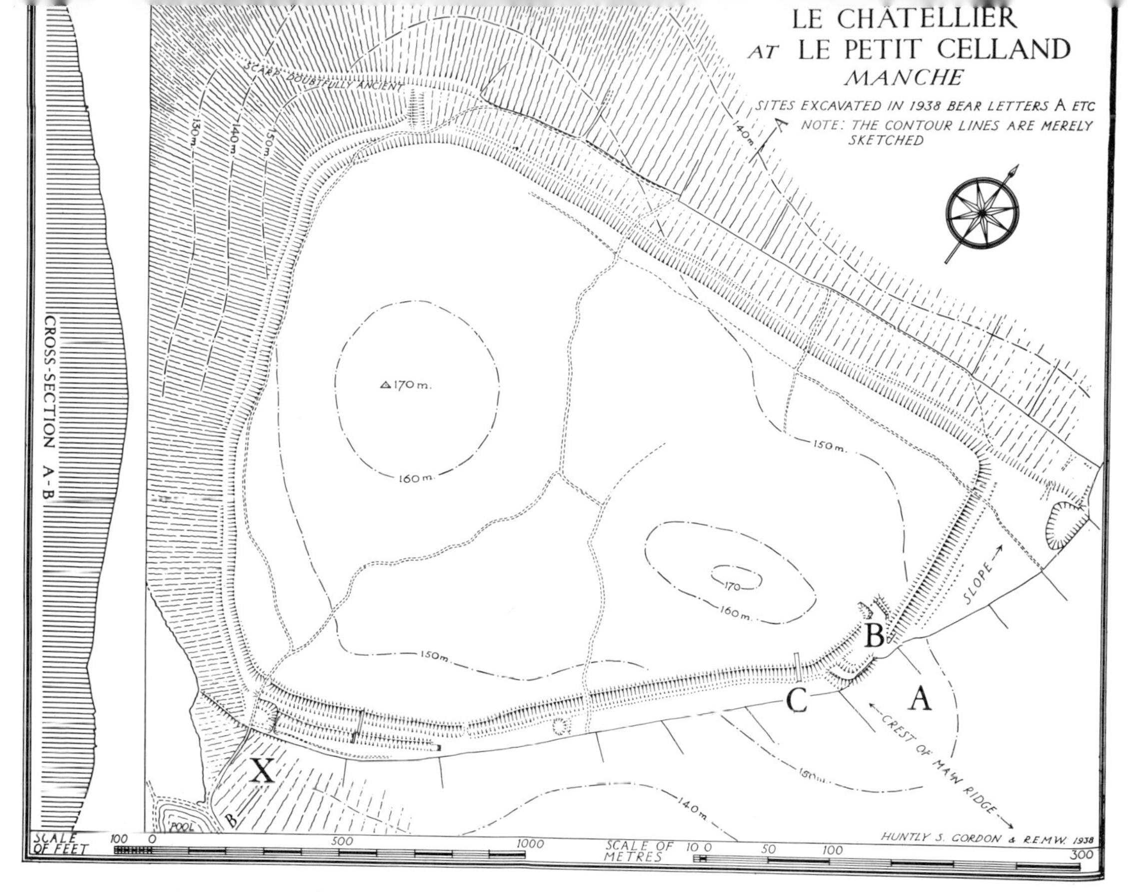

125 *Hill fort of* ***Le Petit-Celland*** *(scale 1 cm : 25 m)*

gateway was at the eastern end (B). It had an oblique entrance and the banks were inturned. It was further defended by an L-shaped hornwork (A), again unfinished. The entrance had been destroyed by violent fire.

Coins found near the gateway date to 56 BC. There is evidence to suggest that the occupation was short-lived. In all probability the camp was thrown up by the local Celtic tribes against the Romans. It could well be the camp that Viridovix, chief of the Unelli, occupied prior to his battle with Caesar's lieutenant Sabinus (Introduction page 53).

Port-Bail

54/11

150 m from the church (which has Roman foundations) is a rock-cut hexagonal font surrounded by the remains of a paving of blue schist slabs. The water is channelled in from the south-east while a lead pipe leads off from the font to a draining well, thus ensuring a constant level of water.

The monument is protected by a wooden roof. To see it, enquire at the town hall.

Rocheville

Les Petites Roches — 54/2
gallery grave — Neolithic
Bricquebec 3–4
315,60/206,70

Fine rock-strewn walking country. From Rocheville take the D 50 south-west (→ Bricquebec), then the first on the left (les Bois de Roches). Continue for 1500 m, following the signs to les Roches. At the unmarked fork keep left and the gallery grave is a little further on, to the left, masked by trees.

The monument is fairly ruined but impressively long, c. 23 m. There is only one capstone still in place. It is orientated west-north-west/east-south-east.

There were two other gallery graves (les Forges and le Catillon) close by, but they have been destroyed.

Saint-Cyr-du-Bailleul

Pierre Saint-Martin 59/10
stone axe-polisher Neolithic
(for the dedicated only) Landivy 3–4
(Figure 127) 369,50/1101,45
At Saint-Cyr take the D 134 north-east (→ Saint-Georges-de-Rouelley) and after 900 m turn right at the signpost to la Gévraisière. Ask for directions at the farm at the end of the track.

A quartzitic rock, 1.4 × 1.2 m with fourteen grooves made by grinding and polishing hardstone axe-edges, and one hollow formed while working the upper and lower surfaces of the tool. There is a much better example at *Saint-James*, Manche.

Such axe manufacture requires water and an additional abrasive such as sand. There is a stream next to the stone.

The stone is still regarded with some awe: according to the farmer his grandfather tried to move it because he thought he might find gold underneath, but even with a team of horses he could not make it budge.

Saint-James

Pierre de Saint-Benoît or 59/8
Pierre qui Pleure Neolithic
axe-polisher Saint-Hilaire-du-Harcouët (West)
(Figure 128) 330,50/1059,0
A fine example but not easy to find. Take the D 998 north from Saint-James (→ Avranches) and after 2 km turn right on the D 363 (Saint-Benoît). Go through the village and past the church, note a turning to the left, then another to the right but keep on and 600 m after this turning, in the valley bottom, to the left of the road, is the axe-polisher. At the moment it is close to a small collapsed wooden cabin but the cabin will probably not be there much longer. It is very overgrown, though only eight years ago the grass all round was well trodden down. The stone was reckoned to have beneficial powers and horses with colic were made to walk three times round the stone and to drink the water in the hollows. It was probably a very good remedy, for the water in the little stream of Longue Touche and in the bordering marshy field is impregnated with iron. Now the horses have gone and the stone is forgotten.

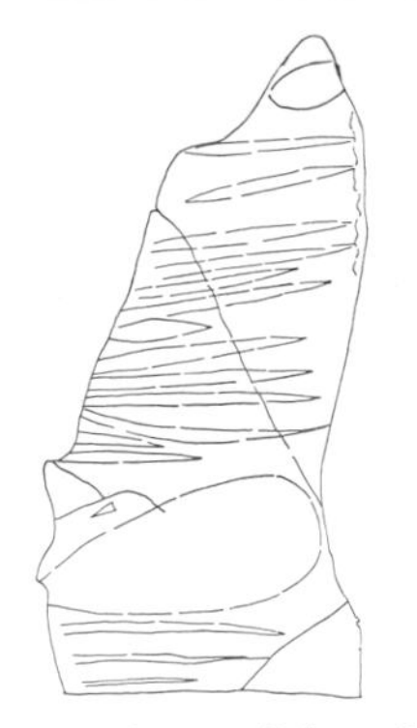

128 *Axe polisher,* ***Saint-James***

127 *Axe polisher,* ***Saint-Cyr-de-Bailleul***

The polisher is of white quartzite, 1.5 m long, and has nineteen grooves and three hollows.

Several hardstone axes, some broken, some half-polished, some completely polished, and a fine perforated jadeite axe pendant were found close by.

Saint-Pierre-Eglise

1 La Longue Pierre 54/2
menhir (one of the Three Neolithic
Princesses) Saint-Vast-la-Hougue 1–2
329,95/225,95
Turn south off the D 116 at Cosqueville onto the D 26 (→ Saint-Pierre-Eglise). After 2.5 m, on the right, by a large farm (Plat Douet) a small signpost 'menhir' points down a track. After 400 m, through the second gateway on the left, the menhir is visible.

It is 4.2 m high and is made of granite.

2 La Haute Pierre Neolithic
menhir (the third Princess, Saint-Vast-la-Hougue
but hardly worth the 1–2
elaborate journey) 331,50/226,50
As above, at Cosqueville take the D 26 south (→ Saint-Pierre-Eglise), continue past the farm of Plat Douet, and at the entrance to Saint-Pierre-Eglise turn left onto the D 316 (→ Angouville/ Vrasville). After

1.8 km take a small turning right (→ Hacouville). Through Hacouville and continue to a small chapel on the left. Turn right—the menhir is visible at the turning—go through the second gate on the right and immediately right again into the adjoining field. The menhir is then just over the brow of the hill!

It is largish, 2.9 m, and made of granite.

Saint-Symphorien-des-Monts

Les Cartesières 59/9
T-shaped gallery grave Neolithic
Landivy 1–2
353,40/1098,30

The monument is in the zoological park next to the village.

An interesting grave, the only surviving one of its kind in Normandy. The gallery section is 10.5 m long and 1.1 m wide at the east end. The transverse section, at the west end, is 8.7 m long and 1.3 m wide.

During an early excavation four Grand Pressigny blades, scrapers, four rim-sherds—one plain, the others with one or three 'ribs', and a great deal of coarse pottery were found.

This form of grave is similar to ones in Brittany and the ribbed decorated ware is like the Breton Kerugou pottery. The coarse pottery is probably Seine-Oise-Marne type.

The park is open from 9.30 a.m. to 10 p.m.

Tollevast

54/2
Church

A small quiet Romanesque church built in the second quarter of the twelfth century. It has several unusual features: no side-aisles, a long narrow choir, an apse with heavy cross-ribbed vaulting and a wide range of decoration, for example on the brackets of the cornice which holds up the roof, on the capitals of the west door and, finest of all, high relief sculpture on the corbels that support the choir vaulting.

Valognes

54/2

Valognes—Alauna—may have been the capital of the Unelli tribe and was probably an important link in the Iron Age tin-trade network. It then became a small Gallo-Roman township.

Vieux Château Gallo-Roman
Roman baths Cherbourg 7–8
325,50/207,70

Take the N 13 from Valognes south-east (→ Carentan) and just beyond the town note a water-tower, on the left. Almost immediately take a small road left, Chemin de la Victoire, for 1 km. The impressive ruins of the baths stand to the right of the road.

These baths were first surveyed in 1765, and the accuracy of the plan was substantiated during excavations in 1954. The excavations uncovered five rooms orientated east-north-east / west-south-west. The walls are made of rubble between facings of small stones; the frames of the bays are made of brick and stone. One of the rooms had a circular bath heated by hypocaust. Water was supplied by an underground aqueduct fed by a spring at le Câtelet.

To reach the Câtelet fountain take the Chemin du Castelet which leads off from the Chemin de la Victoire alongside the baths. Continue for 500 m and the fountain lies to the right of the road.

A theatre lay 800 m from the baths and there was also a temple near by.

Vauville

Les Pierres Pouquelées 54/1
gallery grave Neolithic
Les Pieux 3–4
297,55/225,10

Marked on the Michelin. The monument is hard to find, but involves a marvellous walk. 2 km out of Beaumont on the D 318 going south (→ Vauville) take the small, rough track up to the right, marked, though it is not easy to see, 'Pouquelées'. Then after a kilometre, take the second track off to the right. This is on the summit of the hill, opposite a dry-stone wall. Follow this grassy track for about 400 m. The monument is then 10 m to the left, heavily shrouded in bracken.

Most of the stones are of quartzite. The monument is 16.8 × 1.35 × 1.5 m. Two capstones are still in place and one has fallen inside the monument. In 1870 quarrymen half-destroyed the monument. They were forced to bring the stones back but simply left them lying around.

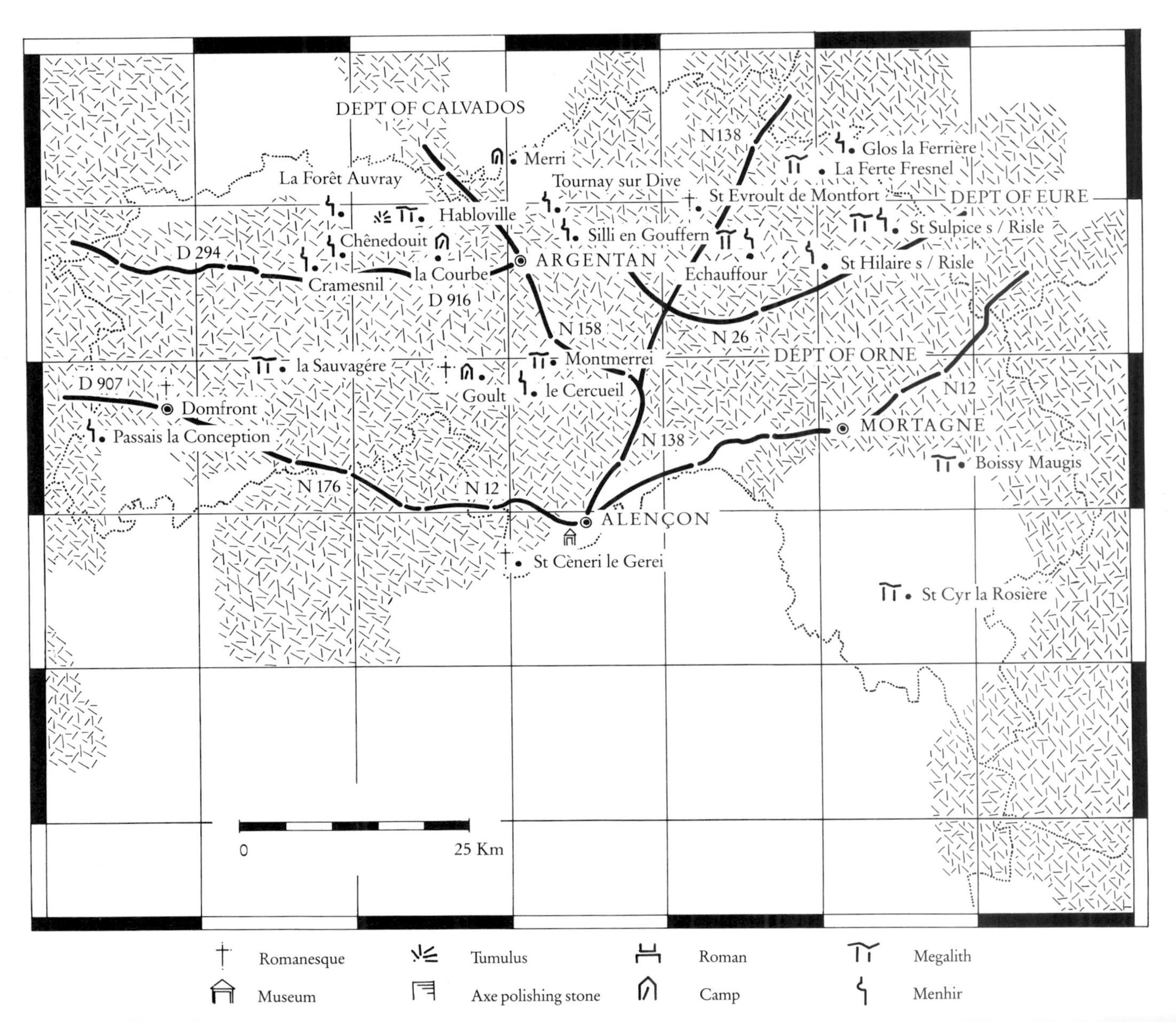

129 Département of Orne

Orne

Alençon

Maison d'Ozé 60/3
museum Museum
The museum is opposite Notre-Dame church in the place de la Magdelaine.

A fine, fifteenth-century house contains paintings, lace and some local archaeology.

Open 16 March to 29 September from 10 a.m. to 12 noon and 2 to 6 p.m.; 30 September to 15 March from 10 a.m. to 12 noon and 2 to 5 p.m.

Boissy-Maugis

La Grosse Pierre or Dolmen du Bois de la Pierre 60/5
Neolithic
dolmen La Loupe (West) 5–6
(Figure 130) 482,72/1086,30
Marked on the Michelin. From Rémalard take the D 920 north-east (→ la Loupe). After 250 m turn left on the small road to the Bois de la Pierre, tarmac for 3.5 km, then gravel. From the beginning of the gravel continue for another kilometre and the dolmen is to the right, in the forest but visible from the road.

A large capstone, 4 × 2 m, rests on four uprights. One of the uprights is of puddingstone, all the other stones are quartzitic sandstone.

Cercueil, le

Pierre de la Tremblaie 60/3
menhir Neolithic
Take the small road going west from the village of Cercueil for 1 km (passing a road right to Montmerrei) to a crossroads. Here, the right-hand road goes to Saint-Christophe, the left-hand to Tanville. Take the cul-de-sac between the two. After 200 m there is a rubbish dump to the right and a field to the left—the menhir is at the far end of this.

A good chunk of sandstone, a respectable 4 m high.

Chênedouit

La Droite Pierre 60/1–2
menhir Neolithic
Argentan 1–2
401,85/112,65 (approx.)
From Chênedouit take the road south-west to the D 21. Turn right on the D 21, then, after 1 km, left on the D 15. Stop at the beginning of the first bend and the menhir is to the left of the road visible from the gate. 2.3 m high.

Courbe, la

Château Gontier, les Vieux Châteaux or les Pierres Brûlées 60/2
?Iron Age
Argentan 1–2
?Iron Age camp 413,60/1118,55
Coming from the east, across the bridge over the Orne, the road climbs to the top of the promontory. Stop at the first farm to the right of the road on the top, and the first two northern ramparts are immediately next to the farm.

A fine site encircled by a tight meander of the Orne on three sides and defended by earthworks to the north and south. At the north end there are two banks and ditches. The main one is 4 m above the interior of the camp, and 5 m above the bottom of the ditch, whilst the outer bank stands 2.3 m above the outer ditch. At the southern end are the remains

130 La Grosse Pierre, ***Boissy-Maugis***

of two banks and ditches and traces of a counterscarp bank on the outer margin. In some places the bank is vitrified.

Craménil

Affiloir de Gargantua 60/1
menhir Neolithic
Argentan 1–2
401,80/1121,80

Marked on the Michelin. From Craménil take the road north towards le Repas, Sainte-Croix-sur-Orne. Then turn right (→ Bruyères, Chênedouit). The menhir is to the left of the road, 300 m beyond the first farm on the right. It is in the middle of the field, and can be seen from the gate.

Red granite, 3.3 m high.

Domfront

Notre-Dame-sur-l'Eau 59/10
Church

The church is in the lower part of the town, to the south of the N 808.

A fine example of Romanesque architecture, lacking, however, a large part of the nave due to a curious decision taken in 1836 to allow the road from Domfront to Mortain to pass through the church. What remains—the transept, choir and belfry—date to the late eleventh or early twelfth century.

Echauffour

1 Pierre Levée 60/4
dolmen Neolithic
L'Aigle (West) 1–2
457,80/1116,45

From Echauffour take the D 932 south-east (→

Sainte-Gauburge). The dolmen is 300 m beyond the last house of the village to the left of the road. The large capstone and the tops of the uprights are visible.

2 Les Croûtes — Neolithic
three menhirs
Directions as for la Pierre Levée (above), but continue down the D 932 then turn left onto a small road (→ Fumeçon). The road ends with a farm, right, and continues as a track. The menhirs are 100 m down the track to the left.

There are two standing menhirs, one 3.3 m high. A third one, 30 m away, has fallen. All are of sandstone.

Ferté-Frênel, la

Pierre Couplée — 55/14
dolmen — Neolithic
Rugles 5–6
465,00/1128,20
Marked on the Michelin. Take the D 14 west (→ Bocquencé) from Ferté-Frênel. After 0.75 km there is a small wood to the left of the road. A track at the near end is signposted to the dolmen and leads through the wood to the dolmen in the field beyond.

The sloping capstone rests on three uprights. The fourth was removed by treasure-seekers in 1825. All the stones are of sandstone.

Forêt-Auvray, la

Pierre Levée or Pierre de la Roussellière — 55/11
Neolithic
menhir
Best viewed from the opposite bank of the river Orne. From la Forêt-Auvray take the D 21 north-east (→ Forneaux-le-Val). Cross over the bridge, and as the road climbs take a small turning right (le Val d'Orne) for 200 m. The menhir can then be seen on the other side of the river.

Cambrian conglomerate, 2.65 m high.

Glos la Ferrière

Pierre de la Broudière — 55/15
menhir — Neolithic
Rugles 7–8
472,88/1128,40
Take the D 919 south from Glos la Ferrière (→ l'Aigle). After 2 km, at the further end of a small wood to the right of the road and almost in an apple orchard, is the menhir.

Puddingstone and 2.2 m high.

Goult

1 Church — 60/2
Church
The chapel of the old priory is now used as a barn. The doorway has six finely carved and unusual capitals.

2 Le Câvalier — ?Bronze Age
earthworks — Argentan 7–8
(Figure 131) — 423,00/103,10
In Goult, to the south of the high street, a steep path goes up to the camp and to the chapel of Saint-Michel. It comes in on the north side of the camp, near to the chapel.

The north-east side of the hilltop is naturally protected by the steep slope down to the river Cance. On the south-east and south the natural drop is reinforced by a bank. On the north and west the bank is further reinforced by a ditch 8 to 10 m wide and 3 m deep.

There is an outlying fortification to the west (la Butte des Sept Puits). It is more or less circular with an internal diameter of 20 m, and is surrounded by a bank, 5 m wide at the base and 1 to 1.5 m high, and a ditch. There are a series of round pits with the remains of interior dry-stone walling, within this enclosure. Each pit is roughly 2 m deep and 1 to 1.5 m in diameter.

Further west again, there are traces of two further enclosures.

The date of these earthworks is unknown and no systematic excavation has occurred. There is vague mention of two socketed bronze axes, part of an axe-mould, two bronze bracelets and some Roman coins.

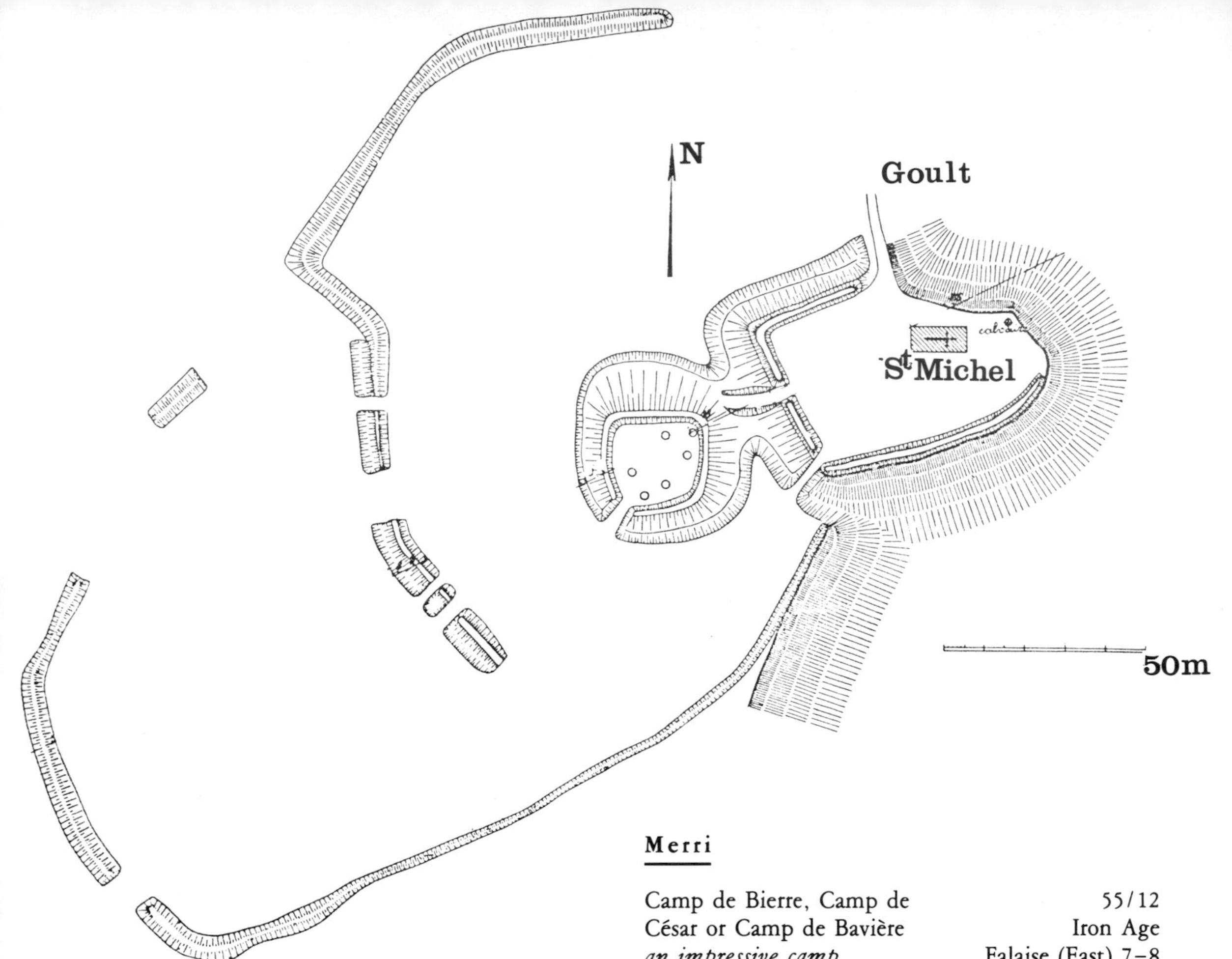

131 Camp de ***Goult***

Habloville

Pierre des Bignes 60/2
dolmen Neolithic
Falaise (East) 7–8
416,30/1125,90

From Habloville take the D 129 northwards. At Frênay-le-Buffard take the small gravelled track, right, signposted to 'la Pierre des Bignes'.

Rather more presentable than most in this département. The granite capstone, 3.2 × 2.9 m is supported by four uprights—two of granite, two of quartzite.

There is a mound alongside the dolmen that has never been excavated and there were two others close by which have been ploughed out.

Merri

Camp de Bierre, Camp de César or Camp de Bavière 55/12
Iron Age
an impressive camp Falaise (East) 7–8
(Figure 132) 424,65/1128,70

Marked on the Michelin (as Camp Romain). From Bierre (south of Merri) take the D 29E south-west (→ Pierrefitte). Just beyond Bierre there is a small track to the left, marked le Camp de Bierre, at first tarmacked then simply a dirt-track. It crosses the stream and eventually reaches the north end of the camp.

Despite a steep natural drop on three sides, the rocky promontory is totally enclosed by a dry-stone rampart. Across the neck of the promontory the defences are tripled with the highest rampart standing 7 m above ground level. The central area protected by the innermost rampart covers about 1.5 hectares, while the exterior rampart encloses an area of over 4 hectares. There is a tower in the north-east corner.

The rampart seems to have been built and rebuilt several times and it is probable that the tower belongs to a later phase of rebuilding. Carbon-14 dates suggest that the camp was first built during the late Bronze Age and was rebuilt and reused during the Iron Age

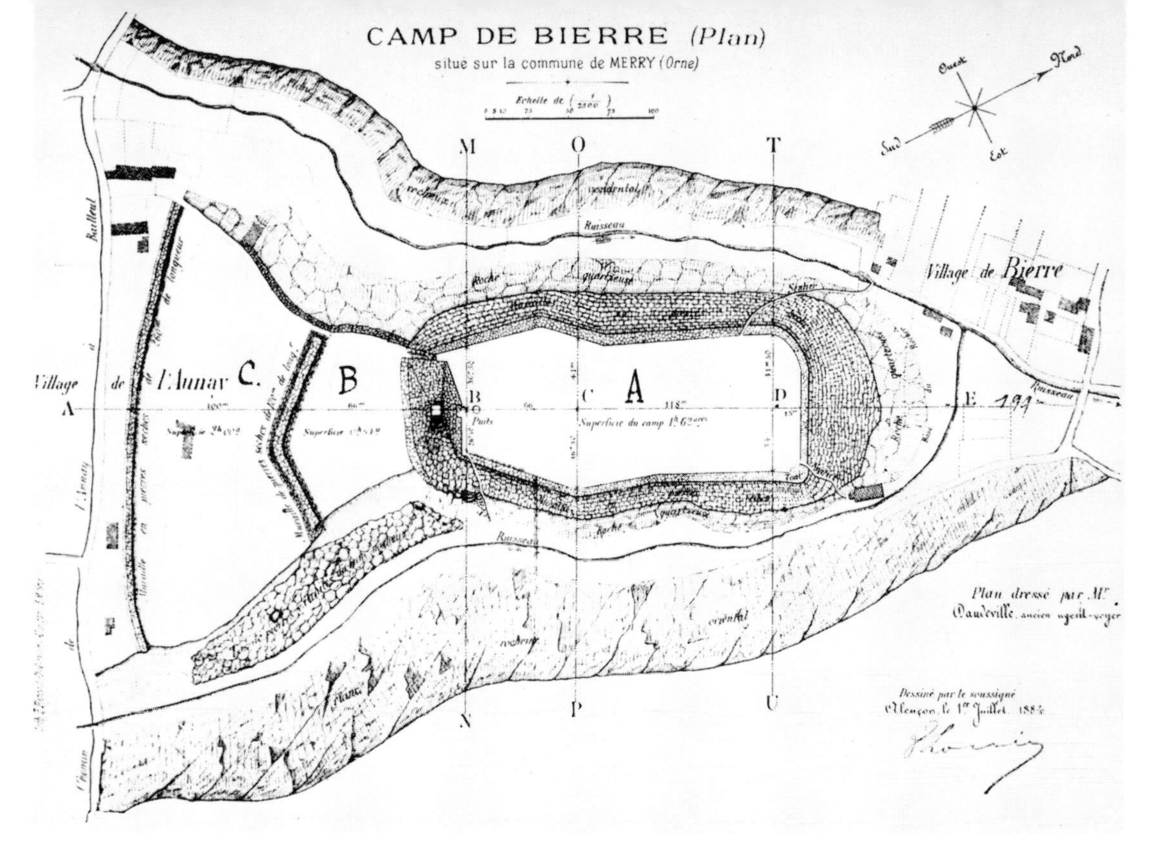

132 Camp de Bierre, Merri

La Tène. The three dates are 790 + − 11 bc (calibrated 965 BC), 370 + − 100 bc (calibrated 435 BC) and 850 + − 120 bc (calibrated 1030 BC). The site was also occupied in earlier, Neolithic times and, later, in the Gallo-Roman period.

Montmerrei

1 La Pierre Tournoire 60/3
dolmen Neolithic
Sées 5–6
429,30/104,50

Difficult to find, and when found not too exciting. From Montmerrei take the C 4 south (→ le Cercueil). Continue for 2 km. The road climbs, then levels out, then descends. 80 m beyond the beginning of the descent, on the left, is a birch-tree with a faint trace of blue paint. This marks the entrance to a narrow path leading to the dolmen.

It turns out to be a large stone, 4.3 × 3.3 m, which is said to rest on three uprights.

Passais-la-Conception

Menhir du Perron 59/20
Neolithic
Landivy 7–8
370,72/1092,60

From Passais take the D 24 south-east (→ Saint-Fraimbault) and then immediately turn right onto the D 21. After 1.7 km turn left (→ le Cerisier). Continue another 1.2 km to a crossing and a calvary. Go straight on for 300 m then take the track right (→ Ferme du Perron). The menhir is 50 m down the track, to the left.

A good 3 m, made of diabase.

Saint-Céneri-le-Gérei

60/12
Church

A beautiful church and a fantastic site. Fine view from the old bridge over the Sarthe.

The monks of Saint-Evroult-d'Ouche constructed this church on the foundations of an earlier building.

There have been later additions—the ogival arches over the north crossing, the fourteenth-century frescos, some fifteenth-century windows and a nineteenth-century west façade—but these are just minor modifications to the fine late eleventh-century church.

Saint-Cyr-la-Rosière

La Pierre Procureuse 60/15
dolmen Neolithic
(Figure 133) Mamers (East) 7–8
473,85/1068,10

From Saint-Cyr take the road south towards l'Hermitière. The Pierre Procureuse is signposted on the outskirts of Saint-Cyr. Continue for 3.3 km to the junction with the C 2 (→ Gémages). Turn down the C 2, again signposted to the Pierre Procureuse, and after 145 m take the first road, left. 190 m along the track, and 55 paces to the left is the dolmen—right in the forest.

All puddingstone; the capstone, 4 × 3 m, rests on three uprights. Other enormous blocks are scattered about.

133 La Pierre Procureuse, ***Saint-Cyr-la-Rosière***

Saint-Evroult-sur-Montfort

60/4
Church

There is a fine twelfth-century lead font in the church, depicting the Labours of the Months.

Saint-Hilaire-sur-Risle

Les Gastines 60/4
menhir(s) Neolithic
L'Aigle (West) 1–2
465,20/1114,30

Quite difficult to find. Take the N 26 in Saint-Hilaire north-eastwards (→ l'Aigle) and on the outskirts of the village, at the calvary, turn right onto a small road for 30 m and then right again to the hamlet of la Métairie. Continue for 2 km, through the hamlet, to the crossroads beyond, and turn left (→ Beaufay). To the left of this road the fields are scattered with rocks. Go into the fields, and up the slope are the menhirs of les Gastines. One of them is dramatically split by a tree. It is over 4 m high.

Saint-Sulpice-sur-Risle

1 Menhir de la Chevrolière 60/5
(Figure 134) Neolithic
L'Aigle (East) 3–4
475,60/1120,72

Go through Saint-Sulpice on the D 930 south-westwards (→ l'Aigle) and the menhir is in a field to the right of the road, beyond the last houses and 800 m before the junction with the N 819. It can be seen from the road, is of puddingstone and 2.8 m high.

2 Dolmen du Jarrier Neolithic
(Figure 135) L'Aigle (East) 3–4
476,70/1120,50

Take the small road south-east through Saint-Sulpice, and cross two bridges and two level-crossings. After the second continue ahead (→ Anglures). The road climbs onto a plateau. The dolmen is 500 m from the level-crossing, to the right of, and 40 m from, the road. It is in a small field obscured by a hedge. If you come to a road junction you have gone 100 m too far!

Again, not too exciting. There is a capstone 4 × 2.45 m and four uprights, all of siliceous puddingstone.

134 Menhir de la Chevrolière, ***Saint-Sulpice-sur-Risle***

135 Dolmen du Jarrier, ***Saint-Sulpice-sur-Risle***

Sauvagère, la

La Bertinière 60/1
or Maison de Fées Neolithic
gallery grave Flers 7–8
395,80/1106,45

From Sauvagère take the D 18 north-west (→ Flers). After 1 km turn left (signpost la Bertinière—dolmen) and go to the end of the road, to a farm. The gallery grave is to the right in the second field beyond the barns (the farmer is not always enthusiastic about visitors).

At last something better. 14.7 m long and between 1.1 and 1.42 m wide. There is a possible divide between chamber and antechamber made of two granite stones. Apparently there used to be another gallery grave called la Maisonette 250 m to the south-east.

Silli-en-Gouffern

La Pierre Levée de la 60/3
Vente de Gouffern Neolithic
menhir Sées 1–2
436,02/1117,39

Marked on the Michelin. From Silli take the road south-east to the D 16. Turn right down the D 16 (→ Almenêches). After 800 m (having passed the Château des Ventes on the left) the menhir is to the right of and 15 m from the road, with woods just behind.

A huge stone, 6 m high, and originally 8 m—before the top got knocked off. Eocene sandstone. Another one nearby has been destroyed.

Tournay-sur-Dive

Pierre aux Bordeux 60/3
or Montmilcent Neolithic
menhir

Not easy to find. From Tournay go south-west for 1 km in the direction of Argentan, then turn left (→ Aubray-en-Exmes). Another 500 m then right onto a gravel track. 485 paces on, to the right, is a field entrance with a barbed-wire barrier. Navigate, and the menhir is at the bottom of this field almost in the hedge.

Sandstone, 3.6 m high.

Seine-Maritime

In the Seine-Maritime there are two great lines of communication. There is the coast, or rather the sea, flanked by high chalk cliffs and long shingle beaches; and there is the Seine, the broad slow-moving river still busy with barge traffic and edged with wooded chalk bluffs. The monuments follow the same two lines: the camps of *Bracquemont*, *Fécamp* and *Veulettes-sur-Mer* along the coast, and along the Seine a mixture of Iron Age camp and cathedral—'la routes des Abbayes'—*Sandouville*, *Saint-Jean-d'Abbetot*, *Lillebonne*, *Saint-Aubin*, *Saint-Wandrille*, *Jumièges*, *Duclair*, *Saint-Martin-de-Boscherville* and *Rouen*.

Bracquemont

Cité des Limes or Camp de César 52/4
Iron Age *camp*
Dieppe (East) 5–6
(Figure 137) 513,38/1249,70

In Bracquemont, at the village green, turn north down the small seaward road which after 75 m angles left and becomes a dirt-track. Follow for 0.7 km and it crosses the ramparts.

A very impressive defence—the banks, coming to an abrupt end at the cliff edge, can be seen all the way from Dieppe. The Germans used it in World War II and scattered bunkers along the top. The site is a shallow promontory with the sea to the north and a valley running obliquely inland to the south. The defended site is now about 48.5 hectares but much land has been lost by erosion. Across the neck of the promontory, on the north-east side, the bank stands 10 m high above the present bottom of the ditch. The dirt-track takes you through the well-defined, strongly inturned entrance. At the head of the valley the defences turn sharply westward and follow the brow of the hill. There is a slight counterscarp for the first 100 m after the westward turn. At the further, western, end the bank swings away from the brow of the hill and has a ditch, a wide berm and a second bank (not marked on the plan). Wheeler suggests that this change may mark the incorporation of an earlier defence system that protected only the western end of the camp. There is in fact a very mutilated and ploughed out cross-rampart which is cut by the quarry ditches of the main rampart.

Between 1822 and 1827 Feret excavated a Gallo-Roman temple which has since fallen into the sea and found an inhumation with a coin of Constans beside the skull, another of Constantine II by the thigh bone and sixty-two Roman coins ranging from Augustus to Vatens; also twenty-four Celtic coins. He also dug up some mounds that contained hearths, rough Iron Age pottery, tiles, copper rings, iron fragments, shells and animal bones. In 1874 more hearths and more Iron Age pottery were found and in 1891 part of the defences were excavated and Celtic and Roman pottery and flint tools were uncovered. Finally in 1926 two more mounds were trenched and produced two pedestal bases, two late La Tène brooches and a Celtic coin. There is also considerable evidence of an earlier Neolithic occupation.

Caudebec-en-Caux

Musée, in the Templars' House, near the quay 52/13
Museum

The house is a rare example of thirteenth-century civil architecture. The contents are various, with a few cases of prehistoric material.

Open from 10 a.m. to 12 noon and 2.30 to 5.30 p.m. Closed Mondays. But the times change frequently.

If you have children there is a curious fairy-tale tree to be visited at Allouville-Bellefosse 10.5 km

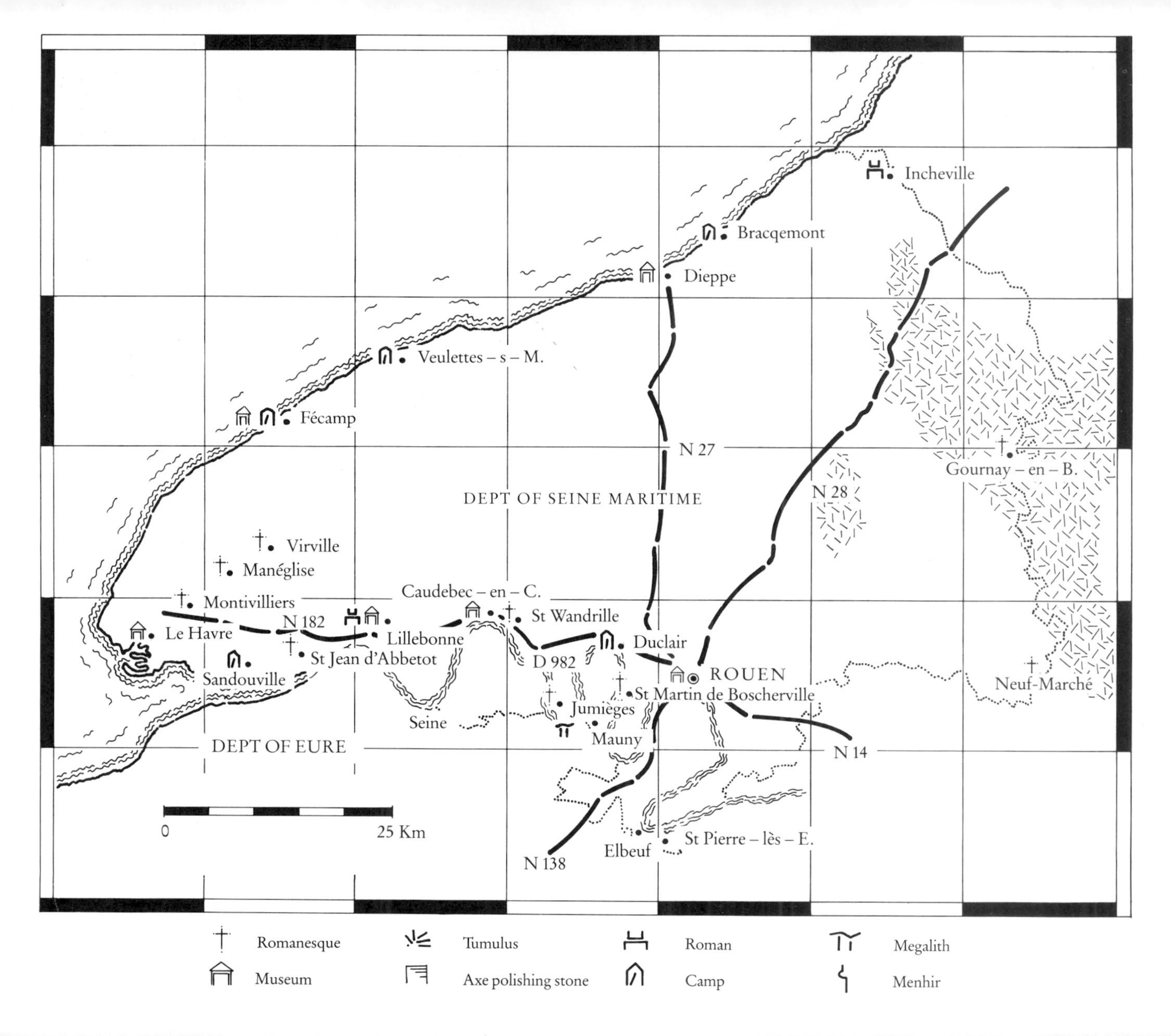

Incheville
Bracqemont
Dieppe
Veulettes – s – M.
Fécamp
N 27
N 28
Gournay – en – B.
DEPT OF SEINE MARITIME
Virville
Manéglise
Montivilliers
Caudebec – en – C.
St Wandrille
N 182
Le Havre
Lillebonne
Duclair
St Jean d'Abbetot
D 982
Sandouville
ROUEN
Neuf-Marché
St Martin de Boscherville
Jumièges
Seine
Mauny
DEPT OF EURE
N 14
0
25 Km
St Pierre – lès – E.
Elbeuf
N 138
Romanesque
Museum
Tumulus
Axe polishing stone
Roman
Camp
Megalith
Menhir

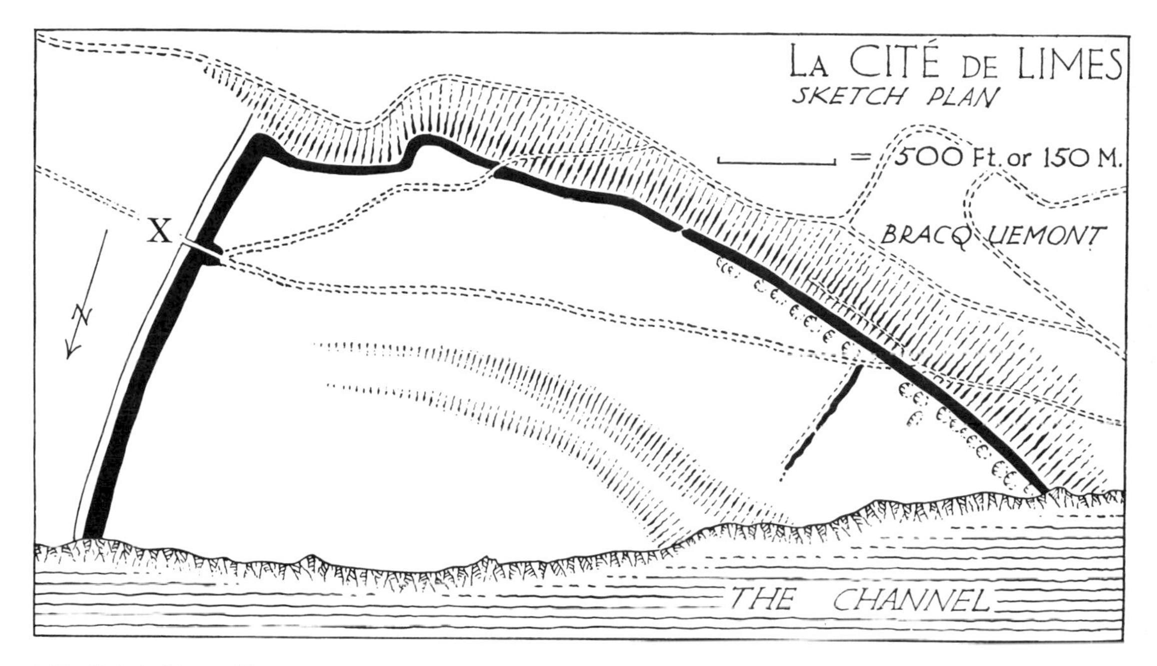

137 Cité de Limes, ***Bracquemont***

north-north-east of Caudebec. A thousand years old they say, with two chapels built right inside it.

Dieppe

Musée, in Dieppe Castle, on the road to Saint-Valéry — 52/4 — Museum

The castle, built around a massive circular tower which formed part of the fourteenth-century town fortifications, is strong on marine history, ethnography etc., with a small section of local prehistory. There is also a remarkable view across the town.

Open between 15 June and 1 October every day from 10 a.m. to 12 noon and from 2 to 6 p.m. 2 October to 14 June open from 10 a.m. to 12 noon and 2 to 5 p.m. Closed on Mondays.

136 Département of Seine-Maritime

Duclair

1 Camp du Câtelier or Châtellier — 52/13 — Iron Age
camp — Rouen (West) 3–4
(Figure 138) — 496,30/199,60

Take the D 982 east out of Duclair (→ Rouen) and then after 1.5 km take the first small road left (signposted Cercle de la Voile)—if you reach la Fontaine you have gone too far. After 75 m the small road widens slightly on both sides and there is a quarry on the left. The further end of the quarry is marked by a stop sign. From there retrace your steps 12 m and get up onto the bank on the *opposite* side of the road. Skirt through the trees parallel to the road for 30 m then turn up a very ill-defined path that goes up the hillside to a sunken track which reaches the camp at X on the plan.

Although it is not easy to get to it is very interesting and well preserved. It is one of the string of Iron Age camps along the Seine between Vernon and Sandouville thrown up against the Roman advance and only briefly occupied. It is protected by the Seine to the south (and overlooks an ancient river crossing),

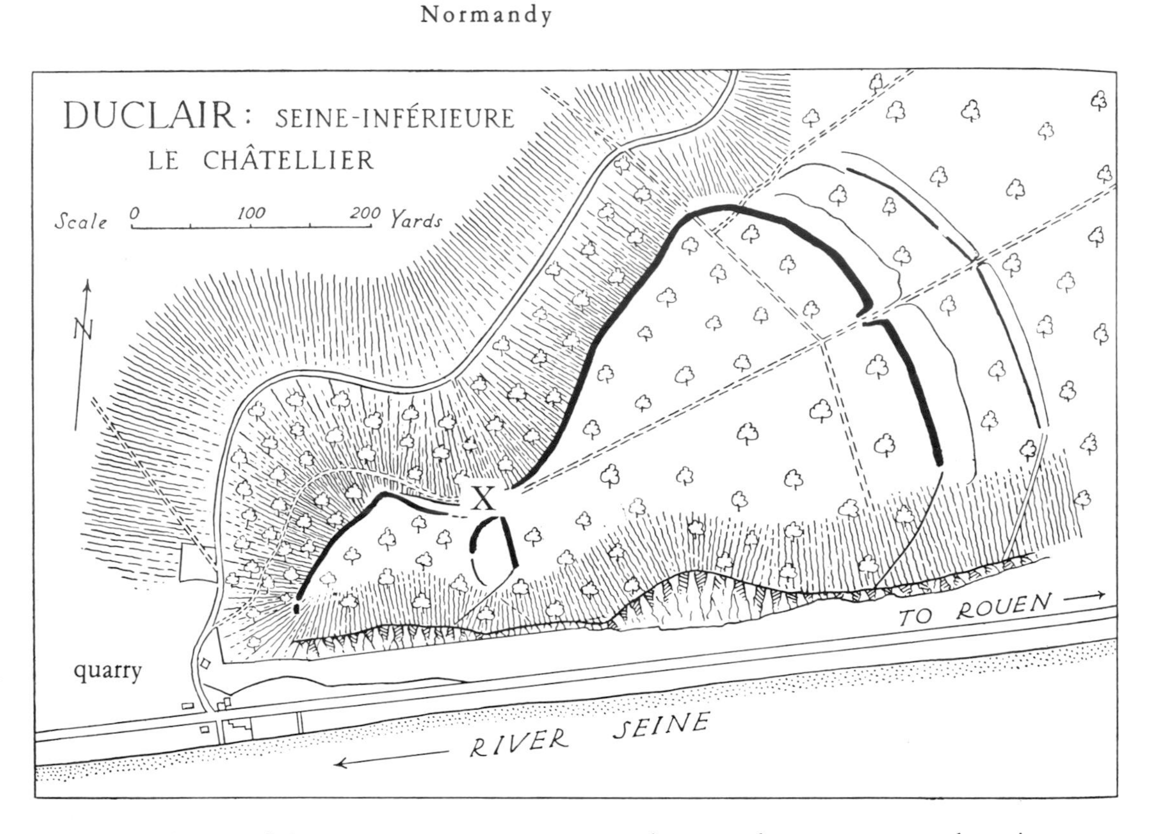

138 Le Châtellier, ***Duclair***

and by the dry valley of the Asnerie to the north. The camp covers 9.8 hectares.

The mainland side has two lines of defence, an outer small bank and ditch, then 50 m further west an inner massive rampart and wide ditch. The rampart rises 7 m above the interior of the camp and 10 m above the ditch bottom. The two features associated with this series of defended sites, which Wheeler called the Fécamp series, are present. The ditch is flat-bottomed, and the entrance through the rampart has strong flanking wings.

There are no defences on the south side where the cliffs give adequate protection. On the northern side the main rampart swings round and follows the valley edge, gradually diminishing in size until it peters out close to the large cross-bank. Beyond this another bank and quarry ditch form a sort of right angle protecting the narrow western tip of the promontory.

Wheeler excavated this site in the 1930s (his trenches across the rampart near to the main entrance are still faintly visible). He found that the main rampart was of 'dump' construction, made up of clay and flints. It had a revetment, a single row of chalk blocks near the top of the rampart, which retained the layer of flints that capped the summit. Within the rampart was a fair amount of pottery indicating that there had been an earlier occupation. Wheeler suggested that there may have been two or even three periods of construction. First, perhaps, the most easterly small bank and ditch, then the main construction, then the westernmost defence. Occupation debris associated with the main rampart suggests a short-lived settlement. It included two developed La Tène brooches and pedestalled and cordoned ware.

2 Saint-Denis Church

The church is on the site of a seventh-century Merovingian monastic cella, and marble columns and capitals were reused when the eleventh-century church was built under the auspices of the abbey of Jumièges.

From the outside, the church looks almost entirely Gothic, fourteenth to sixteenth century. But inside it is more or less untouched Romanesque except for a heavy dose of nineteenth-century restoration. Three of the half-columns up against the rectangular piles on the south side of the nave are from the earlier Merovingian structure and are of grey, green and red marble, and so is the pink marble half-column on the north side. The base of the massive tower rests on four very solid arches, two with decorated archivolts. Again the half-column against the north-east pile is of red marble and is crowned with a fine Merovingian capital of grey marble from the Pyrenees. There is the remains of a similar capital on the north-west pile. The other capitals, with godroons, date to the second quarter of the twelfth century. The belfry is twelfth century, with a sixteenth-century spire.

Elbeuf

Musée de l'Hôtel de Ville, 54/20
place Aristide Briand Museum

A little of everything, including a friendly stuffed dog.

Open on Wednesday and Saturday, from 2 to 4 p.m.

Fécamp

1 Camp du Canada, 52/12
or Camp de César Iron Age
camp Fécamp 5–6
(Figure 139) 461,20/228,80

From Fécamp take the D 926 south-east (→ Rouen) and turn right almost immediately on the D 28 (→ Ganzeville). Opposite the first house in Ganzeville and 100 m before the village sign, take a small precipitous path to the left of the road leading up the hill. Near the top, follow the path as it bends sharp left and shortly arrive alongside the ditch.

The camp gives its name to a whole series of sites in High Normandy, all thrown up—or at least refurbished—against Caesar's armies. This one is a promontory site, 100 m above sea-level, lying between the valley of the Valmont to the east and the Ganzeville to the west. The southern side is protected by an immense bank, ditch and slight counterscarp. The bank is over 5 m above the interior of the camp and 12 m above the present-day bottom of the ditch. Outside and parallel to the main bank is a small bank and ditch. The total area enclosed is over 20 hectares.

The rest of the promontory perimeter, although naturally precipitous, was further protected by a fairly minor bank, shallow ledge and scarp.

Wheeler excavated this site. He examined the main south-eastern entrance with its inturned flanks and found that it was faced with rough flint walls. There were several large post-holes which probably carried either a bridge or a fighting platform. There were five other minor entrances (see Figure 139). The western entrance was also faced with flints and had three post-holes, probably marking the position of a double gate.

Excavation revealed a fair amount of earlier Neolithic material within the camp and extending below the defences. There was a slight concentration of Iron Age material within the shelter of the inturned south-west flank of the main gate with three distinct levels. The upper level has some Samian ware which dates between AD 25 and 50. Below was a level with Belgic sherds including some imitation Arretine forms which probably date to the end of the first century BC. The bottom level is less distinctive but has some Belgic features. It would seem therefore that occupation of the camp just before and following the conquest was uninterrupted but slight. Wheeler suggests that 'the site...was not a permanently occupied *oppidum*; save for intermittent visitation, it was abandoned shortly after construction or was kept in cold-storage for emergency.' This tenuous post-Conquest occupation is mirrored at many of the French camps.

There is more evidence of a localized post-Conquest occupation right in the middle of the camp around the small pond. There is a small area of rough flint paving and both pond and paving are enclosed within a trapezoidal enclosure marked by a low bank and ditch—a feature that is often associated with Gallo-Roman temples. The material dates to between 50 BC and the latter part of the first century AD and includes Samian ware and other Roman pottery, two gold Belgic coins and a Vespasian gold coin.

PLATE XXVIII

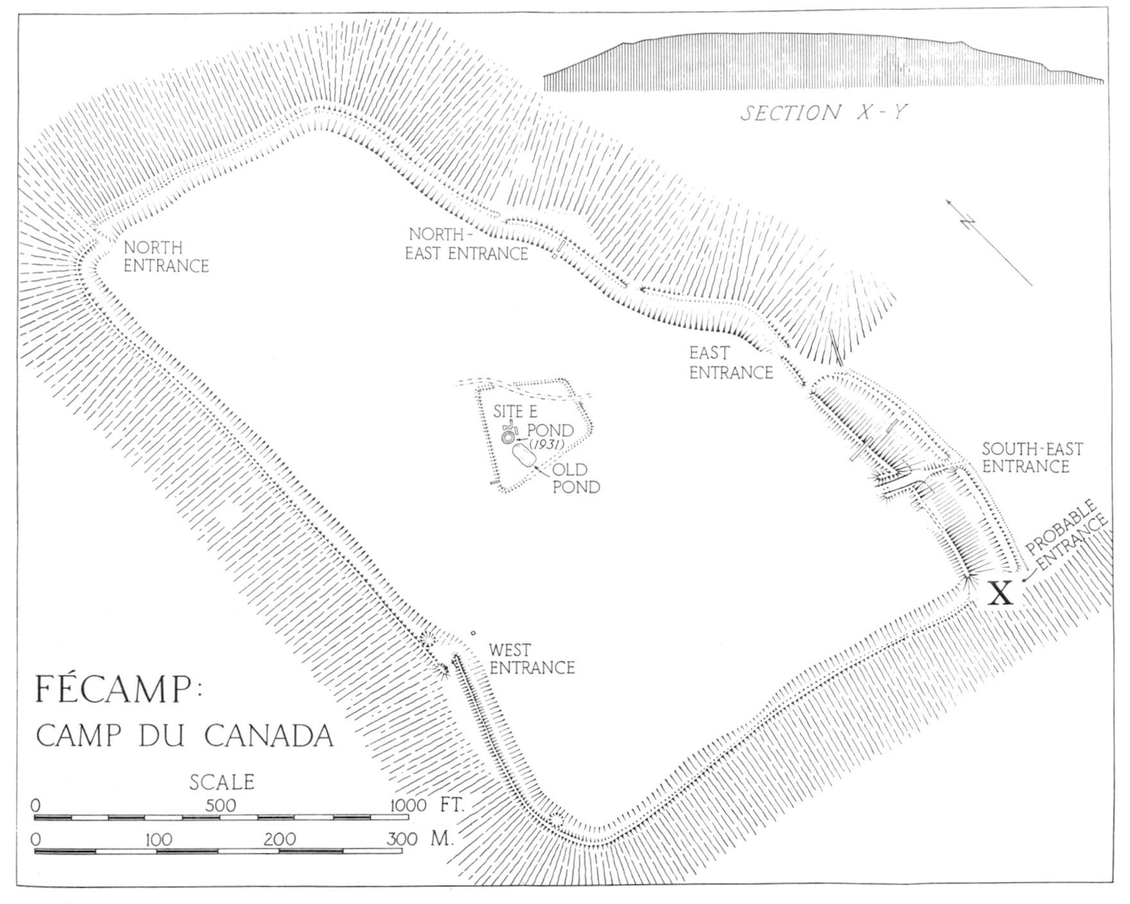

139 Camp du Canada, Fécamp

2 Château de Fécamp

Opposite the abbey, in the centre of Fécamp, excavations have uncovered traces of an eighth- and ninth-century monastery, overlain by a tenth-century palace built by the dukes of Normandy, Richard I and his son Richard II. The original palace was a large hall, an *aulu*, set in a courtyard which also contained many domestic and ecclesiastical buildings. A rampart encircled about ten hectares. A short while later, in the early eleventh century, Richard II replaced the palace with a more magnificent structure, and started work on the abbey. Abbey and palace were protected by a fine wall with vaulted arches and a tower.

A century later Fécamp had lost much of its political importance, and it was the abbey that formed the nucleus of the medieval town. Nonetheless there were important rebuildings, including a major reconstruction of the inner wall, and then the construction of a fortress that incorporated parts of this wall.

Gournay-en-Bray

Saint-Hildevert 55/8

Church

The Second Empire façade and nineteenth-century exterior of Saint-Hildevert mask a twelfth-century church, parts of which were burnt down in 1173 and restored in very early Gothic style. The main interest is the series of carved capitals on the south side of the nave and choir, including some unusual rather rough figures.

Havre, le

1 Musée de l'Ancien Havre, rue Jérome Bellarmato, not far from the Thorenson ferry — 52/11 — Museum

This seventeenth-century house is mainly dedicated to the town's history but does have a room with some Roman and Merovingian material.

Open from 10 a.m. to 12 noon and 2 to 6 p.m. Closed Mondays and Tuesdays.

2 Sainte-Honorine-de-Graville, just off the rue de Verdun — Church

The church is on a hillside with a fine view over the city—or at least an extensive view, le Havre being one of the ugliest industrial towns in France with a fearsome line of oil refineries running out along the Seine and polluting the atmosphere.

The church is at present closed for extensive restoration, the damage having been inflicted not only in the last war but also in the sixteenth-century Wars of Religion. The Romanesque church was built on the site of the sixth-century sanctuary for the relics of Sainte-Honorine—these latter having been removed to preserve them from 'the fury of the Northmen'.

The exterior is not prepossessing. Inside there is an interesting crypt and some carved capitals in the nave, most of which, however, Musset (1974) dismisses as 'banal' or even as 'singularly lacking in skill'.

Jumièges

1 The abbey of Notre-Dame — 55/5 — Church

A magnificent ruin, 'the largest, most splendid and most precocious of the great abbey churches' (Musset 1974).

There are two churches, Notre-Dame and Saint-Pierre, on the site of two earlier churches which were founded by Saint-Philibert in the seventh century and largely destroyed by the Vikings in AD 841. Saint-Pierre was probably rebuilt c. AD 990, while the building of Notre-Dame may have started in the early eleventh century under Guillaume de Volpiano (who also played a part in the building of Notre-Dame at Bernay). It was not finished until 1067. At the very end of the eleventh century, or beginning of the twelfth, the chapter-house was inserted between the two churches. The 'store-house' alongside the façade of Notre-Dame dates to the last quarter of the twelfth century and is early Gothic in construction though retaining Romanesque ornamental features (the most important of which were two fine doorways, removed in Elgin-fashion, by the English ambassador to France around 1825 and haphazardly reconstructed at Highcliffe near Bournemouth). In the thirteenth century the choir of Notre-Dame was rebuilt in the Gothic style (only the two Gothic side-chapels remain); in the fourteenth century much of Saint-Pierre was reconstructed; and finally, in the seventeenth century, the abbot's lodge, now the museum, was built. In 1790 with the dissolution of the monasteries, the monks dispersed, Notre-Dame was used as a stone quarry and an enterprising merchant blew up most of the lantern tower.

The austere façade of Notre-Dame is unlike any other in Normandy. It has three stories and is flanked by two great towers, rectangular at the base, octagonal towards the top, with an imposing series of pierced and unpierced arches. These towers were originally topped with wooden spires.

On the inner side of the façade is a wide loft. The nave, once roofed with wood, now open to the sky, has eight bays with alternating massive rectangular pillars quartered by half-columns and cylindrical columns (a stylistic feature which was taken much further in England and reached its apogee in Durham cathedral). The capitals are hardly decorated though the interior was less austere than one might imagine for there are traces of paint that are probably part of the original decoration. Of the lantern tower only the magnificent west wall remains. The transept has a narrow gallery in the width of the wall and also fine carved capitals. Other capitals, in the museum, are influenced by those at Winchester cathedral. The choir, of which only the outline remains, had a semicircular apse and an ambulatory.

A narrow passage leads from the east end of Notre-Dame to the nave of Saint-Pierre. Only the western end of this church is Romanesque—either a mid-tenth-century restoration of the earlier Carolingian edifice or perhaps a slightly later, end of tenth-century, reconstruction. This part includes the porch, the first two bays of the nave on the north side and the first bay on the south. On the inner side the great entrance arch is surmounted by another large blocked arch which must have been behind a loft or high chapel. There are a series of recessed medallions, repeated also on the north side of the nave, which almost certainly held paintings.

The chapter-house between Saint-Pierre and Notre-Dame has the remains of an early, rather heavy, use of ogival vaulting.

Open from 1 May to 30 September from 9 a.m. to 12 noon and 2 to 6 p.m., and from 1 October to 30 April from 10 a.m. to 12 noon and 1.30 to 4 p.m. Closed on Tuesdays.

2 Saint-Valentin Church
The twelfth-century parts of the parish church of Saint-Valentin consist of the façade (with a sixteenth-century doorway), the austere, unvaulted nave and the remains of the unfinished tower. All these are dwarfed by a huge sixteenth-century choir.

3 Yainville Church
The parish church of Yainville, 3 km north of Jumièges, belonged to the monks of Jumièges. It is an eleventh-century building except for the sixteenth-century façade and north door. It has an imposing square tower and several interesting sculptures.

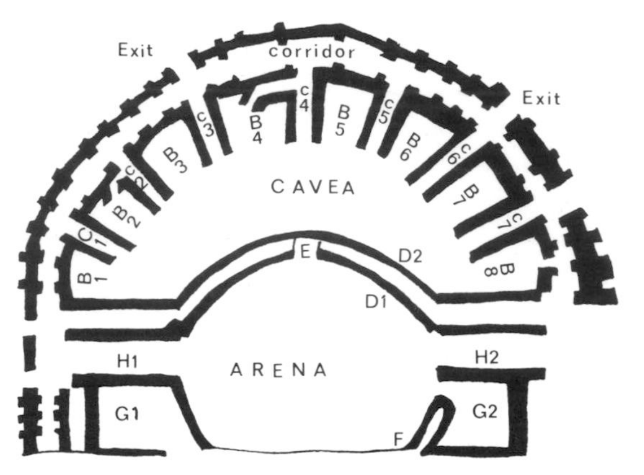

*140 **Lillebonne**, plan of the theatre*
B 1–8 boxes
C 1–7 vomitorium
D 1–2 podium
E sacellum
F pulpitum
G parascaenia
H 1–2 ceremonial entrances

Lillebonne

52/12

Lillebonne (Juliobona) was the chief city of the Caletes on the southern border of Gallia Belgica. The Roman settlement was built in the first century AD at a point on the river Seine that could be reached by sea-going vessels. Goods from the Mediterranean world came via the Rhône-Saone-Seine routeway. The port was in the lower valley, complete with warehouses and shops. On one of the two hills overlooking the port was the fort, on the other, and cut into the hillside, was the theatre.

1 The Musée de l'Hôtel de Ville ('Liberté, Egalité, Fraternité' writ large upon the portal), Place Félix Faure Museum
Opposite the Gallo-Roman amphitheatre, the museum has local archaeological material, including some from the amphitheatre.

Open from 3 to 6 p.m. From 1 April to 30 September closed on Tuesdays, from 1 October to 31 March closed Saturdays and Sundays.

2 Amphitheatre, place Félix Faure Gallo-Roman
(Figures 140 and 141)
The keys and an interesting booklet are kept at the Café de l'Hôtel de Ville opposite the theatre.

A very imposing site. The theatre was built during the first century AD, with an elliptical arena surrounded on both sides by tiered seats (the *cavea*). Those to the south were cut out of the hillside, those to the north (which are now underneath the road) were made up of the material excavated from the arena. Between arena and *cavea* double protective walls formed the *podium* (D1, D2 on plan). The arena would have been used to stage combats with wild animals, probably deer and boar, and would have been strewn with rocks and plants to make it look more 'natural'. There may also have been gladiatorial combats and sacrifices. The small enclave

141 The amphitheatre at ***Lillebonne***

(E) in the *podium* may be a *sacellum*—a shrine to the deities of combat. All the walls built during this period were made of small stone blocks with brick courses.

The function changed, and instead of combat, spectacles, pantomimes and plays were put on. Between AD 125 and 130 the amphitheatre was transformed into a theatre. The northern *cavea* was demolished and in its place a stage and orchestra were constructed. Both these are now under the road, only a small section of the *pulpitum*, the wall that ran between the orchestra and stage, is visible at (F). To make up for the lost seating the *cavea* on the south side was extended. Up beyond the seats cut into the hillslope two semicircular walls and a series of radiating small walls were built. These carried a series of boxes (B1-7) separated by narrow passages called *vomitorium* (C1-7) with a semicircular corridor behind giving out onto two main exits. The theatre probably held 6,000 spectators.

At the same time two great ceremonial entrances (H1 and 2) were built, and were richly decorated with sculptures. In the corner between these entrances and the arena two large rectangular structures served as *parascaenia* (accessory shops). All these later additions were built of small blocks of turf interpersed with layers of bricks.

Then in AD 273 came the first invasions and the theatre was annexed to the fortress. The eastern entrance (H1) was blocked off and the theatre seems to have served as an advance bastion. It was in the fourth and the fifth centuries AD that the small bath, well and pits in the north-east part of the arena were constructed.

A lot of the material is in the Musée départemental des Antiquités de la Seine-Maritime at *Rouen*.

3 Aqueduct Gallo-Roman
Bolbec (West) 5–6 468,00/1202,38
A small section of the aqueduct can be seen on the right-hand side of the road running east from Lillebonne to the Pont de Tancarville (D 982), 10 m beyond the turning right to Saint-Jean-de-Folleville, and 40 m from the main road.

Manéglise

52/11
Church
A lovely rural Romanesque church on the site of an earlier sanctuary. The layout is curious with a five-bayed nave with wide side-aisles and a flat chevet—which must be older than the nave. The capitals have a marvellous variety of sculpted decoration. The choir is covered with an early type of cross-ribbed vaulting (mid-twelfth century). Outside the tower is crowned with a fine cornice with a series of medallions.

Mauny

gallery grave 55/6
Neolithic
Rouen (West) 7–8
496,80/188,55
In Mauny take the D 64A east and after 1.6 km, and just before the river, turn left on the D 265. Continue for 400 m and the grave is to the right of the road.

This modest gallery grave is 7.5 m long and 1 m wide. There is a port-hole stone.

Several dozen skeletons were found, pushed to one side of the grave. Several of the skulls had a round piece of bone removed—apparently these trepanations had been performed by 'an incompetent'!

Montivillers

Saint-Saviour 55/3
Church
Saint-Saviour was once an abbey. Indeed the town name 'Monasterii Villare' refers to the fourteenth- and fifteenth-century urban development around an important monastic centre. The monastery, in turn, goes back to the seventh century when a monastic order for women was established. After the Viking invasions religious life was re-established and the church was constructed at the end of the eleventh century, beginning of the twelfth. In the fifteenth and sixteenth centuries the parochial part of the abbey—the first seven bays of the nave—were extensively rebuilt in the Flamboyant style and this makes for an extraordinary contrast between the different parts of the church. From the outside, at the west end, the Flamboyant porch is flanked by a slender Romanesque belfry (topped with a nineteenth-century spire). Inside, the south side of the nave, the south aisle and the bay closest to the transept are part of the original church. The real glory is the transept with fine sexpartite vaulting separated by decorated ribs, and much sculpted decoration—in particular over the arch in the south arm of the transept. The choir was more or less disfigured in the seventeenth century.

Neufmarché

Saint-Pierre 55/8
Church
The church is predominantly twelfth century though the monastic foundation goes back to the mid eleventh century. It was badly restored in the nineteenth century, bombed in World War II and badly restored again. The nave is basically nineteenth century. The choir is cradle-vaulted—a method hardly used in Normandy— and is flanked by two small chapels, again unusual in the Norman Romanesque. Some interesting fragments of sculpture from the original west façade have been preserved, one on the pedestal of the Virgin Mary in the north chapel, one (a fragment of the tympanum) in the confessional in the nave, and another, also from the tympanum, above the credence in the apse. They all probably date to the second quarter of the twelfth century.

Rouen

52/14
A town worth lingering in. Around the cathedral, many of the old houses remain more or less intact,

while up on the hill in a fine public garden, the Jardin André Maurois, there are two nicely contrasted museums.

During Gallo-Roman times Rouen—Rotomagnus—which had already existed in the Iron Age, probably became the capital of the *civitas* of the Veliocassi. Certainly it was an important trade centre and port; roads fanned out to *Lillebonne* to the west, Paris to the east, and to the Seine to join the road to Orléans and Le Mans. The first quay was built in the first century, a more massive one in the second, and by the late second century Rouen was one of the largest towns in northern Gaul and had superseded Lillebonne as the most important port for the English trade. It covered—although with intervening open ground—over a hundred hectares. There were great warehouses along the quays, administrative buildings and baths in the centre, an amphitheatre that held 20,000 people, large villas, and ramshackle artisan dwellings.

It was affected, but not destroyed, by the late third-century invasions, and a rampart was constructed, protecting about a quarter of the town. It became a garrison town, part of the *litus saxonicum* defences against the northern pirates. Unfortunately nothing remains to be seen of the Gallo-Roman town.

1 Musée des Antiquités de la Seine-Maritime — Museum

The museum can be reached either by the rue Louis Ricard (which is the continuation of the rue de la République) or via the rue Beauvoisine.

It is in the old and beautifully converted Visitandines convent. There are great passages and rooms full of medieval wood and stone work, stained glass and ivory (including the Tau from Jumièges). There is a room given over to the mosaic of Daphne pursued by Apollo and various sculptures from the Gallo-Roman ruins at *Lillebonne*, another to Gallo-Roman small finds, another to fine Merovingian metalwork—much of it from the cemetery at Envermeu, one to Viking and Carolingian material, and one to Bronze and Iron Age objects. This last room has been well catalogued and set in a general context by G. Verron in *Antiquités Préhistoriques et Protohistoriques* (1971), obtainable at the entrance desk. This museum is the finest in Normandy.

Open from 10 a.m. to 12 noon and 2 to 5.30 p.m. Closed Thursdays.

2 The Musée d'Histoire Naturelle is next door — Museum

Up two flights, passed the stuffed pumas and catfish, up two more spiral staircases, past the stuffed birds and detailed human anatomy, and so eventually to a long room where Eskimos and Aztecs peer out among the numerous cases of Palaeolithic flints (from the quarries along the Seine and its tributaries, such as *Saint-Pierre-lès-Elbeuf* and le Mesnil-Esnard) and local Mesolithic and Neolithic material. There are a few rather dusty explanations in the cases in the middle of the room.

Open Wednesday, Thursday, Friday and Saturday from 10 a.m. to 12 noon, 2 to 6 p.m. On Sunday open from 2 to 7 p.m.

3 Saint-Julien — Church

The chapel of Saint-Julien, Petit Quevilly, is surrounded by factories and dumps and is in process of reconstruction. It was built by Henry II in 1160 as an oratory at his residence at Quevilly, and then, in 1183, was turned into a leprosery. Finally it was alienated at the Revolution.

It is a very simple structure, with thick walls, a short nave originally vaulted, now with a wooden roof, and a two-bay choir with sexpartite ogival vaulting. The lower part of the interior walls are decorated with dog-tooth arcades. The capitals are decorated—and much restored. Most unusual are the remains of a series of frescos on the ogival vaulting. These must date between 1183 and 1190 and are already in the Gothic tradition. Outside there is a fine decorated corniche.

Saint-Jean-d'Abbetot

52/12

Church

The choir and the transept-crossing of the parish church are late eleventh century, the nave is fourteenth century. The transept-crossing is circumscribed by four fine arches descending onto decorated capitals. The date of the frescos is obscure but some may date to the Romanesque. In the Romanesque crypt below the church the frescos are certainly later in date—fourteenth, fifteenth and sixteenth century, and heavily restored. But still nice to look at!

It is worth walking round the church and looking at the detail on the outside of the choir.

Saint-Martin-de-Boscherville

Saint-Georges 55/6
Church

The first church, AD 1050–66, was built under the auspices of Raoul of Tancarville, grand chamberlain of William the Conqueror, for a community of canons. The canons were replaced by monks in 1114 and the present church was built, perhaps reusing part of the former church or at least some of its decorative elements. It is a fine example of Romanesque architecture, the nave with its eight bays has Gothic ogival vaulting but the chancel and side-aisles have their original groined vaulting. The austerity of the church is relieved by some very delicate carvings on the capitals in the transept and aisles. There are low reliefs below the balustrades in the transepts showing a blessing by the bishop, and warriors fighting.

Saint-Pierre-lès-Elbeuf

Quarry: Palaeolithic stratigraphy 55/6
Palaeolithic
Elbeuf 3–4
506,05/174,82

Saint-Pierre-lès-Elbeuf lies south-east of Elbeuf. For access to the quarry see plan, Figure 142.

The site is on a meander of the Seine, at the confluence with the Oison. The section in the quarry shows stratified deposits going down to at least the Riss glacial and interglacial formations. The overlying deposits date to the Riss-Würm interglacial and then to the Würm glacial.

Lower Palaeolithic (Acheulian) tools were found in the lower levels, Upper Palaeolithic tools in the top levels.

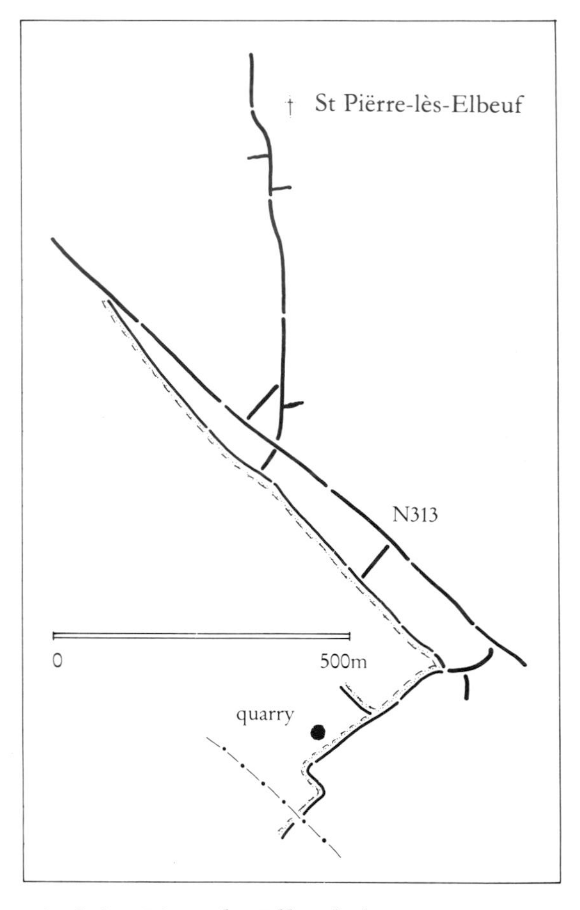

*142 **Saint-Pierre-lès-Elbeuf**, directions to the quarry*

Saint-Wandrille

55/5
Church

Of the abbey of Fontenelle, founded in the seventh century by Saint-Wandrille—God's athlete, both saintly and handsome—nothing remains. It was sacked by the Norsemen, rebuilt in the tenth century, and then demolished. Such ruins as survived the fury of the Revolution date to the fourteenth and fifteenth century.

But continuing down the road past the entrance to Saint-Wandrille, and following the signposts up through the wood to Saint-Saturninius one arrives at a rather heavily restored tenth-century chapel. It is small and trefoil-shaped with massive walls and a heavy square tower. The tops of the three pillars embedded in the base of the tower have a decoration of roses, palms and fantastic animals. These may well come from an earlier Carolingian building.

Sandouville

Camp de César 52/12
Iron Age
Le Havre 3–4
453,62/201,55

From the church at Sandouville the rampart is visible 300 m to the south-west. The easiest means of access is to retrace the road and take the second road to the left. This small road leads to a farm at a right-angle bend and just before the farm the rampart and ditch stretch off to the left and right.

The defences cut off an area of 40 hectares on a flat-topped hill protected by the Seine cliffs on one side and the valley of the Oudalle on the other. There is a single bank 80 m long, with a flat-bottomed ditch. The bank rises 7 m above the interior of the camp and 10 m above the present ditch bottom. It belongs to the Fécamp series with a strongly inturned entrance.

Finds of sherds, coins—including a gold Celtic piece—and milling-stones have been recorded.

Veulettes-sur-Mer

Camp du Câtelier 52/2–3
Iron Age
Fécamp 3–4
474,50/240,60

In Veulettes, at the west end of the beach, take the small road up the hill. Just before the summit a track right leads to the rampart.

The bank stands high and proud but protects almost nothing except some World War II gun emplacements, for the cliff has been heavily eroded. The bank rises nearly 4 m above the camp interior, 17 m above the flat-bottomed ditch. There are traces of a counterscarp. It belongs to the Fécamp series.

Some late Roman bronze coins have been found.

There is a great view across the bay of Veulettes.

Virville

Saint-Aubin 52/12
Church

A small, almost untouched, late eleventh-century Romanesque church—except for the eighteenth-century façade and nineteenth-century sacristy. The main interest is the exterior, austere, with a massive rectangular tower mainly built of roughly cut stones set in mortar. Only at the top are the stones more carefully dressed and decorated with blind arcades and colonnettes.

The Channel Islands

Introduction

In the long perspective of prehistory these islands were more often than not simply part of the fringing coastline of Normandy and Brittany. All through the glacial periods of the Pleistocene sea-levels were so low that Normandy stretched way to the west. Only in the interglacials did the sea intrude and cut off the islands—always first severing Guernsey, which is further away from the mainland and surrounded by deeper water, and then, eventually, Jersey.

Guernsey, island or no island, shows no evidence of human occupation through to the Neolithic. Jersey harboured the occasional *Homo erectus*, and then towards the end of the Riss glaciations c. 128,000 bp, was occupied, at least seasonally, by Neanderthalers living in caves that were scoured out in earlier interglacials and then left hanging as the seas retreated. *La Cotte à la Chèvre* is in the inventory, la Cotte de St Brelade (Figure 143), one of the richest Palaeolithic sites in north-west Europe, with over 140,000 artefacts, is left out since access is extremely difficult (but see also the General Introduction, page 21).

In a landscape of open tundra, Neanderthalers hunted the mammoth, woolly rhinoceros, reindeer, bison, horse, cave bear and brown bear. They piled up the bones, including the great skulls of the woolly rhinoceros and mammoth, below the western overhang at la Cotte de St Brelade. Intermittently over a period of fifty thousand years they built and rebuilt hearths within the cave, hearths that were soon covered with wind-blown loess. During the Riss-Würm interglacial Jersey was cut off and abandoned by both man and animal, only to be repeopled again around seventy thousand years ago. At St Brelade thirteen Neanderthaler teeth and part of a child's skull were found. The caves were finally abandoned around thirty-five thousand years ago, and once again the island seems to have been deserted.

At 16,000 bc sea-levels were more than 100 m below present, but the Würm ice-sheets were slowly beginning to retreat. By 8500 bc the waters were spreading over the island shelf, penetrating between the future islands of Guernsey, Jersey and Alderney (Figure 144). The sea was then 35 m below the present level. By 7500 bc Guernsey was on the verge of becoming an island, and the tundra vegetation was giving way to birch and pine, and some willow and hazel. By 7000 bc Guernsey and Alderney, now covered with temperate forest, were cut off by deep channels. By 4000 bc Jersey was cut off at all but low tide (Figure 145). Between the island and the mainland lay twenty-four kilometres of tidal-flat and rock outcrop. Jersey was still far larger than today and to the south were two low-lying islands, together at least the size of Jersey. Of these nothing remains today except the rocks of the Minquiers and Chauseys. To the north, another, smaller, low-lying island is now marked by the reefs of Ecréhous. Thus most of the evidence that there might have been for coastal Mesolithic gatherer-hunter-fishers exploiting the rich marine resources now lies under the sea.

The human record reopens around 4000 bc (calibrated at 4850 BC), with Neolithic farming groups occupying all the larger islands. One tends to think of islands as being cut off, isolated, developing in rather idiosyncratic ways. But obviously, this 'isolation' depends on how far they are from the mainland, how difficult communication is, and what sort of communication is available. Guernsey, for example,

143 La Cotte de St Brelade, Jersey

is much more difficult to get to in small boats than Jersey. It depends also on social phenomena, how far the islanders relate within a larger network of contacts. It is very clear that during the earlier part of the Neolithic, from the beginning of the fourth to the mid-third millennium bc, the islands played an important part in an extensive network of alliance and exchange that stretched from Brittany to western Normandy and the plain of Caen, and even, though more intermittently, as far as the Paris Basin, southern Britain, Denmark and the Swiss Piedmont. The Neolithic chiefs of Jersey and Guernsey visited, feasted, and exchanged highly valued items and perhaps more utilitarian objects with their counterparts on the mainland (see General Introduction, page 26–32).

Evidence from Guernsey may provide a link between the missing earlier Mesolithic societies and the emergent petty Neolithic chiefdoms. The recent excavation at les Fouaillages, *Vale*, uncovered slight remains of a Mesolithic settlement, and then an early Neolithic structure consisting of a small cairn covering a domed cist, and a circular paved area. Both of these were, by the fourth millennium, incorporated within a large triangular mound with a massive stone façade at one end that gave onto a small slab-built chamber with a semicircular forecourt. The mound also covered an unroofed chamber of slabs and dry-stone walling. This structure looks as though it might be intermediate between the earlier pit-burials in shell middens recorded in Britanny and the more substantial and standardized Island passage graves (General Introduction, page 25). The deposition of stacks of shells in the Island passage graves may be another link to the Mesolithic past.

By the late Neolithic, mid-third millennium bc, the network of exchange and the chiefdoms it supported had broken down, contacts with the mainland

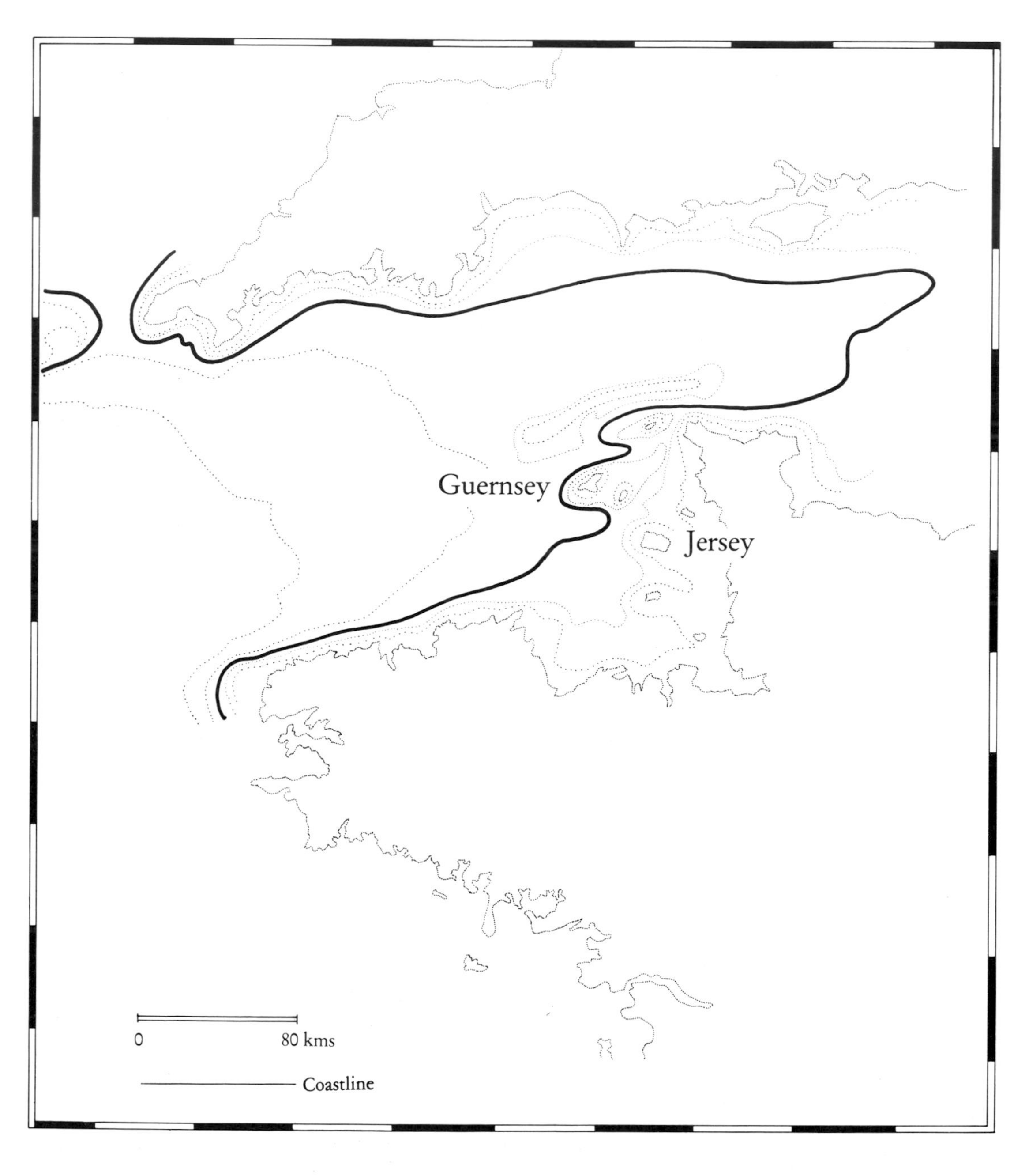

144 8500 BC. Guernsey and Jersey are still part of the mainland

diminished and the island communities became far more insular, and probably more egalitarian. There may even have been a decline in island population. Perhaps some of the more intensive subsistence practices that permitted larger population aggregates and provided a 'surplus' for exchange and ceremony, were abandoned. Only a few communal gallery graves or small tombs were built, or earlier graves reutilized. But the two fine statue menhirs from Guernsey (le Câtel, *Câtel* and Gran' Mère, *St Martin*), and the timber structure surrounded by arcs of large recumbent stones at les Fouaillages, *Vale*, Guernsey (overlying the earlier trapezoidal mound), show that the island people, even if somewhat isolated, had a similar cult of a female deity to that found throughout northern, and part of southern France, and practised rituals centred on stone alignments like their counterparts in western Normandy and Brittany.

This relative isolation in the Late Neolithic may have been briefly broken at the end of the second millennium when again a wide-flung network of alliance and exchange developed along the Atlantic and well into the French interior (and still further afield). This network is associated with Bell Beaker elements which sometimes seem to have been élite commodities seized upon by local leaders to enhance their positions, and sometimes the remains of intrusive groups. On the islands megalithic graves were once again reused for individual inhumations, often associated with copper daggers and fine stone arrowheads, stone wristguards, and with well-made, and less well-made, Beaker ware that sometimes took an idiosyncratic island form—the Guernsey bowl, the Jersey pot. A fine array of island Beaker ware was found, for example, at la Varde, *Vale*, on Guernsey. At les Fouillages, *Vale*, the Late Neolithic timber structure was dismantled, a mound was thrown up over all the earlier structures and a fine series of barbed-and-tanged arrowheads was placed in one of the post-holes. There was a small domestic Beaker site just to the south, and the Beaker élite was probably buried in the neighbouring cist-within-a-circle of la Platte Mare.

Then, once again, in the second millennium, the islands were peripheralized. The flourishing Early Bronze Age trade and exchange network between Ireland, the Wessex kingdoms and Brittany passed them by. Bronze was an élite commodity and the islands saw little of it, only a solitary gold torque from St Helier, probably of Irish origin, or an occasional four-handled pot of Breton origin found on Jersey suggests intermittent contact. So the Stone Age societies probably continued for far longer on the islands than on the mainland, until during the mainland Late Bronze Age, between the tenth to sixth century BC, a few large hoards began to appear. These contained broken implements, lumps of metal, casting jets, as well as finished objects. Such founders' hoards, buried and never reclaimed, suggest both that times were unsettled and that the islands were ports of call within an extensive Atlantic trade network. Two such hoards that relate to the Saint-Brieuc-les-Ifs hoards of Brittany and Normandy were found relatively close to each other on Jersey, one at Mainlands and the other at Bel Royal. The most famous hoard is the one from Longy common on Alderney (in the Candie Museum, *St Peter Port*, Guernsey). It is later in date and contains scythes and other tools that were probably made by the English Broadway group as well as a Norman socketed axe. Iron begins to be used on the mainland in the sixth century but again the islands are hardly affected. There are contacts, but apparently not in terms of such prestigious exchanges. At les Huguettes, *Longis Bay* on Alderney, quantities of pottery were made and the range and style suggest contacts with both southern England and Brittany. But only one iron razor was found on the site. At Ville-ès-Nouaux, *St Helier* on Jersey, there was a small cremation urnfield, and the shape of the cremation urns reflects, probably quite indirectly, the influence of metal forms.

Later, through the fifth to second century, contact appears to be further reduced to the occasional import of graphite ware from Brittany to Jersey. As on the mainland, salt was distilled at numerous small coastal sites (le Crocq, Rocquaine and Catiorec on Guernsey, Belcroute Bay on Jersey, and on Herm) and perhaps some was traded beyond the islands. And again, as on the mainland, small promontory sites began to be defended.

It is not until the end of the second century BC that the Channel Islands are drawn into a more intensive exchange network and this is undoubtedly due to the extension of Roman influence and trade. St Peter Port (King's Road) on Guernsey may have been an important point of entry, both for wine imports shipped in amphorae, and for more local trade items, such as the fine Breton black cordoned, graphite and

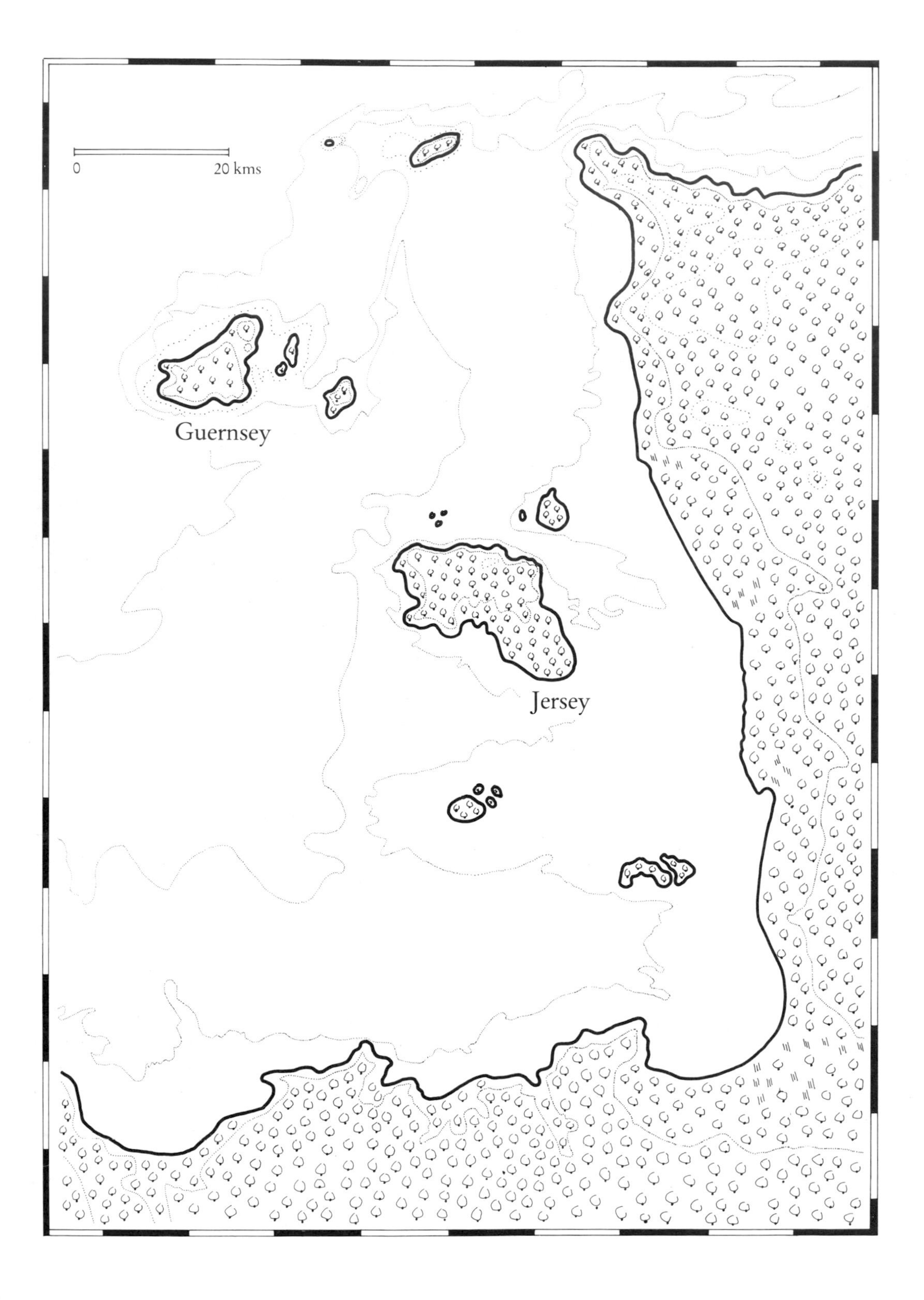
0
20 kms
Guernsey
Jersey

146 Le Pinacle, St Ouen, Jersey

rilled wares. Such trade may have helped to promote and sustain petty chiefs very similar to those in Brittany and Normandy. At least thirty-one 'warrior-burials' have been discovered, mainly on the west side of Guernsey, though one has recently been uncovered at the King's Road site at St Peter Port on the east coast. These consist of extended inhumations in cist graves, with, at St Peter Port, traces of a wooden structure, and some are accompanied by lavish weaponry—swords, spear-heads and shields. More rarely there are knives, or sometimes bracelets and beads.

As the threat of Roman conquest became imminent, the islands seem increasingly to align themselves with the Coriosolites tribal groupings of north-east Brittany and the Norman Cotentin. It may even be that the rich warrior burials represent first century BC mainland refugees. Certainly much of the

145 4000 BC. The beginning of the Neolithic. Sea-levels are at about the extreme low-tide mark of today. The channel islands are true islands

Coriosolites' mint was carried over and eventually buried there. Four great hoards were found at the defended promontory site of le Câtel de Rozel, *St Martin* on Jersey, another great hoard at la Marquanderie, also on Jersey.

In 56 BC Sabinus routed the Coriosolites and their allies on the mainland, probably at *le Petit-Celland*, near Avranches in the Manche. The Romans probably never conquered the islands, and mainland groups may well have found refuge there. At Tranquesous, St Saviour on Guernsey a small Coriosolites settlement of round huts was established in the first century BC. There are occasional Roman imports, at Tranquesous, and at St Peter Port on Guernsey, and two wrecks containing amphorae were found close to St Peter Port. There is also a small shrine at *le Pinacle* on Jersey (Figure 146), but, for all practical purposes, the islands remained outside the Roman sphere of administration and control. Only towards the end of the Roman mainland occupation, as the barbarian attacks grew fiercer, and the Saxons and Frisians raided up the Seine and around the Cotentin, a small Roman fort was erected at the Nunnery site on

Alderney. It may have been an outlier of the line of Saxon shore forts erected in the third century AD. Like them, it was undoubtedly ineffectual in the face of ever increasing channel piracy.

The long history stops short. For the visitor it is a history that is quite hard to find. Mainly, of course, it is the megalithic structures that remain, and even these are greatly depleted. Of Jersey it is said that in the reign of James II there were still 'half-a-hundred' stone monuments, but by the time the Lukis family began to explore and to excavate in the mid-nineteenth century a mere five or six remained. The fate of one monument, the compartmented passage grave of Mont de la Ville is well known. It was presented to the governor of the island, General Conway, in 1787, who duly resurrected it in Henley-on-Thames—'a monument' as Lukis trenchantly noted in 1846, 'to exile and mistaken liberality'.

On Guernsey place-name evidence suggests that the Neolithic occupation was dense and that there were once more than sixty megalithic monuments and thirty menhirs. Now, more often than not, only the name remains, for here as on all the islands both the stone and the land have always been valuable commodities. In 1933, an archaeologist noted that the monuments had been 'sacrificed to one or other of the three major industries of the island, stone-getting, cattle-rearing and tomato-growing. For if in the eighteenth century stone for export was worth its weight in gold...in the nineteenth century even the few feet occupied by such remains were coveted for pasture, while today, those same few feet, for sites for glass houses, are of most fabulous value.'

It is the same story for Alderney—most of the monuments and sites have gone. One of the earliest descriptions of a megalithic grave refers to Alderney. Holinshed in 1587 wrote that 'a priest not long since did find a coffin of stone in which lay the bodie of a huge giant, whose fore-teeth were so big as a man's fist.' That one, too, has disappeared.

Alderney

Begin at the beginning, with a visit to the museum in The Huret, *St Anne's* (see below). Since the island is only three miles long and one and a half miles wide you can locate the archaeological sites on the display map and walk out to them.

A great many sites reported by Kendrick (see Bibliography) and Lukis were destroyed either when the thirteen forts were constructed in the 1850s or by the Germans in World War II.

St Anne's

The Huret — Museum

museum

The museum, which was originally the island school, houses most of the finds from Alderney. Moreover, if you want to visit the (possible) passage grave at les Rochers, which is hard to find, you should seek the help of the museum curator.

Open daily from 10 a.m. to 12.30 p.m.

Longis Bay

1 Les Pourciaux North — Neolithic
gallery grave
From St Anne's follow the High Street and Longis Road.

The grave is much ruined, and capped by a German concrete emplacement. Moreover it is on private land. If, undeterred, you still wish to see it, write to Mr J. Winckworth, les Pourciaux, Alderney.

This grave is orientated north-west/south-east. It was originally 8 m long and 1.5 to 2 m wide, with four or five capstones. A gap at the west end of the south side, with an upright skewed at right angles may be the original entrance, or, more probably, a later alteration. Small cists were found within the chamber, towards the west end of the south side, resting on a pavement. Each contained a human skull and bones but no pottery.

The second gallery grave at les Pourciaux was totally obliterated by the Germans.

2 The Nunnery — Gallo-Roman
Private property, but the outer walls are open to inspection.

This is a square fort, 40.5 m a side with rounded corner bastions. Parts of the great curtain wall still stand over 5 m high, although most of the southern wall and the south-eastern bastion have been washed away by the sea.

The general consensus is that the visible walls are fourteenth century but that they were built on a Roman ground-plan and reused some of the Roman masonry. It is possible that the Roman fort was an outlier in the Roman line of shore forts thrown up in the third century AD against the Saxons.

Foundations of Roman houses have been found close to the fort and a Roman refuse pit was excavated to the north-east. It contained fragments of nearly a hundred pots, a glass bead, glass chips, bricks, tiles, iron nails, two bronze finger-rings, a bronze thimble, a fragment of bone comb, three bone pins and a coin of Commodus. All this material is housed in the Museum of Archaeology and Anthropology at Cambridge.

3 Les Huguettes — Iron Age
pottery-making site
Just inland from the Nunnery on the golf course, up a path off the road from the Nunnery to Fort Albert.

An interesting site where recent excavations have uncovered oval-shaped stone-working platforms surrounded by low dry-stone walls situated among traces of huts. Coarse late Hallstatt pottery was fired on the platforms. As well as quantities of pots, potters' tools of stone and bone were found. There is a carbon-14 date of 490 + 100 bc. At some point the site may also have been used for burials—cremated human bones were found.

The material from les Huguettes is on display in the museum at *St Anne's*.

Fort Tourgis

Roc à l'Epine (marked on the map as Druid's Altar) — Neolithic
tomb
Visible from the road leading from the airport to Platte Saline.

All that remains are two uprights and a capstone (restored), but, according to Lukis (1847) 'tradition bears testimony to the fact that urns, and other articles were discovered beneath it.'

Guernsey

The number at the beginning of each entry refers to the map, Figure 147.

Câtel

1 Câtel parish church — Neolithic
statue menhir
(Figure 148)
This menhir was discovered in 1873, 30 cm below the floor of the chancel and was set up in the churchyard, to the left of the porch. It is a fine granite slab, 2.15 m high, shaped in human form, with a sculpted ridge beneath the head, a U-shaped necklace above two breasts, and a ridge across the back. The face and one breast have been damaged.

Clearly there are links between this monument and the chalk-cut sculptings of the Paris Basin graves, the statue menhirs of southern France and, closer to Guernsey, both the rough anthropomorphic stones found at several Breton sites and the more carefully sculpted examples from Kermené, Guidel, Morbihan; and Laniscat, Le Trévoux, Finistère—with a cast in the museum at *Penmarc'h*, Finistère. See also La Gran' Mère du Chimquière, *St Martin* and the engraved capstone, Le Déhus, Paradis, *Vale*, both on Guernsey.

St Martin

2 St Martin, La Gran' Mère du Chimquière — Neolithic
statue menhir
(Figure 149)
Another powerful stone lady stands between the two gates of the churchyard, on the south side of the parish church of St Martin. This statue menhir was formerly within the churchyard and it is said that there was a slab with two hollows placed at its base. In the nineteenth century offerings were still being placed in front of it, and an over-zealous church warden, fearing a resurgence of idolatry, broke it in two.

The statue is more naturalistic and has a stronger focus on the face than any of the other French Neolithic figures. The reason for this is that the original Neolithic statue was reworked in Roman times. The close-set breasts, arms and girdle are probably part of the original figure, but the face, head-dress and cape are later additions. The vertical row of discs on the left side of the face continues under the chin and was originally duplicated on the right side. The cape has a series of vertical ridges and a row of buttons down the front.

The statue is of local granite and stands 1.67 m high.

148 Statue menhir at ***Câtel***

149 La Gran' Mère du Chimquière, ***St Martin***

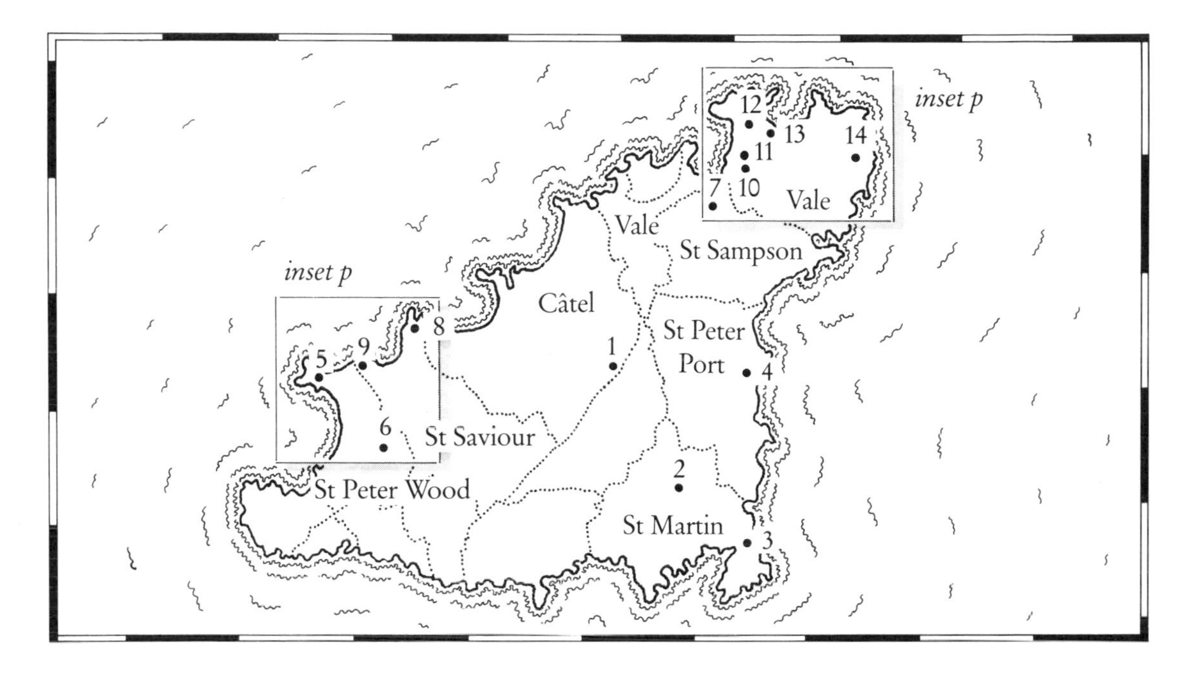

147 *Guernsey, parishes and sites*

Câtel	*1 Câtel, statue menhir*
St Martin	*2 Gran' Mère, statue menhir*
	3 Jerbourg, Iron Age defences
St Peter Port	*4 Candie Gardens museum*
St Peter In The Wood	*5 Le Creux ès Faïs, passage grave, Erée*
	6 La Longue Roque, menhir, les Paysans
St Sampson	*7 Les Fouillages, cists, l'Islet*
St Saviour	*8 La Longue Pierre, menhir, le Crocq*
	9 Trépied, passage grave, Catioroc
Vale	*10 Les Fouaillages, graves, alignments etc., l'Ancresse Common*
	11 La Platte Mare, grave, l'Ancresse Common
	12 La Varde, passage grave, l'Ancresse Common
	13 La Mare ès Mauves, megalithic grave, l'Ancresse Common
	14 Le Déhus, transepted passage grave, Paradis

3 Jerbourg — Neolithic to Iron Age
hill fort — Guernsey 33,80/75,30
(Figure 150)

The Jerbourg peninsula is on the south-east corner of the island. The road cuts across the earthworks by the Doyle column.

The promontory is edged by steep cliffs on three sides. The neck is defended by a triple line of banks and ditches extending for about 165 m. They stay close together for most of their length, but the southern one bends southwards just east of the Doyle column. The most northerly bank is the highest, particularly the west section which measures nearly 3 m from the bottom of the ditch to the top of the bank.

Recent excavations indicate that the original stone-faced rampart dates to the Late Neolithic/Early Bronze Age. This was remodelled, then rebuilt, still within the Bronze Age. Another stone-faced rampart was built early in the Iron Age, c. 600 BC, followed by a second rebuilding and then a rather ineffective reinforcement of earth and turf faced with a thin layer of stone. This last was perhaps a response to the Roman threat from the French mainland. Finally there were medieval reinforcements dating to c. AD 1350 and these were twice remodelled. The stone-

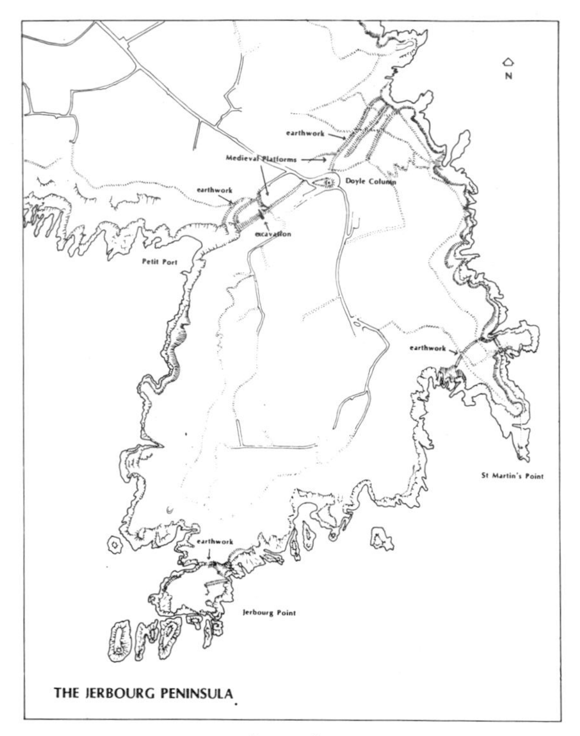

150 Jerbourg peninsula (scale 1 : 2500)

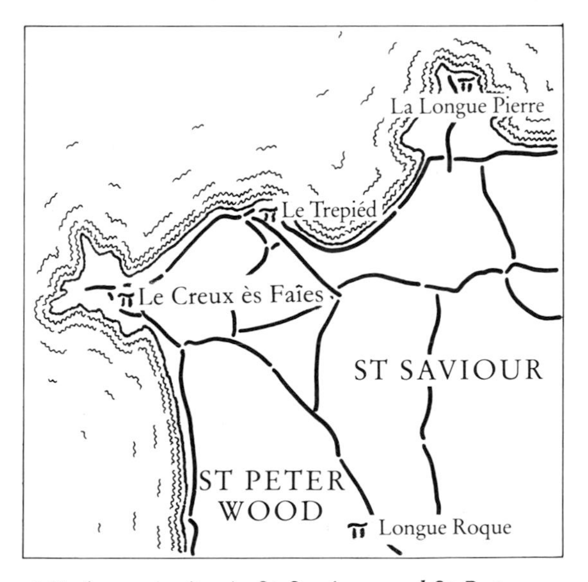

151 Access to sites ***in St Saviour and St Peter Wood***

edged bank which forms the mound on which the Doyle column is sited is part of the medieval construction.

Another small earthwork has recently been discovered running across the southernmost tip of the peninsula.

St Peter Port

4 St Peter Port — Museum
The Guernsey Museum and
Art Gallery, Candie Gardens

Only recently opened this small and very attractive museum, organized around a Victorian bandstand, is well worth a visit. It houses the Lukis collection which comprises a large part of the island's prehistoric finds. The two display rooms have local material from the Neolithic onwards. There is also part of the massive Longy hoard from Alderney. There is a short film that introduces the visitor to the prehistory and history of Guernsey.

Open every day from 10.30 a.m. to 5.30 p.m. (4.30 p.m. between March and October).

St Peter in the Wood

5 Le Creux des Fées or — Neolithic
Creux ès Faïes, Erée — Guernsey 25,10/78,45
passage grave
(Figure 151)

The monument is on the north side of the road to l'Erée promontory, about 300 m from the junction with la Rocquaine road. It is not easy to see, watch for the mound and peristalith.

This interesting tomb is partly rock-cut but is also covered with a mound—used in the last war as a bunker. Some of the large uprights of the peristalith are still visible.

The passage opens to the east. The entrance is uncovered but the remains of the broken capstone lie on either side. The chamber, irregular in shape, has a maximum width of 3 m and is roofed with two large capstones.

Seven or eight Bell Beakers, one rather coarse carinated pot, one large cinerary urn of thick gritty ware decorated with rough vertical incisions, and a disc of Samian ware were found. There were two barbed-and-tanged arrowheads near the surface of the passage fill.

6 La Longue Roque (once known as the Palette ès Faïes), les Paysans — Neolithic — Guernsey 26,55/77,10
menhir
(Figure 151)
Visible from the road.

A respectable 4 m granite, with a further metre below ground.

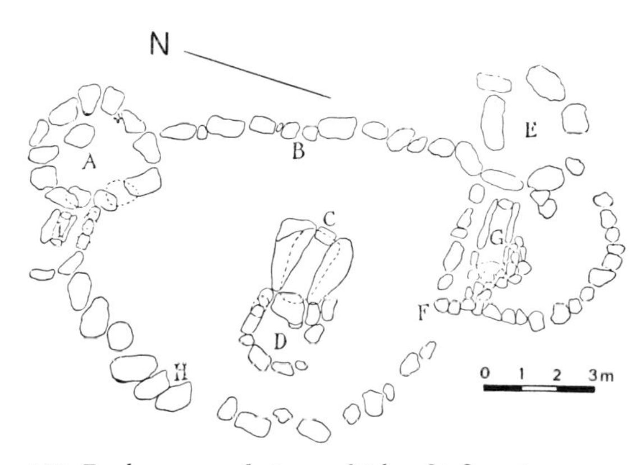

*152 Enclosures and cists at l'Islet, **St Sampson***

St Sampson

(7) Les Fouaillages, l'Islet — Neolithic
cists — Guernsey 33,24/82,23
(Figures 152 and 154)
This site, embedded in brambles and debris, has been much tampered with, the soil has been levelled and most of the stones are now only visible to half their original height.

According to the Curtis plan, reproduced by Kendrick, a circle of boulders 3 m in diameter (A on the plan), abuts onto the main enclosure (B) which contains a central rectangular cist (C). This cist, originally 1.7 × 0.75 m, comprises four uprights covered by a single capstone. At the west end of this is an 'ante-chamber' (D) 1.8 m square, made of uprights and dry-stone walling. It has no cover and opens to the south.

Up against the south side of the main enclosure is another enclosure (F), containing another cist (G) which is 1.55 × 0.52 × 0.6 m, and has six uprights and a dislodged capstone. And on the north side of the main enclosure is yet another very small cist (I), 0.72 × 0.3 m, again with a dislodged capstone.

A fragment of a coarse Seine-Oise-Marne pot was found in (A), a small flat-based pot decorated with two horizontally perforated lugs and alternating bosses was found in (C), a few sherds and a small flint point in (D) and, finally, a coarse sherd in (I).

St Saviour

8 La Longue Pierre or la Pierre de l'Essart, le Crocq — Neolithic — Guernsey 27,10/79,60
menhir
(Figure 151)
Just off the road, down the track leading to the Fort le Crocq. It is to the left of the track, beyond the last greenhouse.

The menhir stands 3 m high within a low boundary wall.

9 Le Trépied (once known as La Pouquelaye du Mont Chinchon), Catioroc — Neolithic — Guernsey 25,97/78,90
passage grave
(Figures 151 (map) and 153)
On top of a low hill, visible from the road.

The bottle-shaped chamber is 5.47 m long with an entrance to the east and three capstones in place.

Three Bell Beakers, one rather coarse carinated pot and two barbed-and-tanged arrowheads were found.

This grave was a famous meeting-place for the Guernsey witches and the Friday night 'sabbats' were sufficiently important for the devil himself to attend. It was often mentioned in the seventeenth-century witch trials.

Vale

10 Les Fouaillages, l'Ancresse Common — Neolithic, etc. — Guernsey 33,50/83,10
multiperiod site
(Figures 154 (map), 155 and 156)
The site is near the fifth tee of the golf course. It is signposted from the car-park on les Amarreurs Road.

The site was revealed after a fire in 1978, and was excavated between 1979 and 1981. It has provided

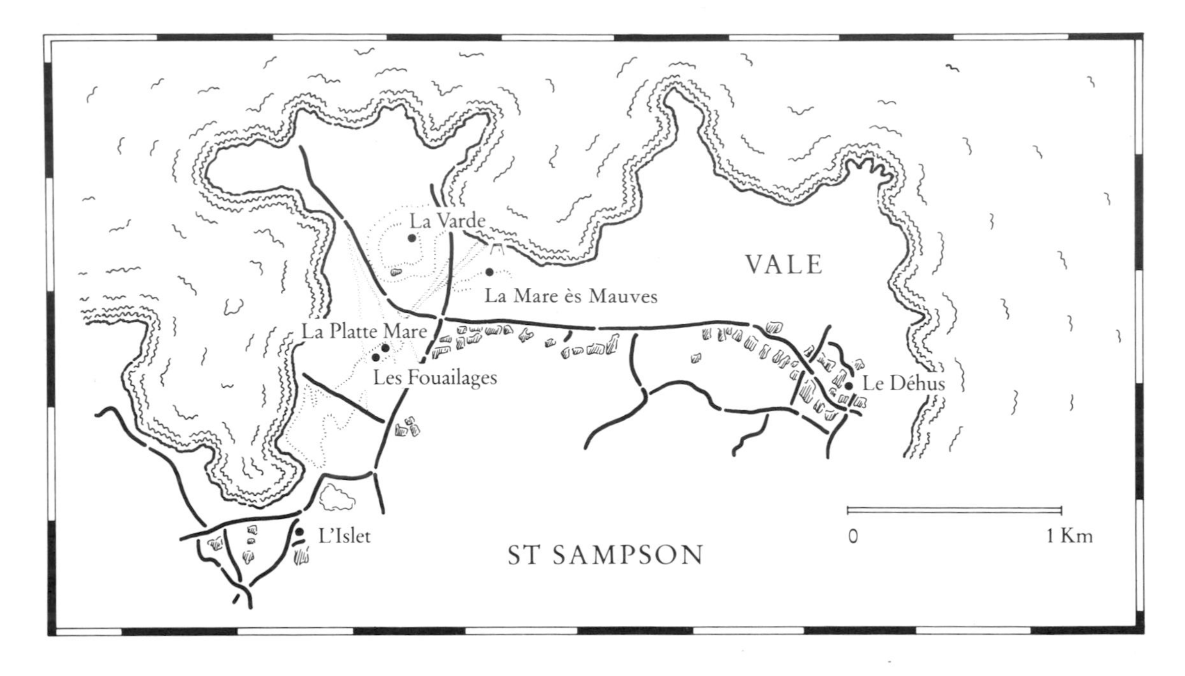

154 Access to sites in ***Vale and St Sampson***

some very important clues to developments within the islands and also to broader problems concerning Neolithic origins and evolution.

The lowest level dates to about 4000 bc, to the time of the first farmers on the island (though there is even a scattering of earlier, Mesolithic flints). A small Cerny settlement, associated with traces of timber structures, was established. Then, after a period of abandonment, the site was reused to build a mortuary-ceremonial structure. The first monument was a small sub-rectangular cairn 1.9 × 1.8 × 1 m with a shouldered menhir or marker slab at the east end. The cairn covered a small domed cist. Close by there was a circular paved area, 1.6 m in diameter, on which there was some burnt material (both these features have now been turfed over).

Somewhat later these structures were enclosed within a triangular mound 20 m long and 10 m wide made of stacked turves with a stone facing. Below this mound, and to the east of the cairn, there may initially have been a sod-lined chamber. This was replaced by an unroofed double-chamber, 2.6 × 1.7 m, made of slabs with dry-stone wall reinforcements. Two stone-packed post-holes mark the entrance; two massive marker slabs mark the rear. To the east again was a small slab-built chamber with three capstones, 1.8 × 0.4 × 0.4 m. This lay behind a small cuspidal forecourt with massive façade slabs which gave onto the eastern side of the mound.

Seven nearly complete decorated Cerny pots, similar to those from *le Pinacle*, Jersey, were found in or near the unroofed chamber and on the western paved areas, as well as a lot of domestic debris.

There are carbon-14 dates of 3640 + – 50 bc (calibrated 4475 BC), 3560 + – 60 bc (calibrated 4415 BC), 3330 + – 140 bc (calibrated 4140 BC).

When the monument went out of use, the unroofed chamber was back-filled, the eastern chamber was filled with clean beach sand and the forecourt was blocked with earth and stones.

Then in the Late Neolithic the site was reused in a somewhat different way. The eastern end of the mound was covered by a semicircular emplacement of layers of packed beach pebbles, earth and boulders. At the centre of this, and using the still visible marker slabs from the earlier monument as focus points, a circle of recumbent boulders, 2.8 m in diameter, surrounded by two semi-circles of boulders, was laid out. Within the circle was a small rectangular

153 Le Trépied passage grave, Catioroc, **St Saviour**

156 Les Fouaillages, **Vale**, *view of the covered chamber at the north-east end*

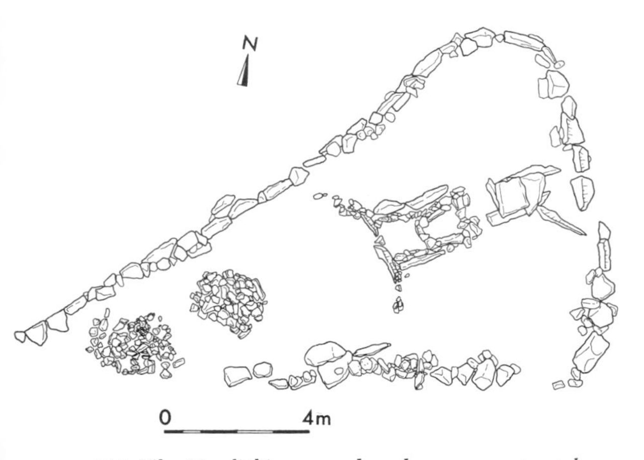

155 The Neolithic mound and monuments at les Fouaillages, ***Vale***

enclosure, defined by low boulders. This may have been associated with post-holes, and may originally have been roofed. The pottery found with these structures was related to the Breton Kerugou ware and to the local Seine-Oise-Marne ware.

Around 2000 bc Beaker-using people dismantled the timber structure. A deposit of eight fine barbed-and-tanged arrowheads (including four of Grand Pressigny flint) was placed in one of the post-holes, and yet another great oval turf-built mound with a foundation of rammed beach pebbles was constructed. It covered an area of 35 × 15 m. Fine and coarse Beaker sherds, including large cordoned storage vessels, were associated with this development, and a contemporary settlement was found on the southern lee of the mound, with post-holes, hearths and sherds of Jersey bowls. This community probably buried its dead in the cist within a stone circle at la Platte Mare (12), 80 m to the north. Carbon-14 dates for this phase are 1900 + − 50 bc (calibrated 2385 BC), 1880 + − 50 bc (calibrated 2350 BC) and 2050 + − 60 bc (calibrated 2595 BC).

At some point after 2000 bc the vegetation covering the mound was cleared by fire and then, probably in the Late Iron Age, between 50 BC and AD 50 enclosure ditches were built in alignment with the mound.

Finally, probably in medieval times, great drifts of sand engulfed the site—providentially conserving it for the archaeologist.

11 La Mare ès Mauves, l'Ancresse Common — Neolithic — Guernsey 34,07/83,55
megalithic grave
(Figure 154)

A hundred metres to the south of the martello tower.

Not impressive. All that remains are four uprights and a capstone. Grinding stones, a quern fragment, two perforated stones and a few reddish-brown gritty undecorated sherds were found.

12 La Platte Mare, l'Ancresse Common — Neolithic — Guernsey 33,60/83,18
cist in circle
(Figure 154)

Not easy to find in among the gorse of the golf course. All that remains of this monument are five uprights and stones that seem to mark the entrance. However, early plans show a rather different layout, and it is probable that the 'entrance' is a recent structure built when the monument was used as a cattle-pen. There are a series of 'cup-marks' on the eastern narrow face of the long low upright that supports the northern

capstone (seven are visible; Lukis recorded eleven or twelve). There is a surrounding circle of low stones, and probable traces of another such circle close by.

A fragment of a roughly made flat-based cup, two Beaker sherds and a polished porphyry axe were found.

13 La Varde, l'Ancresse Common — Neolithic — Guernsey 33,77/83,65
passage grave
(Figures 154 and 157–8)

The entrance to the passage is near the summit of the hill, close to a concrete bunker.

A fine passage grave built of great blocks of local granite. The short passage, with no capstones, opens to the south-east. There is no very clear distinction between the passage and chamber which gradually opens out from 2.5 to 3.75 m and extends for 11 m. The chamber has a recess in the north-west corner. There are six capstones. There was originally a small cist made up of two uprights up against the outside edge of the southern wall.

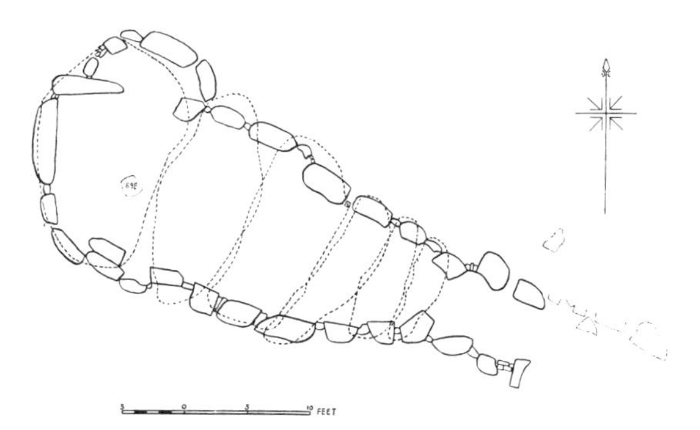

157 La Varde passage grave, l'Ancresse Common, ***Vale***

The mound, 20 m in diameter, is surrounded by a peristalith, and from this a line of stones, protruding only 8 to 10 cm above the ground, curves off to the north-west for about 60 m. Another line, no longer visible, hived off to the south-west of the circle for 25 m. Beyond this line a third section ran in a north-south direction.

F. C. Lukis with his three sons and a manservant, excavated la Varde in 1837. It was his first excavation and his accounts are more than a little confusing. He recorded two levels of paving. The first rested directly on the soil surface and had inhumations and grave-goods placed on it. Then, above a thick level of limpet shells, was another paving of flat stones associated with further inhumations. On the lower paving, and perhaps the upper, there were groups of bones, usually of more than one individual, associated with a pot and surrounded by a ring of small stones. Some of the bones were burnt and it would seem that the unburnt bones were located primarily at either end of the chamber, while the burnt bones were in the middle.

In all, fragments of about 150 pots were found. An unbelievable range of styles suggests constant use and reuse over a considerable length of time. There were a couple of small Chassey pots, two flat-based pots of Seine-Oise-Marne type, a marvellous series of twelve or thirteen decorated ovate pots that seem to be an insular variation of Bell Beaker ware, another four or five undecorated biconical pots of a similar fabric, three or more classic Bell Beakers, a couple of

158 La Varde passage grave, l'Ancresse Common, ***Vale.*** *Lukis' picture of the 1837 excavation*

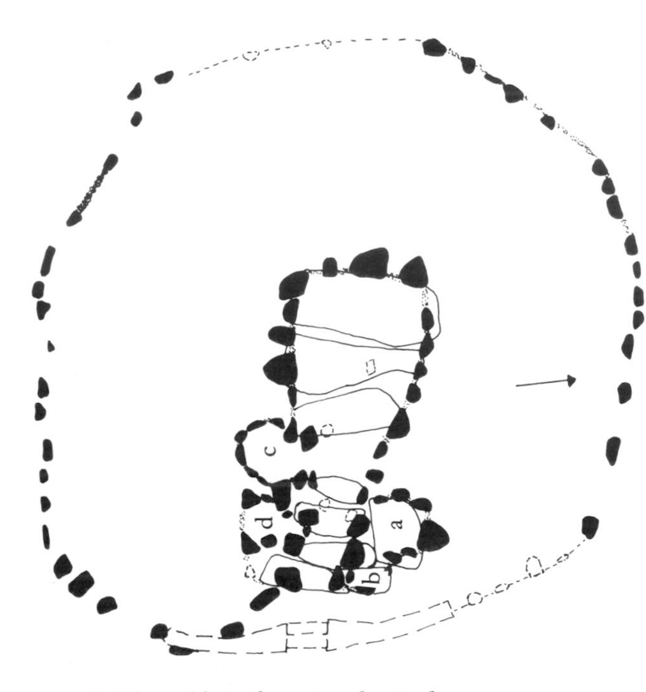

159 Plan of le Déhus, Paradis, Vale

Bronze Age cinerary urns, fragments of La Tène pedestalled urns, some Gallo-Roman ware, and finally, some Samian sherds (these in the top level). There were also two or three fragments of thin bronze plate, half a conical V-perforated jet button, a serpentine crescent and ring and the occasional flint and bone object.

14 Le Déhus, Paradis — Neolithic
transepted passage grave — Guernsey 35,80/83,05
(Figures 154 (map) and 159–61)

A fine monument below a mound 20 m in diameter, originally surrounded by a peristalith of stones of which only a few remain. It lies on the 15 m raised beach, and the vast quantities of limpet shells found throughout the chamber and side-chambers, while certainly reflecting ritual deposition, may also indicate that the monument was built on, or close to, a shell midden.

The passage, nearly 3 m long and 1 m wide, opens to the east and is flanked by two side-chambers on each side. The largest of these is 1.5 m square. The main chamber is 6 × 3.5 m. The two uprights in the

160 Underside of capstone, le Déhus, Paradis, Vale

north-east corner originally stood one on either side of the entrance between the passage and chamber permitting only a very narrow entrance.

On the underside of the capstone in the centre of the chamber is an engraved figure, firmly described by Miss Collum in 1933 as a male with 'hair on the face' and no less firmly, as a 'composite Dispater-Hermes'. In reality it is a female, closely allied to the rock-cut figures of the Paris Basin tombs and certainly related to the other statue menhirs on Guernsey (*Câtel* and *St Martin*) and to the Breton examples. One can make out the face, arms and hands, as well as a crescent-shaped symbol and a straight line with a

161 Le Déhus, Paradis, Vale, anthropomorphic engraving on the capstone of the transepted grave

circle. Some of the lines continue round the edge of the stone, confirming that the stone was engraved before being put into place, and was perhaps a reused statue menhir.

F. C. Lukis, who excavated the chamber on and off for more than ten years (1837 to 1847) started his explorations in the main chamber, and having disposed of 'bushels' of limpet shells, first came upon an upper level of human bones, pots etc., then, separated by yet more shells, another level of inhumations resting on a level of imported yellow clay. This clay lay directly above the land surface.

In contrast, when he dug the side-chamber (a), Lukis found only one level of bones laid on the land surface. He noted that the pottery associated with these bones was different from the material in the main chamber, although sherds from the side-chamber infilling, in particular Beaker fragments, fitted with sherds from the main chamber. If accurate, this description would suggest that the main chamber had been cleared out and then reutilized. Bone points were found in the side-chamber (a), and also, on a ledge to the right of the entrance, a polished serpentine axe.

According to Lukis, side-chamber (b) contained 'two skeletons in a vertical kneeling position' and, he suggested, this 'singular state would easily give countenance to the hypothesis of the two persons having been buried alive' (Lukis' diary 1844). There was no pottery, only a great mass of limpet shells.

Side chamber (c) contained three groups of bones on a paving of flat, irregular slabs associated with round-based ware and the obligatory mass of limpet shells.

Side chamber (d), minus its capstone, had an upper level of bones resting on a pavement of small granite slabs, then a second level again on a paving, and a third level, on the soil surface. This last level consisted of two crouched inhumations and part of a third, as well as an inverted bowl placed over three pieces of stones. Dr Lukis (son of F. C.)—never averse to a bit of drama – noted that the inverted pot contained bone fragments apparently from the fore-part of the chest and suggested that it had perhaps contained a heart 'rudely removed with portions of the parieties'. There was no pottery associated with the upper two levels of inhumations.

In general the pottery from the tomb included Chassey, Seine Oise-Marne, and in the upper levels, Bell Beaker ware. The latter was primarily localized in the main chamber close to the central upright, and a copper dagger was found nearby. Two small bronze rings may be Iron Age or Roman.

The monument is open from April to the end of September from 7 a.m. to 6.30 p.m. During the rest of the year the key can be obtained at the market garden opposite.

Jersey

The map (Figure 162) shows the general location of the sites.

Grouville

At this site there is not only the great megalithic monument of la Hougue Bie but also the Archaeological Museum, the Agricultural Museum, the Occupation Museum, and the Railway Museum.

1 The Archaeological Museum — Museum

There is a geological section in the basement, and exhibits of local Palaeolithic to medieval material in the split-level main hall.

Open from March to the end of October from Tuesday to Saturday, 10 a.m. to 5 p.m.

2 La Hougue Bie *passage grave* — Neolithic — Jersey 68,60/50,25
(Figures 163 and 164)

La Hougue Bie is a very impressive cruciform passage grave covered by an equally impressive mound, crowned by two medieval chapels.

The mound is made of earth and small stones, mainly from the Queen's Valley, 1.5 km to the east. It is 50 m in diameter and 12 m high. There is a splayed dry-stone passage entrance, 3.6 m wide at the entrance, 0.9 m wide at the rear. It opens to the east. It gives onto a passage 11 m long, 0.9 to 1.5 m wide and 1.4 to 2 m high. The passage is made of orthostatic slabs surmounted by seven capstones. Interstices and often the space between upright and capstone are filled with dry-stone walling.

The main chamber is very long, 8.8 × 2.5/3.7 × 1.35/1.95 m, and is covered by five great slabs. Within the main chamber are five large and three small uprights. Side-chambers give off to the north (A), south (C) and west (B) so that the overall plan is cruciform. The north side-chamber is 2.1 × 1.05 × 1.22 m, the southern one is 1.85 × 0.9 × 1.2 m. Both are separated from the main chamber by two uprights and a sill-stone and are covered by a single capstone. On the eastern upright (a) of the north side-chamber are twenty-four cup-marks, and there is another one on the underside of the capstone (A cast of this upright is in the *St Helier* museum.)

The west chamber, at the end of the main chamber is the most carefully made and is separated from the main chamber by a single slab which must have been transported some seven kilometres from Mont Mado. A broken quern, placed upside down, was found at its base. The deposition of a broken quern seems to be an island custom: another was found at le Couperon, and twenty-two at the now destroyed Hougue Mauger.

The remains of at least eight inhumations were found, of which two or three were women, four or five men. The handbook says that 'eminent anatomists...stated that the height...was only four feet nine inches and that these persons were given to squatting' and that 'they had long arms and small brains'! There were bones of cattle, sheep and pig, oyster shell and *Patella athletica*. Also fragments of some twenty vase-supports (often still with charred debris in the saucer), some plain, some with scratched decoration, all very similar to the Paris Basin Chassey forms. In the north-west part of the chamber was a cluster of plain Bell Beakers and, finally, there were a couple of beads, four transverse-tranchet arrowheads, a point, twelve retouched flint flakes and blades and several unretouched flints.

On the top of the mound are two juxtaposed chapels; the more easterly one is the Notre-Dame de la Clarté, built in the twelfth century, while the westerly Jerusalem chapel was built in 1520. In this one, at the east end of the vault, there are two late fifteenth- or early sixteenth-century paintings of

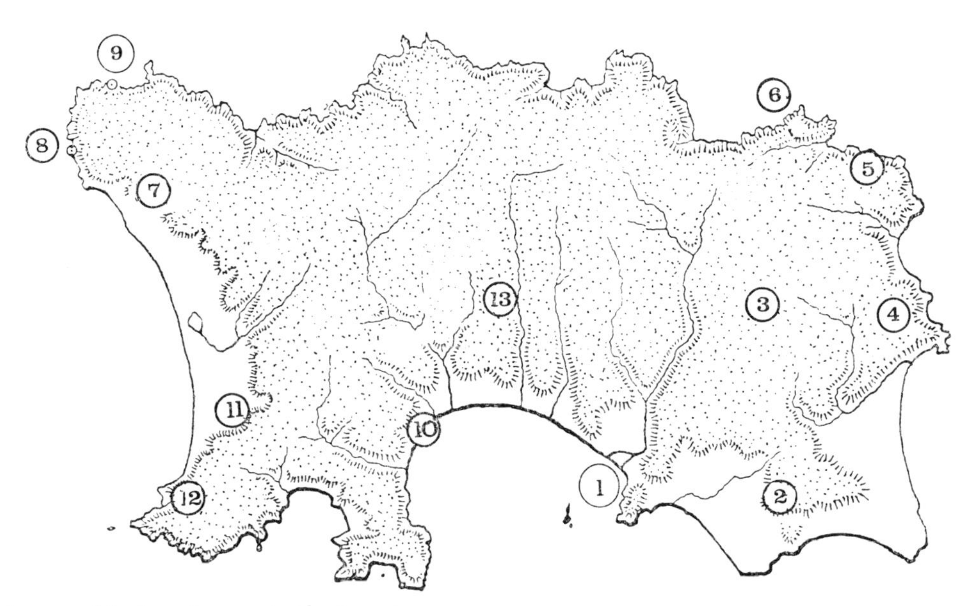

162 Jersey, with sites that are in the inventory

1 *Ville-ès-Nouaux,* ***St Helier,*** *gallery grave and cists*
2 *Mont Ubé,* ***St Clement,*** *passage grave*
3 *La Hougue Bie,* ***Grouville,*** *passage grave and museums*
4 *La Pouquelaye de Faldouet,* ***St Martin,*** *passage grave*
5 *Le Couperon,* ***St Martin,*** *gallery grave*
6 *Le Câtel de Rozel,* ***St Martin,*** *earthwork*
7 *Les Monts Grantez,* ***St Ouen,*** *passage grave*
8 *Le Pinacle,* ***St Ouen,*** *Neolithic-Roman occupation*
9 *Cotte à la Chèvre,* ***St Ouen,*** *Palaeolithic cave*
10 ***St Brelade,*** *church*
11 *Blanches Banques,* ***St Brelade***
12 *La Sergenté,* ***St Brelade,*** *passage grave*
13 ***St Lawrence,*** *church*

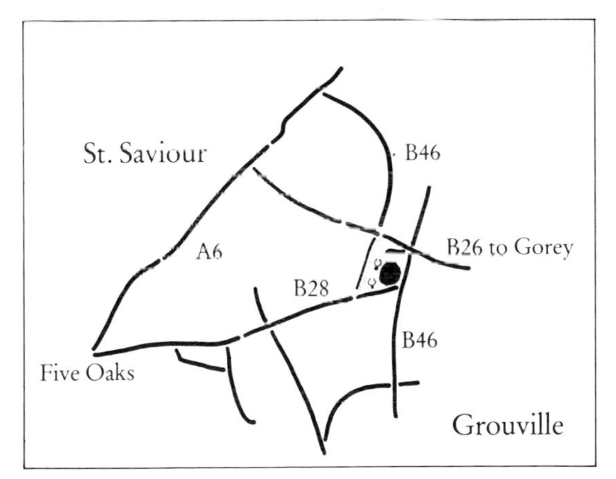

163 Le Hougue Bie, ***Grouville***

angels. These originally flanked a carved figure. The Jerusalem chapel also contains some of the historical documents relating to la Hougue Bie.

St Brelade

1 The church of St Brelade — Church

The earliest parts of St Brelade are the Fisherman's Chapel, of which the lower part of the walls may go back to the seventh or eighth century, and the present-day chancel of the church. The transepts and part of the nave of the church were added in the twelfth century and then, in the fourteenth and fifteenth centuries the height of the walls was increased, the earlier windows replaced and the Gothic roof added. Some part of the Romanesque windows can still be traced on the interior walls. The Fisherman's Chapel also had its walls raised and its roof remodelled in the fifteenth century.

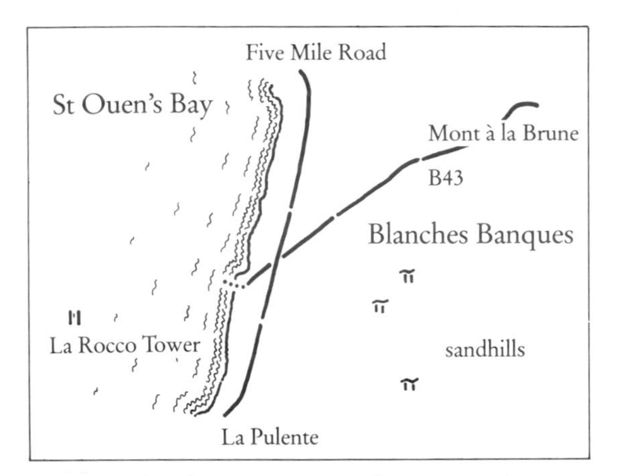

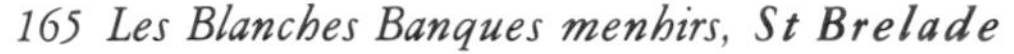
165 Les Blanches Banques menhirs, **St Brelade**

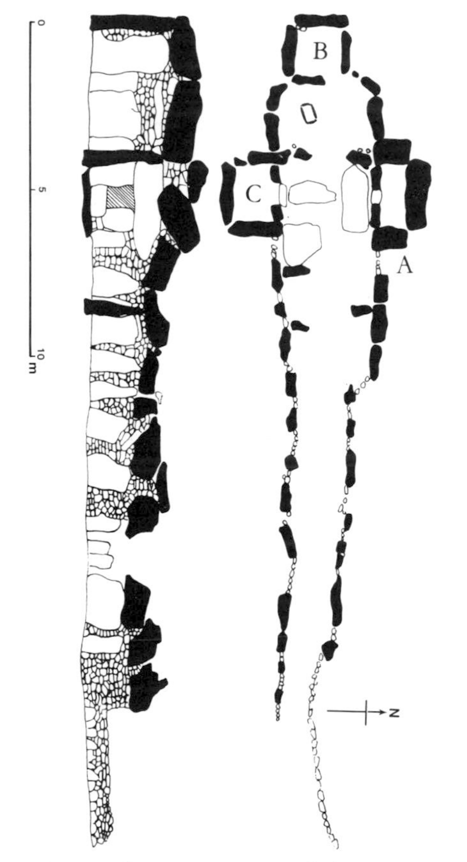

164 Plan and cross-section of la Hougue Bie, **Grouville**

2 Blanches Banques — Neolithic
menhirs and cist — Jersey 57,15/50,00
(Figure 165)

From the car park on the south side of the B 43 strike out southwards across the sandy plain below the dunes.

The Great Menhir is the most southerly stone and is 400 m south of the cist on the slope of the rising dunes. It stands 2 m above the ground. It fell and was re-erected and the setting-stones were found. It is made of granite.

The Little Menhir, granite, 1.75 m high and tapering to a point, is 150 m south-west of the cist. The base has been excavated, the setting stones uncovered, and on the original land surface a tiny sherd of gritty red ware, a thumb scraper and a grinding stone were found.

The Broken Menhir, 30 m north of the cist and 90 m north-east of the Little Menhir, is also of granite. It has been restored, stands 2.75 to 3 m high and has setting stones.

Finally, the cist, modest and restored, once contained the remains of twenty inhumations. They lay in a confused heap along with grave-goods that included one complete Jersey bowl and fragments of a second.

3 La Sergenté — Neolithic
passage grave

Only for enthusiasts. In the Parc de l'Oeillère estate take the upper road and beyond the last houses the road becomes a field track. Take the grassy lane to the left and the monument is about 100 m on, to the right among the gorse.

These remains have often been misinterpreted as a beehive hut complete with bed. In reality, it is a small, once-corbelled, passage grave. The chamber 3.35 m in diameter is of dry-stone walling. The walls now only rise to 0.75 m. At this level—perhaps with a little help from the restorers—they begin to curve inwards. Most of the floor is paved but up against the west wall a curved line of four thin stone slabs, 0.2 m high, partition off an unpaved area 1.5 × 0.6 m. There is a threshold stone between the passage and chamber.

Fragments of four round-based pots, apparently in the Chassey tradition, and unworked flints were found in the chamber.

St Clement

Mont Ubé — Neolithic
passage grave — Jersey 67,70/47,41
(Figures 166 and 167)
Take the A 5 out of St Helier. At the small crossroads *before* the junction with the B 48 turn left (opposite the rue de Samares). Then take the second small road right marked 'Mont Ubé, private residence'. Beyond the last house turn sharply left onto a field-track. 40 m on, left of an overgrown telegraph pole, is the even more overgrown entrance to the grave.

The passage, opening east-south-east, is 5.18 m long and widens towards the chamber. The chamber is 7.3 × 3.05 m and has a slight recess in the south wall flanked by two uprights. All the capstones have disappeared. In 1848, according to Lukis, the west end of the chamber was divided into four compartments by means of five uprights and four low sillstones, and the mound was still visible.

The 'grave-goods' may well be fraudulent—particularly those that were given to the British Museum. There was a typical Jersey bowl, a fine carinated Bell Beaker, plain Beaker ware, fragments of two vase-supports, a grape-cup, sherds of grit-tempered ware with narrow grooves, dots and zigzag incisions. There was also a flint pick, two barbed-and-tanged arrowheads, one transverse-tranchet arrowhead, two Grand Pressigny tools, a grey flint 'rod', four or five perforated pebble amulets, a fragment of a jade-like bracelet etc. A truly eclectic collection!

According to one source no burials were found: according to Lukis there were many.

The material is in the museum of *St Helier*, the Candie Gardens museum, *St Peter Port* on Guernsey, and in the British Museum.

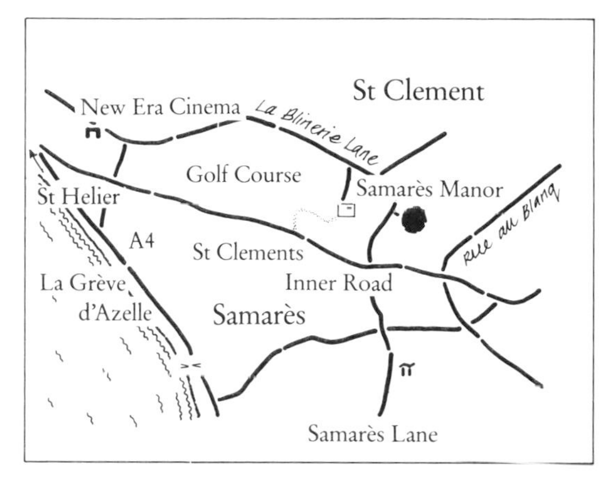

166 *Mont Ubé,* ***St Clement***

167 *Mont Ubé,* ***St Clement***

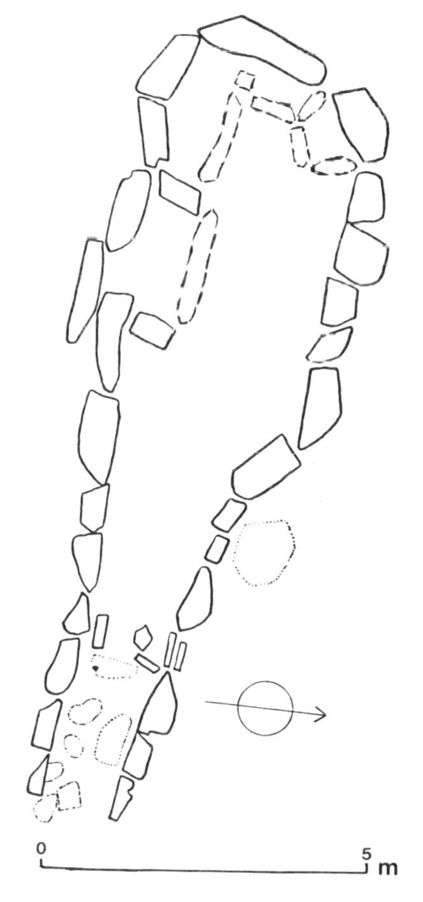

St Helier

Ville-ès-Nouaux, St Helier — Neolithic
First Tower Park — Jersey 63,45/49,90
gallery grave and cist graves
(Figures 168 and 169)
Two rather prim monuments lie within the park.
(a) The gallery grave is 11.75 × 1.27 × 1 m, and is delimited by low orthostatic walls. There are seven capstones still in place and the entrance is at the east

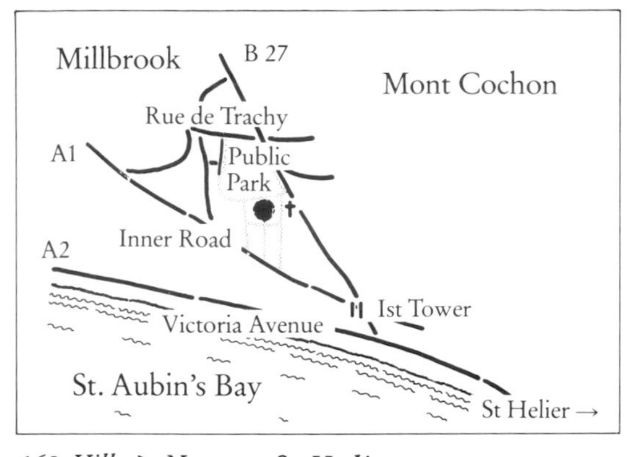

168 *Ville-ès-Nouaux,* ***St Helier***

169 *Ville-ès-Nouaux,* ***St Helier***

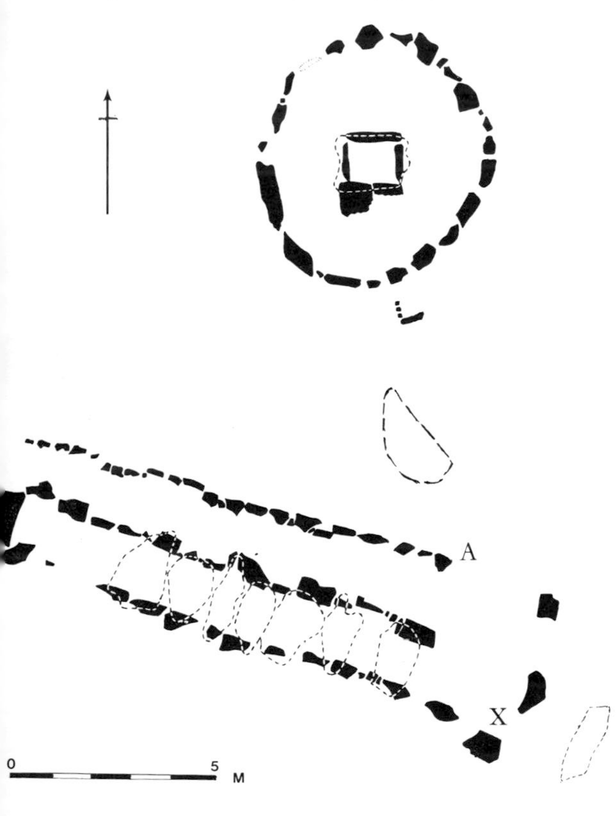

end. One of the capstones may originally have formed an internal divide, and a vertical slab found inside the grave at the west end may have been part of a small cist. There were probably two side-chambers, one on either side of the entrance. The line of small uprights to the north of the grave is probably part of the mound kerb.

Inside the chamber a paving extended for 12 m from the west end. A few limpet shells and fragments of rough Seine-Oise-Marne pottery were found below it, while on top rested a fine group of ten Bell Beakers and six carinated pots placed in tiny flat stone cists. In the centre of this group a discoloured patch of earth probably marked a Beaker inhumation. It was associated with an archer's wristguard, perforated at each end.

In the side-chambers much flint and some pottery and charcoal were found, and outside the grave, at X on the plan, there were several Bell Beaker and Beaker-type fragments.

(b) 5.8 m north-north-east of the gallery grave an oval of stones, 5.8 × 6.4 m in diameter, surrounds a small cist made of four uprights. It has a floor made of a single slab, and is covered by a capstone. At A on the plan a threshold stone probably marks the entrance.

Nothing was found inside.

In a level of wind-blown sand, above the gallery grave and cist-in-circle, a small Early Iron Age cemetery was found, with a series of situla-shaped pots that once held cremations.

St Lawrence

Church Roman

The church of St Lawrence goes back to the early seventh century, but nothing remains of this building. Nor is there much left of the twelfth- and thirteenth-century structure except for the south transept transmuted into the south porch. The nave is thirteenth century, the chancel fifteenth century, and the fine groin-vaulted Hamptonne chapel is sixteenth century.

Within the south porch there is an extremely interesting column which was found in the nineteenth century below the nave. In its first life this column was part of a Roman structure, probably fourth century AD. It was the capital end of an engaged column which must originally have been about 1.5 m high. Later, in the sixth century, the flat top was reused for an early Christian inscription. Finally, probably in the early ninth century one side was recarved with a double-beaded plait. The column is of non-local granite and of course it is possible that it is not *in situ*, and that it was imported in post-Roman, possibly post-Carolingian, and even perhaps post-ninth-century, times. In which case it has little bearing on the island history!

St Martin

1 La Pouquelaye de Faldouet — Neolithic
passage grave — Jersey 71,00/50,70
(Figures 170 and 171)
This tomb is orientated east/west, with the entrance to the east. There is a narrow passage walled with small uprights, then a sort of double-chamber. The first part is about 3 m wide and contains the remains of five or six small cists—much tampered with. The second part is again 3 m wide, has massive uprights and is covered by a great capstone. The mound has a double concentric revetment wall, again heavily reconstructed.

Human bones were found in the cists. The grave-goods, from various parts of the monument, included two fine Chassey pots, a hemispherical bowl, a tiny cup, at least three vase-supports, probably a plain Bell Beaker fragment, two perforated axe-pendants, a polished greenstone axe, and a partly polished flint axe and sandstone rubber.

2 Le Couperon — Neolithic
gallery grave — Jersey 70,32/54,18
(Figure 172)
Take the B 38 and just before it sweeps round close to the sea take the small track right marked rue des Fontanelles. A lovely walk past precipitous potato fields.

The grave is on a high promontory, 38.5 m above sea-level. It opens to the south and the entrance is sealed by a fine port-hole stone. This stone has been in this position *since 1919*. Between 1868 and 1919 it served as a capstone. Its original place must have been within the chamber, creating a divide between ante-chamber and chamber.

The total length of the grave is 8.15 × 1 m and there are seven capstones in place. The orthostatic peristalith can still be seen.

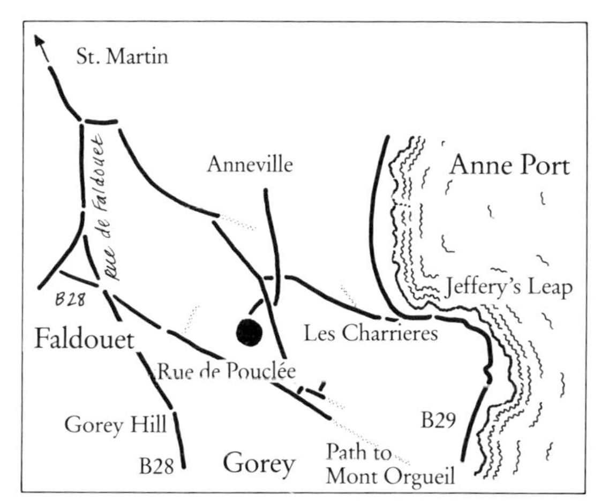

170 La Pouquelaye de Faldouet, ***St Martin***

171 La Pouquelaye de Faldouet, ***St Martin***

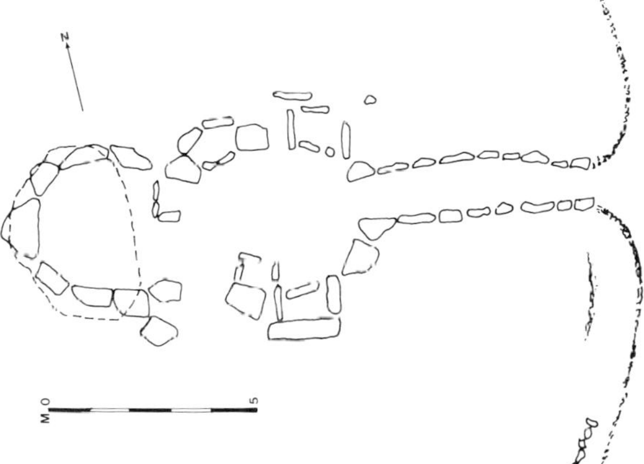

172 Le Couperon gallery grave, ***St Martin***

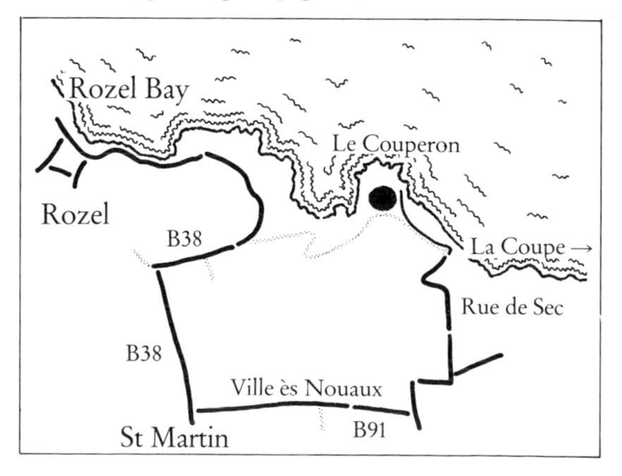

3 Le Câtel de Rozel — Iron Age
earthworks — Jersey 68,90/54,65

From Rozel take the C 39 (→ Pot du Rocher), and near the top of the hill turn very sharply right. Then take the first track on the left.

Le Câtel was a large promontory fort, defended on the north-west, north and east by high, steep cliffs, and across the col, in a north-west/south-east line, by a high earthwork. Originally the earthwork must have extended from Rozel to Bouley Bay, but now only the north-west section running for about 200 m remains. Still it is an impressive section, over 6 m high and 9 m wide at the base. There are some traces of a stone revetment. The entrance was probably in the ploughed-out south-east end.

Apparently Roman coins and bricks have been found in the rampart. More certainly four very large Iron Age coin hoards have been found on the protected spur. They date to the first century BC and in the main were minted by the Armorican Coriosolites tribe (see General Introduction page 53, and Introduction to the Channel Islands page 223).

St Ouen

1 Les Monts Grantez — Neolithic
passage grave — Jersey 56,68/53,68
(Figures 173 and 174)

The monument is in the middle of a field, hidden behind a fairly modern circular stone wall.

The passage, orientated east-south-east/west-north-west, is 3.35 m long, 1 to 1.25 m high. It is made of orthostatic uprights covered by five capstones. The oval chamber, 5 × 3 m, is flanked to the north by a side-chamber, 2 × 1.75 m, covered by a single capstone. The mound is still visible.

One skeleton was found in the passage and another seven in the main chamber (six adults, one child). They were flexed and surrounded by limpet shells, bones and teeth of cattle, deer, horse, pig and goat and by 'special' pebbles. There was also a skeleton in the side-chamber.

There were fragments of at least four vase-supports, very similar to the Paris Basin Chassey forms, as well as a hemispherical bowl, a small saucer, a fragment of a carinated base and two fragments of plain Beaker ware.

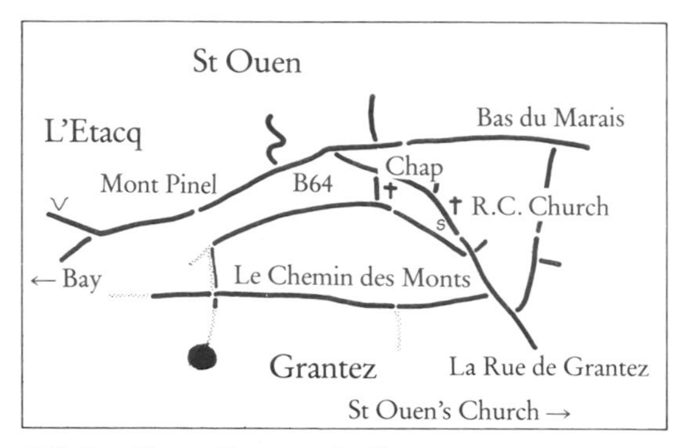

173 *Les Monts Grantez,* ***St Ouen***

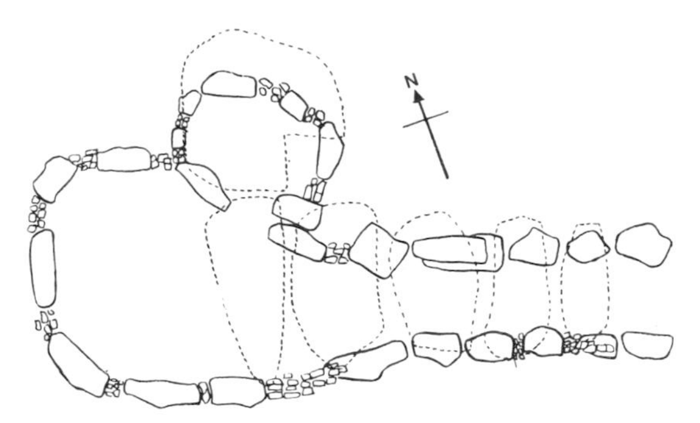

174 *Les Monts Grantez,* ***St Ouen***

2 Le Pinacle — Neolithic to Roman
settlement — Jersey 54,49/55,50
(Figures 175 and 176)

The track ends at a ruined concrete gun-emplacement. Below and slightly to the right a bulbous granitic mass protrudes into the sea and cupped within it is a low grassy col. One can just make out the foundations of a large rectangular building and a low wall. It is well worth a visit—for the view, the isolation and for the feeling that a long, less-isolated history lies buried below the ground.

The col, now 50 m above sea-level, is covered with a thick deposit of head (periglacial debris), clay and boulders, much eroded since Neolithic times. The earliest occupation level, dating to the Neolithic,

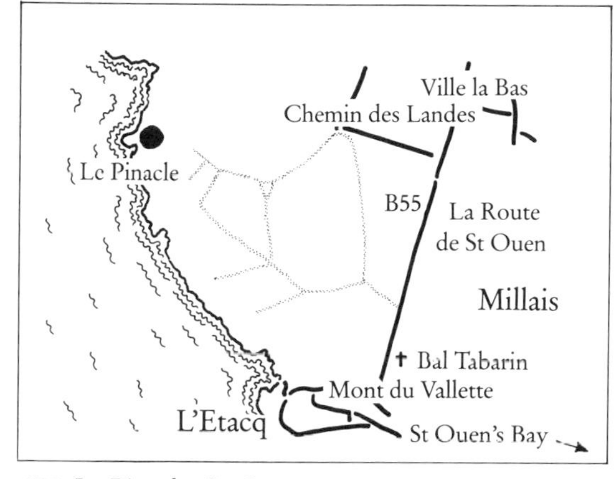

175 Le Pinacle, ***St Ouen***

contained a number of hearths, considerable amounts of cow, sheep and pig bone, the odd nut, and even a piece of 'bread' still adhering to a stone plate. In all probability these Neolithic people also built at least the western section of the inner wall. An enormous number of hardstone fragments were found in this first level, some slate but mainly dolerite. They were made into axes, into ovoid or discoidal hammers, and, an island speciality, into ceremonial droop-bladed picks, often perforated and often broken while being made. There is much waste and many pebbles with battered ends. It has recently been suggested that this site was not really a habitation site, but rather an important axe factory exploiting the dolerite dyke just to the north of the col. It may be that the habitation site was down in the less exposed and more fertile St Ouen's bay to the south of le Pinacle. The original excavators, however, believed that the tools were all made of dolerite pebbles picked up on the shore and that le Pinacle was a farming settlement exploiting the lands to the south of the cliff, now below sea-level. There is certainly a considerable amount of domestic debris—grinding stones and stone baking-plates, and also a more conventional flint pebble industry, including large numbers of transverse-tranchet arrowheads. Either way, the hardstone industry urgently needs more careful analysis, including a survey of the wider distribution of the dolerite artefacts. The pottery from this level is interesting. It has strong Band-keramik affinities, but also decorative features that link it with finds from Mont Orgueil on the east coast and with the north-west French Cerny group.

It seems likely that the second occupation level should really be further subdivided. It is improbable that the Seine-Oise-Marne and the Early Bronze Age materials are really contemporary. This mixed material was mainly located in the area between the western inner wall and le Pinacle. The wall itself was extended sometime during these occupations. Remains of vetch, barley and probably wheat were found. The pottery included both coarse Seine-Oise-Marne ware and finer Breton-style Early Bronze Age four-handled pottery. There were also a few fragments of Bell Beaker, a few pieces of Grand Pressigny flint made into knives and barbed-and-tanged arrowheads, a copper flat axe and bead, a couple of stone beads and the usual pebble flint industry, including a number of barbed-and-tanged arrowheads.

Still later, there was a minor Late Bronze Age occupation, apparently associated with the building of an outer wall made of earth faced with granite slabs. Coarse pottery, a bronze ring and a socketed spearhead with a basal loop come from this horizon.

Then there is some Iron Age La Tène pottery, hand- and wheel-made, with an American coin of probably the first century BC.

Finally, there is the Gallo-Roman structure, the rectangle visible on the surface, with an inner wall 2 × 1.25 m, and an outer wall 3.5 × 2.75 m, and an entrance on the east side. A coin found within the rectangle is of Commodus, AD 180–91. Some black burnished ware manufactured in Dorset was also found. It is generally assumed that the building was a small *fanum*, though no statues were found. An alternative is that it served as a guardroom.

3 Cotte à la Chèvre — Paleolithic
cave site — Jersey 55,13/56,62
(Figure 177)

Hard to find and not much to see archaeologically, but a marvellous walk and view. At the ruins (marked on the map) take the path eastwards (→ Plémont) for about half a kilometre to a concrete pad and then to the second bench beyond. A spiny crag is now visible.

176 Le Pinacle, ***St Ouen***

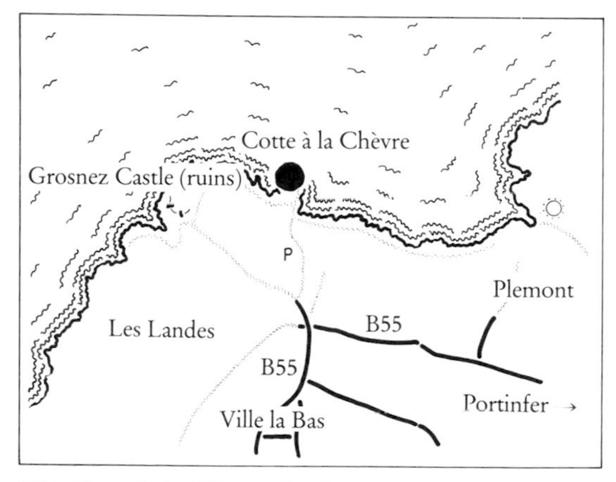

177 Cotte à la Chèvre, ***St Ouen***

Continue another 80 m and take the small precipitous path to the left, which winds down and round to the cave.

The cave, long and narrow (10 × 3.75 × 4.5 m) is now 18 m above sea-level. The lowest level of sand and pebbles is probably of the same date as the cave formation. It is overlain by a white loam level, and then by a level of yellowish loam with a high phosphate content which contains occupation debris and at least two hearths. The high phosphate content may be the result of decomposing bone. Around two hundreds flints were found, mainly a rather crude industry but there was also some Mousterian of Levallois tradition. Although no human bones were found, and there are no carbon-14 dates, the occupants must have been Neanderthalers (see General Introduction, page 21).

Glossary

Acheulian A late horizon in the Lower Palaeolithic, marked by changes in human morphology and tool types.

Anthropomorph Upright stones shaped to human form.

Berm The flat land surface that lies between a bank or mound and a ditch.

Cist A small closed stone structure, often used for burials or to hold grave-goods.

Corbel A domed 'beehive' roof.

Dolmen A small amorphous, stone burial chamber.

Megalith Monument made of large stones—standing stones, stone circles, various types of burial chamber.

Menhir A standing stone, often unworked.

Mesolithic Distinguishes post-Ice Age hunter-gatherers from those of earlier time ranges.

Microlith Very small stone tool, usually part of a compound tool.

Midden A refuse heap.

Mousterian Hunter-gatherer societies of the European Middle Palaeolithic, c. 120,000 to 40,000 bp.

Neolithic Stone-using farming societies.

Orthostat A large stone.

Palaeolithic Hunter-gatherer societies from the emergence of the first hominids through to the end of the Pleistocene Ice Age c. 13,000 bp.

Peristalith The perimeter of a stone burial ground.

Pleistocene The last Ice Age in Europe. It dates from c. 1.9 million years ago to c. 13,000 bp.

Revetment Stone walling used to shore up or consolidate a structure.

Ricasso The nicks placed on either side of a sword blade, close to the hilt, to facilitate blood-letting.

Scories Slag.

Septal stone A sill-stone often placed at the entrance of a chamber.

Stele A carefully shaped standing stone.

Bibliography

I have kept the list short and have concentrated on works that are either in English or are very important general studies in French.

Brittany

M. Batt, P.-R. Giot, Y. Lecerf, J. Lecornec, C.-T. Le Roux, 1980, *Mégalithes au Pays de Carnac*, Edition d'Art Jos Le Doare, Châteaulin

Aubrey Burl, 1985 *Guide to the Megalithic Monuments of Brittany*, Thames and Hudson

B. Cunliffe, 1981, 'Britain, the Veneti and beyond', *Oxford Journal of Archaeology*, 1(1), 39–68

P. Galliou, 1983, *L'Armorique romain*, Les Bibliophiles de Bretagne

P.-R. Giot, 1971, 'Impact of C14 dating on the establishing of the prehistoric chronology of Brittany', *Proceedings of the Prehistoric Society*, XXXCII, 208–17

P.-R. Giot, 1976, *Livret-Guide de l'Excursion A3. Bretagne*, Union Internationale des Sciences Préhistoriques et Protohistoriques, IX Congrès

P.-R. Giot, J. Briard, L. Pape, 1979, *Protohistoire de la Bretagne*, Ouest France, Rennes

P.-R. Giot, J. L'Helgouach, J.-L. Monnier, 1979, *Préhistoire de la Bretagne*, Ouest France, Rennes

J. L'Helgouach, 1965, *Les Sépultures mégalithiques en Armorique*, Travaux du Laboratoire d'Anthropologie Préhistorique de la Faculté des Sciences, Rennes

A. and A. S. Thom, 1978, *Megalithic Remains in Britain and Brittany*, Clarendon Press, Oxford

E. Twohig, 1981, *The Megalithic Art of Western Europe*, Clarendon Press, Oxford

M. Wheeler and K. Richardson, 1957, *Hill-forts of Northern France*, O.U.P., Oxford

Normandy

L. Musset, 1967, *Normandie Romane*, Zodiaque

G. Verron, 1981, *Préhistoire de la Basse-Normandie, 1. Paléolithique et Néolithique, 2. L'Age du Bronze et L'Age du Fer*, Centre Régional de Documentation Pédagogique, Caen

G. Verron, 1981b, *Préhistoire de Haute-Normandie*, Centre Régional de Documentation Pédagogique, Rouen

G. Verron, 1982, *Protohistoire de Haute-Normandie*. Centre Régional de Documentation Pédagogique, Rouen

Channel Islands

J. Hawkes, 1937, *The Archaeology of the Channel Islands, vol. II, the Bailiwick of Jersey*, Societé Jersiaise, Jersey

T. Kendrick, 1928, *The Archaeology of the Channel Islands, vol. I, the Bailiwick of Guernsey*, Methuen, London

I. Kinnes, 1982, 'Les Fouaillages and megalithic origins', *Antiquity*, LVI, 24–30

Books and articles from which illustrations have been reproduced

Batt, M., Giot, P.-R., Lecerf, Y., Lecornec, J., and Le Roux, C.-T., 1980, *Mégalithes au Pays de Carnac*, Editions d'Art Jos le Doare, Châteaulin

Baudot, M., 1943, 'Le problème des Ruines du Vieil-Evreux', *Gallia*, I (2), 191–206

Bender, B., 1967, *The Neolithic Cultures of North-West France*, PhD

Boüard, M. de, 1968, 'Circonscription de Haute et Basse Normandie', *Gallia*, 26 (I), 347–72

Bibliography

Boüard, M. de, 1974, 'Circonscription de Haute et Basse Normandie', *Gallia*, 32 (I), 319–34

Burns, B. and A., 1983, 'A guide to Iron Age sites in Guernsey', *Field Excursion to the Channel Islands*, The Prehistoric Society

Caillaud, R., and Lagnel, E., 1972, 'Le Cairn et le crématoire néolithiques de la Hoguette à Fontenay-le-Marmion', *Gallia Préhistoire*, 15, 137–97

Cunliffe, B., 1981, 'Britain, the Veneti and beyond', *Oxford Journal of Archaeology*, 1 (I), 39–68

Delumeau, J., et al., 1971, *Documents de l'Histoire de la Bretagne*, Toulouse

Drouelle, L., 1959, 'Le Camp de Goult, commune de la Lande de Goult, *Le Pays d'Argentan*, 3 (113), 101–7

Finlaison, M., 1983, 'Guide to the principal prehistoric sites in Jersey', *Field Excursion to the Channel Islands*, The Prehistoric Society

Giot, P.-R., 1967, 'Circonscription de Bretagne et des Pays de la Loire', *Gallia Préhistoire*, X, I, 333-64

Giot, P.-R., 1976, *Livret-Guide de l'Excursion A 3. Bretagne*, Union Internationale des Sciences Préhistoriques et Protohistoriques, IX Congrès

Giot, P. R., Briard, J., and Pape, L., 1979, *Protohistoire de la Bretagne*, Ouest France, Rennes

Giot, P.-R., L'Helgouach, J., and Monnier, J.-L., 1979, *Préhistoire de la Bretagne*, Ouest France, Rennes

Grenier, A., 1960, *Manuel d'Archéologie Gallo-Romaine*, vol. IV, Picard, Paris

Hawkes, J., 1937, *The Archaeology of the Channel Islands, vol. I, the Bailiwick of Jersey*, Societé Jersiaise, Jersey

Kendrick, T., 1928, *The Archaeology of the Channel Islands, the Bailiwick of Guernsey*, Methuen, London

L'Helgouach, J., 1965, *Les Sépultures mégalithiques en Armorique*, Travaux du Laboratoire d'Anthropologie Préhistorique de la Faculté des Sciences, Rennes

L'Helgouach, J., 1966, 'Fouilles de l'allée couverte de Prajou-Menhir en Trébeurden (Côtes-du-Nord)', *Bulletin de la Société Préhistorique Française*, LXIII, 2, 311–42

L'Helgouach, J., 1970, 'Le monument mégalithique du Goërem à Gâvres (Morbihan)', *Gallia Préhistoire*, XIII, 2, 217–61

L'Helgouach, J., 1971, 'Circonscription des Pays de la Loire', *Gallia Préhistoire*, XIV, 2, 363–75

L'Helgouach, J., 1977, 'Circonscription des Pays de la Loire', *Gallia Préhistoire*, 20, 433–55

L'Helgouach, J., 1979, 'Circonscription des Pays de la Loire', *Gallia Préhistoire*, 22, 557–83

L'Helgouach, J., Bellancourt, G., Gallais, C., and Lecornec, J., 1970, 'Sculptures et gravures nouvellement découvertes sur des mégalithes de l'Armorique', *Bulletin de la Société Préhistorique Française*, 67, 2, 513–21

Renouf, J., and Urry, J., 1976, *The First Farmers in the Channel Islands*, MS

Le Roux, C.-T., and L'Helgouach, J., 1967, 'Le cairn mégalithique avec sépultures à chambres compartmentées de Kerleven, commune de la Forêt-Fouesnant (Finistère), *Annales de Bretagne, notices d'Archeologie armoricaine*, LXXXIV, 7–52

Sanquer, R., 1973, 'Chronique d'Archeologie Antique et Mediévale, *Bulletin de la Société Archeologique de Finistère*

Sanquer, R., and Galliou, R., 1972, 'Une maison de campagne gallo-romaine à la Roche Maurice (Finistère)', *Annales de Bretagne*, LXXIX

Thom, A. and A. S., 1978, *Megalithic Remains in Britain and Brittany*, Clarendon, Oxford

Twohig, E., 1981, *The Megalithic Art of Western Europe*, Clarendon, Oxford

Verron, G., 1973, 'Circonscription de Haute et Basse Normandie', *Gallia Préhistoire*, 16 (2), 361–99

Verron, G., 1976, *Livret-Guide de l'excursion A 10. Nord-Ouest de la France*, Union Internationale des Sciences Préhistoriques et Protohistoriques, IX Congrès

Verron, G., 1981a, *Préhistoire de la Basse-Normandie, 1. Paléolithique et Néolithique, 2. L'Age du Bronze et L'Age du Fer*, Centre Régional de Documentation Pédagogique, Caen

Verron, G., 1981b, *Préhistoire de Haute-Normandie*, Centre Régional de Documentation Pédagogique, Rouen

Verron, G., and Fosse, G., 1981, *Préhistoire de Haute-Normandie*, Centre Régional de Documentation Pédagogique, Rouen

Wheeler, M., and Richardson, K., 1957, *Hill-forts of Northern France*, O.U.P., Oxford

Index

I General

Page numbers in *italic* refer to illustrations or maps; page numbers in **bold type** refer to main entries.

Index

II Place Names

Page numbers in *italic* refer to illustrations or maps; page numbers in **bold type** refer to main entries. A–Alderney, C–Calvados, CN–Côtes-du-Nord, E–Eure, F–Finistère, G–Guernsey, IV–Ille-et-Vilaine, J–Jersey, LA–Loire-Atlantique, M–Morbihan, Ma–Manche, O–Orne, SM–Seine-Maritime